I0681191

0

HUSH

The silent scream...

LYNEL COETZER

First Edition: 1 June 2025

CHAPTER ONE

In those moments of trying to enter the panic code on the alarm pad, with his bloodied fingers smearing and sliding on the keypad – 19-year-old Jacques Petersen knew that any moment could be his last. Life was draining from every wound both inside and out – the cold of death was setting in.

Finally, the system beeped twice while the words on the display screen prompted "ON ROUTE."

He stepped back as a roaring silence echoed the house, his heartbeat slamming inside his ears almost deafening. The banging against the front door ceased, for a moment a sense of safety befell him as he slowly sank to the ground against the front door, holding the gaping, blood gushing rip on his left hip. His own breathing was almost echoing in the stillness of the house, and he fought back the tears, the screams – the horror setting in that he may lose the fight to survive while waiting for security to arrive.

The blood was pouring from his hip and inside the madness of his racing mind he knew there was something terribly wrong with the taste funneling up his throat.
He coughed a black spool of blood that plastered his hand as he collapsed to his side on the floor. Tears finally burst through the gut-wrenching pain with a scream he tried to muffle.

The flood of emotions rammed throughout his body, pulsing viciously as he tried not to cry, to stifle his need to scream from the pain.

He had to stay silent, wait for security to arrive and rescue him, the terrorizing realization that the comfortable reality he lived before the *ping* of his phone just a few moments ago was gone forever.

Pressing his elbow to the ground, he heaved himself up as best he could before the stabbing pain of his broken ribs made it unbearable any further and he whined out loudly, toppling against the wall, screaming again – unable to silence it, then, he saw her.

**

Just 30 minutes earlier, his father had winked at him before heading upstairs for the night, a nod back to their chat in the kitchen about Jacques remembering to use protection should his movie date with Ilse heat up.

From the sofa, Jacques smiled, horny as his arm wrapped around Ilse's shoulders – blissful in the reality that he and Ilse had already had sex just earlier that day at her house.
Despite what he'd boasted with his friends, Ilse was the first he'd ever gone all the way with, having struggled with his weight all his life, to be naked and exposed to someone who seemingly enjoyed it, he felt deeply for her and the connection they shared in that moment.

His goal since reaching his teens was to lose his childhood weight and was proud that someone was ok to be with him naked. He could not wait to do it again. Having lived so long with a morbid self-consciousness about his weight – over the already haunting scars of his childhood - having Ilse almost made life feel like it was starting to ease up on its chokehold.

The smell of popcorn hung in the air from the open-plan kitchen and all that was left before the night could officially kick off - was their food delivery to arrive. Jacques looked up the stairs once more, appreciating that his dad retreated for the night to his bedroom upstairs and that they had the bottom of the house to themselves.

For a moment, he was saddened by the thought if his father would ever find another woman to love again, or at the very least come to terms that his mother's suicide would always be something they'd never understand.

He looked down, knowing his father would inevitably read the note again. With him having a girl over he knew his father would have a difficult time not sharing it.

"Are you with me Jacques?" Ilse asked with a gentle smile, taking his hand in hers.
"Don't let it ruin tonight. It's time to move forward!" he thought to himself as he looked into her eyes.
"Yes! Are you ok? Are you comfortable?" His shyness showing in his awkward smile while he reached for the remote.

She squeezed his hand as he slumped beside her into the couch again, the smell of his cologne reminding her of hours ago when she gave herself to him and how intimate they'd been.
"Are you ready for some laughs?" he grinned, pushing play on the remote as he swung his arm back up around her, "I've heard this is pretty good."

The big screen lit up with the opening titles, and he reached toward the side - turning off the lamp to darken the room. With Ilse's hand clutching his he looked at her one more time while he placed the popcorn on her lap.

She smiled to herself as that sense of comfort befell her, sensing that he could possibly be the long term she'd so desperately been seeking since her last break up. He was sweet, yet troubled – free from the arrogance so many other guys had as they matured ready to leave high school. Jacques nuzzled past her long curly blond hair, kissing her cheek softly twice and she smiled.

****

Upstairs, secluded in the main bedroom, his father heaved a sigh as he slumped on the bed, his bowl of leftovers steaming on the nightstand - his laptop already on the bed with headphones ready for his usual weekend binge watch of anything that would take his mind from the harsh reality of the pain that never left his broken heart.

Life had always been rough, and he wore it on the lines of his face, a tiredness that never left no matter how many hours of sleep or how many pills.

He stared at the picture of the three of them just below his lamp, his son was just starting his teenage years, still chubby and red cheeked – they'd taken the picture at a camp site early that morning after a short hike.

His wife was smiling so happily as she clung to them both.

He heaved a soft grunt, hating the picture because of the lies written on her face – while at the same time he was aching to hear her laugh again or to hold her. He hated the picture because he would never have the chance to ask or understand why she chose to leave them behind without any warning or signs.

No pills, no therapy, nothing would ever take away the eternal question, '*Why?*'

He opened the drawer beside his bed and took the note they had found with her body two years prior, when her colleagues had found her – her body hanging from the door of a bathroom stall.
He knew each time that reading it would riddle him with that same mortifying cold agony as always, but he kept reading it each day at least once, trying desperately to understand why she had felt the need to leave them or why leave a note so vague:

I DID THIS FOR YOU & IT WILL ALL MAKE SENSE SOON

There was no making sense of it, he had tried every day to understand it but the torture of failing to do it was his burden forever.

He closed his eyes as he put it away again and slung his feet up on the bed, his palms pressing over his face to force away the weight of emptiness inside him.
He reached to the side for his bowl of food when something caught his eye in the darkness of the ensuite bathroom.

****

"Today was amazing." Ilse smiled cusping his face in her palm while she kissed at his lips, "Thank you for being so gentle, and sweet…"
His face lit up, his cheeks burning red, as his heart raced with awe and excitement.
Smiling, she leaned in and kissed him once, softly.
"Was that your…" he started when suddenly his phone pinged from his jean pocket, "The driver has arrived…"
He got up smiling, eager to move the night along to reach the moments of ecstasy they experienced earlier.
She shifted aside onto the sofa - nervously plucking her shirt back into place and lofting her hair as she wiped her lips.
"I'll be right back." He smiled.

With the movie paused, the silence suddenly felt unnerving, and she looked up at the stairs almost expecting his father to be watching with a stern snarl.

She huffed a sigh of relief as her thoughts returned to the question he was going to ask before his phone interrupted.

When they had sex earlier, she could tell it was his first time, and she bit her lip anxious at what he'd think if he knew it was her third. But she liked him and shrugged the thought from her head.

"It's so strange the app says the driver is here, but I don't see anyone?" Jacques said from the front door, watching as the large electric gate at the bottom of the driveway slid open, "He's not at the gate either."
The night outside was silent, no lights or the sound of a motor running.
He sighed shaking his head while checking his phone again, confirming that the app was in fact showing the driver had arrived.

Without shutting the door, he walked towards the lounge "I'm going down to the gate to see if he isn't parked in the street somewhere. Are you ok?"
"I'm good, thanks please don't worry so much."
"Force of habit, sorry." He grinned with a wink as he left again, heading out - down the porch and down the driveway to the front gate, again rechecking his phone again with frustration.

Outside on the curb the delivery car stood a few feet to the side, out of view from where he was standing at the front door and he huffed angrily, heading towards the car wondering just how useless the driver could be to not make enough effort in bringing the food to the gate at the very least.

The air was warm, and his hormones were on fire, the blatant lack of service was simply not ok.
He raised his phone, clicking the review icon just as he reached the car.
"Would it cost extra to bring …" he paused to peer down at the window, realizing the car was empty with no sign of a delivery bag or driver.
"What the hell?"
Confused, Jacques stepped back looking around the empty dark street.
"Hello?" He called out, to which there was only silence.

He scanned the street for signs of any movement by the nearby homes.
He angrily scoffed, rushing back towards the gate in quick pace, typing his very snarky review on his phone's app.

As he got to the open main gate he stopped again, looking once more around for signs of the driver who was nowhere to be seen.
Inside, he shut the front door and clicked the button beside the alarm pad, closing the main gate before heading to the lounge.

"You won't believe this, the driver…" he paused, Ilse was no longer on the couch, or in the kitchen.
The house was silent, lit only by the light of the T.V.
"Everyone's a damn vanishing act." He teased as he walked towards the downstairs guest bathroom.

"Are you in here Ilse?" he asked, rapping gently on the bathroom door.

It was silent and for a moment he felt a dread seeping on him.

"Yeah, sorry just a sec." she finally replied from inside, trying to hide the awkwardness in her voice. He smiled, briefly regaling her with the mystery of the delivery driver's abandoned car.
"Send him a message, isn't there an option for that on the app?" she asked.
He scrolled, "Oh, yeah good idea let's do that."
"Ok great." She answered from inside the bathroom, nervously pacing, unsure if she should flush and show him that she's comfortable around him or wash her hands and pretend to have already flushed.

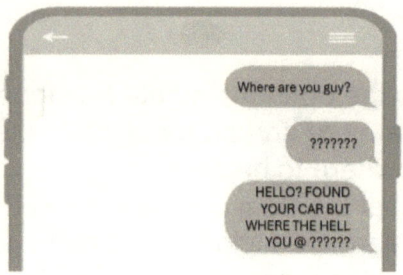

"I'll meet you in the lounge." he said as he headed towards the kitchen when a loud thud sounded from upstairs. Jacques turned, staring through the dim light of the T.V trying to see the staircase. Another thump sounded harder upstairs.

As he reached the foot of the stairs, a crash – this time clear someone had fallen, hard. And without delay, he hurried up the stairs calling for his dad.

The long upstairs passage was dark with only the light from the main bedroom peering out beneath the closed door. In that thin line of light, he could see something moving - breaking the light and he paused in step - realizing the movement was on the *outside* of the door.

"Dad?" he called more loudly, moving his hand along the wall to get to the light switch as the sound of something on the floor thumping and thudding got clearer, an almost gargle type whimper following each movement.
"Dad!" he called again, sensing that whatever was blocking the light from under the main bedroom door was now moving and stammering towards him in the darkness.

He flipped the wall switch at the same moment that something slammed into him, pushing him up against the wall. In a second, a terrible reality crashed over him.

With his face slashed apart and flesh hanging, teeth exposed, tongue almost visible through the torrents of dark blood spewing from his mouth, he screamed as his father's weight forced them both down to the floor, crashing the air out of his alarmed, terrified scream.

As he fought his father's weight from him, trying to get to his knees beside him, crying and screaming

in confusion, Jacques saw that numerous knives were stabbed into his father's side, back, neck and chest – each of them from their own kitchen.
"Help!" He began screaming, unsure where to touch his mutilated father to help as his dad tried desperately to talk to him, his eyes riddled wide and dark.
"Help me!" he cried, hearing Ilse rushing up the stairs, screaming when she saw the massacre before her.

That moment felt like forever, with him wanting so badly for Ilse to save his father, make it all a nightmare to wake from, her standing with her hands over mouth screaming and almost gagging - when with a loud, vicious slam erupted with the main bedroom door flying open.

Storming in a rampage towards them, a tall, dark black figure plunged past and slammed into Ilse with a force so violent that she flew off her feet, backwards into the wall - shattering the portraits as she rolled down the stairs out of sight again.

Jacques got to his feet, his body almost too riddled with terror to move, his lungs unable to gasp air as his eyes stayed fixed on the back of the dark figure who slowly turned to face him, in his hands a small glistening scythe.

"Hello old friend." The voice said in a calm torment, "I did warn you it was time."
Suddenly the events from earlier in the day made sense and as though time stopped, the warnings flashed through his mind in madness:

The first note he found on his way out of the house for school, on the porch – scribbled in black ink: 'IT IS TIME TO TALK'.

He dismissed it, figuring it was something blown in.

The second - a text message sometime later, during recess, from an unknown sender: 'ITS CLOSER NOW NO SORRY WILL CUT IT'

For a moment he felt awkward reading it, a tingle of un-ease shivering somewhere in his soul, but his friends were laughing and joking so, he put his phone away dismissing it for later – forgetting it.

Then the call that came just moments before Ilse's arrival - an eerie whisper *"Truth is journeying up from the grave, buried will it be no more."*

The figure was tall and bulky, clad in a long thick black leather-hooded coat, buttoned shut from the knees to the neck, wearing black gloves - its face hidden by a black gauze mask.
The voice was nobody he could recognize and bore in it a dark hatred that was emphasized in each word.

Jacques's heart was slamming inside, his brain clawing to awaken from this nightmare and his only instinct was to run, as fast as the terror clasping his entire body would allow - leaving his father and girlfriend and just getting out.

He knew this figure was going to make a dash for him, so he leapt over his father's body, into his bedroom and slammed the door just as the figure slammed against it.

Jacques pushed back, forcing the door closed with all his might and locking it. Head spinning and crying, his father's blood fresh on his hands and clothes, he knew he had to think and focus, he had to survive no matter what.

The figure kicked and slashed at the door with the scythe, relentless and crazed.

Jacques rushed to the window, calling for help repeatedly as he swung it open and began to push his body through.

"Open the door fat boy!" the voice screamed, filled with vile rage as its body slammed into the door, the curved blade stabbing viciously through the wood. As Jacques shifted the top half of his body through, the night's cool air hit him and he cried out with a scream, realizing he was awake - there was no nightmare he could escape from on waking.

The nearby houses would surely hear him, and he wailed out again, more desperate, more despair than he'd ever heard in his own voice.

The bedroom door crashed open with the dark, monstrous figure toppling inside over the lower half of the door. Jacques squeezed his waist through the window until he was out on the roof tiles.

Standing up as he looked down at the small garden-shed below, his mind raced trying to figure out his next maneuver to get down when the figure slammed something against the window, and he turned.

Up against the glass was the note from his father's bedside table. His mother's suicide note. He'd seen it only twice, but he knew it well.

I DID THIS FOR YOU & IT WILL ALL MAKE SENSE SOON

And then it struck him, hard and cold. The note from earlier had the same writing.

IT'S TIME TO TALK

Each cell of his being filled with chilling terror and confusion – *did this maniac kill my mother?*

The figure launched backwards towards the door, whipping around the bedroom in a frenzied charge, a vicious lunatic without any stopping.
"Help!" He barely screamed out into the night when the entire window smashed behind him, his desk chair just missing him as it passed on its way down with the glass and window frame against the shed below.

He spun around and the figure was already there, grabbing him by the collar.
"No more running Jelly boy!"
With all his might he flung his fists as they tussled, losing his footing and with the figure in his grip – falling against the roof, rolling once before flinging off and slamming down onto the shed's metal roof with a force that choked his breath.
The figure arose to his knees beside him, pulling the long scythe from within the darkness of his thick leather coat, "Ride is over fat boy!"

There was rage in the voice, violent – fueled by hatred.

Jacques managed to kick the figure's leg, forcing his feet out from under him causing him to topple down with the slam - a blow that sent the roof inward and both of them down into the shed.

Coughing, Jacques had hit the work bench and knew instantly his ribs had been broken because as he tried to roll away, he winced breathlessly in a pain that wrapped his entire chest.

He strained his eyes to find where the dark figure had landed amidst the dust in the air, feeling the impossibility of breathing and moving choke him.

For a moment it was quiet, no sounds of movement anywhere around him or the shed as he coughed and tried to force himself up and find the ability to scream again for help.

But then, huddled beside the door as the dust fell, a man in a red delivery jacket slumped against the wall, his hands and feet bound with tape and his mouth covered.

His eyes were wide as he tried to scream from behind the duct tape which only muffled his terror.

"Help me!" Jacques cried out almost suffocated by the pain around his chest when the sound of his dad's mini wood saw ripped alive from somewhere in the shed.

Before Jacques could even try to distinguish its origins, the figure was at the side of the work bench, immediately ramming the little saw down into his side, ripping and slicing into Jacques' hip.

Screaming out in agony he flung himself off the workbench and onto the floor.

"You all thought it was over, didn't you?" Said the figure, clambering around the debris as it passed the work bench.

"What? Who are you? Why are you doing this?" Jacques rambled in mortified disbelief, his bloody body now stammering for the door.

"No more running." The figure mocked as Jacques slammed against the door, trying to push it open with all the strength he could muster.

The delivery driver was now fighting even more desperately than before to get his hands and feet loose from the tape.

"No more games jelly boy. Everyone you love is gone. Accept it, embrace it." Said the dark figure as he swung the rattling saw forward – missing only because of the delivery driver heaving into him from the side, causing him to topple and the saw to tear into the door just as Jacques burst outward from the shed.

Stumbling to his knees on the grass outside, the adrenaline was losing the battle against pain and blood. He knew he had to force himself to move through the agony encompassing his ribs, to get up and run - find his voice, and scream for anyone to hear from the nearby neighbors.

"Help! Please!" He screamed as much as he could, trying to tumble upward to his feet, squeezing at his hip with both hands, for a moment feeling the bone against his fingers - he cried out.

"Help me!" he called again, stumbling side to side trying desperately to keep himself up. The sound of the little saw being ripped from the wood forced him to turn about briefly, seeing only as the figure brought it up into the air above the delivery driver who struggled to get to his knees – calling behind the tape in muffled screams.

Jacques rushed towards the house, as fast as he could, hearing only the silence of the saw being driven into the driver behind him.

In those moments of trying to enter the panic code on the alarm pad, his bloodied fingers smearing and sliding on the keypad Jacques was crying and bleeding heavily.

He had no idea of knowing where the crazed attacker had gone since the shed. His body ached, the gash on his side ached like nothing he'd ever experienced before, and he felt himself losing enough blood to cause him to collapse.

The display screen prompted "ON ROUTE."

He coughed, violently, stumbling and swaying as he felt consciousness fading. He had to find his phone upstairs, near his father who he had left in the upstairs passage.

At the door beside him, the maniac slammed and rammed against it trying to tear it down with little success. The note haunted him with each drum of his heartbeat in his ears.

The banging at the door stopped abruptly and the house fell back into silence. Tears ran down his face as he slumped down against the front door, fearing that like his bedroom door this door would not contain the vicious psycho beneath the gauze mask.

His eyes had never felt more widely open than they were in that moment - looking at the bottom of the stairs where Ilse lay, still in the dimly lit house. The flood of emotions rammed throughout his body, coursing and pulsing viciously.

"Ilse baby." He said softly, listening with all his might to any sounds from the masked figure, as he heaved almost breathlessly, coughing more and more blood from his lungs.

"Ilse!" he called out.

She raised her head wearily as the pounding in her head drummed and then screamed. Her shoulder had dislocated, and she propped her head down again, still crying out for help.

Then, a coldness jolted through him, stepping down the stairs the attacker appeared from the darkness, again the small deadly scythe was in his hand.

"You have terrible neighbors." It mocked as Jacques scurried backwards – the figure stepping over Ilse and pausing with her body between its legs.

"No!" Jacques cried out, reaching for the door handle above him to pull himself up with. "What do you want? Leave us alone!"

Gripping Ilse's long blond hair in his black gloved hand, the figure pulled her head up to face Jacques. He screamed, warning and crying for the madman to leave her alone as he clambered to pull himself to his feet.

"Do you feel it yet jelly boy? Can you feel the end coming?" he mocked, placing the scythe to Ilse's throat. She cried, begging him to stop.

"Please…" Jacques said falling against the door, fighting to have his legs keep him up, "Please stop!"

The figure moved the scythe's blade to his side with a chuckle - cold and sinister, "I'm kidding I have no reason to hurt her."
Jacques paused, silent, staring between Ilse's frightened eyes, frowning confused, dazed, and bewildered between her and the figure.
Then in a swift swing – the tip of scythe hit her head, and her eyes instantly rolled back as she began to convulse, choking as her body hit the floor shaking violently.

In the distance, sirens filled the night as the security and police combined head towards the house.

It was in those moments everything shattered, and Jacques let out a wailing scream born from pure defeat, agony, and torment - a gut-wrenching cry as though born in the depths of hell.
He felt his body finally surrender to the chaos and mayhem and his knees hit the floor.
"You shouldn't have kept quiet jelly boy. That was a bad call." The dark figure dug into his thick leather coat, removing a homemade knuckleduster with a cluster of nails and screws jutting out of it.
"But you all chose silence. You kept your mouth shut, watching the madness taking over. You all failed, all of you. To be decent!"
Jacques stared up at the mask and suddenly everything began to puzzle together. He tried to scream but the blood inside his throat was now thick, his focus blurring as the figure placed the weapon on its fist.
"Even mommy dearest had to pay for what you did!"

He was forced to make sense of the madness in a short space of time, comprehending that this truly was not a dream and that everything in that moment was real. This monster had killed his mother two years ago.

**

The email was very detailed. Sitting at her desk, Jacques' mother could not believe everything she'd read from the unknown sender.
She was cold, shaking almost as the office around her kept going. She stood up and straightened her jersey, looking around in the hopes of seeing someone, anyone waiting for a response to this terrible joke.
She looked at the email again, the bottom-lines reading:
'*You must die now because of this. Sorry Mrs. Petersen, it IS the only way...*'

She walked to the bathroom, trying hard to smile at her colleagues through the tears that were building inside, disbelief that everything she had read could be true. Every fiber of her body trembled, a cold and wicked shiver.

In the bathroom she washed cold water over her face, staring into the mirror trying to make sense of what to do next as tears ran down her face.
Call the police? Call her husband? Confront Jacques?

Thoughts raced through her mind, but broke when the bathroom door opened and she quickly looked down, hiding her face from whomever was entering, praying they'd leave her alone and not pry.

The thick black rope was around her neck faster than she could realize, struggling and fighting for air while her attacker pulled and pulled - choking her fast as she struggled backwards, pushing them both into the stall.

She could not scream or even move her jaw with the rope so tight, and she could feel it ending as she kicked her legs against the walls until her neck finally snapped.

**

The sirens outside were loud, the lights flashing through the windows, lighting up the dark lounge where the movie was still paused, the lifeless body of his first love was laying only a few steps from him in a puddle of blood. Her eyes wide, tortured. Upstairs his father lay cold, his face shredded.

The figure stood over him, allowing Jacques the last moments trying to make sense of the massacre, the violence, the notes, and the name 'Jelly boy'.
"Please…" Jacques urged, weak and losing consciousness.
The figure grabbed his hair and pulled back to expose his throat.
"Hush now fat boy!" it snarled angrily punching down hard into Jacques' throat.

Jacques hit the floor hard as blood poured and sprayed out across the floor.

The dark figure knelt by him as he lay gargling his last breath, his hands trying to stop the blood streaming through his shredded neck.

Looking at him through the dark gauze, the figure motioned his finger over his mouth, "Sssshhh."

HUSH

- The Silent Scream –

CHAPTER TWO

'*The scene: one of the most troubling, disturbing of its kind – according to officer Gibbs who was of the first to arrive on the scene. We'll have more on this story as it unfolds.*'

The reporter on scene said before the segment cut back to the studio panel, and he muted the television with a heavy sigh, leaning forward against the kitchen counter, placing his unfinished cereal bowl in the sink.

Eric Jansen, almost 22 years old, was dressed in the hand me down navy suit pants and light blue collared shirt his brother-in-law had given him out of the frustration of his inability to land a job since joining their small family in Lynnwood Pretoria.

The small one-bedroom flatlet, at the bottom of his sister's backyard, was quiet and his heart raced as he stared at the T.V.
"I won't be going in today, so you'll need to make your own arrangements. Keith's not well so we're taking a day off." Said his sister bursting through the front door, startling him.

"Gross! It reeks in here, are you still smoking inside? We asked you to smoke outside! You're a guest here Eric! And it smells!" his sister ranted, plucking open the curtains and pushing open the windows.

She was 8 years older than him, tall with black hair just like his, with streaks of red on the tips, still carrying the weight of her first child who had recently turned 12.

"I pay rent!" he snarled, leaning forward as he took the bowl from the counter to finish his cereal, "Also, why are you letting me know on such short notice? How am I going to make my own arrangements now?"

"Call that guy who's always coming around here, what's his name again?" she paused when the pictures on the T.V caught her eye.

"Eric... isn't that your friend from..."

"Jacques, yeah that's him." He answered solemnly, cutting her off as he too stared at the photo of him which the news had on the screen.

His sister turned to him, "What happened to them? Why's he on the news?"

Eric shook his head and he pushed the unmute button.

'With no clues and no eyewitnesses, police are combing the scene with great care and concentration and are urging anyone in the community who may have seen anything or who may have information these senseless killings, to come forward and assist the investigation."

The reporter said as a shot of the house crawling with police and medical teams appeared behind her.

"My God!" his sister gasped softly, "That's just awful! Where was this?"

"Klerksdorp. They must have moved." He shrugged, tipping the bowl out to the trash, wishing like the darkness of the bin, that he could disappear and escape the reality of the life that followed their youth.

"What am I going to do about work now Celeste?"

"Call that guy that keeps coming here, what's his name again?" she said walking to the kitchen with her arms folded.

"Zain." He huffed putting his hands on his hips, "And we don't work anywhere near each other. Can't I just use Kieth's car since he's not using it? Or yours?"

"Mine? You want me to give you the Lexus?" she mocked him rudely as Eric rolled his eyes.

"Ok fine then let me use Keith's car if he's not using it today?"

"I can't. He won't. Just figure it out for yourself for once." She said starting to tidy up the pillows and blanket on the sofa that was also his bed.

"For once?" he frowned, "What does that mean?"

"Look, we've done everything we can for you, and we don't mind helping you out until you have a car of your own, but right now it…" she paused cautiously, "Keith and I feel like you're not taking any of this seriously."

Eric scoffed angrily, "Excuse - the hell - me?"

"You've been here for nine months and only got this job because Keith knows the manager. You live like a pig, and you don't help with anything. And don't get me started on Zeke being under your spell…"

"I'm paying rent!" he quipped back, "And I love Zeke, I'd never influence him!"

"Keith has noticed some changes in Zeke since you moved in and is concerned that if he's exposed to your lifestyle, he'll…"

"He'll what?" he snarled with insult, "He'll what?"

Celeste shrugged her shoulders shaking her head, "I don't know Eric, start smoking or worse maybe?" "I can't believe you think that low of me, no wait, scratch that I can believe it. Keith hates me and he's using Zeke as a tool to…"

"No, he's not!" she defended, "Look Zeke adores you and we just…We want a good example for him! And correction, mom and dad are paying your rent."

"So, I'm a bad example?" he scoffed, "Because of I'm an addict and my parents are helping me get on my feet?"

His sister rolled her eyes, "Everyone is proud of you Eric, you're two years sober that's great, but we're all just tired of bailing you out. I'm just asking you to figure out one simple thing to get yourself to work before you lose this job as well. And you turn it into something like you always do. You're always angry."

"What the hell are you talking about?" he snarled with flabbergast.

"You heard me, you're always angry and have been since you were a kid. Nobody can talk to you without you spiraling out of control."

"Talk to me." He said folding his arm, "Go on, talk to me about how I'm a bad influence on Zeke, or how I'm incapable of making decisions, especially last-minute decisions made by other people which are outside of my control! Talk to me about how I'm sponging up mom and dad's money because trying to make a life as an addict is hard, but I do it anyway…"

"This isn't about mom and dad." she said heaving a sigh.

"I pay my fuel, I don't eat with you guys, I do my own thing. And I haven't gotten any money from mom and dad, they pay you directly. The rest is on my own paycheck! Which is barely enough for anyone to really live on unless I hit commission targets, which I can't because I suck at sales. But it's the only job I can get so I try, I wake up every day and I try my best!"

Eric sighed breathless from his rant, "I don't know what more to do, I stay out of your hair, I stay hidden, so Keith's precious community doesn't even know I'm here and all I need is just a ride to work. That's it. But you come in here and you berate and belittle me and expect me to just smile and wave?"

Celeste huffed, "Act your age, Eric."

"Act my age?" he laughed, "What are you talking about? It's Keith, isn't it? He wants me gone, isn't it?"

"This isn't about Keith."

"Because he knows this would start a fight and wedge us apart."

"This is about all of us having to deal with you!"

"What do you want from me. God damn it!" he yelled, slamming his fist against the counter of the small kitchenette that caused her to jump as a silence fell over the small flatlet. She stepped back almost nervous about how angrily he raised his voice at her.

The news brought it all back to him, he felt a surge of the same toxic dread that drove him to his mistakes to begin with and there was no other outlet, he did not know how to deal with seeing Jacques on the news, the massacre, and the murder – it brought everything back.

"This is not ok." She said softly, finally braving the tension, "You don't get to yell at me in my own house."

Eric sighed looking down, fighting the urge to throw away 21 months of sobriety and numb his thoughts to the adrenaline surging.

She wiped her cheek as she stepped away from him.

"I'm sorry. I can't undo any of it. All I can do is try every day and it's not easy, but I do it. I literally do everything I can to stay out of your way other than drive to work with you because you literally work in the building across the street! It made sense, and as for Zeke I love the little guy. But I understand and I'll make my own way going forward."

"Eric that's…" she tried when he continued.

"I'm sick of hearing your husband berate and belittle everything about me, I feel his eyes on me everywhere I go, his judgmental beady little eyes on the back of my neck. It is suffocating and I don't want to do this anymore."

Again, a silence hung, and he looked down, tears filling his eyes as he shook his head grinding his teeth.

"That's not what I meant Eric. I just wanted to…"

"I just need some time to figure things out and I'll be out of your hair." He said walking towards the door, grabbing his small backpack and heading out.

Celeste sighed and slumped to the counter shaking her head. She took a deep breath and lifted her head, staring at the photo on the refrigerator of Eric with his group of friends – Zach, Bobby, Jacques, Marcus and his sister Odette, Carla, Matthew and his sister Magaret and Leigh-Anne.

The photo was taken 11 years ago shortly after his birthday party, and she remembered that day, she remembered her little brother and the big smile on his handsome face, his hair as black then as it is now.

She could hear their laughter echoing in her memory, it was the day Eric got his first Mountain bike, she had bought him a cover for it, and she could still remember him hugging her so tightly.

He was always so happy, his friends seemed to be the world to him.

Then suddenly everything changed, and Eric became lost in a darkness he refused to speak with anyone. Friends fell away, and everything that was once filled with hope became solemn and morbid, eventually leading him to his addiction. She wondered if the same fate would befall her son and sadness fell over her as she shut her eyes, with a mantra to calm her mind in order to figure out how to make the next move without anyone, or anything, falling apart.

"I heard all of that. You could have stood your ground a bit better." Her husband Kieth said entering at the door, "But otherwise, I think that went well, I'm happy with the outcome."

She rolled her eyes and turned to him, "This wasn't what I wanted. I just wanted him to…"

"He is nothing but rubbish" Keith said, putting his arms around her. He was heavy set, with a round beard, older than her by 10 years with a strong Afrikaans accent.

"He's, my brother." She defended carefully.

"Yes, but he said it himself – he is a black sheep. I know he is a bad influence on Zeke." Keith scoffed, looking at the flat with utter disgust on his face, "I think we have done our part, but we cannot continue having him poison our home, our son with whatever it is. Everyday Zeke is becoming more like a hooligan, making the wrong friends."

"He's a teenager, he's growing up." She sighed rubbing her head in frustration.

"Under what spells or voodoo fumes and what have you?" said Keith putting his hands on her shoulders, "This is for the best, let him go and whatever must be, will be. Nobody can expect us to have that rubbish so close to home."

"He's always going to be my little brother Keith." She defended again, moving out of his grip, "And this wasn't how it was supposed to end – pushing him right back out there. I just wanted him to figure out how to be responsible!"

"Exactly, you came here to have a nice, quiet talk and everything he does makes a big explosion out of nothing."

"An old friend of his…" She said gesturing her hand towards the refrigerator and the old photo, "It doesn't matter. I just think today was the wrong morning for this, that's all."

Keith frowned shaking his head, "Maybe, but it happened. I am happy it happened because now we can live our lives when he moves out and not hang our head in shame to the neighbors."

"They don't even know who he is or what he did unless you told them." She huffed angrily, tears of frustration in her eyes, "Why are you so harsh with him, but you always preach about being a good person without allowing him the chance to be a better one?"

"See!" Keith growled, "Now he has us fighting against one another. This is what I've been saying all the time Celeste. He is bad news. Negative energy, and he lives in it like a sponge. How many chances must he be given? By your parents? By us? There can only be so much before he needs to catch a wake up and live for himself."

Celeste heaved a sigh, and again Keith put his hands on her shoulders forcing her to face him.

"We took the day off, let's just enjoy it and not let him spoil it." He smiled.
"Ok." she said with a weak smile, as he leaned in and softly kissed her on the forehead.
"Come why don't you go make us some lekker coffee? And then we have an enjoyable day as planned."
"Let's do that." She managed a smile, "But I need to call my mom and try to figure out how to handle this before something bad happens or god forbid."
"No, you make the coffee." Keith insisted, "We can't have misunderstandings and people in panic for nothing. We'll see what Eric does in a few days. Maybe now we can discuss me using this space for my things?"
She turned to him, pausing, staring into his eyes deeply and he shrugged his shoulders.
"Yes or no on the gym?"
Her eyes narrowed and she turned away, walking out silently screaming inside.

Keith sighed, turned to the T.V, then headed to the sink and took the remote to turn off the T.V before heading out, shaking his head in disgust as he looked around the small flatlet.

****

As Eric walked down the street towards the main road a few blocks away, he slung the backpack around his shoulder, with a lit cigarette in mouth. He'd really tried to shake the past in all ways he could, even surrendering his addiction to move forward to live a cleaner future, but nothing was ever enough for anyone. He felt worthless again, the cravings poking at him.

His phone toned a message, and he quickly replied.

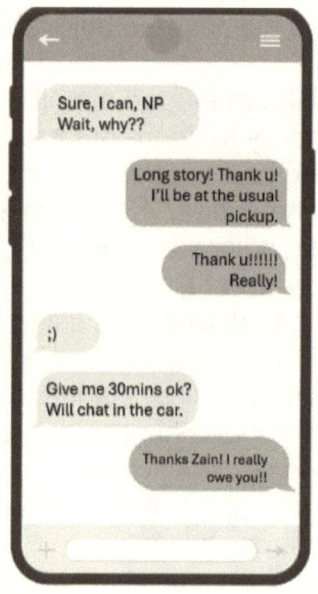

Seeing Jacques' photo on the news had lifted open the very heavy doors to history so utterly thick that it made his stomach tense, knotting tight. He felt it crawling on his skin - the dread, the fight to shut out memories from the day that changed their lives. The brief and almost vague news of the murders was trembling at nerves that he had hoped were long since numbed.

He had not seen Jacques in almost eight years - their last conversation was bitter and fueled with anger, regret, and rage. He knew even in their last engagement that their shared past would always link them together but now Jacques and his father were brutally murdered, and now that link was gone forever which left him feeling sad.

"Hey! Eric!" a voice called out from the other side of the road. It was his sister's son, Zeke, leaving his friends at the bus stop to rush towards him.

"Hey little man." He smiled, fist bumping his nephew then putting a smoke to his lips, "You good ?"

"Yes. How are you?" Zeke grinned up at him, "Dad says you came home late last night and were probably out doing drugs again..."

Eric scoffed shaking his head, "Your dad needs to be mindful of what he says to people who are easily influenced. My opinion."

"Dad just wants everyone to be like him, he's tough but he means well." Zeke said maturely, "I know because it's the kind of thing he says about my friends, my sport, my hobbies...so I get it."

Eric laughed, "Yeah - he does mean well in his own unique way. Look I have to run, or I'll be late for work, ok?"

"Ok...My friend Conner has the new Lord of Battle disc, we were wondering after school if we could play in your room? Your flat I mean!" Zeke grinned brightly, "If we play in the house, dad's going to have something to say and chase my friend away again. You know how he gets sometimes."

"Yeah, I uh…" Eric paused awkwardly, "I will be somewhere tonight, at a friend. Reading some biblical stuff and chanting, so maybe another time yeah?"

Through his deep disappointment Zeke laughed, "Well we can try tomorrow if you're free? We really want to play it without my dad around. We won't bother you! I promise! Plus, I'll make you coffee!"

"Uh, I might not be staying there any more Zeke." He shrugged, "So let's see how things go."

"What do you mean?" Zeke gasped worriedly, "Why? Because of my dad?"

"I need some space, so I'm going to hang with some friends for a few days and see if I'll come back to the flat or not." Eric puffed smoke into the air, "I don't know really."

"What did my dad say?"" Zeke pressed angrily, "He ruins everything!"

"Nah…" Eric managed a smile, "I just need to chill with some friends for a bit, you know?"

Zeke shook his head, "Sometimes I hate him."

"No, hey, don't be like that." Eric insisted, "I decided this, I just need a break so give your old man some slack, ok?"

"But I don't want you to move away."

Eric winked as he dug into his backpack again, "Here you can have this for the time being. Give me your hand."

Zeke held out his hand for Eric to place his flatlet key inside his palm, "It's all yours anytime you want to have some privacy or just need to catch a breath, ok? But open the windows and let the smoke out before you sit in there."

Zeke's eyes lit up at first, then quickly dulled.

"Dad wants to make your flat a gym. So, this won't last."

"But it's a space to chill out whenever you can. Life hands you little miracles one at a time, be grateful when it does." Eric smiled, "I got to go, I'll see you later when I come get some of my stuff. You good, right?"

Zeke nod, smiling again, "Thanks uncle Eric."

"No no…"

"Sorry, Eric. Just Eric." Zeke giggled.

"Good stuff my man." He smiled back, fist bumping again before heading off, leaving Zeke with a large smile, and the key to kingdom he'd very often wished for, eagerly rushing back across the road to his friends.

****

Stepping out of Zain's two-door Ford Fiesta, nerves riddled through him at the inability to shake off the dread from seeing the news. He shut the door as Zain got out of the car. The basement parking lights gave a good enough reflection for Eric to quickly double-check that his dark black hair and outfit were still in order.

From the outside, the bustling city sounds of Pretoria meant that it was alive, and he was late.

Zain was a tall, slender built Indian 20-year-old, with glistening black hair and a small chin only patch of beard. He carried himself straight to almost everyone but a very select few, something his upbringing imposed on his subconscious.

With Eric he felt a sense of comfort in being himself, not second guessing every move or motion that would signal his sexuality to others.

"You seem more rattled than you should." Zain remarked as he rounded the front of the car towards Eric, "Brothers and sisters fight all the time, this will work itself out. Until then, my door is always open." "I just don't want you to read too much into this, but I don't have anyone else to go to." Eric said almost nervously, "I mean I don't even know what we are yet."
Zain smiled as he reached for Eric's hand, "We both know I'm way more into you than you are in me, and for now that's ok. You need help so I'm giving you what you need, ok? No strings attached. But sexual favors will not be turned away and there is no bargaining when it comes to that."
Eric nodded, managing to smile at Zain who laughed teasingly - admiring how bright Zain's eyes were with hope while his own drowned in a pool of secrets and lies.

"I have to get going, so I'll be here around 5 to pick you up, ok?" Zain said heading back to the door, "Now chin up and go close some deals! Earn you some money so you can show that fat old man you don't need nobody."
Eric smiled, slinging his backpack over his shoulder while waiting to wave as Zain drove back out of the parking garage. It was 08h12.

The call center floor was buzzing as it always did after the morning meeting, with sales consultants working hard and eager to close their quotas for the day.

As he rushed across the vast open-plan floor, Keith's good friend and his manager Gerrit Moolman, rushed towards him from his glass office cubical in the middle of the call center floor.

"I'm sorry, I know I'm late but it's my first offence in the 3 months that I've been here and…" Eric started as the broad-shouldered man interrupted.
"Here are the notes to this morning's sales meeting." Gerrit spoke loudly over the noise but smiled, "We're all human and entitled to one bad day a week, chin up and get those targets flowing alright? Good man."
A smile broke over Erics face, "Thank you Gerrit." Gerrit had already turned to walk across the sales floor with vigorous enthusiasm, encouraging his team to get up from their seats and talk to their customers with more energy.

By 11h30 the energy in the call center had not ceased even a bit, the energy was still vibrant in each cluster and the electronic chart kept counting the sales closed by each team. In his cubicle the air was thick, negative - he hadn't had one successful call all morning.
"Come on Eric pull yourself together." He huffed, leaning forward to grab his headset again, opening his line that auto dialed the company's database of insurance leads.
"Is this Mr. Drummond?" he forced a smile as he brushed his hand through his thick black hair, "Great good morning to you sir, my name is Eric Jansen and I'm calling about our fantastic new…" The small notification on the bottom right of his screen popped up, forcing his distraction and he

froze as the person on the line kept asking for clarification on the call.

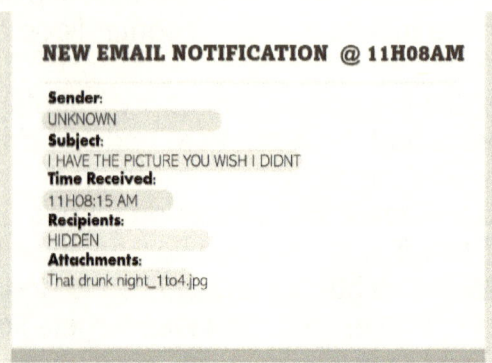

NEW EMAIL NOTIFICATION @ 11H08AM

Sender:
UNKNOWN
Subject:
I HAVE THE PICTURE YOU WISH I DIDNT
Time Received:
11H08:15 AM
Recipients:
HIDDEN
Attachments:
That drunk night_1to4.jpg

He stood up slowly, nervously unable to keep his face from showing the fear within him. His eyes carefully scanned the floor, circling to ensure nobody behind him would have eyes on his PC. Every thought possible tore through his mind as he sat down, careful to open the email without any eyes on his screen.
With his days of being slammed out on drugs, he knew anything was possible to exist in the circles he kept at the time, and the thought of anyone having something on him clenched his stomach.

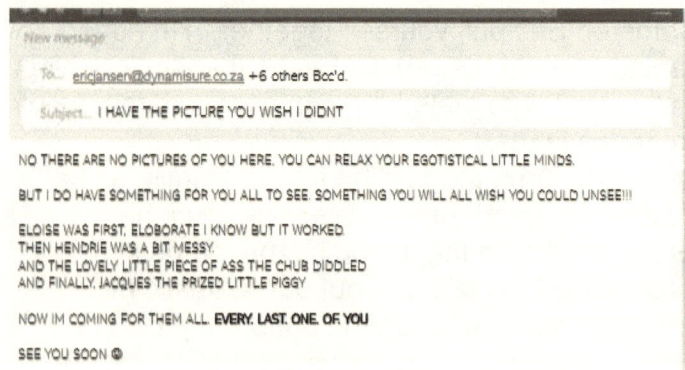

New message

To   ericjansen@dynamisure.co.za +6 others Bcc'd.

Subject   I HAVE THE PICTURE YOU WISH I DIDNT

NO THERE ARE NO PICTURES OF YOU HERE. YOU CAN RELAX YOUR EGOTISTICAL LITTLE MINDS.

BUT I DO HAVE SOMETHING FOR YOU ALL TO SEE. SOMETHING YOU WILL ALL WISH YOU COULD UNSEE!!!

ELOISE WAS FIRST, ELOBORATE I KNOW BUT IT WORKED.
THEN HENDRIE WAS A BIT MESSY.
AND THE LOVELY LITTLE PIECE OF ASS THE CHUB DIDDLED
AND FINALLY, JACQUES THE PRIZED LITTLE PIGGY

NOW IM COMING FOR THEM ALL. **EVERY. LAST. ONE. OF. YOU**

SEE YOU SOON ☺

"What the hell is this?" he said under his breath, his eyes scanning the text again and again, before moving his mouse to the attachments linked to the email.

"Oh my god!" he gasped out loud, his voice drowned by the floor of vibrant sales agents around him.

The images were set to play the next automatically and as horrible as they were his eyes were glued to the screen in disbelief and terrified shock. With his heart racing, an icy cold shrouding his skin as nausea built within his gut.

The images were taken of the crime scenes, first Eloise Jansen – Jacques' mother. Her pleasant face a pale whiteish blue, her lips almost black with her eyes rolled backwards. The marks around her neck were something torturous.

4 seconds later, it was Jacques' father lying sprawled out on his back in a pool of blood, the horror of his flesh ripped face glaring at the camera, his tongue hanging outside the side of his mouth.

4 seconds later, it was a photo taken on floor level of Ilse, someone he'd never met but whose terrible head wound made vile rivet in his stomach, and he gasped.

4 seconds later it was Jacques, an old friend whose terrified eyes stared wide at the photographer.

It began to re-play, but he couldn't, it was terrible. He stood up, head spinning, stomach churning.

The vomit spewed out of his mouth into his hand as he tried desperately to cover his mouth while he coughed to the floor behind his cubicle. Those around him noticed the commotion and stared at him in alarm, raising their hands to alert Gerrit.

His head was spinning violently, filled with terror and alarm he crumbled back down against his desk, trying desperately to stop the reply, to close the file but it would not. He placed his hands up over the screen, trying to block as much of it as he could when another bout of vomit erupted out over his keyboard.
"Eric?" Gerrit called rushing over while a few of his colleagues began to remove their headsets and stand up.
"Stop!" he screamed, slamming his hands against the monitor.
"Eric what's going on?" Gerrit asked in alarm as he and four others reached Erics desk, his hands desperately over the monitor, the vomit running down the desk.

The screen went blank, and his laptop began to beep one long beep, seemingly at no end until it went silent.

Eric gasped in alarmed confusion, wiping his mouth, looking at the cables to see if someone had pulled it out to stop the terror from leaving the screen.
"Eric!" Gerrit yelled now, grabbing him by the shoulders and pulling him away from the desk to face him as the entire cubicle's laptops began to beep with each screen going dark.
"What the hell?" Gerrit frowned bewildered and the sales team grew quiet with consultants asking their

customers to hold as the screens across the floor went off, preceded by the beep.

Eric spun around shaking his head as he pushed past his distracted and confused manager, rushing towards the doors to the bathroom.
"What the hell is going on?" Gerrit demanded, "Someone call IT, now!"

****

By 1pm a section of the sales floor was operational again with new laptops plugged in, while the rest of the crew began carting their laptops out to the IT floor below them.
The stench of vomit hung in the air, and even though he'd been given a few glasses of water since, he felt he was still going to pass out as he did on entry to the men's bathroom.

Vik, one of the HR administrators who helped re-awaken him after being found in the bathroom, stood with arms folded beside the seated company's General Manager, Taryn Graham in her dull Indigo colored dress suit, a napkin covering her mouth.
"You haven't given us much to work with Eric." Gerrit huffed from beside him, "Whatever you opened crashed every single laptop."
"Companywide!" Mrs. Graham scoffed, "And you say it was just porn? Do you have any idea how much trouble you are in Mr. Jansen?"

Eric looked up at her, "Would our IT not have any way of recovering the files or email that caused this?"

"You want to recover your pornography Mr. Jansen?" Mrs. Graham hissed, "That's really what is your main concern here?"

He shook his head angrily, looking at the floor to avoid an outburst.

"IT suspects the file or site you visited contained a type of Zeus virus, they're pretty sure all the laptops have been totally wiped along with the servers linked to them. We'll need an excessive amount of manpower and allocation of additional funds to try to recover any lost files that were not backed up prior to 10am this morning." Vik explained.

Eric sighed, keeping his head down as he forced the nauseating images from his mind.

Vik stepped forward while nicely a copy of Erics employment contract across the table.

"Pornographic content is expressly forbidding on the company servers, stipulated on page 8, point 11a of your contract with us. How you got access to the site is beyond me."

Eric shut his eyes, looking down at the floor still. His leg was shaking visibly as he clutched his hands, trying to stay quiet and just wait for the opportunity to get out of the building and run - find help or solace from the madness scouring through his mind.

"Coupled with your inability to achieve targets for the duration of your employment following the extensive training provided, and your short employment with the company there unfortunately is no way we can even remotely consider assisting you in any way Mr. Jansen." Vik continued cautiously, "We will however suggest that you find yourself support in any form of support group or otherwise, for any sexual addiction you may have. Do you understand Mr. Jansen, or would you like to reconsider having this conversation with a representative of your choice present?"

Eric reached for the water again, trying desperately to calm the tremors inside him, "No, I understand what I've done is really bad."
"Bad?" scoffed Mrs. Graham from behind her napkin, "You're summarily dismissed with immediate effect, pending additional criminal charges once our finance department can determine the scale of loss we've suffered as a result of your disgusting porn!"
Vik cleared his throat, "Do you understand Mr. Jansen? We need to be sure you clearly understand what we are saying, your rights, our rights and that we won't need to re-argue this in court later if you feel you've been treated unfairly."

Eric sat momentarily wondering if he should just speak the truth, tell them the horror of what transpired. The images were obviously taken from the killer's point of view and could potentially lead the police to something useful.

But it would shake everything to the ground of why he had received the email to begin with.

A years-old friendship link to the victim would not be enough to clasp as a non-motive. Then there was the reason why their friendship hit the rocks, ended so violently abruptly.

The secrets they shared as kids, the truth behind what really happened back when they were young teens and what that would do if it were to come to light in the investigation at all.
He wanted to scream, erase the horror from his mind that he saw every time he blinked.

But would that make any difference to keeping his job? How would he prove this to them, to the police? Would anyone have the funds and resources available to find that email again? Those terrible images. Who was the sender? How did they even have the company email address that only existed for three months? Who were the other recipients Bcc'd on the mail?

Eric shook his head and cleared his throat from behind the disgust haunting him from the images, the total shock in which he found the reality of even receiving the email and now losing his job – a sort of scoffing laugh escaped his lips, acting as the emote of his disbelief.
"You have the nerve to sit here and laugh?" Gerrit snarled angrily, "I cannot believe this, old Keith is going to be very disappointed in you."
"You know what?" Eric said looking up again, "Please - please just shove this shit, honestly."
Jaws dropped and he nodded almost politely to Vik as he stood up from the seat.
"Thank you, Vik. I do understand fully. If you press charges against me, go ahead. I have nothing to pay you with anyway, since I'm homeless, broke and God knows what is going on right now."
He almost burst into tears of desperate confusion as he moved from the seat towards the door, his head

still spinning and his entire being trembling from the core.

"You are making this a lot worse than it needs to be Mr. Jansen." Vik said causing him to pause and turn back to face them.

"I have nothing left to lose sir." He said defeated, exhausted and dirty from the vomit that still felt wet against his shirt and pants. "I have bigger problems apparently, and you know what? I hated it here, that's why I sucked at targets in the first place Gerrit, so shame on you for keeping me here as long as you did!"

He huffed and shut the door behind him with a slam, walking as fast as he could towards the elevator, already texting Zain - 'EMERGENCY CALL ME'.

****

From her office in Midrand, a city on the outskirts of Pretoria, bordering the great metropolis of Johannesburg, Carla Wilson stood in her black pants suit, arms folded as she stared out of the window in the boardroom.

In the morning sun that glimmered on the large glass windows her fiery red hair seemed to be flaming, her eyes fixed on the horizon while her mind raced in thoughts of freedom out beyond the skyline, where the noise from the city would drown and she would find a job to sustain herself where she could enjoy her mornings instead of dread the abuse of her arrogant boss.

At Mulder & Seuns Trading her job was to assist the head of sales manager, but as a mid-life crisis facing, divorced and balding man his only objective each day was to remind her that she was his slave. When she started with Mulder & Seuns fresh out of high school in admin, she pictured her future with the company vastly differently and as she stood there staring out across the city she tried hard to un-regret the choice of applying for the position when it arose.

The door behind her opened and Mthato stepped in, her bright smile shining behind bright red lipstick. "They've arrived, should be at the elevator in about 10."

"Oh crap!" Carla huffed, snapped back to reality as she quickly rushed to finish placing the meeting files around the 8-seater boardroom table.

"You want to come to the mall with me at lunch?" Mthato asked, rechecking the tea trolley, "I'm in need of something for myself, you know? I think it would do you some good too."

"You're the assistant to the CFO Mthato, you have it good, I might be reduced to wiping gum from his royal highnesses shoes by lunch time, who knows."

Mthato laughed while she leaned in to hug her, "Oh darling. You just need to tough it out a little longer. He eventually will warm to you the same way he did to Eve."

Carla laughed shaking her head, "Eve still quit."

"After a year at least. Come on! Be my shopping buddy!" Mthato urged playfully.

"I can't, I'm having lunch with my mom today. She's at the hospital remember?"

"Oh god that's right!" she recalled as they began to head towards the hallway, "I forgot you said she'd be in town for her operation this week, sorry I just forgot, you know me – all about Mthato all day, every day."

Carla laughed, shaking her head as they stopped by the elevator.

"Is this the first time you're seeing her?"

"No I saw her last night, briefly. She was still foggy from the surgery but was doing alright." Carla smiled, "We're doing lunch today and if all goes well, she'll be discharged by this afternoon."

"Will she be staying with you or heading back to Secunda?"

"She'd never stay with me I don't think, I mean she's seen my place there's no room."

Mthato nod, "What was it again? Her hip, right?"

"Her knee." Carla corrected, "Nasty thing. She's always had it and I guess she's just over it. It's no big deal there's no reason for her to not be ok. Hell, I'd trade places with her for some anesthesia at this point – some deep sleep could be great."

Mthato laughed but before she could reply, Carla gasped in shock, "Oh shit I forgot something!" and rushed off down the hallway, disappearing around the corner just as the elevator opened.

Down the passage to the right, Carla moved as quickly as her heels would allow, rushing into her boss's office - grabbing the large binder on his desk.

By the time she reached the boardroom, she was already flustered, trying to catch her breath and compose herself as she watched the meeting approaching, riddled with regret that she was late entering.

Their heads turned when she entered, their eyes briefly gauged before returning their attention to the CFO who was doing the introduction. They all knew her, they were management in the company, so passing glance, quick smile and back to the meeting.

But it was Reginald Wiese who's scolding glare remained fixed on her as she round and quietly handed him the binder, mouthing "Sorry" before quietly moving to sit behind him beside Mthato who was against the wall taking minutes.
"Leading me to hand over the floor to the man with a possible solution to save on our current expenses on both these projects." The CFO smiled, "Mr. Wiese can you take us through your costing summary for the existing projections and we'll then compare with the upcoming projects?"
"Yes, thank you Frans, I just want to apologize for my assistant's interruption as well, but luckily I have my file with me." He said flipping his binder open.
Taking her laptop from the side table, she quickly opened it to start when the notification popped up on the bottom right of her screen.
She frowned and motioned her pointer to open the mail, but instead minimized it, opting instead to focus on the meeting minutes which Mr. Wiese always insisted had to be unique to him as opposed to those shared collectively.

Carla watched him speak shaking her head, trying desperately not to convey the vile dislike she had in him, his bald head, and his demeaning manner of speaking to people like they were unworthy of his time yet with a manner that simply passed his crudeness off as 'old and difficult'.

Then suddenly he turned to her, his eyes fixed on hers and a note in his hand.

Her heart raced as did her mind - *did I miss something? A question? Did he say something or ask me something? Oh god was this even the correct binder?*

She quickly scanned the minutes she'd typed out. "Carla this is yours in my file, please I ask nicely that you do not leave your personal notes in my binders?" he said, demeaning in a politeness to get away with it, "Here take your things so I can carry on. I do not want to waste these people's time." She reached out for the note, and he scoffed an apology before continuing. She looked to Mthato who simply shrugged and shook her head, before returning to taking her minutes.

Carla sighed nervously, irritably - feeling a heat within blood as she unfolded the note, a handwritten scribble in dark black ink:

TURN ON THE NEWS CARLA
YOU DON'T WANT TO MISS THIS!

She shook her head confused and crumbled it up, shoving it into her jacket pocket as Mr. Wiese proceeded with the meeting. Heaving a deep breath, she turned her attention again to the meeting minutes. Inside her anger was boiling, being almost sure he had deliberately put the note in his binder to cause the scene for his own amusement.

But wait, he gave me the file to take home last night to recheck.

She thought - her typing stopped.

Was I supposed to watch the news last night? This morning?
Is he upset that I didn't? Did he leave that note as a trick to see if I took the binder home last night?
She shook her head, looking up at his balding head as her thoughts raced.
No because he only messaged me this morning to remind me of the binder. What game is this exactly? Why is he even doing this? Why bother playing games in the first place!

She looked back down at her screen and immediately re-opened the email notifications.
A knock at the boardroom door brought everyone's attention to the tall IT manager with glasses, smiling almost clumsily with a wave, apologizing for the interruption.
"May I steal Miss Wilson for only a moment, please? It's rather critical." he asked. Everyone turned to her, and she froze looking at Mr. Wiese uncomfortably.
"Go sort out, please we are only being held up by interruptions by you." he scoffed, dismissing everything else as he continued with his briefing.

In the IT office, the head of IT stood with his arms folded behind her as she stared at the screen that held a coded version of an email sent to her, which their security systems tracked and were able to freeze.

"Any idea who the sender is?"
"No, none." She looked up at him, "What are the attachments? Are you able to see it?"
"If that gets clicked everyone and everything on the server will be shut down, it's a virus. A serious

virus." He explained, "We're lucky it got picked up before you reacted to the mail. If Felix didn't run the network scan when he did, we may have well all kissed our jobs goodbye."

Carla shook her head, "Can you trace who sent it, or where it comes from?"

"We'd rather not mess with the mail at all just in case it has tracking software or hidden bugs that can cause damage to our servers. There are clickbait viruses, programs that could possibly be imbedded in the email itself. This virus is a real threat, not your normal spam. You're going to have to fill out a report with us, and we'll have to include management in this to boost up our security." He explained as she got up, "I just needed you to know, because the email is still live on your inbox, so we need your laptop for Felix to secure before we give it back to you, so you'll have some free time coming your way."

Carla smiled awkwardly, knowing that this would simply be another kicker for Mr. Wiese.

****

While her daughter's world raced with its own challenges, Claudia Wilson sat up in her hospital bed finishing her oatmeal breakfast, shaking her head up at the news on the screen above her. Even without headphones she knew the story was grim.

"Such a terrible, cruel world we live in." the old woman beside her spoke in disgust as she tossed her headset to the side, "I can't watch this anymore. The world's gone mad man!"

"I actually knew them." Claudia said, placing her bowl on the tray, managing a smile.

The old lady paused, "Then this tragedy is even worse when it's close to home!"

"It was a long time ago. Our kids grew up together and my ex-husband was Hendrie's drinking buddy at the club." She said moving the blanket off her leg which was trapped by the knee brace, "It is terrible what people do to each other, your right about that." The frail old lady stepped out of the bed, her right elbow bandaged and made her way across the 2-patient ward to the bathrooms, "The Lord should take us all, end this madness!"

Claudia managed to smile, shaking her head as the bathroom door shut, shifting off the bed to reach for the drawers.

On her cellphone she began a message to Carla, who years ago was part of the inseparable group of kids that today lost an old friend in a very violent way, and she wanted to let Carla know she cared sooner rather than only at lunch.

Behind her the drapes began to draw shut, so without looking away from the message, she greeted.

"Morning nurse, time for my discharge I hope?"

Adding the heart, she sent the message and turned but there was nobody. Nothing but the drawn drapes shutting her off from the ward entrance.

She looked back up at the screen, thinking back on the years when her daughter would barely be home outside of school – always out and about with the rest of their group for hours on end. She remembered life was much simpler back then in

Secunda, the world was safer and less savvy to the cruelty of the world outside of the small town.

The blue drapes caved in behind her, over her head and shoulders as something grabbed her - tossing her quickly from the bottom of the bed, over the tray crashing to the ground.
Dazed, she scrambled to escape the drapes that were ripped off and wrapped around her, plucking it away from her face just as the dark figure stomped his boot in her face, sending her backwards hard.

The floor and her head met with a hard crack, and she felt for a moment that no thought could process in her brain, it was only the loud dulling zing - a pain that coursed into her entire face.
"What the hell are you doing?" the old lady gasped from the bathroom door in alarm, huddling backwards at the sight of the tall, formidable figure in his thick black coat and gauze mask.

"Help! Hello help!" she called as best she could while he stomped towards her, quickly rushing back into the bathroom, shutting the door.
"Help!" her old voice called frantically, "Help!"
With all its force, the gauzed maniac slammed his black boot into the door, sending it bursting open, hitting her thin frail body backwards into the shower.

It watched her unresponsive frail body for a moment wondering if she was dead or somehow able to survive that.
"Help!" Claudia screamed difficultly from outside in the ward, trying to get to her feet from the drapes tangled around her, her head screaming in agony

as a warm trickle of blood ran down the back of her neck.

She had just reached the door handle when the figure grabbed her, one black hand on her left shoulder and the other at her side.
The figure tipped her up while raising her and as though she were a rag doll rushed with her in its arms and tossed her violently through the glass.

Claudia Wilson's motionless body smashed down on the concrete ceiling, motionless between the air conditioner fan boxes supplying cold air to the floor below.

The figure hurried back to the door, removing the hooded coat and mask before casually stepping out into the loud hallway, leaving the door swinging open.

****

Staring at Eric in alarmed disbelief, Zain's mouth hung open as a coldness sunk over him, his mind racing to comprehend what Eric had just told him. Eric sighed in emotional defeat as he huffed back on the sofa, wiping his cheeks.
He had not spoken of any of this since he was 12 years old. It had been eating at him all these years, scared and lonely in a territory he still never wanted to accept. Speaking of it seemed to open the flood gates of all the remorse, guilt, anger, pain, and torment he'd endured for so long in his life.

It tore down the walls unlike any drugs or drinks he'd ever taken to numb it. And seeing Zain's blank disbelief forced guilt over him for sharing what happened the day his life was forever changed.

But the cost was now a burden on a friend. He looked down to the ground, his leg was still shaking – now from another terrifying reality: a story he swore he'd never repeat and had not, not in 10 years to anyone despite how wasted he'd gotten, or how rough the burden was to carry within.

He turned to Zain, who stared at him with a confused frown scrawled over his face, still silent, mouth slightly open – words unfound. Eric wanted to reach out and touch him, shake him, push a response – desperate to know if he would still have him in his life after this.
Why did I tell him? He wanted to know, he pushed to know. Why did I tell him?

Zain sat back on the sofa, then leaned forward on his knees, his hands pressing over his face as he tried still to allow it all to sink in and find his inner balance again. His 2-bedroom flat was silent, somehow the silence made the flat more humidly unbearable.
"Please say something?" Eric asked cautiously.
Zain swallowed, his throat was dry and his mind fractured - splintered trying to piece together all the information dropped on him through the past hour. He stood up and walked to the fridge, realizing he was shaking as he poured himself a glass of wine.

He took the glass in one hand, the bottle in the other and shut the fridge with his knee. The room

was hot, musty almost – for a moment he stopped in stride, realizing he could smell things from Eric's story that were just impossible. He handed Eric the glass without a word then turned to the balcony door, sliding it open as he slugged back from the bottle.
"Please say something."

The fresh air was alive, unlike the heated weight of his flat.
Silence hung as Zain took another swig from the bottle, nodding while he stared out, accepting that he had pushed Eric to talk to him and explain everything with threats of calling the police.

"I'm so sorry for telling you."
"No." Zain finally spoke, softly.
The breeze circled and Eric felt his heart racing, his own thoughts trying to understand how after so long he finally just opened his mouth and told him that which they all swore to never again repeat.
"I want you to know that I still feel the same way about you."
Eric stared at him, allowing him time to find what he needed to say.
"What you all did…" he said shaking his head, "I have so many questions."
"I know."
Another long stretch of silence lingered as Zain stared into the chaos of his thoughts, trying to force himself to stop shaking and regain his composure.
"You carried this all these years?" he said glancing over to Eric who simply nodded in thick remorse.
"I still love you." His voice cut the thickness in the small lounge and Eric looked up.
"You love me?"

Zain shook his head, "I don't know what I feel right now, this is a lot to process but nothing has changed between us I mean… how I feel about you. In fact, I pity you."

Eric wanted to smile, but there was still the darkness pushing and lingering.

"I did not expect all of this to come out of your mouth. I thought I knew you."

"I'm sorry I shouldn't have told you."

Zain frowned angrily, "And instead lie to me? Keep it hidden so it eats you alive for the rest of your life? How is that any better?"

Eric looked away from his dark and broken eyes.

"In the 2 years I've known you I've always wondered why you were so deep and stoic, but I never would have guessed what darkness you were carrying and that's why I pity you."

Eric huffed uncomfortably, "I'm sorry."

"Just stop saying that!" Zain snarled with another glare, "What difference does that even make?"

The tension was suffocating with each pause to morbid silence.

"Who else knows?" Zain spoke again.

"Nobody, just the ten of us as far as I know." Eric answered softly, "I don't know what happened after we all went our separate ways or who might have said anything."

Zain shook his head, gripping the bottle tightly.

"Zain, I need to know…" Eric finally pushed cautiously.

"If I'm going to call the police?" Zain finally turned to face him, his voice now even lower than before, "No Eric I'm not doing that. I don't think that would make much difference. I think you're right about what they'd think of you getting that email. So, no I won't

be calling the police, and I won't ever repeat this again."
Zain dropped his face into his hand, wiping hard with a deep breath.

"I should have never called you or involved you. I'm sorry." Eric said when Zain swung down another gulp from the bottle before sliding the balcony door shut. Still holding the glass, not taking even a sip of alcohol in his sobriety, Eric watched as Zain round the small coffee table and sat back down on the sofa, still not looking up at him.
"You..." Zain started awkwardly, "You might be wrong. Maybe it's not linked at all."
"I'm pretty sure it would be crazy to think it's not. There were others on that email, other recipients."
Zain nodded, sipping from the bottle before reaching for Eric's pack of cigarettes.
"If I'm a target then everyone else is too. Whoever did that to Jacques and his father is out there, taunting us." His voice broke, the haunting images again pushing on him.

A silence hung and Zain gulped the wine down, smoking like no amount of nicotine would satisfy the nerves etching inside him.
"Well, we need to warn them." Zain stood up, "Tell them what's going on or what you think is going on."
"I don't even know what is going on! I don't know what to think." Eric said standing to face him.

Zain stepped forward, took the glass from Eric's hand, downing it in one sip, before placing it on the coffee table as he stood to face him.
"I know you are scared. I'm scared for you." Zain said looking at him, "And I certainly won't pretend

that this doesn't scare me, because it does. But all I can think of is what you've gone through all these years. All of you."

For the first time in years Eric felt calm somewhere in the darkness as the sincerity burst through Zain's eyes.

"Eric, I am not going to judge you. Not yet at least because I need time to figure this out, I need to figure out where this puts me or how I feel about you. But I'm here and I'll help with whatever I can, but the most important thing now is to make everyone knows and can take precautions to keep themselves safe."

"I wouldn't even know where to start Zain, I've not seen or spoken to most of them for nine or ten years now."

"Then we find a way. Phone book, internet, whatever it takes. If someone is doing this because of what you all did, then they need to know before anyone else gets hurt. Plus, it will give us an indication of who might be doing this. If it's not one of your old friends, its someone they told."

Eric nodded, "Thank you."

He sighed shaking his head, "Well I'm part of this now, so let's focus on finding them and we'll take it from there. If you got that mail, then so did they."

****

By 4pm, the quaint coastal village of Southbroom with its 860-person population was already silent and tranquil. With his house a mere 500 meters from the property's private beach, Zach Manson had it much easier now than ever before. Simple, quaint, and secluded.

Tall, handsome, with long hair, he stood on his wide porch listening to the winged wildlife abuzz before their dinner, their chirps and squawking a tangible complement to the sound of the waves crashing beyond the greenery surrounding the large, private property.
In Southbroom Village, he could be anyone and more importantly, escape everyone. It was a place where he could wallow in his past in any means necessary without anyone forcing their way into it. No therapy, no rehab, no family.

Almost 23, his life to the few people living in Southbroom was seemingly perfect with an inheritance that bought a luxury most young men could only dream of.
Zach had no need to find work or face the struggles of finding his feet in the world. He was just being – existing in a world where he could splurge on whatever he wanted, smile when required and engage with others at his own pace or need. To the locals, he was the guy who lived in the secluded mansion with a private beach - nobody needed to know anything more, nor did he have a compulsory social obligation to offer anything.

After growing up in an average, relatively middle classed home, his father left his position on SASOL in Secunda to start his own small financial consulting business – amassing a fortune in the years thereafter when the firm grew to an international venture, and their days of living just slightly above the bread line ended.

But he was 16 when they truly began to cash in and still stained by the day his childhood ended – troubled and troublesome through dark internal turmoil. But he'd wear the face everyone expected, hiding everything inside in doses of Valium.

Having come into money showed and created more weights to his shoulders when they moved to Sandton in the city – thrust into a new social web that required a more consistent mask as the new kid in an unfamiliar private school -that was when the weight of everything truly began to crack his mask and his parents learned of his addiction to the pills that made everything numb.

He finished his high school run free of his dependence for almost a full year, and almost immediately got shipped to Sandton Prestige, a college not too far from his mother's watchful eyes. And for a time, he tried, but eventually the social conditions of being the heir to a multi-million-rand company garnered popularity and in the first two months the clutches of his addiction was back - he'd started showing up late for classes, fighting on campus grounds, acting out like a child with a temper tantrum over the most trivial of anything that he could use to release what he felt inside – worthlessness.

Shortly after his 20th birthday, he was already on his last chance with the headmaster when the news of his parents' death reached him.
They'd been killed in vehicle accident while driving back to Johannesburg from a vacation at their favorite place in South Africa – Southbroom.

As their only son, they'd left everything to him - a 20-year-old with almost thirty-eight million rand and 52% shares in the company. Why not disappear?

As Zach stepped off the porch and walked across the green yard, he smiled at the serenity of the world around him, with just the waves breaking in the distance. The past remained a blaring scar, whispering to him haunting reminders at every chance it took but he felt a stronger sense of peace in the small, beautiful village of Southbroom and the solitude it presented to him.

With no one left to care enough about him, it was peacefulness to his scarred soul which he preferred over what was when surrounded by the world out in the bigger towns and cities.
The only people who could possibly force him out of his shell were gone, and those who abused the privileges to him being out of his shell could be shunned away. He was, in a manner of logic, free to simply exist.

The waves rolled to shore, crashing with bright foam as they ran up the soft golden sand. The wind was strong, but warm and the smell of the deep ocean rose with each wave that tumbled in.
A tone from his phone sounded and he dug into his pocket. At first a smile crossed his face but then dropped to a concerned frown.

Love you guys too! Chat soon ☺

NOW

Zach?

Hey aunty Chantal.

What's up?

Have you heard?

Heard what?

See for yourself...

www.000881soutafricasnesw. co.za/clicktoread- 101011.55@locationfinder- Klerksdorp-massacre- 20240514

His mother's sister Chantal, who was also the last remaining relative he had, was one of the five people who had his number. Her message seemed random, peculiar even as it was the first time in almost 9 months that he'd heard from her.

He wanted to click the link almost immediately, but he paused to look up at the ocean again, taking a deep breath – a silent scream to the gods to not be anything that would rip away the solitude he so badly sought. He looked at the phone again, staring at the link as his thumb hovered over it.
Instead, he locked the screen and put it back in his shorts pocket as the fresh air circled around him.

I'll deal with this later.

Classed as a village, the locals living in Southbroom were limited to immediate access to stores, restaurants, and bars without having to drive 15 kms to Margate.

But what was offered to the locals in Southbroom was the Golf Club's pub, and on Tuesday afternoons he'd go sit on the deck overlooking the esteemed, gorgeous golf course that ran along the shore, and enjoy their pizza and quiz night – his semi-detachment anchor to the world of the living.

The sun was setting as darkness began to descend on the village of Southbroom when his Jeep rolled to a stop outside the double garage. His parents bought the 6-bedroom home during their very last vacation, having died before returning to tell him the news. It was a large faded grey double story with sprawling green gardens to either side of the house, and large windows in every room.

The main gate rolled shut and Zach hopped out, grabbing his house keys and cell phone before heading up the stairs to his porch when something large rustled in the thick shrubs on the side and he paused. Staring into the darkness his eyes strained, and another rustle sounded, this time from the other side and he swung around.
The night air was humid, and silent as always – he felt something watching him from the darkness that he strained so hard to see. But after a few moments, the silence stayed - nothing else was making a sound.

He took a deep breath as he stepped up the stairs again, backwards, his eyes still fixed on the darkness beyond the light of his porch.
"Stupid monkeys." He sighed, chalking it up before entering the house.

It was 7.30, and the sun and air had him yawning from before he got into the shower. As he dried off and put on his trunks, he moved through the house towards the fridge where he grabbed a beer and took 2 large sips before opening the front door. The cool air seeping into the humid house.

Slumping to the couch in the T.V room, he gulped again at the beer and put his feet up, ready to scroll for something to watch.

By 7.45pm he was fast asleep as the T.V played, the front door wide open to the darkness of the night, and his phone toned again.

****

Through the noise of the Pretoria General Hospital staff going about their duties, with even the voices of her mother's doctor and the police officer right by her - Carla sat motionless and defeated by disbelief. The strange note handed to her by her boss instructing her to watch the news along with the computer virus, a murdered old friend and now her mother.

"Why would my mom do this?" she asked looking up at her mothers' doctor and the two uniformed officers, "I don't buy the anesthesia brought on some episode. Surely it won't stay in the system for a day before causing something like this, plus I know my mother."
"Miss Wilson, we're all still a little shaken by this." Dr. Sesi Bayloi said, her voice calm and almost reassuring, "I know this is difficult for you, but it is known to happen, albeit very rare."
"Well either way, she's not a killer." Said Carla shaking her head angrily, "I can't believe this is happening."

Just down the passage, near the seating area sat the family of the old woman who was pushed to her death in her mother's ward, and a tear ran down Carla's face.
"Miss Wilson, I need you to understand." Dr. Sesi said sitting beside her, "I'm not allowed to speak to you any further, not about this. Every contact we have will have to be in the presence of a police officer or registered nurse as witness that I only provide you with updates on your mother's medical health, ok Miss Wilson? This is now a legal matter between their family and the police. I will stay on call as the primary GP until your mother wakes up."

Carla shook her head looking up at the staunch police officer, "If this was the medication, then surely the law can't charge her with murder."

"Not pre-meditated murder." He said shaking his head, "Look miss, I will tell you this – that family over there, they're not going to let this go easily, anesthesia or not. My advice, get out of that chair and find some legal counsel."

He offered an attempted smile before heading off towards the bereaved family where his partner stood finishing their affidavit.

Dr. Bayloi motioned to leave too when Carla grabbed her arm.

"Doctor. When will she wake up? It's been hours, should I be scared? I know you said something earlier, but I can't…"

"No, it's alright Miss Wilson." She smiled, waving a nurse nearby over.

Dr. Bayloi continued, "I understand it's been a rough day, so I'm happy to explain again. There is nothing medical for you to be worried about at this moment."

Carla shut her eyes, trying to find solace in the darkness.

"Our primary concern is the fracture on your mother's hip and the severe cerebral contusions on the undersurface of her temporal lobes. The sedatives we've given her are for a medically induced sleep until surgery can be performed. The fractures are severe and could potentially require arthroplasty where we replace the hip. But right now, we need to calm the brain's activity and decrease the swelling so we can perform the surgery. Do you understand?"

Carla nod wiping her tears, "Whatever you need to do, just please make her ok again."

"We'll keep monitoring her and the moment there's anything - you'll be the first to know. Ok?"

"So, I really can't see her again, just one more time type of thing?"

"I'm sorry, there's no way we can allow that. There is a police guard at her door in ICU to make sure she's not at any risk."

"You mean a risk to others or your staff." Carla sighed coldly, "But I get it."

"Miss Wilson, I cannot imagine what you are feeling. I don't think anyone expected today to end this way, but you have my word, you'll be the first to know." Carla appreciated the doctors' courtesy and friendly smile, given that her patient had just murdered another under her roof.

The doctor looked to the nurse and then looked back at Carla, "I must see other patients now. If you need anything, please speak to the nurses. You will be the first to know anything."

"Thank you doctor." Carla managed a tired smile, allowing the doctor to head off.

"Why don't you get something to eat?" the nurse offered, "Let me show you where to get a good sandwich."

She gave a nod and stood up, following behind the nurse as she led the way in the opposite direction from the grieving family, when only a few steps later her cell rang from inside her jacket pocket.

Seeing that it was the office number calling, she shook her head almost declining to answer due to both the circumstances and the time, but before she

put the phone back in her handbag, she instead answered the call – continuing behind the nurse.
"Mr. Weise this is hardly the right time to be calling..."
"Hello Carla."
The voice was cold, gruff, and unfamiliar.

"I'm sorry, who is this?" she asked, turning away from the nurse, and pausing to the side.
"Nice little office you have here, assistant PO Officer. Quite the next step from the little tomboy you used to be, well done."
"Who is this?" she asked, now alarmed.
"You haven't checked my email yet, have you Carla?" the voice asked ominously, "You really should Carla, there's a little something just for you."
"What is this about? Who are you?"
The voice laughed, "Not who. What..."
"What that you tried to shut down our offices with your virus? Yeah, we're on to you."
The voice laughed again, "No, no, no. You haven't been following the breaking story, have you? Your little chubby friend sure squealed like the fat pig he is when I ripped out his throat."
She froze in alarm.
"Yes you feel it don't you? Something inside that wants to be set free..."
She hung up the phone almost gasping as a cold set in over her and it rang again, this time an unknown number.
"Hello?" she asked nervously.
"Oh, I'm more than a virus Carla. I wanted you to know what was coming!"
"Who the hell are you? What is this?" she asked, looking around frantically.

"Can you see me yet Carla?" The voice mocked her, "If you look closely, you'll recognize me. I'm the one who's going to make you scream."
Her eyes darted around the crowded hallway, and for a moment she almost forgot that just around the corner were the police, "Who is this?"

Her legs moved as fast as they could, the fear making them almost blocks of concrete in heels while she moved past the hospital staff and round the corner.

The old woman's family were still speaking to the police, and relief rushed over her as she began to rush forward.
"If you talk to the police, I'll finish your mother off."
Again, she froze, her eyes wide, "What?"
"You heard me, if you draw any attention to yourself, I'll end her, officially!"
She clutched the phone trying to force control over her shaking.
"She's a tough old bitch isn't she Carla? I really thought she was dead for sure, but apparently Mrs. Wilson wants to see the inside of a jail cell. She should have just died like the old bag."
"Who the hell are you?"
She moved again, one more step, her breath almost pressed inside.
"Don't temp me Carla, if you take one more step towards the police, I'll slit her open she means nothing to me!"
Her body jumped and she moved to the side, her back up against the wall, huddling almost.
The voice was stern, "This is about you Carla. And the police won't help you anyway, nobody can. It's

all in motion now Carla. There's no escaping it, not anymore."

"What do you want from me?" she braved back her tears.

"You know that don't you? You felt it when you saw the porker's face on the news, something inside you clicked but you weren't sure, were you? How about now Carla? Or do I need to finish mommy to make a point?"

"No please…" Tears ran down her face as she put her hand over her mouth.

"I'll be seeing you soon…tomboy. Check your mail bitch." The voice taunted, ending the call.

Her legs gave in, and she sank to the floor on her haunches - crying into her hands. Every word, the anger and rage in its menacing threats scoured through her mind and everything of her life began to flash and tear in her mind.

She raised her head, and wiped her face while standing up, remembering who she used to be years before, and she took a deep breath and rushed towards the elevator.

In the hospital lobby, she removed her heels, and hurried across to the front desk, hurriedly grabbing through the selection of newspapers to ensure she had one of each, before retreating to one of the couches in the lobby by administration.

Forty minutes later, she had read every headline and grim story published.

CHAPTER THREE

They were all just kids, early teen years. The whole group on their bikes, riding like the wind as though no trouble or care in the world would ever phase them. Laughing as they rode down the street, crossing the intersections and ramping up the pavements to cut across the fields.

Marcus and Odette shared a bike, her on the seat and him upright on the pedals, steering their adventures. They were alone with Jacques, putting their bikes on the lawn in front of Jacques' house.

"Come on! I want to show you!" Jacques urged, ushering them with his hand as he rushed up the narrow porch stairs ahead of them. But he stopped at the door, dead in his tracks just staring at the shut door.
"Jacques?" Odette asked, "What is it?"
He stood still, the silence of the day growing louder as the light began to escape into darkness.
The porch light came on - she and her brother looked up at it, burning bright above their frozen friend.
"Jacques, what is it?" she urged again, when her brother grabbed her forearm.
"Something's wrong Odette, we need to go!" he urged, his eyes wide in fear.
She looked at Jacques again, he was motionless, staying in the same space without a single movement, and she stepped forward.

Marcus gripped her forearm, really urging her again, "Odette we need to go now."

"Something's wrong with Jacques, we can't leave him Mark." She insisted back, her hand reaching out towards Jacques' shoulder.

"Jacques…" she said, her little bottom lip quivering. Then he turned, fast and suddenly.

His eyes were gone, black blood-filled holes and his chest torn apart beneath shreds of shirt, blood gushing out as Jacques screamed.

Odette sat up in bed gasping –
Her body cold with sweat in her bed. Beside her lay Shane, her boyfriend, naked and fast asleep.
She sat up off the bed, wiping the sweat from her face as she reached for her glass of soda on the bedside table, taking a few gulps before putting it back down.

She looked to him again, his pale white skin against the blue sheets and she shook her head rolling her eyes, wondering what her mother would have thought of her loving someone white.
Growing up under the dual influence of Zulu from their mother and Portuguese father, both Odette and her brother Marcus as kids had to be careful who their mother allowed them to mingle with – still stuck in the stigma of an older world.
She wiped her forehead again, then rubbed around her neck – the nightmare had placed inside her a chill that wasn't going away and tensed her.

Suddenly a hand reached for her, and she jolted around barely screaming.

"Are you ok?" Shane asked nervously sitting up closer to her, "You didn't hear me? What's wrong?" She sighed, "You scared me. I had a nightmare." "You scared me!" Shane grinned as he rolled to turn on the lamp beside him before rolling back to face her, his hand rubbing on her scarred thigh, "Are you ok? Want to tell me about it?"

His company made the cold dissipate and she heaved a sigh of relief, shaking her head, "No I just want you to hold me."

"I can do more than that." He smirked, grabbing her towards him playfully.

"I can't." she sighed, "It was just so…I just need a moment, ok?"

Shane sat up and a silence hung. He swallowed his disappointment and frustration at – again - being pulled from sleep by her nightmares.

"I'm sorry." she said softly. He sighed while forcing a smile, then pulled her towards him, clutching her in his arms tightly against his chest.

"It was just another nightmare - you're safe." he said brushing her hair with his hand. She smiled, closing her eyes as she snuggled against him.

They'd been dating since they were 17, having met at Secunda Highschool and in the 3 years together, he always made her feel safe. Her history was a heavy burden to carry - when she was 17 and throwing herself at any guy who'd take her, she only wanted to feel safe.

But she found it with Shane, and she hugged him tightly, silently praying that he'd never know about all the guys before him or find out the truth about what pushed her to be such a promiscuous girl who used to cut herself on the top flesh of her thigh as a reminder to shut her mouth.

She thought again of her mother who died when she was 9, a blood clot that shot from her thigh to her heart, and Odette missed her. She'd always missed her, through everything that transpired in her childhood and the dark years that followed she'd always wondered if things would have been different had her mother been around instead of their father, a snarly drunk.

She appreciated Shane's love and affection because she knew she wasn't worth it.
Odette understood that she made it hard for him to get rest with her constant nightmares, she knew that her mood swings and penchant to drink herself into a ruthless menace drove him to the breaking point more than once, but he chose to stay with her and accept her.

She silently hated herself for being so weak and for failing at moving past the day that changed her childhood. She wanted to be stronger, non-reliant on anything to face the world, but that part of her died a long time ago – never again to be found inside her.

He hugged her close, and she kissed the small tattoo of her name across his chest as she moved to kiss a little lower on his stomach, then back up again on his chest towards his neck as she moved up closer against him. His body was chiseled from carting around heavy tools and equipment all day. But it wasn't the body that made the man a safe zone, it was his heart and how he loved her, a 19-year-old girl who didn't deserve it.

"You're still going to marry me someday, right?" she smiled asking, pausing her kiss to his lips, "Even with all my crazy?"

Shane shook his head, staring deeply into her eyes as he pulled her face closer, kissing her passionately.

"I'd love you and marry you if you had two size 9 male feet growing out of your cheeks." He grinned stupidly and she shook her head grinning as she leaned into him with a kiss.

By 5.30am the sky above Secunda was already that strange shade of black turning blue, with a few stars still in sight to the West. The small town was quiet still.

Shane was already dressed and showered, putting on his shoes on the edge of the bed when she walked in with two mugs of coffee.

"Don't you ever want to get out of here?" she asked, giving him his mug before sliding onto the bed beside him. Shane shrugged his shoulders, "I think everyone from here wants to get away from here. But we've had this conversation, where would I get another decent job that pays what I do now? We need this, I want to make you my wife and give you everything."

She smiled, "I'd take nothing if it meant being away from here."

He turned to her sipping from his mug, and she quickly teasingly continued, "With you of course."

He smiled and sipped at his coffee. He had always known how much she hated Secunda, that deep inside of her lay a story that explained the reason for wanting to get as far from it as possible. But whenever he'd push, she'd shut down, explode, and drink herself into a stupor – arguing and berating him before retreating to her cocoon of self-loathing before they'd be able to make up or even talk again. It was a cycle every few weeks. She was tormented and it controlled her, which was hard for him to watch.

"Secunda has too many ghosts." She said matter-of-factly.

"Well, isn't that why you're seeing Doctor Blomkamp? To face those ghosts?"

She heaved a sigh, nodding, "I hope so."

"Well at a hundred and ninety rand an hour, I'd hope she's a Ghostbuster!" he mocked.

"Hey, don't be like that. I've only seen her a few times since you said we could afford it. It'll get better." She said nodding earnestly, "I will get better. I just need to figure out some things. And if it's too expensive I'll stop going until I get a job of my own."

"No." he said sternly, looking away as he put down his mug to carry on tying the laces of his work boots.

She sighed irritably, "You said you understood."

"I do."

"Then you need give me time. I'm just a plain girl. What do I know about therapy? It takes time, you don't..." she paused.

"What, I don't understand?" he turned to her over his shoulder, "No I don't Odette."

A silence hung between them as he took a few more sips of his coffee before standing up for the bedroom door.

She closed her eyes, the flashes of the past sending chills through her core, showing on her skin and she rubbed over her arms.

Seeing everyone else flee Secunda at the first chance they got, one after the other, reminded her of everything even more – worse, it reminded her that she was stuck there with the sinister shroud everywhere she went, like claws reaching from the past never allowing her to move forward.

"I don't want you to leave angry." She urged getting up behind him, "Not after such an amazing start to the morning."

He sighed and managed a smile, leaning in for a kiss.

"I want you to be ok, no more nightmares, no more flashes or whatever." He said as he caressed her cheek, "And I do know that therapy is a thing people like us know very little about. But it's expensive so the sooner the better, you know?"

She nodded, "I love you, Shane."

"I love you. Always." He kissed her again, a long passionate kiss before stepping back, "I should go before I stay."

She laughed as she followed behind him down the stairs of their 2-bedroom duplex apartment. At the front door he lifted his lunch bag and safety helmet, then turned to her again.

"Listen, I do understand. Kind of... Obviously not really, but I know that whatever it is that makes you..." he paused trying to figure out what terminology would be less harsh, when she interrupted.

"Crazy? Mad?"

He grabbed her hands pulling her close again, "Whatever makes you hate this town so much." Shane kissed her again, staring into her eyes. "Whatever it is, it won't make me love you any less or change my mind. I will make you my wife Odette Gallagher, nothing is going to change that. Whether you tell me, or tell your doctor, I just want you and me to grow old together. Without the baggage, only smiles and little kids to keep us busy."
She kissed him again, knowing that despite what he was saying he too only had enough limit for so long to tolerate the nightmares and her episodes.

Therapy was her only hope to say out loud what ate away at her, but she wasn't ready to say it. Ten years was not long enough. She had thought of telling him a thousand times, but she was too afraid of losing him, so she kept it buried to a point where it was suffocating.

She went upstairs again, taking her coffee from beside the bed then standing at the window watching as he reversed from the carport and drove towards the complex gate.
She looked up at the sky as the orange glimmer began to show on the horizon, when three hard slams echoed from the front door downstairs.

The house was still quiet, and although she knew it was impossible - she called for Shane anyway, confused as to what could have made such a loud thump. She opened the curtain beside the door but outside was quiet with nothing in sight. She stood still with her ears pricking while she moved between the lounge and kitchen, turning on the lights. Nothing had fallen.

She looked out the window and their small yard was quiet.

She turned off the lights, dropping her head and wondering if she was experiencing another episode as she made her way up the stairs.
Pausing halfway, she looked back at the front door, deciding to walk down and open it.

Her heart jolted and she gasped, the cool morning air circling around her as it passed into the house - logged into the door a small axe, with a black handle.
It's sharp silver blade pegging the corner of an envelope into the door.
She shut the door, locking it and rushing away into the middle of the room, her hand up in her hair while the other held her eyes shut, panting breathlessly.
It's not real, it's not real!

Her thoughts raced, and she moved to the door again, careful to unlock it quietly before yanking it open again. *It's real!*
She instinctively grabbed the handle, pulling as hard as she could until it finally un-wedged sending her stumbling, and the envelope dropped to the floor.

She shut the door, locking it and rushed up the stairs again. In the bedroom she hurriedly dialed into her cellphone, the envelope gripped tightly in the same hand holding up the phone and the axe in the other, white knuckles.

"Babe." She gasped as he answered, "Where are you?"

"Just cleared at security. Look I'm about to go through the dead zone so we may cut off." he answered as the line began to crackle.

"Babe, can you hear me?" she urged, "I need you to come home, please quickly!"

"What? Babe I'm almost at the..."

The line scratched, and the call ended. Signal lost.

"Shit!" she snarled, dropping the phone to the bed, then looking at the axe still clenched in her hand before dropping it to the floor and taking the envelope - ripping it open.

It was a set of photos and a note.

The first photo - her older brother Mark walking on the wharf by the boats, behind it scribbled in black ink the date – four days ago.

The next was a photo of Jacques, taken from a distance - at night. He walked away from a delivery car parked in the street. His face riddled with anger and his phone in his hands. Behind it, the same date as the murders from the news. Her heart was racing now, and a heat filled her body.

The note was a thick white paper, folded neatly. On it, scribbled in the same black ink:

TICK TOCK· TICK TOCK·

****

The roads of Boksburg, a suburb of Johannesburg, were busy with heavy traffic as the day broke into full swing.

The R21 offramp was synonymous with being easily backlogged or congested, and sitting in his white, double cab Toyota Hilux pickup, 22-year-old Matthew Jonah nodded to the music playing from this stereo. He was tired, having barely slept with constant tossing and turning trying to erase his mind - bringing it back to the place it was before seeing the news the day before. He spent most of the night on his phone watching videos trying to distract the morbid upset of it all.

After leaving high school, Matthew discussed with his parents the option of taking a year off before following his sister Magaret into university, when his father suggested he intern for a year at their civil engineering business.
He'd enjoyed it so much, things soon became permanent and before he knew it, he was getting a full-time salary, studying through online college while growing up in the real world.

But it was not the studying that kept him from sleeping, it was an old friend's murder in Klerksdorp that had shaken him.

In all the years since their childhood friendship ended, he'd only run into Jacques once again, a year ago during a site meeting with his father in Klerksdorp.
Jacques was at the same fuel station and their encounter, although brief and awkward, was adequate for the time. But now it plagued him, the 2nd death of their old friendship group while they were all so young. The first was Bobby who died when his motorbike was hit by an oncoming vehicle.

It was tragic hearing of it two years ago, but somehow the consolation was that accidents were exactly that - unexpected events that occurred beyond anyone's control. But with Jacques and what happened to them in Klerksdorp, he could not shrug off the pre-considered brutality, anyone would have to do something so terrible.

His phone rang from the seat beside him.
UNKNOWN NUMBER.
"Matt hello?"
"Hello Matt." The voice sounded excited.
"Hi, who is this?" Matt asked, his phone's battery beeping low battery 3%.
"It's good to hear your voice again Matt. I'm almost excited."
Matt frowned with an uncomfortable grin, "Ah, ok?"
"You don't check your mail much do you Matt? I've been trying to get your attention."
Matt checked his beeping phone again.

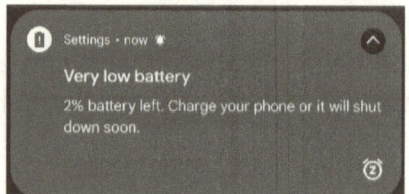

"I'm sorry, who are you?"
The voice chuckled, "Oh you'll find out soon enough. I've been doing my rounds, been very busy."
Matt looked at his phone again. UNKNOWN NUMBER.

"Look guy, I don't mean to sound rude but I don't know you so how about you tell me who you are so we can have a conversation, alright?"

"Say, how's your sister Magaret?" the voice asked, when Matt snarled but before he could speak his phone beeped again, quick in succession.

The call was over.

Later, his Hilux rolled through the main gates at the construction site where he and a team were to spend the day doing revisions of the planning with his father coming to sign off.

Heading across the site towards the container offices, he greeted the guys with smiles, the irritation of the call already out of his mind. He loved what he was a part of, always eager to be on duty even when sleep had eluded him, and a headache was throbbing.

Siviwe, the surveyor, was already pouring herself some coffee from the pot when Matt walked in and she smiled brightly, "Good morning, want some?"

"Do I ever say no to coffee?" he smiled, placing his things on the small desk, "Do we have any outlets in here, my phone died."

She gave a nod towards her satchel, "I have a power bank in there, should give you a good boost."

"Life saver, thank you." he said, going over to her bag.

"So, word is the client is asking for a new brick mason to be appointed. Did you hear?" she mongered,

"The guys a joke if you ask me. He was out of line and way out of his depth." Matt shrugged, "I don't go to an accounting firm and tell them how to run their books, so he should have known his place."

Siviwe laughed, nodding in agreement as she handed him a mug, "You're going to have to tell your father that. He's putting Nkosi on paid suspension."

Matt sighed, shaking his head before sipping his coffee before pulling out his laptop.

The door opened and they were greeted by a tall, heavy-set man with a long beard – Andreas Christodoulopoulos, the landscape foreman.

"Are we are doing this or what?" his voice boomed as he reached for the mug in Siviwe's hand, taking it as though she had offered, "Some of us are here to get paid sooner rather than later."

"Excuse you." she scoffed, reaching for her mug again just as it was about to touch his lips. Andreas was everyone's anti-favorite Greek - filled with pranks and loud chuckles at times, while on other occasions the most stubborn and arrogant of men, particularly over petty things.

Matt shook his head, waiting for his laptop to open while Siviwe and Andreas gossiped about the site's latest news while Andreas poured himself coffee. A message toned from his cell, charging to the side. It was a voice note from his sister Magaret.

Outside, on the side of the container office, he put a lit cigarette between his lips, about to play her voice note when at the gates he saw someone he immediately recognized. He frowned, straining his eyes as he stepped forward, watching the security talking to a face he'd not seen in a decade.

"Is that you Eric?" he called moving around the bulldozer towards the gate, "Eric Jansen?"
Eric smiled nervously, as the security ushered him to meet Matt at the fence.
"Hey Matt." Eric smiled, "It's been a while."
"You can say that again. How are you?"
"Good, good. You?"
"I'm good, doing great, working with my dad." Matt smiled, "What brings you here?"
Eric looked back to the car where Zain sat watching them, he was nervous and unsure how to approach the reason for his visit.
"Well, we've been trying to reach out to you. well, anyone actually... From the old days." Eric mumbled, "My friend Zain and me. That's him over there in the car."
Matt frowned, looking at the car and then back at Eric's awkward nervousness. The unsettling energy vibrated off his old friend heavily, and following the phone call earlier he began to feel almost threatened, in danger.

"What are you talking about man? Was that you who called me earlier?"

"Uh, no. No, I don't have your number. But Zain and I were able to find you online, and you tagged this location a few days ago, so I was hoping you would be here."

"Why?" Matt asked bluntly, rude even, "Why are you stalking me after all these years man, I haven't seen you in forever and you're here with some guy at my work..."

"I know, I know!" Eric pushed calmly, "I just, we need to talk."

"About what man?"

Eric turned to the car; his body was shaking now from the difficulty in trying to explain everything.

"Is this about what happened to Jacques?"

"Yes, maybe."

"Bro what do you mean maybe?"

"Did you get the email yesterday?"

"What email man?"

Eric lowered his voice from the security guard, "The one with the murders?"

"What?" Matt gasped almost laughing, "What murders? Eric, what the hell is this about me?

"It's all over the news Matt." Eric said still talking softly, "I got an email... it has pictures, terrible pictures of the crime scene."

A silence hung briefly, Matt scanning his old friends' face, trying to figure out the complexity of their sudden, awkward engagement.

As a kid Matt would often bully Eric relentlessly and Eric felt nervous again as though afraid that Matt would lunge forward with his brutish force and pin him to the ground in a headlock while performing a wedgie.

"Look Eric, this is a little strange. You are showing up here all cryptic and shit…"

"Did you get the mail or not?" Eric asked forcefully.

Matt shook his head, taking a step backwards, "Look I don't know anything about your email ok, maybe it's in my junk, I don't know. This is weird, and I'm already having a pretty weird day!"

"Don't walk away from me Matt." said Eric pleadingly as Matt stepped away.

"And to be blunt, you're being weird and creepy! And I'm not appreciating this at all man. There's a reason your mail is in my junk folder dude, we aren't pals anymore, you cannot just show up all weird and out of the blue like this."

"I just need a few minutes! I think…" Eric noticed the security guard reacting to them and he again lowered his voice, "Look can we just talk in private? Come out, sit with us so we can…"

"Hell no." Matt scoffed, "Tell me what you want or get out of here Eric. You and your friend."

Eric looked back at the car, Zain's face trying in vain to hear them, the security guard motioning a step closer.

"I think Jacques' murder has something to do with us." He said abruptly, loudly even. And Matt's mouth dropped open, the smoke just waning out.

In those brief moments as he stood there, he felt himself being sucked back ten years into the past, it was compressing and suffocating.

Eric sighed shaking his head, "We need to talk."

"No. No we have no reason to talk, especially about that. Now get out of here Eric." He stepped back, "I can't go through this with you, it's been years and I just...I can't. Tragic things happen and that's just how it is, alright. Now go away."

"Matt, we need to discuss this!" Eric urged.

"No!" Matt snarled, "Get out of here. Get him out of here, please get him off site."

The security motioned to Eric, taking him by his upper arm, "Please vacate sir."

"Matt!" Eric called as he watched Matt heading across the site and out of sight, the security guard still tugging him politely - violently towards the car.

"Wow." Zain laughed while Eric got back into the passenger seat with a heavy and defeated sigh. "You didn't handle that very well."

"No kidding."

Matt checked inside the office, there were now just a few more waiting inside for the superintendent to arrive for them to start. But he was shaking, upset and unsure so he stepped back to the side lighting another cigarette, shaking his head angrily as he replayed their encounter.

Getting any communication from his sister was out of the ordinary as they barely spoke since she'd left for Cape Town University, and since he'd opened the voice message, it was followed by several question marks - prompting urgent response. He pressed to listen.

Look asshole, I got your letter and whatever this is, I'm not interested, and I want you to leave me alone! Ok? God - do you have any idea how awkward it was getting called in for this and the 20 questions about it? You're a child! I have no idea

*what this was for or why you'd even do this at all?
It's crazy, you are crazy and I'm furious at you!*

She continued, leaving Matt shaking his head in
confusion. He'd not sent her anything – ever.

*I don't even understand the concept behind
something like this! I've done nothing to you, God
we barely speak, and you prop out of nowhere with
this shit? You sent this to the head of the board
marked life or death urgent. Are you kidding me?
Do you have any idea the fuss they would have
gone through to get that letter to me? I want you to
go back to leaving me the hell alone. Don't ever
contact me again!*

He shook his head angrily, and hurriedly typed
back:

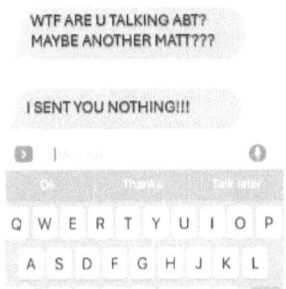

A few seconds went by, and he pulled hard at the
cigarette, staring at his phone trying to imagine if he
had been roped into a pranking show or if his world
had suddenly become Bizarre Central.
Her anger was alarming.

As kids they were almost inseparable, just two years apart and part of the same friends' group. But since the day everything happened, they'd never been the same despite trying and failing to be one another's support pillar through the years.
Despite a brief time of trying, it was evident that no matter what – they would never again gel, she'd always look at him the way she did that day, and it was too much for him to bear amidst everything he did trying to bury it. Her scowl was a reminder of everything he didn't want in his world anymore.
The app indicated she was replying by voice note so he anxiously watched for it.

Look I don't have time for this I have enough shit to deal with, unlike you! Whatever this is, whatever you thought you'd accomplish – it's not going to happen we'll never be as close as we used to be Matthew, that's over! God, I cannot believe you did this Matt! God how humiliating! And for what Matt, for what? Why would you do this? I don't know what this is about, but I want you to leave me alone. Got that? LEAVE ME ALONE!

She was angry, and he was confused. The frustration in her voice was pure, legitimately convinced he sent her a letter. He stood shaking as he quickly typed his reply.

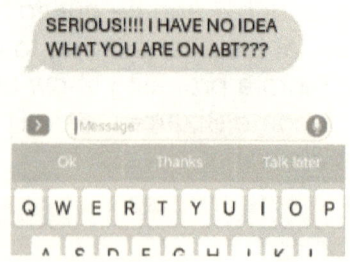

He paused for a moment, watching anxiously for the four dots but nothing came, so he aggressively clicked to reply via voice message.

"Ok…I for real have no idea what you are talking about so stop snorting whatever is messing up your brain and get your shit together before you harass me with your bullshit. How's that?"

He shook his head, taking the last drag of his smoke before tossing it to the ground, stepping it into the dirt.
He closed his eyes, taking a deep breath, then checked the phone again - four dots and he shook his head, rolling his eyes while he waited for it to come through.
His phone toned, an image, then another:

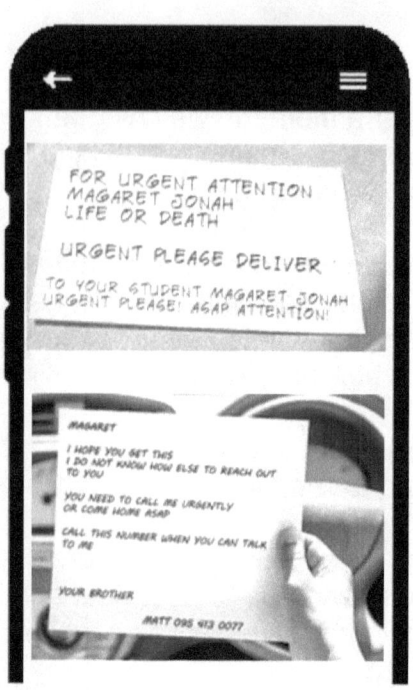

An ominousness befell him, a tingle deep within the coursing blood in his veins as he hurriedly dialed to call - but she cut the call, and he typed as fast as his thumbs could allow:

He heard his father's laugh, and he looked up to see his dad approaching while greeting the team in stride. Matt hurriedly typed again:

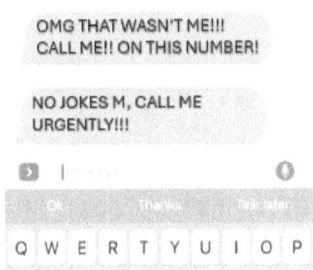

His dad's smile was broad, his dark hair combed neatly in a side path, and he reached out to shake his hand. He was proud of his boy working with him, taking keen interest in everything he built.

"Ready for a big day son?" asked his father Steyn Jonah, his voice deep but kind. Matt heaved a deep breath, forcing a smile as he walked to meet his father.

****

Even as the early sun heat her four door Golf, the long stretch of black road leading into the primary entrance to the large Sasol compound and everything beneath it, Odette's body stayed cold. She was frantically scanning all the cars coming and going at the main gates, waiting desperately to see Shane's pick up.

Beside her on the seat the pictures and the note, stuff into the envelope with the black handled axe wrapped in a dish towel.
She'd been waiting for 40 minutes, with impatience growing - in the back of her mind she knew how

large the site was and how many hoops he'd have to go through for clearance to leave, but her panic forbade her from any more tolerance.

Inside, her stomach was knotted, and she knew she'd need to eat something soon because the growling was becoming worse. Finally, a van stopped, it was him. He got out and walked to the gate, chatting to security, pointing at her in the car. She clasped her hands, so desperate for him to hold her or better yet - wake her from this fear. They opened the controlled pedestrian gate allowing him to walk out.
She leapt out of the car in a rush toward him, gripping him tightly.
"What's going on babe?" he asked confused, his dirty hands pulling her to see her face, the tears on her cheeks crushing him and empowering his concern.
"Can't' you please just come home?"
"Eddie won't let me. We are too behind and there is no one that can come stand in for me."
"Someone came to the house." She said, taking his hand and pulling him towards the car, "I think something bad is going to happen…I don't know what to do."

Several minutes later, they were inside the car with the axe and envelope contents on his lap – the picture of her brother Mark in his hand. He was quiet, having heard her explain where it came from, and he raised the axed, turning to her, concern written all over his face.

"Someone put this through our door?"

"Into the front door."

He was silent again, staring at the axe.

"I don't know what to do." Her voice was shaking, "I've tried to reach Mark but he's not answering or reading my messages."

"We need to take this to the police." He said now angrily, "Someone dares to come threatening you at our home! We must go to the police! They can get fingerprints off this stuff."

"Ok, ok." She nodded her head up and down, almost her whole body agreeingly.

"Who is this guy anyway?" he raised the photo of Jacques.

"That's a guy I used to be friends with when I was younger, his name was Jacques Petersen." She said nervously almost, "I've not seen him in years, so I don't know why I'd get this? I don't understand any of this!"

He nodded, then paused for a moment as he connected the name, he was certain he heard before and once the data in his mind pieced together, he turned to her.

"Jacques Petersen, the guy from that massacre in Klerksdorp?"

She nodded. A short silence hung in the car as he figured out how to swallow another untold truth handed to him by her.

He'd gotten home talking about the story – carried over from everyone at work discussing it and sharing what they'd read in the various papers. She never said anything, nothing.

"Will you come with me?" she asked nibbling on her thumb nail, "To the police? Will you be able to…"

"Are you ever going to be honest with me Odette?" he faced her, speaking clearly, frankly.

"What do you mean?" she asked cocking her head to the side – being caught in her own frantic thoughts to realize that not mentioning to him earlier was hurtful.

"You knew the guy?"

"When I was like 12 or something yeah, we were friends."

"You knew the guy?" he asked again, more irritably. She frowned, "Why? What do you think that means? Am I next?"

Shane huffed angrily biting his lip, his hands pounding his leg as he spoke.

"You knew the guy? This guy! This guy - whose whole family got brutally murdered, and you didn't mention that to me yesterday. It didn't occur to you say - hey Shane, you know what? I knew the guy?" He scoffed chucking the pictures at her, "So what the hell am I supposed to be thinking? Are you next? Are we safe? All I wanted was to live happily ever after with you, as hard as it was going to be it was going to be enough for me! But every time I think there's a chance to have that, it's taken from me. _You_ take it from me with your secrets and your goddamned bullshit! Odette…I…I can't do it anymore! I don't know what to say to you anymore! You're unbelievable."

"Baby let me explain." She said reaching for his hand, which he plucked away angrily.

"Explain what? How you spent over an hour sitting with me yesterday and talking about this horrible thing that happened, and said nothing that you knew the guy? What - did you screw him or something?"

Her jaw dropped. She'd not seen him so raw towards her before, his face was red, his hand on the door gripping it tight.

"Was he the one who made you become a slut throughout high school?" he attacked, staring at her - glaring without more charade or tolerance.

Tears ran down her face, and where it usually ached him to see her crying and would soften him – it didn't.

Since Shane had realized that he had felt something genuine for her two years ago, all he did was work hard to making sure he could provide her with what she so desperately needed – love and security.

He worked long hours in a tough job to give her that and even stopped speaking to people he once considered friends. He was angry now, but the anger stemmed from the expensive therapy sessions in the hope she'd figure out how to stop with her nightmares and come to terms with whatever tormented her into having her drunken sessions.

"Yeah, yeah Odette - I know. I know about what kind of girl you were around the time that we met." He said sternly as a sadness broke over his face, "I've known since the night we met at Jenny's party. And through all of that, all your drinking and your goddamned nightmares I've stayed. I've tried to save you."

"You can't save me!" she screamed, her voice reverbing out of the closed car so loudly that the security turned to them.

"So, what I didn't tell you that I knew Jacques?" she

snarled, "So what Shane – you met me that night thinking I'd be easy enough to get laid? And what, you just enjoyed it so much you stayed for another two years?"

"I can't do this. I can't go through this anymore." He opened the door, "I know how this ends and I just, you won't ever change. Nobody can save you, that you got damn right Odette."

He stepped out, "I'm done Odette, we're done! I can't live with a girl who has old boyfriends waiting to chop holes in my door."

The car door slammed.

"To hell with you!" she screamed, hitting her face and head while kicking at the floor of the car as she burst into tears. She cried for only a few seconds before swallowing it, biting down on her teeth, and wiping her face – history had taught Odette Gallagher to hide pain - she knew exactly how.

****

Two hours had passed since he'd gotten out of the car, leaving his heart with a broken girl. Shane sat on the work bench with all his colleagues bustling about lunch, trying to shake off what he'd left her with – an axe and a threat.

He'd broken, become something else and was exhausted by what she'd brought into his world, despite loving her with all his heart. Shane sat with his sandwich in his hand, staring at the ground trying to figure out if she hadn't brought all of this to him out of some ploy to simply avoid being alone during one of her episodes.

Could she be that far gone? That messed up?

She'd pulled many tricks before, forcing him to leave work for emergencies only to arrive home and find her hammered drunk with cuts on her leg on some incoherent outburst.
"Hey Shane!" a voice called from up the top stairs, "Boss wants to see you."

****

With bottle in hand, Odette stammered out of the car and leaned up against the carport pillar.
She'd been at The Cold Fridge – a dingy tavern on the outskirts of Secunda where she'd always escape, drink herself comatose when the demons of the past would crawl into her living world and escape the cages she'd keep constructing inside.

The carport pole was hot from the midday sun, and she quickly fumbled away, struggling with the keys to get the car locked before heading towards the front door.
She stopped – the gash in the wood stood out clearly, and for a moment in her almost dazed numbness she felt the nerves creeping back in, but she swung the Vodka back with a gulp, pushed open the door and stomped inside.

The curtains were all still drawn shut, she'd not opened them in her haste to get out and she looked at the door wondering if she'd even locked up before leaving.

"Oh well no crying over spilt Vodka now." She mocked, swigging another gulp before fumbling over to the stereo and putting it on, slinging the volume high.

"To hell with you. I don't need anyone. All I wanted was some support, I'm going through something here. But did I get it? No!" she said heading up the stairs, the bottle still in hand.

"It's fine, I have myself I don't need anyone! TO HELL WITH YOU SHANE TOBEY!" she yelled, "Bastard! Your own parents died getting away from you! ORPHAN!"

The dark flat boomed with the music, hiding her shouting and ranting as she tripped into the main bedroom.

***

Her immediate neighbour to the right was a work from home online tutor, Elizabeth Vermaak – Bets. She was a short, chubby single woman in her early 40's with long dyed blonde hair that was tied tightly in a ponytail, wearing gym slacks and woman's golf shirt.

She tried to get through her lesson, hiding the displeasure of the blaring music from next door as she spoke, but soon her online students began raising virtual hands and delivering comments about the music.

Although each duplex apartment had a small walkway separating them, the music was loud. Bets knew she'd have to use the brief gap between the end of her class and the start of the next, to go bang on her neighbour's door yet again in the hopes of getting some respect.

***

Plucking open the cupboards in their bedroom, Odette began pulling her clothes out from their hangars with her free hand, chucking them towards the bed as she slurred crude and cruel rants about him knowing the sordid rumours about her.
When their childhood fell apart, Odette and Mark were barely able to live in the same house without there being terribly violent fights – which she most of the time started - her way of expressing the torment inside of her, and she'd physically lash out at Mark to rid herself of it.

After her mother's death, their father fell into a deep depression, and soon became permanently drunk, but after their lives changed – it somehow felt harsher and harder to withstand because they had both lost the friends that drew them out of the house, who gave them purpose and hope away from their pathetic father.

Their father was working on the mines in the neighbouring town during the short hours that he was no longer drunk. It was in those quiet hours after school that the haunting thoughts of what they'd done would begin scratching at the walls of their morality. As things changed and friendships faded, Mark secluded himself mostly, getting lost in books while she sought out both comfort and trouble which she found with boys who had no regard for her than anything but a toy.

She wanted a man to love her because she remembered how safe everything was when her father was sober, and her mother was alive. She craved safety from the demons of their decisions. She craved that feeling of a man holding her tightly and knowing that every moment, no matter how dark, would be ok.

Staring at the empty cupboard, with only Shane's clothes remaining - hers sprawled out across the floor and bed, she realized that everything she feared losing in Shane had indeed just been lost.

"You're pathetic!"
The voice startled her, and she spun around, the tall dark figure in thick leather standing at the entrance to the bathroom in the darkness.
"Hello Odie." It mocked showing her the scythe.
She screamed in her rush for the door, falling over from the jackets tangling at her feet.

Grabbing her by her hair, the figure plucked her up to her feet, shoving her up against the wall, pinned.
"You *are* pathetic! Just like your father!" He snarled, forcing a blade down across the left side of her face and she screamed.
The figure let her go just long enough for her to grab her face as the blood poured over her screams.

It grabbed her again by the back of her hair, punching hard at her face with its gloved fist to shut her up, then again and again before dropping her to the floor.

Dazed and bloodied she rolled to her stomach, clasping at the rug to get towards the door.

"No." it said, grabbing her legs and pulling her back as she screamed.
"Hush now!" the figure snarled, kicking hard into her side forcing her breath out as she rolled on the floor by its feet.

"You think you know pain Odette?" The figure reached down, grabbing her, and spreading her legs to expose the cuts on her thigh, "That isn't pain, that is what secrets do to you."
"Please don't!" she begged in a breathless whimper. The figure dug in his coat, pulling out the same axe used by the door and swiftly slammed it down into her inner thigh. She wailed out into the music, crying as she held the open tear in her leg.

It reached own and grabbed her by the throat, raising her up while squeezing harder at her neck as her eyes widened being choked, before tossing her across the room towards the doorway and into the passage.
Blood gushed from her leg, her throat damaged and her screams barely passed the blaring music as she crawled towards the stairs on bloodied hands.
The figure stepped out of the room behind her, placing the homemade knuckle duster over the black glove, carefully stepping behind her watching her fight for her escape through the gauze mask.
Suddenly a loud knock wrapped the front door.

***

Outside, Bets stood with arms crossed, her face puffed up shaking her head.

"Trouble in paradise again?" a man sounded from behind her, and she turned.

It was Bernie, the 66-year-old caretaker of the complex, stepping out from the small garden gate at the tenants across the way with one of his garden workers Thomas beside him. He walked with his chest outward, his arms slightly further from his side then believable – and a snarky grin always chiselled into his wrinkled face – believing he still had it.

"Every few weeks, the same thing." Bets shook her head as she walked to meet him at the edge of the sidewalk. She, like numerous others within the complex, were sick of Bernie and his failure to deliver anything without disappointment or at the least – smoke & mirror filled stories negating around his failures - weak attempts to 'run' the complex.

Bernie laughed, "Don't be so miserable Betsie, it's a beautiful day let the young be young."

"Don't give me that Bernie, this is ongoing for too long and I'm not the only one sick of these tenants disrupting the complex with their drinking, fighting and now this again. Lots of us work from home, we can't like this."

"I've spoken to the Trustees countless times." Bernie explained, his face changing now to that of an old man doing his best while being defeated again and again by the Trustees, "If I had more authority, I'd have them evicted long ago!"

He immediately turned to Thomas, back in God-mode, "Trim these hedges nicely, smooth and in one line." Bernie instructed Thomas who knelt with his sheers at the hedging.

Bets turned back to the noise disrupting duplex behind her, "How have you been unable to evict them after all the noise complaints Bernie?" Bets scoffed, "This is not acceptable! If you don't do something I will."

"Calm down Betsie." He said taking her by the shoulders – to which she shrugged away.

"Let me go speak to them, get that music off and then I'll speak to the trustees again. Let Bernie handle this, you know I always make a silver lining." Bernie said as he round past her toward the short walkway towards the door.

"Careful, this one can be wild trouble!" Thomas added with a chuckle.

Bets looked down at him angrily, "You better do my hedging better than this Thomas, I don't want to sit with a bush that won't grow because you are chopping it like a hooligan."

He nodded and continued sheering as Bernie reached the door, staring at the gash in it angrily having only a few months ago replaced their door due to previous blowouts that caused panels to break and chip the frame.

Confrontation was never his strong suit, and as he stood there, he felt a little crackle in his nerves.

He looked back to Bets who stood watching him with beady eyes and he puffed out his chest, folded his fist to bang against the door twice more.

The door opened with the 2nd blow, slowly creaking - the music roaring out past him into the warm afternoon air. He looked back to Bets who ushered

impatiently at him to go in, "Go on show us! Show us Bernie the fixer."
Thomas grinned eagerly, "If she's offering beers, get us each one!"

Bets shook her head in frustration, just wanting to finish her last few lessons so she could go for her wine and gym session with the girls, "Just go in there Mr. Caretaker. Take care of this!"
Puffing out again, Bernie grinned and turned back to the flat - carefully sticking his head into the dark house.

"Hello?" he called to no response, "Hello - can you please put off your music and come to the door? It's uncle Bernie. Hello?"
Only the roaring metal music blared at his face as he carefully took a step inside - the radio just a few steps from the door.
"Hello!"

Outside, Thomas grinned shaking his head, "That lady is going to donner him going in there with dirty boots."
Bets scoffed, checking her wristwatch as the heat began to slam her.

Bernie took a step forward announcing as he left the doorway, "Ok I'm coming inside, it is Uncle Bernie do not be alarmed I only want to make sure you are alright. Hello?"

The door slammed almost immediately behind him, causing both Bets and Thomas to jerk. Through the music they could hear something, a clutter of sorts as they watched the flat nervously – unaware that inside, the dark leather clad figure had slammed Bernie into the kitchen counter with his arm tightly around his neck forcing out only silent screams and gasps.

Bernie shoved back, pushing the figure aside, and lunging a desperate but weakened punch at the gauze mask sending the dark figure stumbling backwards.
"What the hell are you doing?" Bernie yelled, his body shaking in alarmed despair, "It's me Bernie!"
Outside, Thomas stood up nervously, "Do you think she attacked him?"
"I don't know." Bets said shaking her head, "With those people anything is possible."

In a brawl - stumbled into the kitchen, the figure's grip on his neck was strong but Bernie he kept on punching and punching with all his might until eventually the figure released his neck to block the powerful blows to its face and head.
In the chaos and ruckus of the music blasting so loudly inside the flat, it was in a small moment that Bernie saw the opportunity to grab a dirty pot from the sink and swing it at his attacker.

The blow hit against the mask from the side, forcing the figure backwards up against the refrigerator. Bernie puffed out again, chest forward as he swung a second and third blow against the figures head, forcing his assailant down to hands and knees in the small kitchen.

Breathless, Bernie tried to kick at him, but the figure grabbed his leg in quick move, immediately slamming the knuckleduster into Bernie's knee.

The nails and screws bore through the cartilage and against the knee bone as the figure rotated his fist side to side with Bernie wailing out in pain over the blaring music. He toppled down onto his back on the kitchen floor, clutching his leg – his old, withered face red with agony and terror behind his cries and the figure immediately began punching away at him. The homemade knuckle duster tearing deep into the flesh with each strike.

Upstairs, Odette clawed towards the stairs, trying to scream through her damaged larynx as she made her way passed the spare bedroom, Shane's 'Boys Room" where he had his PC rigged for games, and then her hands reached the first step where she clung to it - pulling her body forward with all her might only to see the figure standing up in the kitchen – the brutal attack on the old caretaker leaving nothing to recognise.

She cried out, as loudly as she could over the music, and her head dropped in defeat – surrendering to the reality that her heart could no longer keep her going. Laying listening as the figures heavy feet made their way up the stairs towards her, shutting her eyes and praying for the pain to end.
"Last chance Odette." The figure snarled at her, "Tell me the truth."
Her eyes rolled back, her body barely clinging to life.
Plucking her up like a doll to her feet, the figure slammed her into the wall and began delivering countless, violent punches to her stomach before tossing her into the spare room where she hit the

table and slung down to the ground as it watched from behind the monstrous metal mask.

She was dying, slowly and painfully on the floor, with copious amounts of blood pouring from the slice to her face and thigh, and holes in her body. "I want you to know." It said standing over her as it removed a large hunting scythe from the inside of its thick coat, breathing heavily beneath the gauze mask.
"I *will* kill your brother Mark too. The same way you lay here choking on your blood so will he. I want you to die knowing that everything you tried to live for is gone. You had time to free the secret, but you chose silence. Now it's too late."
The figure lunged down with the scythe fast, ending Odette Gallagher.

The figure walked down the stairs and towards the radio, switching it off so a silence could fall within the small duplex again. Then to the couch where her bag lay, scrummaging through for her cell phone. It put the phone inside the coat and made towards the door removing the hood and mask when the door handle shook. Like a gazelle, it moved just as the door opened covering it.

"Hello?" Bets called out with her eyes wide and unsure as she stood at the doorway, calling twice more – Thomas just a few steps behind her with his shears in hand. Bets stepped inside carefully, her eyes wide as it scanned the dim room where silence roared loudly now.
"Go home, I think you must call the police." Thomas said pulling her back. She nodded fast as she dashed back towards her unit, leaving Thomas at

the doorway clutching the garden shears tightly in his hand as he very cautiously entered the dark and haunted duplex.

He was two steps inside when the movement in the corner of his eye got him to swing around, finding Bernie shredded and gargling his last breaths on the kitchen floor.
He screamed in terror, when the door shut.

CHAPTER FOUR

"I'm not sure, he just said he wanted to use the house phone." Jana Jonah said to her husband across the dining room table as he sat down in front of his plate for dinner.

"There's always something brewing between Maggie and Matt." She sighed, "Why they refuse to get along is beyond me. Did he say anything to you today at all?"
"No, actually Matt rushed out of a meeting and didn't come back." Said Mr. Jonah digging into his couscous salad, "He just grabbed his laptop and shot right out of there. I haven't spoken to him since."
"I wonder if it has anything to do with that friend of his, do you remember little…" she started when Matt entered the doorway still holding their cordless house phone.
"Hi dad." He managed to smile through the trembling in his body as he saw him sitting at the table.
"Oh, so you can use my house phone but not call me when I'm looking for you?" his father scoffed, "I'm very disappointed in your behavior today, Matthew."
"I'm sorry, I just wasn't feeling well."
"That is not how you handle excusing yourself from a meeting, you are twenty-two years old, you should know better. That was strange and embarrassing." He spoke harshly, "I am not there to cover for you, Rodwin is very upset. That is your responsibility to

sort it out. I made it clear from the start, no favoritism for my son."

A silence hung as Matt placed the receiver to the side table, "I will dad, sorry."

"So, Matthew, what did your sister say?" his mother broke the silent tension.

"Still can't reach her, just goes to voicemail."

"What's going on Matthew?" his mother asked with a concerned sincerity, "Would you like to sit down and have something to eat with us?"

"No, I'm ok mom. Thank you." Matt tried to smile, as he aimed to force the images from the email out of his head and to allow the conversation with his sister to settle in his thoughts.

His mother carefully placed her fork to the side of her plate, "It's about those murders on TV, isn't it? You're friend Jacques from Secunda?"

He looked up, the voice inside of him screaming to be released.

"This province killer thing?" His father frowned in confusion, "You knew someone?"

"Don't you remember little Jacques, his father worked on the mine, Barry Petersen. When Matt sprained his wrist so badly out in the field then his father brought him home?" his mother said putting her hand on her husband's forearm, "They grew up in Secunda, they were all friends at a stage."

His father nodded, "Vaguely yes, the fat one?"

Matt cleared his throat, "So, I am trying to reach Maggie and just check in with her. But she's not taking my calls."

"Matthew I'm sorry I didn't realize." His father sympathized, "Please, come and sit down."

His mother urged, "There's more than enough for you to join us? A good warm meal will do you a world of wonder."

The sight of the pork in red wine sauce was enough to make him vomit again, so he shook his head politely declining.

"Thanks mom, but I have to head out."

"I'm sure your sister will phone eventually you know how busy she gets." Said his mother offering a smile.

"Son, we're here if you want to talk about it?" his father added smiled. '

"No, it's ok. I'm good, I just really need to speak to Maggie so if she calls back or anything, please you need to ask her to call me, ok?"

"We will son." His father nodded.

Matt forced a smile, then turned again for the front door, quickly hitting the button to open the main gate outside.

"Love you." his mother said as the front door shut. "Shame I don't remember these kids. I did see something on the news, but I didn't know he knew two of them, that's terrible."

NO JOKES M, CALL ME URGENTLY!!!

NOW

WE NEED TO TALK! PLEASE CALL ME!!!!

Outside in his Hilux, Matt put his phone away, his nerves shaken by the reality of the email and images replayed in his mind. He heaved a deep sigh, reversing out of the steep driveway with his thoughts loud in his mind.

"Oh!" he gasped, braking just moments before hitting another vehicle just inches from the entrance to his parent's gate, "Sorry!"

The old Ford pickup, matt black, stood idling as the gate began to slide shut.

"No, no, no, no!" Matt urged in panic when the gates sensor stopped it from rolling open.
Matt huffed, "Can you reverse so I can get out?"
The black pickup stood still, its powerful motor rumbling.
Matt waited in frustration while the gate slid open again, and still the old pickup did not budge.
"I don't have time for this." He scoffed angrily, gearing the Hilux into drive when the pickup slowly reversed enough for him to maneuver out.
"Well, there we go, that wasn't so hard now was it." Matt moaned, gearing back into reverse, and pulling out into the street.
"Thanks so much, really glad we can be decent!" He waved to the rearview mirror sarcastically, gearing into first and speeding off, leaving the faded old Ford pick-up behind him by the open gate. The pickup moved forward, its engine growled low as it turned in by the gate and slowly crawled up the steep driveway.

"It's a very small world if you think about it. I mean you hear of these things everyday but when it happens to someone you know it brings it closer to home you know?" His mother continued with a shake of her head, digging into her steamed vegetables.

A knock rapped at the door.

"That's odd." His father said standing up to it, "Matt?"
Another knock, and he stood up going to the front door, seeing that it was still unlatched, he frowned, looking up at the small stained-glass window in the door.
"Matt?" he asked again, unable to see more than a blurred dark image moving.
"Matt is that you?" he asked again. An eerie feeling filled his body as he carefully reached for the door handle, the figure moving away.
"Steyn is everything ok?" his wife called from the dining room.
He flung the door open to the crips air of the early night and nobody was in sight.
"Matt?" he asked, stepping out onto the porch, checking to the sides, before seeing that the gate at the bottom of the yard was standing open. "What the hell?" he said walking out onto the porch.

"Steyn?" his wife said from the dining room table, listening inventively through the eerie silence when behind her, the figure quietly stepped out from the kitchen.
"Matt?" he asked now almost angrily, stepping down from the porch onto the paving, seeing the black

pick-up in the shadows of their driveway. An icy cold befell him, and he rushed back inside.

"Jana?" he called, rushing into the dining room where she lay face down on the floor beside the table, barely conscious.

"Jana!" he gasped, rushing to her, lifting her lifeless body into his arms to find red bruises around her neck.

"Oh my god! Jana!" he cried when the figure leapt out from the entrance hall behind him, strapping a black rope around his neck.

"No…" he gargled, scuffling backwards, slamming his attacker into the wall as his face reddened and his fingers desperately clawed at the rope burning into his neck – finally falling to his knees with the figure standing behind him, pulling at the rope. He felt everything draining, fighting to get to his feet when the figure's knee pressed down on his back.

"Sssshhh." It whispered, and with a hard tug snapped his neck. His body slopped to the floor with a thud just a few meters from his wife.

****

By 9pm the city of Pretoria was lit up, still alive for the night as Zain's Ford Fiesta cruised along the streets towards the police station.

Since their awkward encounter with Matt, they'd spent the remainder of the day trying to track down anyone else through internet and social media searches, also arguing a giant portion of their time about everything they could and should possibly do about the suspicions they carried.

Zain had taken numerous painkillers throughout the day, desperate to rid himself of the headache stemming from his neck up into his skull that arrived with Eric's story and refused to leave. Stress had killed his mother at an early age via stroke and heart attack, it was something he knew ran in his family – the headaches from hell.

The car rolled slowly into the car park in front of the police station and a chill filled them both.
"This is the right way to do this." Zain said with a calm certainty, "Other than your friend Matthew, who I believe will have a restraining order against you, if you try approaching him ever again, and Vid-Tube master Mark Gallagher – we're not getting anywhere. We need to involve the police."
The car was silent, hot even with both windows open.
"Alright, let me do this." Eric said, opening the door as he stepped out.

The city's bustling in the air circled him – the night so vibrant that he felt the craving for strong drinks and any music to drown the noise inside his mind.
"You know Zain." He said leaning in after shutting the door, "If I could go back to stop myself from telling you, I would. I'm sorry."
Zain stared at him for a moment and Eric rapped on the door before heading into the station. Watching him walk up so confidently, albeit electrified with stress, a bright smile crossed Zain's face.

Although they'd spent the day together confined first inside the car between Boksburg and back, then within the confines of his apartment – he felt further from Eric than before. The more they searched and probed rationality, the more he felt the severity of Eric's story eating away at him, putting between them a giant hole that may not ever be filled. For a few hours he'd been thinking about just kicking Eric to the curb, protecting himself and getting away from whatever mess this all was.

But he also knew he was tired, exhausted from the unwavering rush of thoughts and doubts, searches of names and articles. Deep down he already knew he loved Eric, because there was a connection between them that felt unlike anything he'd had before. But now work was put on hold through lies of sick leave, he was part of something he wasn't sure he'd even understood at all - because of the guy who made him feel alive for the first time since coming out to his family in his last year of high school. He'd been alone since then, unable to figure out who and what he was about, scared to be gay in the world without any family or friends who would support it.

His parents had paid for his apartment almost immediately after his high school results came in and organized his work through associates – as far away from them as possible, in the big, strange city. He'd not seen or heard from his family since he was 18, three years no contact - and of the friends he had back in Pietermaritzburg had moved on, forgotten about him already.

When he met Eric, they'd been in the same doctor's waiting room and could still remember how he felt.

He'd caught Eric looking at him with wide curious eyes a few times, but until they started hanging out and getting to know each other more, he'd never guessed that Eric was open to the possibility of a kiss.

****

At 20, Leigh-Anne Roos had already travelled through most of South Africa, having nabbed a modeling contract shortly after her 18th birthday. She'd dreamt of the stage since she could remember and aimed to use modelling as a step towards acting.

Posing for the camera's, Leigh-Anne was the poster of any typical model, long legs, tall, perky breasts, and full lips complimented by thick flowing blonde hair.
The shoot was outside the Fourth Raadsaal, one of Bloemfontein's famous landmarks, where the shoot only had permission to utilize the premises at night long after being closed.

Opened in 1893, the buildings renaissance style was a total contrast to her provocative, barely concealing outfit as she leaned against the pillar as the camera rolled.

"Ladies, don't become history – be HIS STORY."
She grinned walking down the steps.
Noticing her persona had shifted, the director Max-B raised his hand and politely asked the 9-person crew for a reset.

"Did I say it wrong?" she asked as he walked up towards her.

"What's happening Leigh-Anne, you're saying words but I'm not feeling it. This segment must match the same energy as the first and third." Max-B explained removing his cap and scratching his head, "It has to flow, or our 25 seconds means nothing."

She sighed, "I wasn't aware that my energy dropped, it's just…"

"Do you need a little something?" he asked, lowering his voice cautiously.

She shook her head in disgust, "No it's not that at all I just caught a segment of the news on Cheryl's phone, and it upset me."

"Well, this is South Africa, the news can upset anybody darling." He joked, "Shake it off and carry on like the rest of the country."

"There's been a string of murders and I…"

"Ah yes, I've seen that yes. We must remember Leigh-Anne, bad things enter people's homes every night on their televisions, on their mobiles and laptops. We have a 25 second window to turn their attention away from what they hear to buy what they think they need."

She managed to smile, but inside her core was still reeling with the shock of seeing her friend on the news, the once chubby boy who was the first boy she kissed in a game of spin the bottle.

"You are the woman the ladies aspire to be, that men want their wives to be." He continued with a grin as he watched her heaving breasts, "And we want them to rush out and buy Seductress, don't we?"

"Yeah, I know, I'm sorry."

"Camera is reset, we can go again." The camera operator yelled from the side interrupting her.

Max-B grabbed her by the shoulders, "Let's get this wrapped up so you can take a hot bubble bath back at the lodge, sound good to you?"

Leigh-Anne managed a smile again as he ushered her back towards the steps.

****

While Eric sat waiting for a police officer to talk to, he rubbed at his temples desperately trying to get rid of the headache and the images that he could not unsee each time he closed his eyes. He hated himself for everything and felt a rage bubbling beneath his heart desperate to escape - beat himself up for all of it. His childhood, his past with alcoholism and drug abuse, now for the agony of knowing what he'd dumped on Zain and brought into his world.

He even hated himself for puking and not being able to handle what he'd seen, for being so violently haunted by it even now in a musty, dirty police station. He sat back in the uncomfortable stool while laying his head back, wishing he could indeed go back in time to undo everything including his own existence.

On the outside he came across almost tough, and together but it was not at all who he had grown up to be deep down. With his eyes closed, head back – his mind wandered back ten years.

As a kid he was the adventurer of the group, daring - with enthusiasm matched closely by his friend Zach as the two of them raced with their bicycles through the field, ramping and doing tricks – their eyes wide with life, their laughter booming in the wide-open fields of adventure and possibilities.

Alive and vibrant, the 10 of them were carefree in all their escapades, with nothing to stop them from living a wild and carefree childhood to the utmost fullest.

"Jansen?" a voice pulled him back.
In front of him stood a tall, well-built 40-something year old policeman in plain clothes, reaching out to shake his hand.
"Bandile Dladla." His voice was firm, hard.
"Thank you for seeing me, sir, I'm Eric Jansen and I..." he looked away, around the station. Dladla nod his head watching the clear fear jive from the young man's skin, "Let's go sit down and talk."

****

Luna's was one of the many hangouts in the small fishing town of Lamberts Bay on the western coast 280 kilometres north of Cape Town. Popular with tourists year around, the town always had people passing through and Luna's catered almost specifically for the locals, fishermen.

It was a quaint pool bar, fitted with high wooden stools and tables, wood panels decorated with the town's popular memorabilia. It always smelt of fresh sea from the fish brought in to serve with pub style lunches and there was always 70's or 80's glam rock and roll playing.

Mark followed his uncle here shortly after his father's suicide. With everything already soaked into him and the burdening torture that chewed away at him, his father's death was what drove him away, as far as possible from Secunda. Like his sister, Mark missed their mother and in his teenage years grown to despise his father for being the pathetic drunk he was, always abusive and berating them. Hearing the stories about life at sea after the funeral, Mark knew then that he had the opportunity to run as far away from Secunda and the darkness of his childhood as possible. His begging and pleading for his uncle to take him back to Lamberts Bay didn't take much since his wife was not able to have kids of their own, but Odette was two years younger and had to stay in Secunda with their father's sister Cookie Venter to finish high school. So, he left, something she'd never forgive him for.

He was 15 when he first started on the boats, and in the 7 years since he'd built a good name for himself with the locals and the other trawler crews. He was strong with tanned skin, dark brown eyes, and long dark hair, always wavey from the wind at sea. He'd found his passion for Vid-Tube after being subjected to it through a tourist family a few years prior – he'd had a brief fling with their daughter who was always scrolling through the videos of its content creators. Realizing he'd have ample to share with the world from the long hours out at sea, he'd created an account and within a few months his video's garnered over 3000 followers.

He'd get requests from certain places to do paid promotions with his clips, but as he had zero expenses living with this aunt and uncle, everything he made was already saved and simply lying in wait. His videos were traditionally Point-Of-View style clips of the ocean, their encounters with sea life, the huge draggers and rubbish too often contained in their nets. And every so often, depending how far out they'd head, he'd capture hilarious moments of the crew slipping, slanting, and tossing around on board as the ocean shook the boat, only on some rare occasions would he face the camera and talk to his audience about life as a fisherman.

He and the rest of the 4-man crew had been out on the water since before 3am with his uncle at the helm, yet they continued to drink even with the exhaustion settling in. It was tradition to do so whenever they'd have three consecutively successful days' catch.
Bobbing his body to the music, Mark loved how simple the world was since leaving everything behind all those years ago. He was happy, saddened only by knowing his uncle had been diagnosed with lung cancer, but who chose to live whatever years were left with unwavering vigour and gumption.

At the bar with him sat 55-year-old Robb who was the loudest, gruffest, and most bearded of them all, and also one of the longest serving men with his uncle's charter. Klooster Botha, in his thirties who never wore anything that showed skin other than his hands, thin but strong who hid scars from the fire that cost him everything and their crews newest addition Greaser was finishing a game of pool with his uncle.

They called him that as a reference because of his long black hair that was always thickly greased backwards and who despite working in a somewhat dirty job kept coming onboard with a white T-shirt.

His uncle Gordon finally got to the bar, grabbing his beer mug, and raising it for a toast, his cigarette hanging from his lips, "May rod and line never part, drink up now for early morning again we start!"

They and half the bar raised their mugs in cheers. Suddenly a hand tapped on his shoulder, forcing Mark to turn and face his aunt Jo-Anne with a surprise.

Behind him, his uncle spat the smoke out of his mouth and out of sight.

She was a large woman, stern faced with her hands clasped by her waist, a weight across her face and her eyes red from crying.

"Markie, I just got a phone call." She said over the music, ignoring what she'd seen, "We should go outside and talk, Gordie, you are coming also."

Outside the night air was humid, but the strong wind eased its warmth as he and his uncle followed her towards the sidewalk, away from the entrance.

"Markie...." She said turning, her face sad as she spoke, her bottom lip quivering.

"What is it Jo, what's wrong?" Gordon pushed around Mark and took her hands, "Tell me."

She sobbed shaking her head, turning to face him. Even at 22 she still saw the young boy who first came to her home as the son she'd never been blessed with. But his dark eyes glared to her, desperately wanting to know why she'd come all this way from home to talk to them.

"I got a call from my friend Cookie in Secunda Markie." She said through her tears, trying hard to get the words out.

"It's Odette, your sister's…she's…. she's been murdered."

****

It was 09h53 when Eric exited the police station, drained and exhausted.

In the car, Zain had fallen asleep in a bundle against the window and door but jolted up right when Eric tapped on the window to be let in.

"My god it's been hours!" Zain said as Eric slunk into his seat, "Are you ok? What happened?"

"I told him about the email, and that it had those pictures." Eric said, his voice dry and tired, "But turns out they sort of already knew about the email by the way, seems Andreotti Insurance opened a case against me for crashing their servers."

"What?" Zain remarked, "Well I guess it figures they'd do that after how you left things especially."

"Yeah well…" A yawn broke out, his eyes heavy, "So then I had to sit with the police guys handling that and explain to them that I got the mail and what it had on it. Of course, they all looked at me like I was the murderer or something, and then they got the cop from Klerksdorp on a video call, and I had to re-explain that I'd gotten a strange email, and on it was those images. I didn't know why or how and that I was scared for my life. So now they're going to reach out to another division of police who is handling this stuff and will come through to question me again."

"And until then?" Zain asked worriedly, "They're just going to leave you without protection?"

"Well, I don't know – maybe they're not convinced that I'm in any danger. And to be honest I don't even know if they believe me about what was on that mail. I got the feeling they think this is some desperate play because of the case Andreotti Insurance made against me."

Zain swallowed the disappointment.

"So, I don't know, but I gave my statement and those other cops going to come through tomorrow and meet me at your place, if that's ok?"

Zain nod watching him, his hand on the keys ready to start the car, pausing to state, "So, you didn't tell them *everything*?"

Eric turned to him with a stern confusion, "You know what would happen if I did?"

"Yes - but when you realized they weren't taking you seriously, didn't it cross your mind to elaborate even just a little bit?"

"Are you crazy Zain?"

"But you're saying they're not going to do anything?"

"I don't know what they're going to do Zain, I am just telling you how I see it."

There was a tension growing in the hot car, the air becoming thick with moodiness.

"Well let's hope whoever comes to see you can do something, before something bad happens." Zain said finally starting the car, "I just think that without the whole story Eric -how will they believe you're in danger? Or even start helping in anyway? Now you're just coming across as a possible nut job without any proof of anything until we're both cut up into pieces on tomorrow's front page!"

Eric huffed angrily, yelling "What is it that you were hoping for coming here exactly Zain? Because this is what we discussed was the plan!"

"But it doesn't feel like this was helpful in anyway and we're running out of time. I must go to work in a few hours, I have a life and responsibilities outside of this bullshit Eric - so excuse me for being a little on edge about all of this!"

"What do you want me to do here Zain?"

"It doesn't matter Eric. Nothing matters because this is just all too much."

"I'm sorry I…" Eric started when Zain turned the engine off again and cut him off.

"I don't want to hear it again, Eric. I get it. I know that it was therapeutic for you to get it all out and share it with me, and I'm touched that you felt close enough, even comfortable enough to tell me, but…Eric I am…. I just…."

Zain heaved a sigh dropping his head and pausing, "I don't know how much more of this I can take... I can't do this. I thought I could but…I can't and I'm sorry."

A heaviness clouded the car, the humidity visibly sitting on them.

"Yeah, I figured." Eric said softly – emotionally drained in all ways possible, "I understand. Just… Just drop me off by Celeste's place for the night and I'll get my stuff tomorrow. We're both very tired."

"That's not what I meant." Zain scoffed, "I just…"

"No I get it Zain, I do. I think we both just need to breathe right now."

The quiet between them lingered for a few seconds before Zain spun the ignition on again.

By 10h37 Zain's Fiesta slowed into the driveway at Celeste's house that stood dark and quiet in the still night.

"So, you'll be there before I leave right?" Zain asked, avoiding eye contact with Eric who stepped out.

"Yeah, all good." He tried to be courteous.

"I don't need to pick you up?"

Eric rolled his eyes as he shut the door, walking up the driveway and around the side of the garage, out of sight.

Clutching the steering wheel, Zain watched him disappear into the darkness angrily. Angry at himself, tired and filled with regret.

****

The backyard was lit only by the spotlights of the main house, leaving most of the big open yard hidden by the shadows of the night, including the small path to Eric's flatlet.

"Please be open, please be open." He whispered nervously to himself as he drew closer to the door beside the grape vine that separated his view of the main house, having recalled leaving the keys to his nephew and fearing being left in the scary night by himself. When the door opened, a strong relief covered him and for a moment he wasn't scared because the lights inside were still on, something that irked him as he shut the door.

When he rounded into his small lounge, he jolted to find Zeke sitting playing.

"What are you doing in here Zeke?" he said tapping at his shoulder, causing Zeke to spin in fright, plucking the headset off from his head.

"Oh, hi Uncle Eric!" he smiled casually. "What are you doing in here? Do you know what time it is?"

"I know, I know! I'm sorry!" Zeke sighed, "I snuck out about an hour ago, this game is just so good!"

"If your mother finds out you're in here this late it's going to land on me with your dad."

"I just need 10 minutes to finish this level to save, promise!"

"Alright but don't do this again so late ok?"

"Thanks uncle Eric!" Zeke's eyes gleamed, putting on his headset and turning to finish his game.

"No, I thought we agreed it's just - Eric." He said when from behind him the door clicked, causing him to turn.

Stealthily, the door slid open, quietly halting against the stopper and Eric stood staring with bated breath as the cool night air seeped into the flatlet. There was nothing, just the dark leaves of the grape vine beyond his door. His heart raced as he moved to close it, knowing that he had not locked it but fearful of what would have caused it to click open.

At the doorway, he paused, then stepped one foot out.

"Can we talk?"

Zain's appearance to the side scared the breath out of him as he jumped back in alarm, pummelling his elbow into the door frame and stammering forward clutching it in pain.

"Shit! Sorry!" Zain offered, "Are you ok?"

"What the hell Zain?" Eric snarled heading back into his flatlet, his funny bone echoing in agony.

"I'm sorry I just didn't want to leave us like this." Zain said walking in behind him and stopping by the doorway, "I figured work can wait while I sort out my other priorities."

The need for sleep began to wear on his whole body as he opened the fridge, leaning in for the cool air to awaken the strain of sleep on his eyes.

His phone toned a message from his jean pocket.

"And scaring the shit out of me was the way to go?" He scoffed rolling his eyes while he scanned the refrigerator.

"Your arm is collateral damage. I just don't want to leave it like this."

Again, Eric's phone toned a message. Seeing Zeke on the sofa in front of his game, headset on, Zain shrugged off any awkwardness of his presence in their conversation and closed the door behind him.

There was nothing in his fridge but an already opened glass jar of pickles, and in that moment, it was enough for Eric, who grabbed it and shut the door.

"I don't know what you want from me Zain, I can't say I'm sorry and other than that I have nothing else I can say."

His phone toned as he leaned against the counter trying to open the jar when his phone toned again, and he frustratedly took it from his pocket.

"Who would be messaging you so late anyway?" Zain huffed, almost crossing into suspicious jealousy territory.

Eric's face dropped and he tapped to open the video file from the unknown sender, his body falling cold as he watched the clip taken of him just moments ago from through the dark vine, talking to his nephew on the couch.

"What the..." Eric gasped in alarm when the door slammed open from a forceful kick outside.

He could barely see the dark figure stampeding in, but at Zain's scream - Eric leapt forward, shoving him aside and up against the back of the sofa just as the handheld scythe's 5-inch blade slashed through the air, slicing into his shirt.

The gauze masked maniac slashed again, but with the glass of pickles, Eric rammed it against the side of its head then tackled forward, slamming the black clad monster up against the wall beside the door. Zain grabbed Zeke's arm, plucking his attention to the scuffle, and trying to usher him past it and out the door to safety.

The figure forced Eric against the wall, hand over his throat and the scythe drawn above him trying to stab down past Eric's grip on its wrist.

Zain released Zeke's hand and dart into the attacker, slamming him away from Eric who dropped to the floor as they wrestled with Zain trying to keep the scythe from entering him.

Bravely, Zeke dashed for the corner of the small lounge where Eric kept all his odds in an old laundry bin.
The slicing blade tore across his chest from just above the nipple across up his shoulder, and Eric forced himself up just as Zeke rushed over with an old wooden baseball bat.

Zain screamed and the figure hurled him against the wall, just in time grabbing at the arm of the madman in the terrifying black hood with all his might to block the blade from coming down.

With its other hand, the figure grabbed at Zain's throat – pressing hard while it slammed his head into the wall again, and again.
"Leave him alone!" Eric snarled, slamming the bat into the back of its head and upper back as hard as he could.
The thickness of the long leather coat guarded some of the blows, but not the hood over its head and the figure's force loosened enough for Zain to kick free, shoving the figure down as he almost dove away to the floor gasping.
He swung again and again, hitting the arms and side of the dark figure until the scythe flung to the side - then swung three more times until the attacker was down against the floor cowering behind the mask.

"Come on, let's get out of here!" Eric warned, grabbing Zain to his feet, and plucking again at Zeke who sat hunched in shock by the bottom of the couch.

As they rushed across the dark lawn the backdoor flung open to Keith and Celeste in their night clothes, Keith also holding a bat of his own.
"Get inside!" Eric yelled, "Call the police!"
Celeste grabbed her son and ushered him in through the back door as Keith grabbed at Eric as he and Zain tried to pass.

"What the hell is going on?" he snarled as only a confused, frightened father would. Looking back to his flatlet in the shadows of the yard, the only light through the vine from the open door – Eric shoved Keith backwards.
"Get inside and call the police!" Eric roared, darting down the steps and running as fast as he could to the flatlet again.
"Eric don't!" Zain urged, rushing onto the grass after him.

Burning from the slice in his skin, Eric had one goal to end the chaos - he needed to shut the door, lock inside whomever was under that cloak, behind the mask.
With only a few steps to the door, the figure slunk out against the frame, holding the side of its head as both Eric and Zeke stopped cold in their tracks. His heart raced, wondering how he could stop this masked maniac, and trap whoever was attacking them.

The figure stumbled outside, the scythe back in its dark hand.

"Eric! Run!" Zain called in panic, to which Eric skid around and rushed back to meet him on the grass, running together towards the back porch door.

"He's coming!" Zain called frantically.

Keith stepped back slamming the door shut on them.

"No! Open the door!"

"Keith! Open the fucking door man!" Eric rammed against it with his fist, "Let us in!"

"Help us!"

"Open the door, Celeste!"

Zain grabbed his arm, tugging him to the side as the masked figured lurked closer. They propped down the side of the porch and around the dark side of the house towards the front.

Following with a fast pace, the figure laughed behind the mask.

Zain and Eric thumped against the front door, calling and yelling.

"You son of a bitch!" Eric screamed angrily kicking at the door, "You asshole!"

"Come on!" Zain tugged at him again, lunging them forward towards his Fiesta in the driveway, grappling for his keys in this pocket as the figure stalked out of the darkness towards them.

The engine roared to life with Zain's clutch grinding as he tried putting it into reverse in fear while staring at the maniac who slashed the scythe down into the hood of his car.

The car shot backwards, veering into the middle of the road with a screech.

Again, the gears grind as Zain saw the figure rushing towards them.

The scythe pierced into the roof and the car shot forward – tyres spinning as it sped up, the figure clinging to the handle of the scythe blade as it ran beside the car, until finally heaving itself upwards and on the roof.

"Oh god!" they freaked from inside at the thumping against the roof. Zain tore the car across the corner yard, veering side to side to evict the maniac from above them.

"Zain!" Eric warned, "Watch out!"

Just as the oncoming SUV swerved to a sharp stop, Zain slammed the brake and the Fiesta skid to a violent slide stop – sending the figure flying off onto the concrete in front of the car.

For a moment everything was silent but the running of the engine as they sat gasping inside the car on the dark and quiet street. They looked at each other as though seeking comfort that they would soon wake up from the bad dream.

"What the hell is wrong with you? Is everyone alright? What's going on?"

The voice tore their attention forward. It was a man standing outside his SUV, holding his hand up to the lights of their car trying to see. Then as though cutting through their headlights, the figure arose blocking between the man and them.

"No, no, no, no!" Eric gasped, scrambling out just as Zain gripped him by the belt across the seat.

Screams filled the night, echoing down the dark road.

The man toppled to his knees, ripped from chest to belly and Eric gasped in terror as Zain screamed - pulling at him to get back into the car.

From inside the SUV a woman screamed covering her face as the figure turned to face the Fiesta, the hunting scythe oozing thick red blood. Unable to see its face, Eric knew in that moment that the madness behind the mask had just elevated to a rage. In that faction of a second - every question surrounding all of it began swirling inside his mind. "Eric! Get in the car!" Zain yelled, to which Eric clambered back into the Fiesta, slamming the door as Zain sped forward and around the SUV.

The figure lurched up into the driver's seat of the SUV, turning to face the screaming wife who only screamed more seeing the splatter of blood on the dark gauze.

"Get out!"

She clumsily fumbled for the door not once taking her eyes from the mask.

"Get out!" the figure roared angrily reaching over her screams as it pushed the door open, chopping at her arm, neck, back and shoulder forcing her out. The SUV veered forward, crashing over the sidewalk as it spun around in pursuit of the Fiesta.

Bleeding with wide terrified eyes, the woman reached out and screamed into the night, "My baby!"

****

Tearing down Lynnwood, veering past the few cars still out – the Fiesta reached 90km's and staring behind them, Eric tapped on Zain's shoulder.

"It's ok, it's ok slow down we're ok."
Zain's eyes were wide, terror stricken – his mind in a place he never knew could exist.
"Zain, it's ok, you need to slow down." Eric said softly, grabbing him by the shoulder. The car slowed, veering to the side coming to a stop at a bus bench.

Zain turned to him with wide, dark eyes as his legs and arms trembled.
"Are we safe?"
"We're ok." Said Eric taking his hands from the steering wheel, "We're ok. It's going to be ok."
"You're hurt."
"I'm ok."
Nausea filled Eric's mouth again, and he looked down, heaving breathlessly still.
"That poor man." Zain said softly as tears filled his eyes.
"What do we do now?" Eric asked fearfully, "I don't know what to do!"
After a silence, Zain cleared his throat, "We need to get help."
Eric nodded his head bravely, wiping his cheeks when the sound of screeching tyres echoed behind them, and they flung around to find the white SUV barrelling down towards them.
"Shit!"
"There's no stopping this him!" Zain sneered, frantically gearing as his Fiesta flew out on to the road.

The SUV swept across the black tar, racing up towards the back of the Fiesta – it's lights flashing and flashing. The other cars on the road honked as the two cars motored passed at high speed, approaching the large intersection from the highways on and off ramps.

There were cars up ahead, the traffic light red with a truck en route to crossing, in an instant Zain had to make a decision - terrified and screaming, he veered into a turn - the tyres screeching. The Fiesta slid to the gravel beside the road, cornering as stones and sand shot into the air as the Fiesta cornered back onto the road ahead of the truck.

The SUV followed the same manoeuvre but slid to much going off the tar and it bounced back to the road, slamming and scrapping into another vehicle at the light but pressing on as it tore against the front car before turning behind the truck. The figure clenched at the steering wheel, pressing the accelerator to the floor.

"Where are we going Zain?" Eric asked, clutching at the dashboard to the car hitting 115kms.
The offramp would lead to Johannesburg, and going straight would be a stretch of dark road out of Pretoria. Zain watched the mirror, seeing the lights of the SUV forcing past the truck and he instinctively released the pedal.

Seeing a few cars coming off the highway ahead, the truck driver honked as the SUV coursed to pass it. As the cars past them, watching from the Fiesta that slowly rolled to 20km's, Eric thought they'd have a gap to get away, but the SUV stayed its course in passing the truck, sending the first car to the side and into a barrel roll off into the darkness.

"Shit!" Zain gasped, slamming on the breaks - watching as the second car's brakes lit up - it tried to swerve just as the truck steered off to the side, but the third car slammed into the second with fury. Parts of metal and plastic flew through the air as the truck barrelled into the field - the white SUV bolting around the calamity - still veering towards them. "NO!"

The Fiesta jolt forward, but in the wrong gear and shuddered to a skew stop in the centre of the lane. "Zain!" Eric yelled in fear while the lights from the SUV lit up the inside of the car, roaring across the darkness.
"No!" they screamed, but the tyres of the SUV screeched, burning the rubber as it swung out, skidding and dithering from side to side, screeching to stop just a few meters ahead of them.

Breathless, cold – they watched as the SUV roared forward, lining up to face them.
The lights flicked to high beams, and they sat frozen, terrified.

For a few seconds the figure watched from behind the mask, seeing their terror in the brightness of the lights and relishing at the destruction and mayhem it caused behind them in the crunched metal that sprawled the darkness. The figure knew then that the real game had begun now, terror was instilled - soon everything would happen as planned. Then the baby cried from the back seat, and behind the gauze mask it smirked, gripping the steering wheel angrily with its black gloves.

The sound of the SUV's tyres spinning away on the tar tore through the air. Zain fumbled to restart the car, jolting forward only a few centimetres before cutting out again.

The SUV head towards the Fiesta, where their screams echoed as the gears grind – the lights blinding. Another jolt, the Fiesta sprung forward – still the wrong gear – as the SUV slammed into the left side with a loud crunch.

The windows on the passenger side shattered inwards and the Fiesta bounced, its metal crunched as it slanted back down onto the front of the SUV. Panicked, they flung around but the SUV was stopped, sitting silent with the airbag inflated up on the drivers' side. It was silent, the engine no longer running. The SUV's bumper and some of its grill had almost fused with the rear of the Fiesta just behind the wheel, the metal twisted and crunched.

The road was quiet again, no traffic coming or going. Just the distant sounds of the truck driver trying to assist in the mayhem. Eric shoved at the door with his shoulder.

"What the hell are you doing?"

"We need to get out of here!" he urged, shoving, and pushing, "Maybe he's in there! Damn it's stuck I can't get it open."

Zain turned the key and the car started up, he shifted the gear and the car motioned backward, pulling away as the two metal bodies tore lose from each other.

The remaining headlight of the SUV fused out, and Eric could see into the SUV, urging Zain to stop.

"He's not in there."

"What?"

"He's not in there." Eric urged, staring at the empty, dark SUV.

"Then he's out there." Zain nod out into the darkness around them. Staring side to side, around the car at the emptiness of the night, the terror remained clutched.

Sirens sounded in the distance, and they turned to each other, staring worriedly for an absolution that neither could offer.

A moment later the car jerked forward, heading off towards the highway in quick pace with a buckled back wheel.

****

With sunrise, the town of Secunda was already abuzz as news crews began swirling the town, while police cruises patrolled the streets.

News had quickly spread of the macabre crime within the community and the opportunity for news agencies to cash in were plenty, with it already being referred to as the Secunda Slayings.

Coupled with the brutal massacre in Klerksdorp matching details of the crime scene, articles and reports dubbed it as the 'Province Slayings'.

The story was all over the television, and as he sat motionless at the desk of sergeant Duncan, Shane's face glistened from the tears that seemed to never stop.

He was numb, breathing, and existing only because there was no switch to turn it off.

It had been hours since he got the call, and he still could not comprehend that Odette had been taken from him, nor accept that he'd always carry the guilt of being responsible for leaving her on her own. He was thirsty, his lips cracking already but he could not drink. He wanted to suffer and eventually die from it because that is what he deserved after what he'd left her to live through in her last hours.

He died in those words, 'She's been murdered'.

Perhaps had he not heard the reporters talking or caught glimpses of the T.V playing in the station foyer he'd have simply believed she was murdered, an idea unknown. If he'd not seen a glimpse into the macabre, he would have somehow been able to accept that she had died non-violently.

But he'd raced down the narrow roads of the complex which had been clogged off by police, fire, and ambulance services – reaching the front door of their house before he was grabbed by the officers.

He struggled, calling for Odette as they tried to usher him to the side but for only a moment – in the arms of the police, from the sidewalk he glimpsed inside their home – the grisly blood-splattered walls, drenched stairs, and smears on the upstairs walls. The home he'd only for a minute of his life shared with someone he loved.

He kept playing that moment over and over in his head as the police explained the details of the crime to him - sparing certain gruesome details.
He'd told the police everything he could but still sat wondering if he'd even known himself. Nothing felt real, he barely felt alive much less awake.

"Sir?" sergeant Duncan said softly from the side, watching the tears that rolled down his face. He'd left an hour earlier under the idea that someone would be there for Shane, to take him home and deal with his loss. But here he sat, broken and alone.

"Mr. Tobey." He said lowering to face him, "Sir, do you have anyone who can come get you?"

Shane looked up at him, his eyes blank and hollow.

"Sir, is there anyone our team can call or anywhere we can take you?"

Shane's eyes dropped again, looking off to the side – lost in agony.

****

Carla watched the news from the booth at a takeaway burger store, on her phone. Tears running down her face at the latest picture shared on the news of her old friend Odette Gallagher - a beaming smile across her golden-brown skin, in the arms of a boy whose face was blurred out.

A small smile broke over her mouth - happy that Odette had found love and happiness, remembering the day she and Maggie sat showing Odette how to polish her nails while Mark played outside with Matty and Zach.

Her smile dropped their friendship had ended so abruptly back in Secunda before she left just weeks shy of her fifteenth birthday. She'd often wondered what had happened to Odette after hearing through the old connections from school that Mark had left to stay with family not long after their fathers' suicide.

She had always understood that Odette and Mark had suffered a lot of tragedy even physical pain after the loss of their mother. Sitting there, with her tablet in her hand Carla felt the eerie reality sinking to her core - that if she didn't find the others soon, her face would join the news. She shivered, longing for the days where the sun shone differently, with hope. She brushed off the heavy frost of fear and swiped the news to the side of the screen to return to her internet search:

Although she'd previously, tried to search for him and found no traces of him anywhere online, she tried again.

This time with a very different motive, hoping that it would bring anything back but again it was as though her Zachary Manson did not exist in South Africa, the only mention ever being the obituaries 'survived by son Zach Manson' or articles about his inheritance over his father's company.

She sighed disappointedly after browsing three search pages, she cleared and paused to recall the names of the past for her next search.

pretoria_localfeed.infohub.co.za
Published 45 minutes ago – Presumed link to the Province Slasher.
Missing local men now confirmed key suspects in the murder spree, Eric Jansen and associate.....

****

By 10am, Mark had landed at the airport in
Johannesburg and was waiting at the car rental
agency for keys to start the two-hour drive through
to Secunda.
Standing there in the cold basement of the airport,
he realized that he had still not succumb to any
sadness or tears for his sister.
He looked down to his hardened hands, wondering
if the life he'd chosen to destroy his haunting past
had hardened him beyond compassion at all. Then
he saw the newspaper stand and the headings of
each front page, the pictures of old friends sparking
a chill across his skin.

Mark quickly scrolled through the notifications on his
phone, dismissing them all before scrolling through
his phonebook, clicking on a contact he'd not used
in a few months – Zachary M.
He held the phone up, he would be the first person
he'd talk to about his sister's murder since leaving
Lamberts Bay.

****

Outside in the cool air as the sounds of nature lulled
over Southbroom, Zach was in his sprawling back
yard beneath a carport type roof he'd had erected
over a slightly raised wooden deck where all his
gym equipment stood safely behind massive glass

windows. It had everything an official gym would host, apart from the large hammock he had put up just outside of his fancy glass shed beneath a large Cussonia tree.

He was wet with sweat from both the humidity the coast boasted and the physicality of his work out as he punched at the long red bag when a knock rapped at the door. It was Penny, his all-in-one housemaid who lived on the property in a separate cottage further down in the back yard.

She handled all the cooking, cleaning and oversaw the stocking of groceries and sundries needed for him to live. Initially he never wanted to share his life with anyone, but he'd met Penny early on in his life in Southbroom and decided to take advantage of her skills and figured having someone to share his life with wouldn't be that bad if it was only on rare occasions.
He opened the door to her smiling as she handed him the phone, "It's Mark."

They would talk every 3 or 4 months since Mark had reached out following his parents' death and listening as his old friend spoke his stomach sunk and he slowly walked out into the sun seeking warmth to shed himself from the cold dread.
"There's more." Mark said, "Have you seen the news about this Province Slayer?"
"No, I haven't." he said when Mark continued to explain.
As though spinning, with all the weights from his gym against his chest, Zach listened with wide eyes, his mind racing at the sudden and alarming information.

"I'm heading to Secunda now, if I know more, I'll let you know." Said Mark on the other end, "Are you with me Zach?"

"Yeah. Yeah, I'm here." He said forcing himself to breath, "It's just a lot to take in. I'm so sorry to hear about Odie."

Mark managed a smile, "If there is anything else I'll let you know but I figured you would want to know."

"Of course I do, I'm "just… I'm so sorry about Odie." Zach said, "Do you need anything? Anything at all?"

"No, I have to do this." Mark sighed, "But thank you. I'll check in with you later."

"Stay safe, ok?"

Zach hung up and for a moment simply stood still beneath the sun as his heart drummed inside his ears, banging on his chest.

"Is everything ok?" Penny asked looking up from the chopping board as he entered the white marbled kitchen.

"Penny, have you seen my other phone? The silver covered one?"

"I found it yes it's on the shelf by the book stand in your room." She smiled, "Which you need to start filling with actual books or pictures, this house is too empty not much for me to keep cleaning."

Like most of the large house, the main bedroom was yet to be decorated with more than just his enormous bed and some odds and ends. The air in the room had gone, filled now only with the drumming of his heartbeat in his ears.

He dropped the phone to the ground at the foot of the empty bookshelf that stood on the side of his large white bedroom, heart racing.

He turned and slunk down on the bed, putting his hands into his long hair as he tried to find a stillness to the roaring digging of the past.

****

Hiding inside the car parked in a loading zone bay behind the grocery store across from Zain's complex, they sat quietly nibbling at mini sausage pies. On Eric's lap lay the plaster and white gauze Zain had gotten from the chemist to close the cut on his chest.

They were watching and waiting for the police to arrive as per the commitment made the night before. They'd each tried to take turns resting, sleeping in only short bursts. The fear had them under its control.
They were riddled with guilt, nausea, dread, and exhaustion – eating only to gain whatever energy their bodies needed to stay awake long enough for them to see the police and attempt to make contact without being cornered or taken in.
"Are you alright?"
Zain turned to him, "I think so."
A silence hung again, for the duration of Eric packing away his leftovers while neatly placing the remaining plaster and gauze in this jacket pocket.
"If you need to crash for a while, I'll be alright."
Zain nod, clearing up his lap from the crumbs while shoving the papers into his door before getting out of the car with a hard shoulder to the door, and climbing into the back seat.

Before leaving, Zain taped his old cellular to the inside of the security gate by the front door, the number they'd call when the police arrived.

"You know…" Zain said from the backseat, "When this is all over - if we make it - it's only fair you repair the damages to my car."

A grin broke Eric's concentration across the street and he turned over the seat.

"Don't say it." Zain huffed without even looking up.

"Say what?"

"Sorry. Don't say sorry."

Eric nodded smiling, "I was going to say you only have about an hour because I get lonely."

Giving a subtle laugh, Zain snuggled his face away from the sunlight and Eric looked back towards the complex's main gates ready for the wait when suddenly a silver BMW X1 SUV pulled to a stop in the visitors parking. It was the first car to approach the entrance all morning, the rest was vehicles leaving. Then the car door opened, a girl stepped out, jeans, a light blue crop top and flaming red hair that flayed in the wind as she threw her jacket on.

"No ways!" he exclaimed in awe, "It can't be."

"Who?" asked Zain sitting up in alarm, "Is it the cops?"

Eric shook his head, starting to shove against the door, "No, that's Carla. Carla Wilson."

"That's Carla?"

"Will you please just help me get out?" Eric snarled pointing at the door that remained stuck.

****

Carla shut the car door, nervously looking around her with the voice from the call still chillingly reminding her '*I am everyone, I am everywhere*'. She knew that approaching someone wanted by the police was a long shot, but he was the closest person to her from what her searching found, and she needed to get help urgently. She could not stop worrying about her mother.

"Carla?"
The call shook her, and she spun to the side, seeing on the other side of the road a face she'd not seen in ten years. "I thought that was you!" Eric said, a big smile over his face.
She managed to smile back at him as a relief encompassed her.
"What are you doing?" Zain grabbed Eric's arm tugging him away from the sidewalk, "Everyone can see your face."
Carla nodded her head, raised her hand and ushered that she'd be bringing her car over.

Having parked her X1 BWM two loading bays and a large rubbish skip away, to the front of the beat-up Fiesta, Carla unlocked as Eric and Zain hopped up into the back seat.
"Carla oh my god." Eric said relieved, hugging her over the middle console.
"It's good to see you again Eric." She smiled pulling away, looking to Zain.
"This is Zain." Eric grinned as Zain shook her hand, "My…boyfriend."
Carla paused in surprise, remembering that when they were kids Eric was always under their radar of suspicion of being gay in the way he'd often get caught gawking at Zach or Mark.

"Nice to meet you Zain." She greeted with a cautious smile, "I'm so relieved you're here actually, I wasn't sure with this whole thing that you'd even be home.

"How did you find me?" Eric frowned confused as Zain leaned forward suspiciously.

"Because this is my place, not his."

Carla shrugged explaining, "I actually tracked you through the internet, to your sister's house."

"You saw Celeste?"

"I called her."

"Did she say anything about last night?" Eric asked assertively, "Are they ok?"

She sighed, realizing that they'd not been aware of the news, and she cautiously stated, "She didn't say too much Eric, you guys are on the news, did you know that?"

"What? Why?" Zain gasped in alarm.

"Someone's after you, aren't they?" she said matter-of-factly to which they both nod tensely.

"They're after me to, I got a phone call."

"A phone call?" Eric seemed confused, bemused even at the fact that she'd tracked them down over a phone call after what they'd gone through.

"There's more…" she explained, "…I've been trying to reach out to anyone from the old group and I found you were closer than Matt…"

"Excuse me!" Zain pushed, "Can we go back to the fact that we're on the news please? What is it saying exactly?"

Carla turned to the glove compartment, taking out her tablet and doing a fast search, handing it to them as she rested over the front seat while Eric and Zain watched.

'…with police now confirming this morning a total of 10 victims in the so called 'Province Slayings', a deadly murder spree currently shaking the nation into a state of panic and uproar with everyone wondering when will it all end? Starting with the senseless murders of the first known victims in the spree – 53-year-old father Barry Peterson and his 19-year-old son Jacques were found slain in their home in Klerksdorp along with 18-year-old Ilse De Kock and 26-year-old Hannes Van der Merwe…'

They all sat silent, their heartbeats pounding loudly inside their chests, breathing tight - watching as the report placed pictures of the victims on the screen.

'…To the streets of Secunda 300 kilometres away where the tragedy struck a quiet residential complex, with victims included 19-year-old Odette Gallagher, Bertie Bernard - the 67-year-old resident caretaker and his young assistant 22-year-old Thomas Smith. But the onslaught didn't end there…'

Tears welled on Eric's face as he stared at the picture of Odette, recalling how she was the first girl who ever decently spoke to him about the possibilities of him being into guys and understanding that which the other's often joked about.
It ached him to remember her now under the circumstances in the madness suddenly entering their lives.

'…the authorities, as early as yesterday, were struggling to find sufficient leads or eye- witness accounts in both provinces, another rampant spree

hit the streets of eastern Pretoria last night following a strange visit by one Eric Jansen to the police in Lynnwood station.'

He gasped as a picture of his boxed up onto the board behind the reporter.

'...claiming to have detailed information about the murders in Klerksdorp, Eric Jansen approached the Lynnwood police department late last night offering local police information he believed would help solve the case. According to a police spokesperson earlier today, Eric Jansen stated that he was in fact in possession of crime scene details of the Klerksdorp murders, claiming that he had physical evidence and knowledge of surrounding both the crime scenes...'

That's not true!" he snarled angrily, his heart racing rampantly against his chest, his mind spinning. Zain clasped his hand tightly, his stomach knotted and aching.

'...however, when police tried questioning him further to get enough to legally detain him, Eric Jansen managed to flee the police station and just moments later, would go on to terrorize his sister's family in the quiet neighbourhood of Fairie Glen, attacking them in their home, before fleeing the scene...'

"Oh my god! the words blurt out of his lips as the report cut to a clip of an interview with Keith from the driveway of their house.

'It was probably just before midnight when we heard screaming from the flat behind the house. Eric and his friend were storming the house. I didn't want to let them in because I didn't know if they were on drugs at the time.'

"That is such bullshit, what an asshole!" Zain snarled as an image of his face now joined beside Eric's on the bulletin, a CCTV image taken off him at the police station when he had gotten out of the car for a moment to stretch his legs.
"Oh my god my father's going to kill me!"
"Why would he do this?" Eric shook his head in alarm, "Zeke was there, he saw everything."
Carla shrugged shaking her head while the report continued from the tablet.

'…shortly after fleeing the residence in a white and blue Ford Fiesta, the two young men then hi-jacked residents Clive and Donna Fourie just a distance away as they returned from a late gathering with friends. The couple was found in the very early hours of the morning by a group of joggers deceased in the street. Based on other reports that flooded the police station earlier, it is now believed that Eric Jansen and Zain Naicker had murdered the couple before taking off for a joyride through the city streets with the couple's 4-year-old daughter in the back seat.'

They both gasped, Zain dropped his head into the palms of his hands, "Oh my god."

'…Lisa-Marie Fourie was luckily found safe and unharmed following what appears to police as a high-speed race, causing chaos through the streets

of lower Lynnwood towards the Simon Vermooten offramp, where the pair caused a further loss of lives in a multi vehicle accident, involving three vehicles and a truck.
Stefan Northam, long distance driver for Carassco Group, informed police that the SUV tried overtaking his truck despite oncoming traffic, causing the vehicle carrying Pieter Jaco Buys and his 17-year-old daughter Lorena to veer off the road, killing Pieter Jaco Buys instantly and trapping his daughter who tragically succumbed to her injuries before paramedics could evacuate her from the wreck. Another two vehicles were also involved in the crash, killing 31-year-old Abongile Mzamane, 29-year-old Olwethu Mandela, 38-year-old Claude Vermaak and 41-year-old Dalton Adkinson.'

A heaviness filled the car, both Eric and Zain feeling as though they were not able to breath, their chests constricted by the weight of guilt and anger.

'As this tragic spree of mayhem and murder unfolds without any viable leads, it leaves the rest of South Africa wondering: where will these so-called Province Slayers strike next?'

"This is such bullshit!" scoffed Zain angrily tossing the tablet to the floor angrily.
"You must believe me Carla, none of this is the truth! We were attacked last night!" Eric insisted.
"Yeah, I figured, else do you really think I'd let you into my car?" she managed a comforting smile.
"What are we going to do?" urged Zain in full panic, "We have to prove we're not the killers!"
Eric grabbed him, "We're going to be ok, alright you need to trust me."

Zain heaved a heavy sigh shaking his head, cusping his face into his palms as he toppled backwards in the seat. Eric felt again the weight of regret for involving Zain into the mayhem of his past and present - his head fell into his hands in defeat.

"We probably need to get you guys out of here." Carla's voice broke a short silence.
"I can't." Eric looked back across the street and then pausing as his mind wondered.
"What is it?" she asked staring at the complex now as well.
"This doesn't make any sense. If we're suspected to be the slayers, then why haven't the police been to Zain's house yet? We've been here all morning and not once did anyone enter the gates, not once."
Zain sat forward again, "Yeah, that's true.
"So, what does that mean?" asked Carla. "It means hopefully that the reporters have it wrong, that the police are just saying it's us because they need someone to save face for the public, right?"
Eric was almost excited in how he spoke, "Maybe we can still go to the police and tell them everything this time."
"Everything?" Zain urged behind his dark brown eyes.
Eric looked to Carla nervously, "Maybe it's time we tell the whole story."
She stared at him with a slight frown trying to piece together Zain's involvement.
"You told him?" Carla snapped in surprised alarm. Eric nodded.
"Look I'm not here to judge, ok? I have enough of that in my own life." Zain defended.
"Oh my god!" she huffed, getting out of her car, and slamming the door.

Eric hurried out as she walked while he rushed after her, grabbing her wrist.

"Listen Carla I..."

She spun around with fist swinging, a powerful right hook that sent him tumbling back up against the back of her car.

"Oh snap!" Zain remarked in alarm, quickly getting out of the car.

"Are you crazy?"

"How could you?" she stared only at Eric with her dark blue eyes tearing at him, "Do you know how many times in my life I wanted to tell someone? Do you have any idea how this has eaten away at me my entire life, but I said nothing! I kept it in, I honoured the deal! I honoured the fucking pact!"

"Carla I..."

"No!" she yelled stomping back to the door of her car, slamming it behind her as the ignition immediately roared to life.

"Damn she got you like a pro!" Zain said watching her car pull forward.

Eric shook his head in defeat and the BMW X1 braked to a stop, the reverse lights on and it reared backwards.

Staring at the window from the side of the car as it stopped in front of them, Zain prepared himself in front of Eric defensively while the window rolled down.

"There are cops at your house." She said rolling her eyes.

Behind her – across the street a white police car parked, with three people heading to the gate, one of them in uniform – officer Dladla from the night before.

****

Brutality was something they'd be exposed to every day; it was their job as members of the Unique Crimes Unit within the South African Police Service. Handling killers with deranged senses of mentality and broken morals is what they were trained to do, so the 'Province Slayings' was nothing out of the usual.
The viciousness of the murders, the almost too clean crime scenes, and the macabre reality that people who sat planning these crimes existed in everyday world was no surprise, they would find the killer and bring justice for their families thereby restoring a sense of hope in the community.

Walking to the security gate, special Detective Anele Dekka found herself thinking of her ex-husband who was also in the UC Unit and very irate that she had been given the case despite his insistence to superiors to take lead, citing her age and experience in the unit as inferior.

Their divorce was much like their marriage, over quickly.
She'd decided to take on her maiden name, dropping his and as she stared at her badge readying it for the security gate she grinned.
Her partner on the case was Clayton Malik who walked rubbing at his neck that ached still from the previous case he'd worked where the gang they were after attacked them, shoving him down a flight of stairs. He was tall, with dark black hair and a short, clean-shaven beard.

At the security gate, they showed their badges and were allowed in with guidance to the flat of Mr. Zain Naicker by the head of security.

"Remind me again…" Dekka said as they head down the walkway, "You did not physically see Mr. Naicker at the police station last night?"
"No, he was only mentioned as the person who was waiting outside in the car." Officer Dladla confirmed, his tone riddled with irritation.

"…yet somehow, as of 11h14 - which is now." Detective Malik said defensively while checking his wristwatch, "Nobody from your department has been to this premises at all, despite snitching to the media their identities as plausible suspects, I find that very peculiar."
"Look." Dladla sighed stopping in his stride as he faced them, "I have told you a hundred times, I don't know who got wires crossed between the boys visit to the station or the attack on their house. It wasn't me."
"I will remind you officer Dladla that your presence here is only to derive a sense of comfort from Eric Jansen because he met you." Dekka warned as she turned to continue.
"To confirm, you are sure the tenant hasn't checked in at the gate at all?" Malik asked the security guard ahead of them.
"Not since tagging out yesterday afternoon no. This is it."

At the door, Detective Dekka knocked between the bars of the security gate.

"Open it up." Instructed Malik stepping aside for the guard when Dekka reached out stopping him.
"Hold up." She lowered staring at the security gate, seeing the tape and phone.
"Is it a bomb?" Dladla asked in alarm, startling the security guard who hopped backwards. Putting a white latex glove on her hand, Dekka rolled her eyes, "No it's clever way to…"
The phone rang - both Dladla and the security guard jolted, much to Detective Malik's amusement as Detective Dekka quickly unwrapped the tape, freeing the phone.

"Mr. Naicker I assume?" she answered putting the call on speaker.
"This is Eric Jansen."
"That's him!" Dladla outburst pointing at the phone. Dekka rumpled her mouth angrily, prompting Malik to usher both the officer and the guard to the side out of earshot.
"Look I didn't…WE didn't do any of those things they're saying on the news."
"We'll be the judge of that Mr. Jansen." She said as her partner regained his position at her side, "Clever idea with the phone. Where are you? You must be nearby enough to see us?"
"Look I went to the police for help, we're innocent you have to believe us."
"Why the elaborate cell phone trick, if you're innocent why not come talk to us face to face?" she said while her partner hurried along with the officer and guard to try spot them inside the complex.
"Look I've seen the news. I know you guys want to put all of this on us."
"If you're innocent, then come talk to me. We'll figure it out."

"No thank you!"

"You're disappointed in the police, seems fair enough - if you're telling the truth."

"Well, you <u>are</u> the police - aren't you?" he scoffed, "I left the phone because I need someone to understand and want to help us, not chase us and lock us up while the real killer is out there. So, are you willing to be that person?"

"My name is Anele Dekka from the Unique Crimes Unit. My pay grade is a little higher than the police. I don't have a need to do anything without evidence and right now all I have against you is that you and your friend Mr. Naicker are the only people who anyone can place at a crime scene linked to the recent murders."

"Someone attacked us! He is the one who killed everyone and now he's after me and my friends."

"Mr. Jansen we should be speaking face to face. I know this is going to be hard to believe, but I am on your side. Neither of you are not in any trouble, there was a leak at the station and the news ran with it. Why don't you just hang up and come talk to me, let's figure this out together."

From the back seat, Zain grabbed the phone and pressed it against his leg.

"Maybe we can trust this cop?"

"If we go to the police, people will die." Carla warned.

"How do you know that?" Eric asked, "You heard her! There is no evidence just people who place us at the crime scene. We're like eyewitnesses or something."

Carla recalled the cold words from her call in the hospital, and her mother slid into her mind.

"He said he'd kill my mother if I went to the police."
She said candidly as tears welled in her eyes, "And
we have to approach the same with you Eric. We
don't know who or what we're up against."
"Then what? What are we doing this for?" appealed
Zain when Eric grabbed the phone.

"Mr. Jansen are you there?" Detective Dekka asked
for the fourth time.
"Look we're in trouble here lady. Someone is after
us, we've been threatened, we've been attacked
and there is no way you can convince me to come
out with my white flag here."
"Then talk to me Mr. Jansen. You went to the police
for a reason last night, talk to me."
"I got an email at work. I don't know who sent it or
why. It had pictures of the murders in Klerksdorp on
it." He said as the cold crept over his skin again, "I
knew it was some kind of warning."
"But you never told your employer what crashed
their systems?"
"You know I didn't. I didn't know how to explain it to
them."
She nodded, "Then you got attacked."
"Yes."
"Do you have any idea who might be doing this? Or
why he's after you?"
"No. No I don't know. He's in a black jacket with a
mask."
"A mask?" she asked almost unconvinced.
"Yes, a black mask and a leather outfit. I don't know
the face or the voice. My nephew Zeke saw him,
he'll tell you."
"We already have your brother in law's statement."
"No Keith thinks this is because…I'm an addict in
recovery, two years sober. Speak to Zeke, he'll tell

you what he saw." He sighed as the phone scuffled again.

"Mr. Jansen are you there?"
"The email was sent to me and a bunch of others, if you can track that mail, you'll find the killer."
"We're working on that." She nodded, "Are you with the other recipients of the email now?"
"No. I don't know who it was sent to, but it wasn't just me."
"Are you with Mr. Naicker at the moment?"
"Yes."
"What is his involvement? Did he receive an email too?"
"No, he didn't." said Eric with a sigh, "Look, if you don't find a way to trace that email then more people will die. Whoever got that email is going to be a target just like I am and…"
The phone scuffled again.

"Alright." He said coming back, "That's all I can tell you, because that's all I know. We were attacked last night and almost killed. So, you need to trace the email and speak to Zeke to get the truth."
The call cut.

There was a silence as her partner, the officer and guard returned all shrugging their shoulders in defeat.

"Anything?" asked Detective Malik wiping his brow. She turned to Dladla angrily, "Your department screwed this up for us. Our one potential lead is too scared to come in."
"So, what now?"

"Now?" She said stepping aside and ushering the guard to open the door, "Now we have to work double time."

"I want to meet with the Mr. Jansen's employer and IT division about that email. And I want to interview the sister and her son." Said detective Malik as Dekka looked down at the phone again, her eyes lighting up.

In the BWM they sat quietly as Eric handed his phone to Carla to charge, it had 14% battery that they'd been saving for that call. Then it rang and she turned to Eric in surprise, holding it up for him to see the number on display.

"You didn't put off caller ID?" she vented angrily, "Are you brain dead?"

"Now they can track us or something!" Zain added angrily.

Eric grabbed the phone, "I'm throwing this away so…"

"One question Mr. Jansen?" the Detective asked when they connected.

He looked at Zain and Carla who both shrugged their shoulders infuriatedly, and the Detective posed, "Did you know any of the victims Mr. Jansen?"

Eric hung up nervously.

Carla shook her head and hurriedly put her seatbelt on, driving out of the loading bay and heading out of the shopping centre's parking lot.

****

Since entering Secunda in his rented VW hatchback, Mark felt the lulling drum of the past resurfacing as he past sidewalks, streets, and homes he once used to speed past on this bicycle with all his friends and the laughter of it haunted the car in soft echoes.

When he drove past the police station, a batch of reporters crowded on the side of the entrance and he watched them, curious for the reason of their presence, accrediting it to a possible norm in towns larger than Lamberts Bay.
As he pulled into his aunt Cookie's street a stronger flood of nostalgia entered his mind, and it was when he turned into the driveway that he recalled the last time he'd been at that house.
It was the day of his father's funeral.

**

Her home had always been warm to Mark and Odette as kids, warmer than the coldness of their own house, resulting in them often ending up with her while their father got drunk or stayed away on binges.

But that day the house was cold despite the sun shining outside. Aunt Cookie never left him or his sister alone since hearing of her brother in laws death and offered copious amounts of hugs and kisses throughout the days leading up to the funeral. But putting him in the ground took more from her than she anticipated, and when they got home, she had broken down to her own guilt encompassing her.

Unlike Mark, who sat aside for the most part stayed to himself while everyone made their rounds for finger snacks and condolences, his sister Odette was serving plates and drinks to the uncles, enjoying the attention. Seeing her smile, he felt hatred for his sister, believing that she had somehow managed to forget the past and that despite the terrible situation with their father that he was still in fact, their dad. The day felt the same as the day of their mother's funeral and he felt alone.

He went to the window, looking out at the cars in the street in front of the house, and saw a face offering a wave from between the cars on the driveway. He went outside, shutting the door softly while carefully making his way closer to a boy who once was an integral part of his friendship circle, Bobby Minnaar.

"Hey Bobby." He said confused, surprised even that his young friend was now smoking and looked so different.
"Sorry about your dad." Said Bobby almost bluntly, taking a pull of a cigarette as though he was of legal age to do so freely. A smile cracked, "Thanks." Bobby stared at him for a bit, taking two more drags, before turning away.
It was then that he hated Secunda, his childhood, his friends, his parents, and his sister - knowing that he had to get away or he would drown in a pool of black misery with the thought of choking on it any longer forcing him back into the house. He pushed his way to his father's brother Gordon.

A few hours later it was decided and agreed on, so he turned to his sister who stayed silent throughout the conversation and planning phases of his departure around Aunt Cookie's kitchen table once everyone else had left.

"Will you be ok Odette?" he asked staring at her as she stood to the side. At first, she said nothing but stare at him, furious that her schooling bound her to the town that depraved her peace.

"You can come when you're…"

"I don't need you." She said scornfully cutting him off while shaking her head and turning away, "You'll see me when you see me."

**

After parking the car and stepping out, he paused - closing his eyes as the reality of his return hit him, his sister was dead and that was the last time he'd seen her.

He wanted to feel something, cry or hurt but there was nothing.

When the door opened, he was almost as surprised as his aunt was at how much had changed in the 7 years since they'd seen one another.

She was no longer a large chubby woman with bulging curly black hair, but a thinner lady with straight hair tightly in a ponytail, the lines on her face etched from her own tribulations.

"Marcus!" she said grabbing him into a tight hug that lasted briefly, before she pulled away to look at him, her hand examining his dark beard.

"Lord it's so much to take in. Just look at you, a man already!" she said with a burst of laughter through her tears as she pulled him against her again.
"I've missed you too aunty." He smiled, remembering how different her hugs used to be.

An hour later, he clutched the warm cup in his hardened hands at a new table in the kitchen, with her opposite him with teary eyes. She'd told him everything she could about his sister and her life that he'd missed out on while he sat there absorbing the morbid reality.
"I still expect her to come through the door." Cookie continued heavily, "She was happy at times, but at other times she was following in your father's footsteps."
Mark nod solemnly.
"But shame, Shane loved her, he was good for her actually I just hate to say it..." Cookie paused, "She wasn't good for him, not in my opinion at least. Maybe behind closed doors it was a different story. But yes, let me finish my tea and get back to the arrangements for the funeral, it's such a mess with all the red tape the police needing her body and everything."
"Well aunty, you don't have to do it alone anymore, I'm here to help now." He said offering his hand across the table and squeezing hers.
She smiled, "I appreciate it Marcus, that you came all this way, so quickly also."
Mark managed a smile, "I don't have much else to spend my money on, so I have savings."
"Shame I haven't asked Shane yet about any money they might have saved up, or if there were any policies. I doubt it because they were only

engaged not married so we might be looking at a state funeral."

"Don't worry about it aunty, I have money saved up." He explained standing up to the sink with his mug. He put it under the tap and paused staring out to the backyard where he recalled many days of happily playing with his friends – Odette doing nails while he played marbles with his friends under the tree – and to his surprise someone was on the old, rusted swing set by the tree.

"Aunty, who is that person out there?"

"Shame I got so excited having you here I didn't even think to tell you." She said standing up to take a place beside him, "That's Shane. He has nowhere else to go right now, boy has no family like I explained, and their townhouse…. I don't think he is ready to go there. So, I've welcomed him here for as long as he needs."

The air outside was cold and thick clouds rolled in on the horizon as Mark head out through the yard. A smile crossed Cookies face watching from the window as Mark stopped by the old swing set, remembering seeing himself with his sister and all their friends being there.

"Hey Shane, I'm Mark." He spoke softly, having noticed in his approach the torment within the strangers' eyes.

"The brother? Marcus?"

"Yeah, the brother, Mark, it's nice to meet you." He smiled as he extended his hand. Shane looked to the side, the weight of his heartache crushing his chest again, pausing only briefly before standing up and immediately throwing his arms around Mark, bursting into tears.

Finally, a pain struck his chest and tears welled in his eyes as the stranger who loved his sister clung to him, sobbing, and apologizing beneath his breath.

"I'm so sorry Mark, I'm so sorry! I loved her with everything. I should have kept her safe! I should have protected her…I should have kept her safe".

"Don't say that." Mark said adamantly while Shane stepped back wiping his eyes and cheeks, his face raw already.

"I loved your sister Mark." He said straightforwardly, trying to barrier the tears in his breaking voice, "I'm so sorry that…"

More pain struck his heart, and more tears welled to overflow as he watched the agonizing pain in Shane's stuttering, breathlessness.

"I failed her, I failed your sister. If you want to kill me for it, I wouldn't blame you."

"No, I don't. This wasn't your fault, Shane." Mark insisted, now wiping his cheeks too, "I'm sure my sister loved you too and there is no blame here, this isn't your fault."

There was silence as Shane stared up to the dark sky blanketing the town, composing himself and finding the courage to speak his truth while he slumped onto the swing again as Mark sat on the one beside him.

Again, reminders of the past scoured his mind.

Shane spoke through the agony inside him, choking breathlessly behind his tears as he explained everything that happened on their final morning together.

Mark sat motionless, digesting every detail of what Shane explained in his sobs.

"I shouldn't have left her!" Shane said, wailing into his hands as the pain tore from the pit of his soul into the chilling air.

There was a stillness, as though even the breeze had retreated to the pain emerging from them and it suspended the world for a moment, allowing both young men to just exist in the world left behind by Odette.

CHAPTER FIVE

The night had fallen, stars glimmered above the magnificent city of Cape Town as Magaret Jonah and her triage of friends sat down for dinner at a pizzeria. While still managing to smile, the sting of exhaustion dwelled among the four of them – having all been cramming in for their benchmark tests while floating the responsibilities of all their other courses.

"I don't care about the health risk, but I need me some cholesterol." Stevie grinned, "I want cheese, and I want a ton of it!"
Like Magaret, he was also 24 years old pushing his first degree in medical biochemistry. A flamboyance oozed from him and the stereotypical flares of colours he fashioned. "There isn't anyone who can say we don't deserve it after all we've sacrificed the past few weeks." Marlize agreed as she took the menu from the menu holder, "I for one want to feel Christmas meal sick when we walk out of here, I'm starving one, and two - I need comfort food."
She flung back her thick curls, giggling as she licked the side of her lips with a wink. "I could do with a few Sangrias myself." Ola raised her suggestion by flicking her eyebrows up. Magaret slumped back in the booth, "I'm exhausted!"
"Oh! Come on Mags, we have a few days off to recover! We should be lapping up every minute we can before the cycle starts again." Ola nudged at her.

"Come on Mags, you of all people should be keen after the hell your idiot brother put you through." Stevie insisted, "Live a little girl!"
Magaret laughed shaking her head, remembering she still had an unread text from Matt waiting for her attention, simply lacking the energy to invest into it or him after her tough week.
"I'm in." Marelize nod with a giggle, "But I'll do me some red instead. Apples make me gassy."

The group giggled as Magaret opened her phone to 19 new notifications.
9 regarding general social information surrounding their student housing group, dismissed. 7 missed calls, all from her brother, and 3 new emails.
She dismissed everything easily, it was time to relax, to breathe again - but then her thumb paused, one of the email notifications stood out.

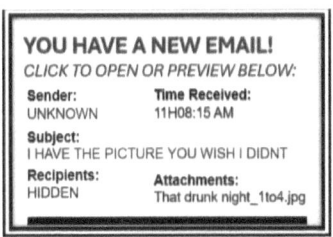

YOU HAVE A NEW EMAIL!
CLICK TO OPEN OR PREVIEW BELOW:

Sender: **Time Received:**
UNKNOWN   11H08:15 AM
Subject:
I HAVE THE PICTURE YOU WISH I DIDNT
Recipients: **Attachments:**
HIDDEN   That drunk night_1to4.jpg

While her friends discussed their evenings meal, she clicked to open the attachment when Hans Babel and his roommate DJ slinked up beside them.

Hans, a tall pale skinned blonde with big shoulders, had been chasing after Marelize since the term started, and while she would have settled for a fun fling, she enjoyed his advances more than she'd craved his pale skin. She enjoyed anyone who thought anything of her.

"If it isn't my favourite brunette." Hans winked across at her, "You guys sure are letting lose tonight, mind if we join you?"

"Sure, you can sit next to me DJ!" Stevie immediately sprung to make space between him and Ola.

Magaret slid her phone back into her pocket, "Or right here since I'm already on the end seat."

DJ was the brooding dark haired quiet type with a brilliant smile that drove both Stevie and Magaret wild. It had become almost a game competing over him.

Ola did not like either of the boys and rolled her eyes as she stepped out for Hans to slide in between her and Marelize.

"Sangrias huh, someone's looking for a headache in the morning." DJ noted with a friendly smile as he sat down beside Magaret.

"We're waiting on jug three so feel free to help yourself." Stevie posed flirtatiously.

DJ laughed shaking his head, "I'll stick to beer thanks."

The little wink he tossed out sent Stevie into a warm flush, gawking as he turned to Magaret – a subtle middle finger in her face as DJ turned to the waitress to order.

They talked, ate pizza, as the jugs of Sangrias flowed with fresh beers and Marelize's dark red wine stained her lips glass after glass.

Coupled with the hint of sleep deprivation and mental exhaustion, they were buzzing, giggling in their booth and by closing time the six of them stepped out into the air of the night - all giggles and spirit when Magaret's phone rang.

It was Matt again and she sighed, clicking it 'End Call' before hurriedly opening her messaging app and scrolling to the unread messages received from her brother.

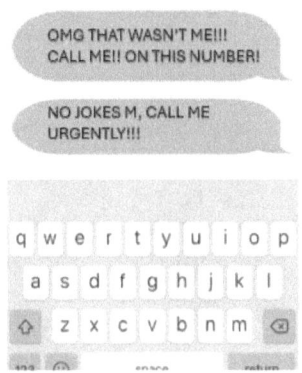

What was previously frustration was now an eeriness that lingered on her skin.
"Is everything ok?" asked Stevie slinging his arm around her shoulders.
She turned to him smiling when Hans, with Marelize's hips in his hands announced that they'd all be heading to the pool hall Crafty's for some juke box and beers.

"You in?" Stevie asked with bright eyes. "I don't think so guys, I have some stuff I need to handle." She declined, much to the groups brief dismay before they turned and started across the street.
"What's going on you seem upset?"
"Just my brother." She huffed. Stevie moaned grabbing her hands, "The letter thing? Still? Girl, you need to build a bridge already. Come on, you've

been buried in books like the rest of us. Let's take tonight to disappoint our mothers and we'll handle little brother tomorrow!"

A smile broke and Stevie' s eyes lit up again, "Sister don't make me get on my knees and beg, you know there's only one reason I put these Versace jeans to the ground, and it *isn't* for begging girl!"

"Fine!" Magaret laughed as Stevie bounced happily, tugging her behind the group.

****

With only an hour to sunrise, the rolling beauty of Bloemfontein hung silent beneath a cold layer of air on its stretching plateau.

The shoot for the night had wrapped up, and the 9-person crew were in the elevator with Leigh-Anne at the quaint, two-story Roses Hotel.

Her silly giggling and pretentious charm at director Max-B's fingers caressing the lower part of her back upset her assigned runner - Patty Cooper. She was also a tall blonde who worked hard to be polite to a girl a fraction prettier than her who scored a modelling contract when all her own efforts fizzled and her only chance at being part of the action was to work as an assistant.

Everyone in the elevator knew what worked to progress any aspiring model/actor's career and to them the flagrant display of inappropriateness was nothing new. It was a job, nothing to invest in, especially with a much sought-after director like

Max-B. But Patty clenched her jaw, rolling her eyes, not only in disgust but also in regret that her morals once placed the barrier in her own path.

When the elevator doors opened to the 2nd floor where the crew had booked 12 of the 15 rooms, everyone parted ways with their gear.
"Until tomorrow then." Leigh-Anne smiled, motioning alongside Patty towards their rooms when Max-B grabbed her wrist, forcing her to face him again.
"What do you say we have a little champagne and celebrate?" he smiled before noticing that Patty too had paused, "Just the two of us."
Leigh-Anne managed a smile, the same smile she'd used numerous times before in similar situations when her desire to achieve was overwhelmed by her virtue.
"I'm real tired Max-B. Maybe another time? Like tomorrow after we wrap the shoot back in Joburg?"
"I see." He stepped back, his demeanour now cold, "Well that's…Good night then."
He moved past her, glaring at Patty.
She'd never worked with Max-B before, and landing the opportunity deserved all she had, personal issues needed to wait.
"I suppose one glass won't hurt anyone." She said, causing Max-B to pause and turn back to her.
She looked to Patty who openly sneered all her disgust in an eye roll before turning and walking.
"Sorry, it's Patricia, right?" Max-B said stepping to Leigh-Anne and taking her clutch purse into his hands. Patty stopped, took a deep breath, and turned.
"Please be so kind to put this in Miss Roos's room, will you be such a darling for us?" he cocked his head, watching Patty who was visibly frustrated

while walked a few steps back towards him and taking the purse, offering the best attempt at a smile she had.

Leigh-Anne felt the girl's judgement, loudly - but as it began to sting, she thought about everything she'd had to endure in order to get this far and would not tolerate it from a second-rate failure she'd only met a few days ago.

Max-B turned to Leigh-Anne, grinning as he held his arm out, leading her to his room, three doors down from where Patty entered.

Patty entered Leigh-Anne's room, switching at the lights only for nothing to happen. She paused, stepped back into the hallway puzzled, pausing to see Leigh-Anne and the director shut their door.

"God, I need therapy." She rolled her eyes going back into the room in a huff.

She tried the lights again. The spotlights that were shining outside and the hallway's dim globes gave just enough light for the room to be more than just a hollow blackness.

"Guess the hotel figured you'd end up in a different room, slut." She said tossing the clutch onto the bed where it popped open, spilling some contents out on the bedding beside a white note under a single dying white rose.

With no-one else expected in the room, Patty stepped to the edge of the bed.

"Keys, balm…tamps and oh look, gum. Food for at least two weeks." She teased shoving the items back into the clutch while reaching for the flower and note.

Her face frowned as she examined the dying flower, then tossed it to the bed before unfolding the note.

DID THE RUNWAY TEACH YOU TO RUN LEIGH ANNE?
BECAUSE TODAY THE PAST CATCHES UP

"That's charming…" She said leaning forward - behind her, almost slithering out of the darkness the figure moved - realizing in only a fraction of a second that the girl who turned around was not his intended target.

Patty screamed but it reacted quickly, stabbing the scythe up into her stomach. An awful grunt escaped her as the tip of the blade tore out of her back while the figure began lifting her off the ground. She grabbed its arms, and her face turned red, her scream drowning behind the pool of blood pouring from her mouth.

Leigh-Anne pulled away from Max-B's tongue ramming at the back of her throat, "Sorry I just, I think I need a minute."

"A minute?" he wiped his mouth clinging to her waist, "What are you talking about angel lips?"

She smiled again as she leaned in to kiss him softly on the lips, then cheek and on the lower part of his jaw, whispering, "I need the bathroom."

He grinned releasing her waist as he stepped back, "Well you better hurry back we have an early flight tomorrow."

She shut the bathroom door, plonking her head against it taking a deep breath.

Max-B slunk to the foot of the bed, removing his shoes when he heard a thud at the room next door, a muffled pair of voices from the boom operator and sound mixer.

He stood up, moving closer to the wall whilst the commotion seemed to elevate – a gargling almost. Then silence.

She knew that to ensure more consecutive contracts and gigs, she'd need to make an impression with Max-B. His directorial status on this campaign would open so many new doors for her and she knew it would come with a price.
As she stared at herself in the mirror, she reminded herself to never let anything get in the way of her childhood dreams.
She took a moment to admire her beauty and adjust her breasts when she heard the door to the room slam open.

Alarmed by the tall, dark figure in its gauze mask, Max-B huddled backwards, "Who the hell are you? Get out of here!"
The figure dug into the thick leather coat, pulling out the scythe and shutting the door.
In the bathroom, Leigh-Anne pressed against the door listening as Max-B called out for help, wrestling, and then the sound of wet chopping that quickly silenced the room.

Terrified she stepped back covering her mouth to contain her cries when the door to the bathroom was kicked in, and she screamed.

The figure plucked her by the front of her dress, tossing her onto the foot of the bed, where she flopped and slid off through – the warm gooey innards from the disembowelled director.

She hit the ground with a roll, looking up as the figure slammed its boot at her - sending her backwards into the cabinet where the rooms TV shook and fell to the ground with a crash.

It was in that moment that the door reopened, two of the hotel's security guards gasping in alarm at the scene before them.

The figure moved towards them when the first guard immediately fired two rounds while the second guard started to yell, "Get on the ground!"

The figure stumbled backwards, almost unphased by the two holes in the dark leather of its coat.

"Stay back!" The first cried out, raising his weapon as the figure plunged towards them again – this time slashing the scythe as another two shots went off – only one hit, tearing a hole in the shoulder.

Screaming as blood sprayed, the second guard hit against the wall – a single slash across his forearms, chest, and lower chin – terror in his eyes as the figure plummet the scythe into his partner ruthlessly until his body slammed against the door, shutting it as he fell dead.

Leigh-Anne rolled to her knees, screaming with all her might as the figure turned to the first guard.

"Stay back! Stay back!" he cried, fumbling on his side, reaching desperately for his gun on the carpet. The scythe's sharp tip slammed down into his back, hooking deep through the bone into his lungs.

"Help!" Leigh-Anne screamed, realizing that she'd never make the door with the guard's body blocking it. She flung herself up and dart to the large wood-framed windows, tearing the curtains aside as the figure flung the guard's body off the blade to the side.

"Someone! Help me!" she banged against the window to the people below, residents and staff who had hurriedly evacuated at the sounds of mayhem. The figure raised the guard's standard issue Glock 22 behind her, aiming it dead at her as it cocked back the trigger, a sound that forced her to turn to face the black gauze.

"Please! Please don't hurt me, please!" she begged, her blood-soaked hands reaching up defensively, "Please! Please!"
The black index finger rose to the mouth of the gauze mask, "Sssshhh…"

One shot and the top of her body swung back, smashing through the glass, and hanging out for only a moment before her body slid, sending her down to the lawn below as the onlookers screamed in horror.

****

The white double-cab Hilux tore across the N1 highway, inside Matt was furious despite the upbeat tunes stemming from the radio. He had called his sister countless times without response and amid the frustration there was the annoyance that he was unable to find Eric who was easily able to find him. Having been following the news, along with the strange and sudden reappearance of Eric – everything made his gut churn as he tried to piece everything together.

Would Eric, desperate to find him, do something so extreme to find his sister?
Had Eric also visited Jacques and Odette prior to their deaths?
Were any of the others in danger?
Was he in any danger? Was his sister?
Could Eric and his friend truly be the murderers like the news implied? Why after all these years would Eric be the one to target them all?
Perhaps he couldn't live with himself any longer and wanted them all to pay.

He'd spent much of the night searching the internet to track down the rest of his childhood friends, and then decided to start his own investigation, hitting the road at dawn.

He'd managed to track his old friend Marcus Gallagher relatively quickly through his Vid-Tube account, but Lamberts Bay was too far a drive. He sent a message via the app but now had to wait for a reply in the hopes Mark would even see it. Finding Leigh-Anne was the simplest with her career in modelling – the internet had her face and name at an easy click. But physical address was obviously never listed. Seeking her out through her agency would prove time consuming, and perhaps even slightly stalkerish, so he kept looking. Through a general internet search, finding Carla Wilson wasn't too hard – tracking her to Midrand's Mulder & Seuns Trading, where the internet boasted her picture as one of their employees with a short bio. He'd found absolutely no trace whatsoever on the others who may know anything about the recent spate of murders.

'Tragedy has struck South African's again this morning, as the Province Slayings continue, this time at the Roses Hotel in Bloemfontein, where police were greeted by a horrific scene that had unfolded in the early hours of the morning according to eyewitnesses staying at the Hotel…'

Matt put the radio louder.

'The entertainment industry this morning is rocked by the tragic death of Max-B, the well-known director of award-winning films such as 'Meisies op Strande' and last year's 'The Dinner'. It's been confirmed that the esteemed director was on location for a commercial shoot when he and three members of his crew were attacked along with two security guards from Roses Hotel, who also suffered the onslaught of the attack while trying to defend and protect.'

The air inside the Hilux felt thick, cold, and ominous.

'Surviving the attack, relatively known young model Leigh-Anne Roos fights for her life this morning at the Bloemfontein Mediclinic, the only surviving victim of the Province Slaying so far, whom police are hoping against time will recover soon to provide them with more details. A statement was released this morning by special Detective of the Unique Crimes…'

He realized that he was not focusing on the road at all, so he flipped the radio off.

Dazed almost, the speed of his pickup's wheels on the tar reduced, and he was hit with a sudden thirst, feeling almost choked as he veered to a stop in the

emergency lane. His heart raced, pounding against his chest.
"What the hell Eric, what are you doing?" he gasped.

****

With a considerable crowd of reporters assembling around the premises of the Roses Hotel as their car pulled in, detectives Dekka and Malik got out of the car to a barrage of questions being shouted across the yard at them - dulling the significant beauty of the rows of roses leading to the entrance of the hotel.

The pressure was mounting with police stations across the country trying to collaborate without releasing any sensitive information, while reporters were relentlessly pitting against one another for any sordid detail or scoop they could get from paramedics, officers, and eyewitnesses.

"Detective Malik, Detective Dekka. I appreciate you coming out here before heading to Secunda." Colonel Ronald Preston addressed them as they entered the hotels foyer, where a few fold-out desks had been set up earlier for the witness testimonies.

He was a very tall, broad shouldered man with grey hairs ebbing through dyed dark black.
He was their direct supervisor, who had arrived just twenty minutes earlier following a visit from the station in Botshabelo.
They both greet him with a strong handshake and subtle smile while he turned to introduce the Hotel

manager Scottie Innemann, explaining that he was just questioning him as he was inside the security control room when calls flooded in distress to hearing screams.

"At first it was calls from their colleagues in the rooms adjacent to where it happened." Scottie Innemann explained, his old face riddled with exhaustion from a full day of questioning, "Then the gunshots, everyone heard those! That's when most of the visitors began rushing from their rooms to get outside. Some stayed in their rooms to afraid to come out even when the police got here."

"And the hotel has CCTV surveillance?" Dekka asked checking her notes from the telephonic briefing the local police provided en route.

"As I've said numerous times we have sixteen cameras, but your colleagues have already gone through everything there is." Innemann turned, leading them around the front desk into a narrow passage hidden from guests.

"Sixteen camera's and nothing?" Malik commented to his superior in surprise.

"Nothing as yet, there is a team still combing the footage." Colonel Preston replied as they entered the large security control room where they were met by five uniformed police officers and two of the hotels' guards hovering over their shoulders to assist with examining the video footage.

"Also Mr. Innemann to confirm…" Malik paused to check her notes, paging back and forth quickly, "…the only other entrance to the building were already locked by the time the attack occurred?"

"That's right. Our security is very tight here, I've told the other policeman too. We have the main entrance and the side entrance where we get stock deliveries. The rear entrance was sealed up years ago to make provisions for an entertainment room for the kids."

"With this setup you can welcome the King." Dekka remarked stepping over to one of the screens, "Is that also the reason your reaction officers carry firearms?"

"Look this is Bloemfontein sir." Innemann stated zealously huffing, "But our establishment is often visited by VIP clients. But we want everyone who passes those doors to experience a unique and safe stay in the Rose."

"Except the guests last night." Colonel Preston disparaged stepping beside Dekka by the monitors. "Mind you sir, this never would have happened if the police already caught this madman!" Innemann flared up aggressively when Malik stepped between them.

"It's been a very long day for you Mr. Innemann we can only imagine how you feel having lost two of your security agents as well." Malik spoke gently, "We really do appreciate all your help, and your team. Can you tell me a bit more about the security detail throughout the course of the day starting from when the doors opened until the incident, anything strange or out of the ordinary?"

Innemann shook his head, "Absolutely nothing out of the ordinary. This is Bloemfontein, nothing ever really happens here. Not like this, nothing like this ever happened, not once in the sixteen years I've been at the Rose."

"We need to issue an update to the hounds at the gate Detective Dekka." The colonel stood with his hands behind his back while the two detectives continued to scan the surveillance screens.

"Where are you with the Jansen matter?"

"We're working on a warrant to have the cellular location tracked." She said, her eyes scanning the four screens almost simultaneously, "But as I've mentioned sir, I don't believe Jansen or Naicker is responsible for this."

"Ah yes, the man in the black mask."

"It's more than we've had to go on before." She said raising her eyebrow.

"If there was a man in a mask moving about, someone would have seen something." He said adamantly, "Nobody has seen anything like it. Even so, the media want some kind of break in this case, and we need to give it to them. Even if it buys us another week."

"Another week and more bodies will pile up and we'll still be in shit creek without any leads." Dekka said quickly realizing her candidness before clearing her throat and returning her attention to the monitor.

Preston grinned, "I want that phone tracked and I want them found. The press must know we're doing something. Until Miss Roos is able to speak to us herself and recount what happened here last night, they're the closest thing we have to understanding this mess. Where are we on the email?"

"The authenticity of its existence is corroborated by the company Jansen works for, but the damage it did to their servers means it's a good wait to get our eyes on it, if the virus hasn't already destroyed all traces of it."

"The minister of police wants answers, and the press is having a field day tearing the unit apart. We have a working-class father with his face shredded

off, a teenage girl mauled to death, hell I have the Allied Union up my ass for the garden worker who had his garden sheers shoved down his throat."
She sighed shaking her head as the stress pressed against her neck.
"I think it's a mistake to waste resources on them sir, they're not the ones doing this." She said matter-of-factly.
"We don't have time. The UCU doesn't have time. Jansen and Naicker will stay on the top of your priority list Anele, the moment that phone is tracked you make the arrest!"
His voice was hard now, but her response threw him off guard.

"Wait!" she said pointing to the one screen, "Rewind it 10 seconds."
The officer took the tape back, on the screen the footage taken from outside the large, roofed parking port behind the Hotel.
"See something Dekka?" Malik asked standing beside her now.
"Take it forward to just after 5am." She instructed.
"What do you see Anele?" pushed Preston.
She held her finger up, watching as the footage continued at the time frame, playing for 40 seconds when she yelled, "There!"
"What do you see?" Malik asked staring at the screen where there was nothing but the quiet parking port without any movement.
"Show me the controls." She said leaning over the officer who quickly explained how to control the player.
"At nine fourteen last night." She said pausing while the tape rewind, pausing on the front of the parking

port, where two cars were entering, and another was exiting.

"This black pickup enters the parking." She pointed as she slowly played the tape, showing how the black vehicle entered the parking back past the valet.

"Then leaves at five twenty-six." She paused again to forward the tape, pausing at the same spot of the empty parking port, but pointing to the far side just at the back of the port a black object moved out of vision.

"It left out the back of the parking?" Malik turned to Innemann who shrugged his shoulders.

"The parking bay has a one-meter wall surrounding it, there is no chance anyone got a vehicle through that without being heard."

"Were all the vehicles were accounted for by your team?" Preston turned to Malik.

"Yes sir, every last one of them."

One of the local officers from the side added with a strong certainty, "Every single one of them. There's not black pickup."

Accompanied by one of the security guards and two uniformed officers, they exited the large doors on the side of the building, across the large patio, down the stairs to a section of the large driveway that led around the rear of the building.

"So, everyone checked out?" Malik asked almost in surprise as they reached the large carport.

"Would you stay here with a killer on the prowl?" Innemann said with a heavy heart, fearing that the Rose would lose its stature and dwindle to nothingness in the months to come.

Splitting in two teams, detectives Dekka and Malik began walking the circumference of the one-meter-high brick perimeter wall, while Preston and Innemann walked at a slower pace closely behind. "A five-star accommodation with a carport? Hardly seems impressive."

"The original garage was demolished about four years ago with the intention of replacing it with another, before the hotel changed owners. It's supposed to be done but you'll have to ask the owners when." Innemann said as they reached the wide parking port.

A few minutes later, having very briskly rushed along the wall, Dekka called out.

At the rear, between two of the large metal beams holding up the metal roof structure was a partition of brick wall where a large section was standing in façade with all the cement between removed. As Preston and Innemann approached, she kicked it and the bricks toppled outwards.

"Very clever." Grinned Preston, suddenly realizing that their perpetrator was a patient but very determined to stay out of jail maniac, "He chipped it all away."

"To sneak out the back without anyone being any wiser." Dekka said as the uniforms assisted her up over the small wall following Malik who simply hoisted himself over.

Colonel Preston looked over as Innemann and the uniforms stood watching while Dekka and Malik pointed out the thick tyre tracks hidden in the field grass, leading off to the side where it undoubtedly met up with the road again.

"Like I said sir, with all respect." Dekka said nodding, "Jansen isn't our "suspect.""

"Then he's a victim. Either way, we need him."

****

Near midday, the sun scorched the city of Midrand, where inside her townhouse, Carla sat on the edge of her bed, with her phone up to her ear listing for the latest update on her mother's condition.

"The surgery was a success. She's recovering nicely, but we are monitoring her." The doctor explained, as a rush of both relief and fear triggered confusion to her thoughts when Eric tapped on the bedroom door.
"Are the police still guarding her?" she asked ushering him inside.
In his hands was the packet she'd brought back for them after having gone out earlier for fresh clothes and some bread to feed the two of them as they slept.
"Unfortunately, there's been no update regarding the other family or the charges against your mother, so yes there is a uniformed officer stationed at the hospital."
"Thank you doctor." She said politely, "I'll call later, thank you."
"Everything ok?" Eric frowned worriedly, standing shirtless with the wound on his chest exposed.
"Yeah. I suppose for now." She got up, "You guys will find towels in the cabinet beneath the sink."
"Hey Carla." He took her by the arm, "I'm sorry for everything."
She tried a smile nodding but the weight was still raw and heavy as tears broke to her eyes. Eric

pulled her against him in a hug as she softly sobbed behind her hand when Zain entered behind her.

"I can't tell you what it means to Zain and me that you're helping us out like this."
"Yeah, we're in shit river with holes in the boat." Zain added, "Don't know what we would have done if you hadn't found us."
She smiled stepping back while he continued, lifting his packet up, "I promise we'll pay you back for these when all of this is over."
"Let's get through alive and without a mental break then we'll call it even, alright?" she joked ushering him past her.
"Sounds good to me." Zain grinned slipping between them and into the bathroom where he shut the door. She looked to Eric again.

"I just wish all of this wasn't really happening you know…" her voice trailed softly, "My mom, Jacques, Odette…All those people…"
"Yeah, yeah I know."
"Who's doing this Eric?"
He shook his head rubbing the ache on his neck with a hard grip, "You know my brain keeps on trying to figure this out. The more I try the more I come up with nothing. But if it's not...that, then why else?"
"It's that Eric, it's the only thing linking us all." She said unpretentiously, her voice certain, "I mean look at you. You told someone, maybe someone else did?"
From inside the bathroom, Zain slanted out of the running shower listening.
"Look I get it, ok? I should have never spoken about it." Eric was almost defensive, "I should have never

dragged Zain into this, I wish I hadn't. But I kept my end up for years. I stayed quiet, letting it eat me alive and putting me in places you'd be shocked to understand. But you don't know how it was seeing those pictures, Carla. It was vile, I've never imagined such terrible…"

He trailed off, closing his eyes as he clenched his jaw – forcing the reminder from his mind's eye.

"I was in a bad place, a place I'd not been in for a long time…Zain was there…and I love him."

In the shower, Zain slipped in shock, grabbing the wall to prevent his fall.

"Like real deal here Carla, I love him. And for me, to have that after all these years of hell…I don't know."

He stalled shaking his head as he realized he was veering off.

"Look Carla, I wish I could go back and say nothing. But I can't. I know you don't trust him I respect that you have no reason to. You don't even need to trust me, God it's been years since we were friends. But we're here now, together all three of us. And I don't know who is doing this, I don't know why."

A silence hung between them in her bedroom, and Zain too slipped back under the hot water.

"My point was that maybe someone else knows, and now someone's trying to make us pay?" Caral said finally, "Or it's one of us."

Eric huffed a deep breath shaking his head.

"You've thought about it too, haven't you?" she stepped forward.

"Yeah, I've thought about the possibility yes. But Carla, who and why after all these years?"

"Ten years." Her voice was stern, "Sunday is ten years exactly. I remember the date. Every year."

A solemness befell her, and she turned to the window, now also rubbing her neck beneath her red hair as she stepped into the afternoon sunlight breaking through.

"You speak of going to bad places, but you're not the only one. I know what it did to me, and now I know what it's done to you."
Eric looked down awkwardly, filled with shame and regret.
"Bobby, Jacques, and Odette are dead, so that leaves us with 5. And then there's Nathan and Wessel."
"Nathan wont…"
"I know." She said interrupting with a grunt of frustration, "But I'm turning over every stone here. Whoever has any idea of what happened that day is a suspect."
She turned to face him again, "So, we need to find the others and get an idea of where they are in their lives so we can narrow this down and end this thing before anyone else gets hurt."
Her cellular toned with a new email and she rolled her eyes as she moved towards the door, "I'll leave you to shower."

Eric heaved a burdensome sigh and opened the bathroom door.

Zain reared his head out of the curtain grinning, "You want me to leave it running or...?"

"You heard that didn't you?"

"Heard what?" he cocked his head to the side convincingly, "Something happen?"

Eric shook his head, "No, we've just been talking." Smiling as he stepped out of the shower, Zain put his towel to his face when Eric said his name. "What's up?" he asked trying to hide his delight as Eric paused stepping into the shower to face him. A subtle smirk broke over Eric's face while he stepped back out, grabbing Zain and pressing him against him as his lips planted to his.

It was the first time he'd ever kissed anyone with that level of intensity, and safety he felt in the past few weeks. As they kissed the sorrow stabbed at his heart for knowing that he'd put this person in the line of danger, and then Zain pulled back as an awkwardness lingered in the steam between them.

"I'm sorry, for all of this." Eric said standing back, touching the dark bruise on Zain's upper arm, "I never meant to..."

"Look the past few months getting to know you, getting close to you... I've never felt this way about anybody." Zain said nodding, speaking earnestly and direct as he stared up into Eric's eyes, "And I know this is crazy Eric, I know the future is uncertain in so many ways but dude... I don't want to be anywhere else, not with this was going on. I know what I know, and we need to figure it out."

Carefully, Zain put his hand over the tear across Eric's chest, "So, I don't want you to feel obligated to protect me or save me or anything. I'm here and we're in this together. You have nothing to apologize for, not to me."

Eric sighed nodding his head and after a pause, Zain smiled standing back, "When this is all over, we'll revisit what this kiss meant just now, but until then keep your emotions in check. We need to stay focused, alive, and out of jail..."

Eric smirked as he turned back into the shower.

****

By late afternoon, a thick blanket of summer rain clouds draped the sky over Secunda, the wind was strong as it twisted its way around the VW hatchback and up along the stoned path from Cookie's porch to the driveway - holding closed his blue jacket to protect from the chill in the wind, with Shane morbidly following behind him.

As the car head through the small city, a silence lingered between them, having stayed up without sleep talking about Odette and gaining a perspective from the man she loved into the life of his sister.

Mark knew that Shane would get lost to the madness of his own guilt and die questioning everything that transpired in those final moments together at the Sasol gates. Mark had been there before he ran to the ocean to escape it.

Within their conversation in the dark hours of the morning, they came to the ominous realisation that whatever pictures she'd received had unquestionably not been found at the crime scene, or the police would have wanted to see Mark for questioning even before his arrival. The need to understand and know if the police had missed it was set alight at the breaking news from Bloemfontein – no longer a strange but horrifying coincidence but a terrible reality.

The dread Mark felt since hearing of how the murders at Odette's home were the second in a string of attacks chocked at him - even harder now that two more names he knew had been mentioned in the same grisly news, Eric Jansen and Leigh Anne Roos. The anxiety gripped tightly, twisted around his gut and up his trachea, constricting his breath as it reached up stabbing at his mind, picking open memories and emotions he'd long since suppressed.

The rental rolled to a stop on the dry road where once a string of modular homes stood on the far outskirts of Secunda. The area was desolate, overgrown now, with nothing but vague reminders of shapes that were homes and rusted fencing that surrounded them.
"Why are we here Mark?" Shane asked confused. Mark took small steps forward as the wind snaked cold through the long grass and over the dusty streets and then turned to face him - his eyes burdened in deep suffering.

In flashes through his mind, he recalled the day they all swore to never speak of it, when 10 great friendships shattered. Then the email with the attachment he'd opened on the plane – the terrible images of his friends butchered.

Everything inside of him was screaming silently, and he could not make sense of any of it. The world felt smaller than ever, cold and without air.

Looking at Shane again, he could see the distraught and broken shell of a young man that once had ambitions and hopes for life.

He knew the feeling, too well. It was the feeling that made him run to the water.

"Why are we here?" Shane pressed again.

He could feel the torment within Shane, a physical suffering he could almost touch – as though it were draped over his shoulders like a blanket. Mark knew that every day after, with Odette and Jacques dead – there was no reason to leave Shane to exist in such a miserable darkness of questions and guilt, and he opened his eyes looking at Shane.

"I needed to bring you somewhere…where I could talk and get it out." Mark began, "It's something that happened ten years ago."

****

"What's wrong?" Zain asked entering the lounge where Carla sat waiting with her phone in one hand, the TV remote in the other – her whole being almost desolate and her face pale.

She looked up at him, "Is Eric still in the shower?"

"Yeah, he'll be out any minute, are you ok? What happened?"

"I'll wait for Eric." She said sternly, folding her legs up on the cough, holding them in her arms.

Zain sat on the sofa across from her, "I get it Carla, you don't know me. You don't want me knowing your business. But..."

"I don't care what you think of me you know." She spoke rigidly, "I know you have a lot of judgement against us for what we did but..."

Zain interrupted with an irritated huff, ", I have no idea what happened out there that day, not really. I wasn't there."

"Either way Zain." She interrupted back angrily, "I don't know you, you're a stranger."

"Ok I was thinking about what you said." Said Eric entering the open plan room and heading directly for the kitchen, "If it is one of us, we need to look at who's the hardest to find."

He opened the fridge, "Which would be Zach, he is literally off the grid. And I mean why? But also, what about Wessel, all his friends died that day so that's a motive, isn't it?"

They both looked at him as he opened the cupboard for glasses and he paused awkwardly, "What's going on?"

"I got an email from our company's 'Meet the Team' platform, it's from Matt."

Eric cocked his head in surprise, and she continued, "He explained your weird visit the other day, and asked if we could meet up, but there's something else."

Carla paused, looking to Zain and then back at Eric, before aiming the remote at the TV and clicking to start the snippet she had recorded from the news.

Eric stood by the counter, a death like cold riddled over him as he stared at the report on the Bloemfontein attack, a coldness that physically ached his skin. It was clear now, screaming silently at his core, that someone was after them, all of them – coming with a violent and relentless vengeance for what happened ten years ago.

****

Tagging at the gate felt like it was the first of the hardest things he'd ever need to do again, knowing that Odette would not be waiting for him at their small starter apartment. Shane sat softly rubbing over his fists, his knuckles were red and bloodied, like the cuts on Marks face.

They had not spoken since the raging scream erupted from Shane's lips, before his vicious attack that Mark had not even tried once to defend or block, instead laying on the dusty sand allowing Shane's fists to swing freely again and again. When the words left his mouth through the distraught sorrow – Mark again wanted to suffer, even die now that his sister had suffered the wrath of their childhood ignorance.

The sedan slowly rolled down the narrow roads in the complex and Shane pointed at the parking bays where Odette's Golf stood just to the side of the small duplex apartment where the yellow crime scene tape flailed in the wind.
"That's hers."

The VW eased into the open parking bay beside it and Mark stepped out, leaving Shane to move only when he was ready to.

He held his side, the pain from Shane's blows were tender with each movement. He stared at his reflection in the Golf's window for a moment – all beaten and bruised but, in his opinion, not nearly punished or destroyed enough to absolve him of all the guilt inside.

The inside of the Golf was empty, no signs of any axe or of any supporting envelope or pictures.

He felt for the door, it was open, and he slowly motioned into the driver's seat - sitting where his little sister had sat, he could not help but want to smile at how much taller than her he'd always been.

Inside the car, Shane stared at his fists still, unable to look at the car or the house.

His broken heart now riddled with wrath. He knew staring at his broken fists that nothing would ever vindicate him of the guilt he felt for leaving her at the gates, or for the unkind words he thought he meant in the heat of the moment. He'd carry it for eternity, in everything the world offered because she was his world, and nothing would ever change that.

The state of his fists proved that, aside from everything he'd learned about Odette and what set her onto her path of bereft angst where her only solace was booze, the only person who deserved to suffer was himself for leaving her to die without knowing how sorry he was. But he would need to wait until the person or people who did this suffered even more for stealing the sun from his life.

The wind howled beneath the zinc roofing, as Mark shut the car door and turned to face the duplex – the yellow crime scene tape that had withered out of place around the yard from the strong wind remained intact across the front door.

His dark eyes filled with tears, and he took a deep breath when Shane's door flung open as he stepped out into the cold air.

Mark paused with uncertainty, then asked "Are you sure you're up for this right now?"

"I'll never be up for this." Shane said, his voice dry and broken, "I can't go in there."

Mark walked to him, hands in his jacket pocket as the cold wind slithered across his battered face.

"I'd rather we know if they found it than never know if they even care to find who did this." Shane held out the house keys, his bottom lip shivering from the intense cold her death left inside of him. If there is any proof in there that will help them find whoever is doing this, we need to find it. But I can't go in that house."

Nodding, Mark took the keys and walked towards the front door, pausing at the tape, his fists clenched in both bravery and fearful turmoil.

He pushed the door, allowing it to carefully swing open - immediately Mark choked in alarm, tears streaming down his face, and he looked away in sobs behind his hands. To the side, Shane closed his eyes, recalling the vivid moment he'd seen into their home.

Mark turned his back on the house, staring at the sky, catching air to the raw aching reality that stole every breath behind his tears that he fought bravely to control.

With his eyes shut still, he turned back to the doorway when Shane's cellular rang, the wind carrying it loudly and he turned away from the house as Shane spoke.

"Yes, alright aunty Cookie thank you." He hung up looking at Mark.

"Aunty Cookie says there are police coming to the house, they want to speak with you."

****

The Midrand Mall hummed with the sounds of shoppers as Carla made her way up the steps from the basement parking, along the wide walkway past the ATM's and to the left towards the food court. While she walked, she remembered a time when they had all decided to try their hand at fishing at one of the dams near Evander -the 10-kilometre bicycle trip it took to get there on an icy cold June morning. Danger and caution barely existed in their world, life was pure adventure, trust, and companionship. She longed for that and still with each step, with all the noise in her mind, she could not stop herself from wishing she would awake from the nightmare thrust into their lives.

If she had one more chance to be a child again with her friends and do everything differently, she'd take it.

The food court lined either side of the wide floor way, with numerous restaurants bustling and filling as she paused near the centre, where a large wooden deck stood for persons buying from the carts could sit.

She felt her pocket and remembered that she had left the car in so much of a hurry – her phone was still laying on the dashboard. She sighed, scanning the faces of everyone in around the restaurants, food carts, benches and deck trying to find Matt like they had arranged. She could barely recognise his voice when she called the number on his email, and as she felt herself spinning from side to side anxiously seeking him, she realized that like his voice his face too had changed, and she was no longer looking for the boy she shared a life with.

"Thank god, where the hell have you been?" Matt snarled into his phone as he made his way through the mall.
"Severely hung over." Maggie explained sitting up in her bed, her mouth dry and her head groggy from their overextended partying.
"Look what do you want Matt?"
"The letter, it wasn't me." He urged, "I think someone else…"
"I don't even care anymore." She said slopping her legs off the bed, "I've drank my problems away and have a serious hangover that needs attention. Whatever your games are little brother, I'm over it…I'm over you. I told you not to contact me."
"Have you even seen the news?" he said pausing, "Maggie?"
"No, I haven't seen the news! I'm twenty-four, not forty-two." She mocked leaning forward and putting her spinning head into her hands.
"Odette and Jacques are dead Maggie."
She took a deep breath, allowing air to funnel to her brain that remained sore and hazed and then frowned, "What?"

He scoffed angrily, "They've been murdered Mags, by the province slasher or whatever they're calling him."

"What?" she tried to think through the blandness in her head.

"Where have you been?" he scoffed, "Maggie we think we might be in danger."

"In danger?" she frowned still struggling to get over the bitter taste in the back of her very dry mouth, "What are you talking about Matt?"

He sighed angrily, trying to find a way to tell her everything while walking through a crowded mall. Then, across the way he saw the face of Carla Wilson, her red flaming hair almost impossible to miss.

"Look take a shower, something for the headache and then call me, ok?" Matt said walking again, "Please Maggie, I need you to call me!"

"Alright!" she insisted, "I'll call you just calm down."

"There is something going on that links to that day Maggie." His voice sending coldness over her, "So I need you to call me, ok? You hear me?"

She nodded as the dread lingered, "Yes I'll call you."

He hung up, leaving her to sit and adjust to hearing him referencing a day she never thought she'd ever have to speak of again.

"The fire that leads the way." Matt said to her side, reciting something they'd often say as kids because of Carla's strong will and spirit for adventure.

She smiled turning to face him, "Matty."

He smiled shaking his pudgy stomach, "A few to many beers over the years, I figured you'd maybe not recognise me."

"How are you Matty?" she said cautiously leaning in for a hug, unsure if he'd welcome it or not.

"It's been a minute, thing called life I suppose we all found a way to cope." He said hugging her as she studied his face.

"I'm glad you reached out to me."

"Carla I'm assuming you've heard all of it on the news and that's why you called me?"

"You said in your email that you suspected Eric of…" she paused, looking around to be sure she was out of earshot of anyone else when he interrupted.

"I believe he's the killer yeah. Him and his pal from the news are knocking off our friends one by one and I think I'm next."

"What?" she gasped taken aback, "Why would you be next? Did something happen? Did you get a call or something?"

"What? No. Eric came to see me two days ago – acting *really* creepy!"

"I know, it's not what you think that was." She sighed shaking her head and he took a step back.

"What do you mean you know?"

"He was trying to find out if you were also being threatened because the killer sent him an email."

"An email?" Matt's face mocked her the same way it always did.

"Eric was trying to track us down so he could warn us."

Matt shook his head in alarm, "You're with Eric, aren't you? He's here, isn't he?"

"He's not the killer Matty."

"Carla, I can't be talking to you. He's wanted by the police!" he stepped back, his voice growing louder.

"Matt, you need to listen to me, we need to stick together!" she urged.

"Look I don't know what's going on and…"
"Matty, someone attacked Eric and his friend two
nights ago, almost killing them. The same person
who went after Jacques, Odette, and Leigh-Anne."
She spoke softly, but with a stern aggression as she
moved closer to him, "The same person who went
as far as throwing my mother through a goddamned
window. So, nobody is safe! We need to stick
together! Now more than ever."
His eyes scanned her suspiciously, then crossed
the bustling around him nervously.

"I know you've put the pieces together Matty." She
said leaning closer to him, "Otherwise you wouldn't
have reached out to me."
"I don't know what to think." He huffed, "This is all
really bad."
"We should go, we need to talk somewhere private."
Matt's face spoke volumes of internal conflict, and
she sighed, "Where's Magaret? Is she safe?"
"She's fine." He paused uncertain if he should tell
her his sister's whereabouts in fear that soon the
Province Slayings would seep into Cape Town.
"You've spoken to her?"
"I got some cryptic messages from her after Eric
showed up, then I heard about Odette, now Leigh
Anne."
"Is Magaret safe Matt?" she pushed again, and his
demeanour lowered from defence to defeat.
"I can't reach her." He chose to leave her out of it as
far as possible, for the moment at least.
A heaviness circled over them as the mall continued
around them, and she stepped forward again,
"Listen to me Matt, the news is wrong. Eric and Zain
are not the one's doing this. And if there's a chance
that Magaret *is* in danger like the rest of us right

now, then the four of us need to figure it out who before anyone else gets hurt."

He nodded nervously, and then looked up at her, "Alright."

****

The basement, like the mall, was buzzing with shoppers and cars coming and going. Inside the BWM, Zain sat up against the backdoor with his legs stretched up on the seat and Eric was slightly reclined in the front, the tablet in his hands searching for Zach Manson.

"So, tell me about this guy nobody can find." Zain said yawning, "Do you really think he might be the one doing all of this?"

"A few days ago, I wasn't sure which shirt made me feel suitable for my job, today I'm not sure if I'll live to see tomorrow." Eric huffed negatively, "So I don't know what I think anymore."

"That's one way of putting it I suppose."

Eric tossed the tablet to his lap, heaving a defeated sigh.

"Everything was so different when we were kids. I believed it was a friendship that would never break apart, at least before…" he paused shaking his head, "Zachary was my best friend, well we all were. Mark and Zach were like brothers but when I came along, Zach made me welcome and I don't mean just like another kid to hang out with, the three of us were the first you know? At a stage we were inseparable to the point where our mothers just expected where one was the others went too.

When the group grew it became something legendary – a sort of family."
Zain smiled seeing Eric's face light up as he spoke.

"All of us were just different from all the other kids. We sought adventure in everything, always on the go, always tearing through the fields on our bikes. God the games we'd play. The world was so different back then, we weren't afraid of anything or maybe we were, but we had each other so nothing seemed impossible or scary. We had each other and our imaginations."
"And after…" Zain asked carefully, "You and Zach couldn't stay friends?"
Eric shook his head solemnly, "None of us could. Not really, we tried but nothing was the same. It became harder to talk to each other or even look at each other. Too much blame and guilt and everyone was just…."
Suddenly the phone on the dash rang and Zain sat up.
"She left her phone."
It continued to ring, and Eric reached for it.
"Are you going to answer it?" Zain asked almost anxiously after seeing the display reading the same name from Carla's story – UNKNOWN NUMBER.
It continued to ring, then went off and the missed call notification popped up.
What felt like relief befell the silence of the car for a moment, then the ringing started again.

"What if it's Carla calling from this guy's phone?"
Eric nod, answering, "Carla's phone hello?"
"Who is this?" the voice was cold, "Is this Matt?"

Eric's eyes grew wide, "Who's this?"

"Oh it's you, Eric." An icy giggle, "Who would have thought you'd go running to a girl to save you."

"Why are you doing this?" he snarled now gripping the phone angrily.

"It's a passion project."

"Who are you, asshole?"

"An enthusiast."

"Stop with the games dickhead!" Eric yelled into the phone, "What do you want?"

"Eric Jansen! Carla Wilson! Zachary Manson! Matthew Jonah! Margaret Jonah and Marcus Gallagher!" the voice roared violently, pausing as it switched to a cold calm giggle, "Oh then there's still Leigh-Anne Roos, maybe. And for the fun of it, I'll include your little friend."

"Go to hell asshole!"

It laughed, "Oh the gangs getting back together. Isn't it amazing how a little madness, murder and mayhem brings everyone closer?"

Eric stared across the basement as Carla and Matt exited the stairs into the parking garage alongside another couple and he turned to Zain in alarm, "He's here!"

Zain scanned the basement parking, where a few people were at their cars, nobody specifically on the phone.

The voice was adamant, "Get out of the car Eric, let's play their lives for yours. All you have to do is tell the world the truth."

He froze cold shaking his head and the voice taunted, "Get out of the car if you want to save them!"

"Why are you doing this!" Eric raged into the phone.

"Time to speak, let it all out."

"Who are you?"
"Time's up!"

Somewhere in the basement tyres screeched
loudly, forcing Eric to look up, seeing Carla and Matt
spin around to the sound of a matt black Ford
pickup veering out of a parking bay, swinging into a
turn with engine roaring as it sped towards them.
"Run!" screamed Eric from inside the car, his hand
slammed up against the windshield.

Carla grabbed Matt's arm, pulling him with her while
rushing towards her parked BMW, the other couple
behind them also darting to the side as the engine
roared closer.
She and Matt slid between her SUV and the car
beside it, while the pickup swung a right, heading
deeper into the back of the parking basement
behind rows of cars.

The fear retreated as they pant breathlessly
between the two cars, trying to see where the
roaring engine sound faded while the other couple
who dart aside stepped back out in alarmed
confusion, glaring at Carla and Matt in disgust.
"What the hell was that?" Matt exclaimed looking
first to Carla then to the window at Eric inside.
Carla, looking at the terror in his eyes and the
phone in his hand, knew.

Suddenly another screech echoed, and the engine
roared. There was not enough time to know where it
was coming from when the matt black pickup
barrelled into the other couple, spitting their bodies
out beneath its thick wheels.

Carla screamed, her hands up in front of her mouth and Matt stood jolted in time, his eyes wide with terror as the pickup veered away into the basement again.
Eric got out and stepped closer, staring at the mangled bodies in horror.

****

Speaking from the podium in the boardroom full of news crews, Colonel Preston stood chest out, shoulders back – proud of the badge and earnest as he concluded in his media address.

"…everything in our power, and South African's can rest assured that the attacker will be caught. He or they, *will* be brought to justice."
Journalists raised hands in the air as camera's recorded from multiple stations and media outlets.

"Colonel Preston, has the UCU been able to determine if these attacks are being carried out by a single individual or group? Should South African's be concerned about the rise of a cult?"
"As I've said, this is an active and ongoing investigation, any information is closely guarded to avoid unnecessary panic and false media. The combined efforts by all police stations across the country are hard at work to find anyone responsible for these crimes, but I can state that there is no evidence to suggest that this is the work of a cult or otherwise." Preston answered, pointing to the next reporter.

"Referencing your statement earlier, is it plausible at all to believe that this is the work of a single individual, able to seemingly be in two places at once?"

"That is a factually incorrect way to state your question and supports our concerns regarding the media and what's currently being published regarding this case. I will reiterate, the South African Police Service's stance regarding fake news – we cannot tolerate the spread of unnecessary fear and panic." He spoke harshly to the reporter, "We are in the business of catching human beings, criminal minds who are flesh and blood, not chasing ghosts. There are sufficient travel arrangements that can be made between provinces, and I suggest the likes of News Hound research the facts relating to the case before publishing conspiracies."

The reporter stood gobsmacked, standing aside with her face down as the rest of the media called out with hands raised.

"Yes, you in the front." He pointed outward.

"Thank you, Colonel Preston. Are we to assume that there are still no details available regarding the arrest of Zain Naicker and Eric Jansen and that they are still at large?"

"Again, we want to avoid false media and I'll reserve my comment on Mr. Naicker and Mr. Jansen's involvement in this case for a later time when we have sufficient comment to deliver. Next question please?"

"Are there any other suspects at this time?" the same reporter asked.

"Next?" he said more sternly now.

"If the UCU is unable to apprehend known persons wanted by the police for questioning…" The same reporter pushed arrogantly, "…how can we as the public consider sleeping safely if the real killer is able to cross provincial lines so easily? Ghosts or not colonel, the SAPS and UCU seems to be having difficulty in catching anything while distraught families await justice."

Preston leaned to the podium, "Next question please."

"Interprovincial travel arrangements noted but does this mean security at airports have been put on alert and a more thorough passenger search is underway before boarding?" another reporter asked stepping forward.

"Airports, toll booths, trains and busses have all received the same communication, as I said the search is on. We will apprehend the person, or persons, responsible and bring closure to the families."

****

The park off the R55 was almost empty by 6pm, Carla's BMW the only car in the parking with a few others roaming in the distance across the vast lawn with their kids at the playground.

The sky was cluttered with thick clouds and the wind had grown chill.

The four of them were by a bench, Matt sitting beside Carla while Zain and Eric stood. They had all now shared their stories with Matt who sat leaning forward with his head in his hands, quiet as it sunk into him.

"We can't turn to the police, or my mother will die." Carla continued, "So we need to reach out to Mark and Zach and figure out how to end this."

"End this?" Matt stood up with a laugh as he strutted about in a circle, shaking his head, "Are you all suffering from a bop to the brain? Secrets and lies is what got us all into this mess to begin with! Now you want to keep doing the same thing. End this? Please! You mean handle it under the table and sweep it under the rug just like when we were kids."

"So, what do you want to do Matt? Wait for more people to die? For Maggie to…" Eric started when Matt flung around.

"Don't you say it! Don't you say it, Eric!"

"Or what Matt? You going to bully me? I'm not a kid anymore." Eric stood with his chest out.

"Oh! Big guy now huh? You don't scare me Eric, you're still the same wasted pathetic loser you've always been!"

"Guys this isn't helping!" Carla raised her voice. Eric swung a right, connecting Matt's side and the retaliation forced them into a grip and an all fists swinging, legs flailing scuffle began as Zain and Carla pulled them apart.

"Stop! Will you both just stop!" Carla yelled, her voice loud in the emptying park.

"To hell with you Matt!" Eric scoffed, "You've always thought you were above everyone else."

"I was better than you! Look at you man I haven't seen you in years and you still the same. We know how you had to sell a little of yourself to get some cash and we know it wasn't ladies."

"Shut up!" Eric snarled as he lurched forward again, but Zain pulled him back and Carla stepped between them.

"Will you just stop! None of this is relevant!" she warned again raising her voice, "We're not children anymore and this doesn't matter right now! Two of our friends are dead while the other fights for her life!"

"Yeah Carla?" Matt scoffed spitting blood to the dirt, "And how many more people must die so your mother can live?"

"What?" she gasped when Eric shoved him again. "Shut your mouth, Matt!"

"Bring it on, washout!" Matt shoved back when from the side, Zain flung forward and grabbed Matt against the chest of his shirt, shoving him off his feet and down into the ground hard. Bewildered, Eric and Carla froze as Matt winced from the pain of his air being knocked out.

"You both need to shut the hell up!" Zain snarled angrily, "Two innocent people just got flattened in front of us, don't you care? Are you so immune to running away from death that this doesn't bother you?"

"Hey…" Matt tried when Zain continued over him.

"No, people are dying. Not just your friends, but innocent people. Whoever is doing this has no fear and is coming hard. Somehow tracking us and you guys don't seem to care about anything but arguing and refusing to believe that we're all in *serious* danger here."

They watched him as he spoke, his face filled with a desperate rage.

"We need to do something, and we need to do it fast! You all saw him mow down those people like they were nothing! Imagine what happens when he gets to us, and he will if we don't do something quickly. So, check your macho ego and let's figure this shit out! This is only getting worse, and I'm sorry about your mom Carla, I really am but how many more people are going to die while you all refuse to accept the fact that you did this!"

"We know what we did!" Carla roared behind tears, again Zain simply talking over her as he stared them down.

"Then accept the fact that its not going to end until each of you are dead or you come clean. That's what this is about. It's about him wanting you all to pay. So, for the love of God please can you all get over it? It's done, the past cannot be changed anymore it's too late for that. Because if you don't start acting like the group of friends that started this, you'll never end this on your terms, and we all know it's going to end badly."

Cold reality hung as Zain huffed back down on the bench leaning on his knees, "We're a rag tag bunch of nobodies and whoever is doing this is out there, watching us and waiting to make his move."

The cold wind howled through the park's trees, the area eerie and desolate.

"Who are you even dude?" Matt asked getting to his feet.

"We know the three of us weren't driving that pickup." Carla spoke finally, moving to sit on the bench too, "Leaving Maggie, Mark and Zach."

"Also, there's still Nathan, and Wessel." Added Eric rubbing his neck to ease the pain that lingered.

"As suspects?" Matt gasped in a chuckle, "It's not my sister."

"Targets, or victims." Eric folded his arms, "We won't know until we get hold of them. For all we know they're looking for us."

"Maggie's a lot of things but she's no killer." Matt was certain, "She's landing in a few hours, she'll tell you herself. Besides she has a solid alibi – she's on campus so we can take her off the list entirely."

"We'll take her off the list when we're certain it wasn't her." Carla said sternly.

Matt rolled his eyes shaking his head, "And as for Mark, he's off in the water somewhere, he won't have time to do all of this, he posts content religiously."

"Maybe it's old videos posted to be an alibi?" Eric suggested as he offered Matt a cigarette as Zain huffed back up to his feet in frustration.

"Didn't it occur to anyone that this Mark guys sister is dead? Surely, he'd be coming to the funeral or something. If he's so Vid-Tube famous, then we should be able to reach him."

"I've left messages via the app." Carla said as the wind iced her face.

"I have too." Matt nodded.

"If he knows what's going on, he'd probably be heading to Secunda the first chance he gets." Said Carla.

"Maybe he will resurface now with Odette's death. Can anyone remember the name of that aunt and uncle back in Secunda?" Matt asked.

"Cookie something, I don't remember I've already tried searching online and in the phone book." Carla sighed shaking her head.

"Then that leaves Zach." Suggested Zain, "He is the only other person know knew right? Why is nobody able to find this guy?"

"A millionaire serial killer?" Matt again chuckled bellowing smoke into the cold wind, "Look we need to be real here, if the theory is that it's one of us, the only logical suspect would be Bobby."

Eric and Carla turned to him in confused surprise, "Bobby?"

Matt nod inhaling.

"I thought he died years ago?" Zain asked also perplexed.

"Again, who is this guy?" Matt pointed dismissingly.

"What are you saying Matt?" Eric insisted, "Bobby's dead."

Matt shrugged his shoulders, "Maybe he faked his death, and spent the last few years planning all of this to get back at us."

"Sounds far-fetched to me." Carla mocked shaking her head, "There were other people out there that day who make a lot more sense."

"True, but let's face it Nathan is the least likely suspect here, I'm sure we all agree." Matt said looking at them when Zain frowned confused. "Why?"

"But I agree with you, we don't rule anyone out until we're certain." Matt said, dismissing Zain with a glare out the corner of his eye, "And Wessel, if he was ever going to say anything why wait ten years? For effect? I don't think so. I think he's already dead, the drugs probably killed him years ago."

"So, your logical choice is Bobby? Our friend who died when he turned nineteen?"

Carla scolded, "Anyone could have told someone, including Nathan or even Wessel or Zachary."

"Does it sound as far-fetched as Zach Manson spending his time killing people instead of touring the world and boning gorgeous women across the planet?" Matt posed seriously, "As far-fetched as the fact that someone is out there trying to kill us all? You were just implying that my sister had the ability to mow down ten people a minute ago. And I hear you Carla, I really do – there were others there that day, but they didn't know what happened in that shed. So as far as I'm concerned, Zach isn't far-fetched. You just can't come to terms that your boyfriend may be a serial killer. Or that your best bud tried to kill you and your boyfriend."

"He was never my boyfriend Matt."

"But you loved him, we all knew it." Matt said shaking his head, "Because anyone else who has a grudge against us is either dead or untraceable."

Eric sighed in defeat, "I don't know who else would know enough to come after us, if they knew anything they would have said it already."

"If anyone outside our group knew, why sit on it for ten years?" Carla added, "That doesn't really make sense. But we should check out all the options."

"Or go to the police." Eric said, "Come clean and…"

"And then? Our lives will be ruined." Matt insisted angrily, "We're not doing that."

"We can't fight this ourselves either, we don't know what we're up against here."

"But we know why." Carla defended, "We need to figure it out, because Matt's right. If this comes out…"

There was silence as their thoughts began to piece together sense in his wild theory.

"All I'm saying is, we know it's not me. And it's neither of you losers, it's not this guy." Matt pointed at Zain again, "It's not Leigh-Anne, Maggie, Odette, or Jacques. And Mark wouldn't take out his own sister."

"We don't know Mark anymore, who knows what he's capable of." Said Eric with a heaviness, "We can't rule him out, remember?"

"For all we know Mark and Zach are already dead." Added Zain looking up at Carla, "Look at what happened to your mother, nobody knows anything, and they could have faced the same fate."

The sky drew darker as thunder moaned in the distance.

"But you're right, we're going to need to figure this out before anyone else dies." Matt murmured beneath the façade that was fading with the light of the day.
"So, what do we do?" Zain asked standing up.
A moment lingered, each of them puzzled and confused with fear preying on their skin with the cold wind sweeping easily through the park.
"If none of us saw Bobby go into the ground, then making sure is worth a shot." Suggested Eric as he walked towards the car, "And with any luck you're right, Mark will surface for Odette's funeral so we may get two birds with one stone here. And maybe we can trace what happened to Nathan and Wessel too, someone there would know."
"Secunda?" Carla said unhappily.
"We'll pick up Maggie from the airport and then road trip baby!" Matt teased, ushering to the driver's door, "Come on fire, lead the way."
"Shut up Matty." She rolled her eyes opening the door.

Realizing his second first impression was lacklustre, Matt nod and round the car where Eric stood with his leg up into the car and his arm slung over the open door.
"So, it's like that?"
"It's like that." Said Eric nodding for him to get in the back.

Inside, Carla and Zain both sat annoyed watching their stare off, and then Matt raised his hands laughing.

"Sure thing, you're the boss." He said opening the backdoor when his phone rang. He dug into his back pocket, his screen was cracked from the shove to the ground, and he leaned in, grimacing a death stare to Zain before answering.

"Hello?" he answered when his face dropped.

"What?" Matt stuttered, his body slumping against the car with his legs weakening in shock as he began to cry, "No, no…"

****

A storm was forming over Secunda, the sky dark, ablaze with lightning as thunder raged far along the horizon in booming echoes. The UCC's black Nissan Patrol was parked in the driveway next to Mark's rental, and inside Cookie prepared coffee while Detectives Dekka and Malik sat with Mark and Shane in the lounge.

The house was warm, and the aroma of coffee lingered.

Mark sat forward resting his elbows to his knees, having just explained to them that the wounds to his face resulted from a fall.

Their eyes were unconvinced.

"So… you haven't seen or spoken to your sister in years?" Dekka asked sensitively, to which he shook his head without saying anything.

"According to you Mr. Tobey…" Malik said scouring his notes, "The victim received a threatening letter with…"

"Odette." Shane corrected bluntly, "Her name was Odette. Not a victim on a list, a person. Who deserves justice."

Dekka looked to Malik scornfully and he apologised. "You said Odette received a letter stabbed into the door of the house before meeting with you at work to discuss what was inside." Dekka took over, "In your statement you said it was a picture of her brother, Mark, and Mr. Jacques Petersen from the Klerksdorp murders."

"Did you find it?" Shane asked looking at them, "The axe, the pictures, the note?"

Swallowing a sigh of tired defeat, Dekka shook her head, "Nothing was found no, but Odette did meet you at the entrance at your work just like you said, that is confirmed. Also confirmed is the gash in the door at your home. So, I'll be frank with you both, in a manner of speaking Mr. Tobey you are the only witness, in all these scenarios, with anything relevant to help us do our jobs and find the person or people responsible."

The stove top kettle whistled from the kitchen and Cookie turned off the gas at the small bottle on the counter by the stove.

"We believe that if there is a link or connection between your sister, and the murders in Klerksdorp, as well as the attack on Miss Roos in Bloemfontein, then there is a link to everything else. And in the middle of this web sits the spider everyone wants squashed." Malik nod in agreement.

A silence hung briefly before Cookie entered with a tray of coffees for each of them. As Mark sat there, he felt the oxygen draining from his lungs, his world compressed. After trying to outrun, bury and forget everything from the past 10 years – the walls were closing in on him now and he wasn't sure if he was as ready as he felt, laying in the dirt letting Shane beat him up.

"I'll be in the kitchen if you need anything." Aunt Cookie smiled, heading out, allowing chance for the two Detectives to sip at their coffee.
Malik's cellular rang inside his jacket pocket and he stood up to excuse himself.
"You can take it." Dekka said with a sigh, relieved that she could at least enjoy another sip of the piping hot, strong coffee her body so urgently craved.
"Odette knew Jacques and Leigh Anne." Mark said nervously, his hand trembling.
Dekka lowered her mug and Shane sat forward, almost nervous himself.
"We…"
Suddenly Malik re-entered the room excited, "We've got a hit on the BOLO for the black pickup."
"Can't this wait?" Dekka stood up angrily.
"CCTV footage from a hit and run in the basement of the Midrand Mall, vehicle matches and forensics believe they'll be able to trace the treads on the scene. And there's more."
Dekka sighed shaking her head, then turned to Mark, "Will you give us a minute or two?"

Outside, Dekka shut the door as Malik led her to the side of the small porch.

"He was about to tell me something Clayton, that was very unprofessional!"

"CCTV has Eric Jansen on the scene." He grinned and her eye flared in surprised disappointment.

"We need this while the iron is hot." Malik insisted, "The brother and the boyfriend are dead ends."

"No, they're not. His sister knew Jacques Petersen and Leigh Anne Roos." Dekka raised her eyebrows, "That's the link."

Mark leaned against the door while Shane listened by the window as Dekka confirmed that the link was a relationship between victims and agreed to part ways and handle each lead separately.

Shane tugged Mark towards the couch, "You realize what you're doing right?"

The front door opened, and the cold wind funnelled in.

"I'm sorry about that. My partner needs to leave urgently." Dekka offered a smile as she closed the door, "I'll have a patrol vehicle pick me up."

Mark nod nervously and watched as she sat down again.

She could sense that both young men were riddled with a fearful apprehension at her presence, and she shook her head, reaching for her coffee again, trying to ease her persona so to allow them to regain a level of comfort to ease them into opening to her.

"You were saying Mr. Gallagher?"

Mark looked up at her, with all fibres of his being wanting to speak but the words were inside choking away at him. He looked down again at his hands, heaving a deep and heavy sigh as quietness filled the spaces between them.

"Look Mark, whatever it is, you can tell me." She leaned forward. Shane looked at Mark who kept his face down, breathing slowly in the enduring silence. Dekka heaved forward, placing her mug on the table.

"My name is Anele Dekka, I'm thirty-seven and have seen the worst in people, both professionally and personally. I have trust issues, but everyone says it's part of the job. I've been divorced, very recently in fact. And most of the time when it's just me alone in my apartment I cry. I cry because I live the unjust every day of my life and I've made mistakes and sometimes just because I'm afraid."
They watched her speak, a radiant exposure of honesty.
"I know you think the police aren't doing enough, but the truth is…Whoever is doing this is very, very smart, and very dedicated. I see now that a lot of thought has gone into each of the attacks. And the scary thing is, we don't know where the next attack will be or who he's after. But I do know this…" she looked up at them, "You know something. And I want to help you, not prosecute you. Let me help you and put an end to these murders."
"Detective Dekka, the link you're looking for is that Odette knew two of the others. Jacques and the Leigh-Anne." Shane spoke cautiously when Mark's phone toned to three messages shortly after each other.
He reached into his pocket.

"But she also knew you." Dekka said turning to Shane, "And you Mr. Tobey."
"Don't look at me, I have nothing to do with this." He shook his hands up in angry defence.

"To do with what Shane?"

He shook his head, biting hard that the muscle of his jaw probed out and Dekka turned to Mark who was now staring at his phone with wide dilated eyes.

The notifications were for his Vid-Tube account where he'd been tagged into four videos'.

The first was 15 seconds of Carla and Matt talking in the mall, the hashtag below reading: *#oldfriends*. The second was a 10 second clip taken from inside a car racing behind them in the parking lot and before he could see the third, Dekka's voice drew his attention back to her.

"What is it Mark are you alright?" she asked, watching him curiously. He shook his head standing up anxiously, quickly clicking on the third video.

"Mark what is it?" Shane stood up to, "You look like you've seen a ghost?"

It was a 7 second clip of Detective Malik heading to the car while Dekka re-entered the house. Below the video the hashtag: *#welcomehomemark*

Dekka stood up frowning suspiciously, "Show me your phone Mark."

He rushed to the door, bolting outside and into the middle of the lawn, scanning the road and yards in the street.

"Mark!" Dekka said stepping out behind him with her hand on her side holster, "I need you to turn around Mark."

Aunt Cookie clutched Shanes arm by the door watching.

"Mark, I need you to turn around. Slowly." Dekka repeated, when Mark finally looked to her.

"There is someone out here." He said adamantly, "Someone filming us."

Dekka frowned as he stepped towards her scrolling to the first clip and held the phone up.

****

Sitting on the porch of their parent's home, the noise inside of both Maggie and Matt's heads raged loudly as the quiet world around them droned in a deafening stillness. The afternoon sunset was dwindling through the cloud scattered sky while the wind held the foreboding scent of rain.

Everyone had either come by the house or called, and as their closest relatives engaged inside, they simply sat together in silence, a drowning silence of torment. He needed to talk to his sister, but he couldn't find the words to bring forward everything he barely believed or understood – explaining a nightmare that had come to life and set up the death of his parents as a suicide.

Maggie simply sobbed into her hands, trying to understand how her life went from carefree campus shenanigans to the sordid reality that her parents were both dead. The words from the police who had left just an hour ago still ringing in her ears 'murder suicide'.
It was as though her world had not stopped spinning since her feet left the plane and she saw her brother's broken spirit glaring at her behind his eyes.
Sitting there now beside him, she realized just how alone they had sudden found themselves in the world, her younger brother was really all she had

left now – the brother she gave up long ago in her own pursuit to escape the past.

"What is this all about Matt?" her shattered voice finally spoke as she looked to him, "Is this what you were trying to tell me over the phone?"
He shook his head, wiping his eyes, "Not exactly."
"Why would dad do this?" she cried, "He loved mom so much."
"He didn't do this." Matt spoke adamantly, "This was made to look like he did."
"What are you saying Matt?" her head was reeling, "What is happening?"
He turned to her, taking her hands into his, "We need to get out of here."
"What?"
"We need to go. I'll fill you in on the way." He said standing up, pulling her up with him, "We need to go to Secunda."
"No!" she pulled away angrily, "What the hell are you talking about? Secunda? Matt our parents are dead!"
"Maggie for once I need you to listen to me." He grabbed her hands again, "Please I need to tell you something. Something that's been happening."
Her legs were still not able to keep her body up and she slumped back down to the steps, crying into her hands. "We both know dad didn't kill mom and then hang himself." He said through a broken voice as he fought back his tears, "But I do know that someone is out there trying to kill us for what happened in Secunda ten years ago."
She looked into his eyes, the noise in her head now roaring in further confused chaos, "What?"
He knelt by her, taking her hands in his, "Maggie, you and I don't see eye to eye, but we need to go,

please. I need you to get up and come with me, it's not safe here for us. We need to go, and I swear I'll tell you everything on the way."

Wiping her eyes and her nose, she looked back to the house where she could hear the talking from inside, all the relatives were living close enough to come through stood talking through tears.
The disbelief and shock were almost as cold as the air moving through the yard, into the morbid house. "Dad didn't do this." She said turning to face him as she continued to wipe the tears from her face, "I want to know everything."

****

With only dim streetlights to break the darkness of the cold streets of Secunda, a faint drizzle began to fall as the dark sky continued to rumble overhead.

Inside aunt Cookie's house, Mark and Shane sat in the lounge when Dekka re-entered from the kitchen, hanging up her phone then standing with her arms folded as she stared at them.
"The patrol vehicle is almost here."
Shane looked up at her nervously, ""Are we going to jail or something?"
Detective Dekka shook her head, moving to the window beside the front door, peering out.
"I have nothing to arrest you for Mr. Tobey, we just need to take a formal statement down at the station. You however Mr. Gallagher I have a good mind to book you on tampering with a police investigation."

Mark shook his head angrily and Aunt Cookie held his hand tightly.

"But I won't, not yet at least." She turned to face them, "If we'd known about the connection between the crimes, we would have been able to pre-determine any possible attacks, short list potential victims and save lives."

"Investigating is your job!" Mark stood up abrasively, "The fact you people didn't pick this up yourselves is a testament to the thorough police work, well done Detective!"

She stared at him puzzlingly, so young yet his large presence was commanding and almost threatening.

"Arresting me for doing your job sounds like a stretch, and I think with someone out there taunting us we have bigger problems, don't you?"

"Calm down Markie?" Cookie asked nervously reaching up at his hand from the couch, "Please sit with me."

He managed a smile while taking his seat beside her again, her hand clutching his tightly as she smiled wearily, pushing up against him for comfort.

"Look, I've literally just got here." he said talking calmer now, "I've snoozed most notifications, you should give me my phone back so I can check in case there is something else."

She had forgotten that his phone was in her coat pocket, and she dug in, "So to be sure I'm getting all the details here, and doing my job – is there any connection to Zain Naicker or Eric Jansen?"

"Eric's not your guy." Mark said candidly, "You're barking up the wrong tree."

"So, you know him too?" her voice carried dark resenting frustration.

Shane watched angrily as Mark nod.

"How do you know he's not the one doing this?" Shane stood up, "He's the only person the police have connected to all of this, and you didn't think that was relevant to tell me?"

"What about Zain Naicker?" she asked forcing intermission between them.

Mark turned to her shaking his head.

"Have you spoken to Eric at all in the past few days?" she said finally handing him his phone.

"No. I got back to shore then almost immediately came here. Today was the first time I've checked notifications since I got the call, the rest were all just dismissed."

She nodded watching as he unlocked his phone, then turned to do another quick look outside, anxious for the patrol car to arrive.

Shane resumed his spot on the cough, his arms folded, and face riddled with frustration.

"Will I be in any danger here by myself?" Cookie asked nervously from the couch.

"It would be best if you could find an alternative place for now. Otherwise, I can see about arranging a patrol car for the night."

"Do you have anywhere you can go?" Shane asked.

Cookie paused, "I could give Iris a call? Maybe it won't be too much inconvenience with Terrance working night shift, I'll call her and make my arrangements."

Dekka nod, "That would be best."

Cookie stood up and headed down the hall while Mark turned back to Detective Dekka in alarm, "You should see this!"

His eyes were alive with horror, he'd finally opened the email he'd received days ago. She met him standing up, taking the phone.

The first image was a woman, dead and pale with black lips and marks around her neck laying in what appeared to be a cubicle, the second was victim Jacques Peterson.

Mark turned away, holding his hand over his mouth as a cold slithered on his skin and Shane stood up worried, "What is it?"

As Dekka held the phone, her heart raced as the third image appeared on screen, Ilse De Kock - then the final victim Jacques father who face was all but shredded. It began to replay, but she quickly locked the phone, lowering her arm.

The patrol vehicle rolled to a stop in the driveway behind the rented VW and uniformed officer Suzelle Coetzer got out.

She had not even shut the door when the figure appeared behind her, the ferocious scythe swinging upwards and tearing into her plump stomach just below the rib cage.

She tried to scream but the only thing pouring from her mouth was dark blood as the figure raised the scythe upward, hooking her ribs and lifting her against the side of the car - her blood dripping onto her shoes that dangled inches off the ground.

****

The boom of the front door crashing in happened so fast, but Shane was the only one who saw the shadow across the curtain before the large dark figure crashed into the house.

Dekka had just swung around when the figure collided with her, immediately grabbing her, and swinging her through the air into the TV unit -

crashing down the entire structure as her body hit it, the television crashed on the back of her head.

The dark figure turned as it flipped open the black scythe - and instinctively, Mark leapt for the attacker, slamming with all his brute force against it. With one hand pushing the scythe against the wall, his arm pressed against the figure's chest and throat - face to face with the black gauze.
But it was only for a moment that he had to imagine this figure being the one behind the murders, when Aunt Cookie rushed in, screaming in alarm.

Using this distraction, the figure kicked Mark backwards and threw a strong left hook, sending Mark crashing into the wall – the figure raising the blade into the air above him.

"No!" Shane leapt up from the Detective's side, the figure slashing just inches from his chest. "Help us!" Aunty Cookie cried out, rushing back down the passage.

The figure swung at Shane again and again, forcing him backwards when Mark managed to grab hold of its arm, swinging the figure to face him as he started pounding his hard right hook at its mask. He swung a left, then another right before the figure blocked and grabbed his hand – headbutting hard down into Mark's face sending him down to his knees almost instantly.

Shane rushed to the side of the couch, grabbing the pot plant from the small table and with all the vengeance thriving alongside his adrenaline, chucking it at the figure, smashing the pot against the side of its head. He then rushed to the small shelf just before the kitchen's entrance, grabbing vases, pictures, and ornaments one by one in a frantic rage.

"Get some asshole!" he screamed as he pitched them all at the figure one after the next. Mark stammered to his feet, swaying with blood gushing from just above his left eye as the figure made his way over to Shane amid the bashing and breaking against its arms.

The scythe tore through the air, it was closer than Shane could gauge, and its deadly curved blade sliced across his right arm - sending him aside screaming, holding it as blood already streamed out. The figure bounded forward, stabbing him in the stomach with two fast jabs, and Shane fell to the ground in writhing screams.

Screaming as he rushed forward, Mark connected with the figure again in a tackle, crashing into the kitchen floor against the small table.

The figure slid aside, the thick black leather jacket squeaking on the tiles as Mark stammered up against the table, the blood from above his eye now obscuring his vision as he saw the figure moving towards him, almost unstoppable in its madness.

He reached blindly for the knife block he'd seen standing on the counter near the small gas bottle, grabbing out the boning knife.

In the lounge, Cookie shoved the TV off from Detective Dekka as she helped the Detective upright amid the broken wood and glass, her face covered in slits.

A scream and scuffle ripped through the kitchen forcing Cookie up, bound to run when Dekka grabbed her, stopping her as she stumbled to her feet.

"Go get help! Run!"

The edge of the scythe blade stabbed into Mark's side as the figure rammed him into the counter, Marks strong hands fighting it from going any deeper as he screamed.

"You should have just told the truth. Goodbye Markie boy!" it snarled from behind the gauze mask.

"Screw you!" he scoffed in pain, stabbing the kitchen knife down into his attacker's shoulder, forcing the figure to withdraw backwards as Mark slopped to the side.

"Enough of this!" The figure raged angrily, grabbing the handle, and quickly ripping the kitchen knife from its shoulder angrily, "Time to die!"

As she rushed across the yard as fast as her deteriorating hips would allow, Cookie paused at the sight of the gutted officer laying by her vehicle and she screamed.

"Hey!"

The figure turned just as the shot from Dekka's 9mm flared, the bullet hitting its chest sending the figure against the counter.

She fired again, the bullet hitting the kitchen cupboard door above its head, and as though primitive instinct – the figure threw the scythe at her. She managed to cower as it flew past her, lodging into the wooden counter.

Before she could fire again, the figure was by her, the boning knife stabbing down into her forearm, her sidearm falling to the floor with her scream that was quickly choked by the figure who grabbed her by the throat.

"You have the right to remain silent Detective!" the figure mocked, squeezing at her throat, and pushing backwards, up against the cupboards.

Dekka tried desperately to fight the hand, gripping her throat and scream, but she was only gargling as the vein on her forehead pronounced itself.

"I said quiet!" it said, ramming her head backwards into the wooden door, then again and again before tossing her over the table and to the floor.

The figure cocked his head watching her choke for air in a daze on the floor, then turned to Mark who hunched on the ground side, desperately holding the wound on his shoulder as blood covered his hands.

"Are you enjoying this Mark?"

"What do you want?" he said trying to force himself to his feet through the pain stemming from the hole in his side, "Who the hell are you?"

"Who are _you_, Mark? Markie? Fisher 'underscore' Mark?" The hooded figure shook its head, tauntingly alluding to his profile name on Vid-Tube, "I know the real you, unlike your followers who only see the big strong man with a lot to say."

The figure reached down, plucking Mark to his feet in recoiling pain, and placing the bloodied scythe against his neck.

Staring at the black gauze mask, Mark's eyes strained to see anyone behind it, but the darkness beneath its hood seemed endless.

"You had the chance, and you chose silence. So now it's time for you to stay quiet Mark, something you're good at." The figure said putting the blade against Marks lips, "Sssshhh…"

Mark hit the table going down to the ground as the shots ring loudly above him.
At the doorway, relentless in his desire to end the maniac with each pull on the trigger of the Detective's gun, a blood-soaked Shane screamed, "Die!"

The figure slung backwards as some of the bullets hit into its body while others pierced the cupboard doors, the stove and the kettle waiting on the stove.

The firing stopped, Shane toppled to his knees, dropping the gun, and placing both his hands over his shredded stomach before collapsing on his side out into the lounge.
"Shane?" Mark said clambering to his knees towards him.
His eyes were wide, his breathing short quick bursts in and out, and blood riddled out as Mark tried to help push his hands down on the black tears.
"You need to put pressure, ok? Stay with me Shane!" Mark urged.
"You should tell the truth…" Shane gasped.
"Put pressure here, ok?" Mark insisted, moaning as he reached for the gun and got up, quickly moving over to the Detective who tried to lift herself up, mumbling in agony from the hellish pain in her arm. When he grabbed her under her arms, she jolted in fright at first, easing only as she saw past the blood over his face, asking in a daze, "Did you get him?"

"Nope! Missed me!" the vicious figure leapt up with the small axe in hand, the long thick leather coat riddled with holes – the hood off its head exposing a black sparring headgear to which the black gauze was clipped.

It took only a second to absorb the reality that the monstrous demon slaying its way through their lives was nothing but a human with sufficient protection to keep itself safe, and Mark flung the gun up. One shot hit the upper arm, the other hit the kettle on the stove.
Another second flashed and with all his might, through the pain of the hold in his shoulder, Mark forced his other arm up, gripping the gun with both hands and fired again.

One shot was left in the chamber, and it fired - piercing the small gas bottle on the counter beside the stove with a loud 'pop' that sent an eruption of flames outward with a roar that scorched up along the walls towards ceiling, spiralling flames through the air as it fell back down onto the stove top where the entire canister burst.

The blast sent the figure down and a blanket of flames across the kitchen, searing over Mark who fell to the ground.

****

The night sky was torn with vicious strikes of lighting that webbed out across the dark clouds as thick black smoke rose up.

The sirens of the fire department were loud, honking as they entered the street where police were trying to push residents back from the scene.
On the side, Cookie stood held up by her neighbours, tearing up while her house of 34 years went up in flames but relieved that the nights mayhem was over.

"Thank you." Dekka limped to the back of the ambulance where Mark stood watching as the paramedics rushed Shane inside.
He looked at her, wobbling through the pain, then back to the flames flaring out into the wind as fire teams rushed towards it.
"We didn't get to find out who it was." He said as the flames flickered in his eyes.
"We will." She said putting her hand on his shoulder, "We will."
"Sir, sir we need to get you looked at." A paramedic hurriedly wrapped the silver mylar blanket over him, ushering him aside as another rushed to tend to the Detective.
"Steady sir." The paramedic said helping Mark up onto the stretcher behind the ambulance, "We'll take care of you now sir, you can lay back."
Aunt Cookie hurried to his side, taking his hand in hers as they rolled him to the ambulance. A loud groan stemmed from the flaming house, and he looked back, watching as the ceiling beams caved in bringing the roof down with a loud crash sending the flames and sparks high up into the darkness.
Mark closed his eyes, slowly lowering down onto the stretcher.

CHAPTER SIX

'Shocking footage from Secunda this morning as fire and rescue teams begin the search for the so called, Province Slayer, who is presumed dead inside the rubble at the home of Secunda's Cookie Venter, where just 10 hours ago an epic show down occurred between SA's relatively new task force the UCU – Unique Crimes Unit, and the Province Slayer. In what reads like a true battle between good and evil, Detective Anele Dekka, lead UCU agent on the case, survived a harrowing showdown when the home of Mrs. Venter was attacked late last night, ending in a bloody blaze, with the suspect still inside the house at the time of the explosion that rocked the once peaceful streets of Secunda. As police comb the premises this morning, many South African's anxiously await confirmation that the spree of terror is finally over. While the smoke settles, we confirm that the latest attack has tragically ended the lives of 22-year-old Marcus Gallagher, the brother of Odette Gallagher, the teenage victim of the Secunda Slayings, and 21-year-old Shane Tobey the deceased girl's fiancé. More on this story after the weather.'

Detective Malik switched the TV to mute and moved towards the window of his hospital room where he sat on the bed tightly bandaged around his waist with a large white patch above his eye.
"So now I'm dead?" He grinned over to Aunt Cookie who was on a seat beside his bed, "That's oddly comforting."

Dekka, seated in a wheelchair with her arm in a cast, sighed shaking her head, "We're just playing it safe, to protect you and Shane."

"This just buys you some breathing room. Eventually you have to tell us everything." explained Malik rested at the foot of the bed, "This just provides you with a certain level of safety, we'll clear it up when the time is right. For now, we need confirmation that the Slayer was killed in the fire."

"You don't believe that do you?" Mark looked to Dekka nervously.

She looked down at her arm, replaying the attack and the fear that twisted her gut.

"I think whoever that was last night is serious about what he's doing, methodical in his preparation. You saw the headgear, and you know how many bullets hit him. We must brace for the worst-case scenario."

"So what? I stay dead while he keeps going after my friends?"

"Speaking of which." Malik stood up, going to the door, and peeking out, "You can come in now."

Mark frowned as Carla, Eric, Matt, and Magaret entered in a row, wearily but excitedly smiling. His eyes lit up in surprised confusion, "What…"

Carla leaned in, hugging him tightly, "It's so good to see you, Mark. I'm so sorry about Odette. And I'm glad you're ok."

Her hug was warm and tight, a reminder of their youth when she'd always cared deeply about the neglect he and Odette faced under their father, offering them sandwiches whenever she could – sometimes enough for them to keep for when they were home.

He had the biggest crush on her, always caught up in her fiery red hair and the ocean of her blue eyes, something he withdrew after a short but meaningful romance with Maggie who was two years older.

"Hey Mark, wow you got so much bigger." Maggie managed her first smile, looking at his ripped upper body that bulged behind the large white bandages around his torso. She hugged him tightly and fought back the tears at the still very raw reality that she found herself in the past day.

He laughed awkwardly while she stepped back, taking his hand into hers, "I'm so sorry about Odie. I'm sorry about what happened to you." She said, looking at his big hard hands, remembering the day she asked him to let her practise kissing and how they grabbed her behind as he'd seen in the movies.

"I can't believe you're all here. What are you guys doing here?" He said looking up at Matt who stepped forward.
"Well hello to you too dipshit." Matt grinned as he shook Mark's hand, his bravado glistening, forced outward at the sight of how strong he'd gotten since they were younger, seeing his strong arms and hardened hands while remembering a time that Mark stood up to him for a prank on Eric and he'd wrestled him to the ground, tearing up his knee and bloodying his nose.
"Hey bro." Eric smiled pausing awkwardly and then finally moving in to hug his old friend, who always protected him like a big brother.
"I'm glad to see you." Said Mark patting his back, "I'm happy you're ok I heard on the news about what happened in Pretoria."

"Yeah." Eric stepped back glancing over to the two detectives cautiously, "And I'm sorry about what happened to Odette."

"I appreciate that. I still can't believe you guy are all here right now." He laughed, wincing, and holding his side.

"I can't believe how big you all got!" Cookie said moving to the bottom of the bed, as they all hugged her excitedly, greeting her and complimenting her weight loss.

Malik leaned over his partners shoulder, "Should we give them a minute?"

"He saved my life. I think it's the least we can do." She nodded.

"For the moment at least." Malik agreed as he wheeled her out the door.

"God bless you all, you are all so big my stepchildren." Cookie teased laughing through her tears as she wiped her face before re-hugging Carla and Matt tightly.

"What are you all doing here, I thought you were wanted by the police?" Mark asked still perplexed and surprised.

Eric shrugged his shoulders boyishly, "Yeah always in trouble you know me, bad boy for life, right?"

"Yeah right!" Matt scoffed tearing open a small pack of peanuts and raisins, "You know why we're here Markie boy. Until the fire we all thought you were the one doing all of this, or at least you were one of our suspects."

"What?"

"And if not you, then we'd make sure Bobby's in the ground where he's supposed to be." Matt said bluntly when Maggie nudged him.

"He's been through a lot too Matt." She said shaking her head before turning to face Mark again, "We were coming to see if you were here, and we had some other suspicions too."

"Well since our parents are dead, I'd say we don't have time to ease him in here." Matt was crude, his eyes dark and tired, "We need to get to the point because maybe this guy is still out there? Maybe Mark failed to burn his ass alive?"

Maggie nudged at him again and Carla immediately turned to Aunt Cookie, asking her to give them a minute in private before the detectives returned.

"Of course, I'll go downstairs and organize some coffee from that shop." Cookie smiled heading to the door, "And I'll buy you time as best I can."

"What?" Mark asked confused, "Your parents?"

"Yeah, the cops say it's a murder suicide, but we know it wasn't." Maggie explained softly, fighting back the ache in her heart that opened the water gates to her eyes.

"It was him. He did this to us the same way he tried with Carla's mom."

Mark shook his head, a thousand thoughts going through the pain and headache as he tried to look at them all and grasp their presence after 10 years.

"I'm so sorry..."

"Yeah, well you should be, we all should be." Matt scoffed, tossing peanuts to his mouth trying to simmer the rage inside, "We can cross Mark off the list now, but that leaves more work. I say we leave now and go dig up Bobby."

"What are you...Dig up Bobby?" Mark shook his head puzzled, turning to Carla, "And what do you mean the police are taking you away?"

"Hey, look we have a lot to catch you up on." Eric sat carefully on the edge of the bed as the others began to settle too, "But first tell us, did you see who it was?"

"Yeah, was it Zach?" Matt asked, again bluntly, "We kind of need to get to a conclusion here so we can stop this son of a bitch!"

"Zach?" Mark almost sat up before the pain shot through him and clutched his shoulder, "Why would Zach be the killer?"

"Matt will you please just shut the hell up?" Eric scoffed, "We're all sorry about what you and Maggie are going through here, but can you give the guy a minute?"

"You need to be quiet, seriously." Magaret huffed at her brother, "Please?"

"Look what the hell is going on?" demanded Mark, "Someone talk, one thing at a time. And who is this?"

"I'm Zain. I know everything, I'm with Eric." He said with an awkward wave, softly from the side. Mark remembered his face from the news and sighed looking down and shaking his head, anger was somewhere in the turmoil of his battered thoughts beneath the pain from his shoulder.

"I never saw his face." Mark said softly, "I don't know who it is."

"Well let's play pretend the killer isn't dead in that fire." Matt said again, "We need to be ready for another attack. All of us in one place, we're like sitting ducks."

"We have to speak the truth, if he's not dead we have no choice." Said Mark softly.

Matt shook his head angrily, "No. We've covered this, we're not here to say anything to the cops."

"Then why are you here?"

There was a pause as they all looked at one another.

"We can't find Zach, he's the only one left of the group that nobody can find." Eric explained, "We figured he might be the one behind all of this."

Mark shook his head with resolute certainty, "It's not Zachary."

"Look I know I need to shut up and be quiet, but…" Matt said chewing, "We all know you and Zach were tight, even after everything went down, so we can't shoot down the idea out of some kind of loyalty or something."

"It's not loyalty Matty." Mark said adamantly, "This guy is strong. He's fast and big and nothing keeps him down, nothing."

"Well, he kicked your ass, and you grew up to be quiet the hulk." Matt said sarcastically, tossing his mouth open as a peanut flew up.

"We also had this crazy idea…" Eric continued through his annoyance, "…to look into Nathan Bekker and Wessel, do you remember him?"

"I don't think so…" Mark said trying to think through the millions of thoughts raging in his head.

"We also want to look into Bobby." Matt added again, "As far as I know he was buried here so…"

"Bobby?" he looked up frowning, "As in Bobby Minnaar?"

"We just trying to figure this all out, it's got to be someone who…"

"Someone who knows what happened ten years ago." Mark interrupted solemnly looking over to Zain nervously, "I figured the same thing."

A short silence hung among them, then Mark asked, "Why are the cops taking you guys away? Are you all wanted or something because I can speak to Detective Dekka and…"

"She's already piecing something together." Carla interrupted anxiously, "She called Eric just as we arrived in town. I don't think they suspect him anymore but, she knows something and asked us to come to the police station for questioning."

"Informally, at least for now." Eric added nervously.

"And what is it that you all are planning on saying exactly?" Mark asked nervously, to which the room again hung in an awkward stillness.

"We're not saying anything, at least not *that!*" Carla stood up from the armchair.

"Are we sure we want to do that, even at the expense of people's lives?" Matt asked bluntly, "Because I've been thinking about this and after my parents…"

"No Matt, if we want to stop this, we need to honour the pact and finish this ourselves." Said Eric quietly in the corner, his own demons clawing to surface.

Matt snarled shaking his head, "Big mouth for someone who randomly just tells strangers! I say we call those detectives in here and we just spill the whole story."

"I'm with Matt, we need to tell the police the truth!" Maggie insisted with tears in her eyes, "Enough people have died, needlessly. It's time to come clean."

"Then I'll take it on myself." Said Eric sternly, looking over to Zain with his eyes screaming in certain apology, "I'll say it was all me and now there is someone after my friends."

"Call the sheriff - it's bad…" Carla mocked rolling her eyes, "That's ridiculous Eric, we're not even sure of anything yet. For all we know they find the body in the house, and all of this can be over."

"Why are we all pretending any of this is, ok? People are dying so we can shut our mouths to keep Carla's mom alive?" Matt roared angrily, as the divided room erupted in argument.

"Stop it!" Mark yelled, "Enough, ok, just shut up all of you!"

They all turned their attention back to the bed where Mark sat, and a stillness fell over the room again.

"It's not Eric's place to take this on him. We're all in this together. Always have been."

"Well, I disagree, very strongly." Matt snarled, "First we say nothing because of your mother, now we say nothing, and my family is dead."

"Then we'll vote on it. Like we did as kids." Mark suggested finally breaking the density that hung in the room, "Either *everyone* goes down together or nobody at all, but no one person is taking the fall here."

"A vote?" Matt scoffed at the idea, "You want to put it to a vote? Who made you the captain huh Markie boy? What did Zach pass the baton to you or something? We're not little kids anymore man! What would your sister think of that now?"

"Keep her out of this!" warned Mark, his muscles now clenched and his eyes wild.

"My sister lived in a darkness that she couldn't escape, right up to the end Matt." Mark said softly, "And I know that in our own way, we all did. But speaking now doesn't change Odette not being here, or Jacques and his father, or anyone else who's died because of what we all did. Leigh Anne is fighting for her life and we're here with a choice they weren't given. A choice stolen from them. And I'm sorry about your parents, I really am I feel your pain better than anyone in this room because my sister was taken."

He sighed turning to the window as he spoke, "But it's been ten years that we've all tried to move forward, running from it, trying to get as far away from it. I hope they find him in that house, but a part of me wants him to myself because I want justice for my sister. For everyone."

"We're not above the law Mark." Maggie said softly. Mark shook his head, "No we're not. But I saw with my own eyes, nothing kept him down, not knives, not bullets. He wants us to pay and there's no stopping him. But I'm standing right here, available. I want this to end, I want the truth set free. But first I want him to pay."

"What are you saying Mark?" Matt frowned watching Mark painfully slink back on the bed.

"I'm saying I'd rather not be in a jail cell and that I'd rather face the past or die trying because it's what we do now that will define how we spend the rest of our lives. And I don't mean being free to go back to our jobs... I mean living the rest of our lives free of it, from all of it. I'd rather face whoever is doing this and my reckoning. Because that is what this is about. Nobody else needs to die."

The room filled again with silence as he paused.

The door opened and Detective Malik stepped inside wheeling in Detective Dekka, now with three other uniformed officers at their side and Mark's nurse.

"We're going to need you all to come to the station, now." Malik explained, glancing up at the TV. They all turned their attention to the screen, where behind the reporter on display was a sketch that sent a chill riddling across their skin. Carla hurriedly flung for the remote to unmute the station.

'...as we bring you more breaking news this morning in the Province Slaying massacre, with the fire that supposedly ended it all but failed to yield positive results for the Unique Crimes Unit and the South African Police Services, who just moments ago officially confirmed that despite all their efforts, search teams at the property came up empty handed.
Police spokesperson Colonel Preston in a short statement outside the Secunda police station, confirmed that there was no recovery and that the suspect is still at large. However, for the first time in the case, the South African Police Service has provided a detailed description of the attacker, confirming that the assailant acted alone.
Furthermore, the UCU has provided all news outlets with a sketch of the supposed Province Slayer, as it is now appearing behind me. A glimpse into the horror faced by the 26 victims involved in these tragic attacks.
With police asking anyone who may have information, has seen this individual, or anyone who might see this individual lurking about to call the hotline appearing on the screen below.
With a face to the terror, and continued failure to close in on possible suspects, South Africans in every province feel the fear of this terrifying figure on the streets. We investigate this further with former...'

****

The sky above Secunda remained blanketed with the heavy grey clouds as a soft drizzle soaked the small city below. There was a foreboding uneasiness that lingered in the cold wet air.

At the police station, each of them had been taken to separate rooms or offices where they could be questioned by detectives Dekka and Malik with Colonel Preston present.
Waiting for their turn was brutally morbid, the silence of the police station's rear offices had it hard to fight away their desperate need to regain the hours of sleep lost since the attacks entered their lives.

The questioning was relatively standard for both Maggie and Matt, the police knew very little about them since they arrived in Secunda under the same radar as Eric, Zain, and Carla. Their questioning was short, courteous in regard to their parents recent passing, with neither indicating that the murder-suicide was anything more or associated to the Province Slayings, they both had their questioning over in under an hour.

They had handed over their phones which allowed the Detectives to review the messages received and shared, then were left to sit waiting in separate offices while Eric and Zain's questioning dragged on as they were asked repeatedly to provide a detailed recollection of their respective involvement with the murders, their attack, the killer and the deaths surrounding them.

While Zain recounted the events leading up to the attack, he was careful in how he spoke or what he said. He was placed in a small office with only a desk and three chairs, metal filing cabinets lining the one wall where Preston sat.

It was draining him to stay ahead of his thoughts as he recounted the scuffle inside the flat and ensuing chase. Inside a battle raged, something he worked hard to stifle, but it was increasingly exhausting him. "I think Eric was just scared for the little guy, his nephew." He said, "When Keith shut us out it was like…I don't know, I've never felt so alone in my whole life."

"See that is where wires got crossed accidentally implicating you both in the attack." Dekka leaned across the desk as she glanced at her superior, "Only the little boy saw what you saw, not his father or mother. So, when someone leaked to the media, a lot of details were missing, and conclusions were jumped to."

"Conclusions that had us wanted by the country." Zain scoffed shaking his head in disgust, "I was there when you called Eric, you weren't on our side."

"I was doing my job."

"Knowing that his nephew saw the killer you still made us feel like we had nowhere else to go. You kept it from us the whole call, I heard you."

Seeing him growing increasingly upset, Malik quickly diverted with a question, "How about you tell us why you met with Miss Wilson and Mr. Jonah, why did Eric want to see them?"

Zain rolled his eyes at Dekka before he leaned back into the chair and folded his arms, "How about something to eat?"

****

For Eric - seated in an interrogation room - it was describing the murders of Clive and Donna Fourie – the couple attacked for their SUV on the night of the chase, that got tears to breach his focus. Reliving it was a difficult undertaking, seeing them so brutally and easily slain by the dark hooded maniac.

His body still hurt and the slash on his chest felt bruised with each breath, and having waited so long for his turn, he'd succumbed to about one hours drifting sleep before they walked in.

Sitting there drained, bruised, and exhausted he spoke softly recalling the incident at the Midrand Mall parking garage.

"It's one of the worse things I've ever had to see. I just kept thinking we had to run, and keep running you know? He cut them down like it was nothing, like opening your fridge to take what you want kind of simple. It was the same seeing those two people go under the wheels of that pickup."

"Another scene you chose to flee." Preston spoke harshly with his arms folded, "You tend to bring all the right emotions for us to believe you know only what you're telling us Mr. Jansen, but we have been doing this for a long time."

Eric looked at him heaving a deep breath, "You wanted me to stay and get arrested?"

"For witnessing a crime? I don't think so." Preston spoke sternly.

"Your police force was after me, if I had stayed, I'd be in jail now."

"So, you and Mr. Naicker chose to keep running, straight into the arms of Carla Wilson and Matthew Jonah." Dekka raised her eyebrow, "Something you failed to mention to detective Dladla was your connection to the victims."

"I wasn't sure if it was…"

"What? Connected? Relevant?" Preston pressed in frustration, "Perhaps you should be in jail Mr. Jansen. You fled the scene of both crimes, leaving us to assume your role in all of this. I'll have you know Mr. Jansen; your tears don't fool anyone. We want the truth, a four-year-old child was put at risk because of you! And you still fled the scene!"

"We didn't know about the kid!" Eric pressed back, "I don't know what you want from me? I've done nothing wrong! I saved my nephews life what about that? Where's his story? Because this is my story and I cannot give you anything but the truth, and while we're at it -where's a public apology to me and Zain for branding us the killers? You forget Detectives, I came to you guys, I spoke to Detective Dladla out of my own, before the attack, before everything. And like I said to you over the phone Detective I'll say again, we're victims here so stop treating us like we're anything else."

"You willingly neglected to inform anyone that you personally knew the victims and have yet to prove that you indeed have received vital information on email regarding their murders. For all we know you may be conspiring with the killer carrying out these attacks."

"That's not true." Eric urged, "We have nothing to do with this."

"Then who is?"

"I don't know!"

"I think you do, and you're afraid to tell us." Malik added from the side, "But we cannot figure out why. Why is someone targeting you and your friends Mr. Jansen? The sooner you tell us the sooner we can catch the person or people responsible for this."

"I do not know!" Eric felt the cracks showing on his face.

Dekka shook her head, "Eric, you haven't told us why the Slayer is after you and your friends."

"I don't know, they don't know! Why are you sitting here with me when you should be out there finding him?"

Why the email Eric?" Dekka asked ignoring him, "An email so extreme it shut down your place of work and cost them a lot of data."

"To ruin me? To destroy my career, I have no idea." Eric sighed, "You went up against him detective, why is he still alive?"

A grin broke on her face as she was about to reply when he continued, "How did he escape the fire? Exactly, you don't know."

"Why target you, and your friends and their families?" Malik asked again, "What's the connection here?"

"I don't know."

"But you do know Mr. Jansen." Dekka spoke harshly now, "You were all friends, every one of you! Now there is someone after you, and them! Yet you chose to play dumb. Why would you want to risk that?"

"Unless you're the one doing it." Preston added, "Your statement to officer Dladla in Pretoria referenced that one of the images you received in the email were that of Jacques Petersen's mother?

Why would the killer include that when the cause of death was ruled a suicide?"
Eric heaved a sigh, his mind and body weak and tired.
"Tell us the truth!" Preston slammed his hand to the table.

A silence hung and Eric looked up again, "At first it was Jacques, it was scary because I knew him. Then I got the email, and then I was attacked. Eventually things start making you wonder, and I got scared so I went to the police, and then I was branded a killer."
"No this is not so random as you make it sound Mr. Jansen" Dekka sat back smirking, "You can't keep up this charade forever."
Malik sighed exhaustedly, "Mr. Jansen let's just cut the crap. Just tell us why you and your friends are being targeted, what are you afraid to tell us?"
"I don't know, ok?" he defended angrily, "I don't know, I do not know!"
"But you do know Mr. Jansen!" Preston snarled authoritatively, "And the less you cooperate with us, the more likely that someone else is going to die."
Eric dropped his head down into his hands in defeat, his heartbeat slamming against his chest, "I don't want to do this anymore."
"Stop running from the truth and tell us what we need to know to catch this son of a bitch." Urged Malik leaning on the table.

"Then get me a lawyer." Eric said looking up, "Because I'm done repeating myself over and over and all you want is someone to hang for the media."

Dekka and Malik nervously looked to Preston whose face was riddled with frustration as he stood with his hands on his hips shaking his head.

"We're the law son, we have 48hrs to detain you and you're not under arrest. Are you sure you want to go this route?"

"I'm done, I'm not saying anything else or repeating anything until you get a lawyer." Eric insisted slumping into the chair and folding his arms.

Shutting the door behind her, the three of them stepped into the hallway and Dekka turned to them with a tired sigh, her eye bags showing.

"Well, he's asked, we have to oblige."

"We will, but he's not under arrest. We have 48 hours, let him stew in his thoughts while we speak to Carla Wilson." Preston walked, "I'll make the call to the state for his lawyer when we're done, we have time."

Dekka looked at her partner shaking her head as they followed behind him.

****

Outside, the soft drizzle had become a downpour, drenching the streets with an icy cold wind that made the station's narrow hallways chilly and ached at the bruises on her body as Dekka's limp grew more prominent.

Entering the office, a shared room with two sets of local Detective desks, they took their seats across from Carla after kept her waiting for 4 hours.

She detailed the events at the hospital, Detective Dekka's mind travelled back to everything shared with them throughout the day and the thorn in her mind remained. She felt her stomach burn from the pain killers for her arm while also regretting not ensuring lunch when Zain Naicker had asked.

Carla sighed shaking her head as she dabbed her cheek softly with a paper tissue when detective Malik shifted his weight on the edge of the desk where he sat.

"So, you're saying you got involved with Eric and Zain following an attack on your mother where another patient was killed?"

"That's exactly what happened."

Dekka frowned, scanning the red head's face carefully.

"Miss Wilson, the charges against your mother are barely something to be concerned with, at the most she'll serve a few years for involuntary manslaughter and with a good lawyer, she'll get off on a temporary medically induced insanity plea."

Preston leaned forward, "You cannot expect us to believe this happened in a hospital full of patients and doctors everywhere…"

"Well, it did. He attacked her! And killed that old lady." She leaned forward, "He told me in the phone call."

Preston nodded, his face riddled with suspicion, "Yes the phone call from the unknown number, just minutes after learning that your mother was going to have charges against her?"

Carla shook her head, looking up at Malik, "You took our phones, you have access to my call history. Why would I lie?"

"To save your mother." Said Malik matter-of-factly, "A desperate attempt to shift focus off of what she did while explaining your involvement with Mr. Jansen and Mr. Naicker."

"Which at the time could be considered tampering." Added Preston, "They were key witnesses, and you harboured them?"

"Willingly." Detective Dekka stated from the side, "Which seems irrational given that you are a young woman in a very successful position, earning well. Why would you willingly help them without being certain they were not the killers?"

"They needed someone to help them, so I did." She scoffed, "While the police branded them as suspects without evidence, chasing them down instead of protecting them they needed help."

Preston shook his head as he stood up to stretch his legs.

"Miss Wilson, you have to see this from our perspective." Malik said talking softer, "We're trying to help you, and more importantly we're trying to find whoever is doing this. You are connected to three of the victims, and I'm being honest, an attack in the middle of a hospital seems very unlikely given the description my partner gave us. How can someone like that go unnoticed?"

She shook her head in disbelief, "You know we have no reason to be here, we're here because you asked us to, because we want this to stop. We've done nothing wrong, and I'm done being treated like a criminal for stepping in to help my friend when the law was doing the opposite."

Preston laughed shaking his head, "So you are a victim here?"

"Yes!"

"Who fled the scene of a crime in Midrand?"

She sighed shaking her head in annoyance, "Then arrest me. I wasn't driving."

"Let's talk about Mark Gallagher."

"What about him?"

"His sister dies, he comes home. And you all decide to come through and see him?" Dekka frowned suspiciously, "Big old reunion while people are dying, and families need answers. Again, this seems too random an act. You came here with Eric Jansen and Zain Naicker because you already knew the connection. You already knew who and why this was happening, so you came to warn him."

"We came to warn him yes. To tell him our suspicions."

"And who is at the top of your list Miss Wilson?" Malik frowned, "Who did you come to warn Mr. Gallagher about?"

Carla shook her head in frustration as she leaned forward on her elbows, "We don't know, that's kind of the problem."

"But you came to warn him, about what exactly?" Dekka leaned to meet her eyes, "Tell me what you would have told him Miss Wilson."

Carla leaned back with a sigh, "I would have said that someone is killing our friends and he's in danger."

"No thoughts at all as to who or why?" Malik shook his head in disbelief, "Come on Miss Wilson, you know we can see right through you."

"I'll say it again, slower this time, we don't know who or why."

"And what did Mr. Gallagher say when you all

showed up there at the hospital telling him your suspicions?"

Carla shrugged her shoulders, "He said we need to tell the police if you didn't find a body, and you didn't and now we're here. Which means the actual killer you failed to stop is still out there."

"Then tell us which other friends we need to be warning." Said Preston clearing his throat as he strolled towards her side, "Who else is he coming after?"

"I don't know."

"But you knew for a certainty it was Matthew Jonah and his sister Magaret, isn't that why you convinced them to come out here just hours after finding out their parents are dead? Seems strange they'd follow you all here on an 'I don't know' wouldn't you agree Miss Wilson?"

A silence fell in the room as Carla looked to the side, her mind depleted and tired.

She looked back at them, "What do you want from us?"

"The truth." Said Dekka speaking kinder, "We just want the truth."

****

After the attending nurse tore into him for trying to leave his room, he'd managed to calm her and convince her to let him see Shane, a nurse wheeled Mark along the passages of the ICU floor to the nurse on duty, who smiled and slowly moved him towards the door to Shane's ward.

"He's recovering, but I can't guarantee he'll be very responsive." She reached over him to open the door.

Seeing him on the bed, all bandaged and wired to machines – a flood of guilt slammed Mark, and he felt almost winded.

"Mr. Tobey." She said softly moving to gently touch his arm, "There's someone here to see you."

Unable to turn his head much due to his body being strapped down to mitigate the risk of all the stiches inside and outside of him tearing, Shane's eyes moved to the side as Mark forced himself up out of the chair, leaning against the bed.

Shane's eyes were red, his face a pale white.

The damage to his internal organs, particularly liver, kidney and large intestines were serious while coupled with that - in the rush to get him out of the burning house, further damage was done through haemorrhagic clotting, and the nerves along his spine which had already been slightly severed by the attacker's blade had been affected, causing permanent damage to the functions of everything below his ribs.

With his eyes full of watery pain, Mark shook his head, "I'm so sorry."

He stared up at Mark, a dark hatred for surviving was alive inside him, specifically for surviving as a cripple. He had lost the love of his life, the will to live – but death evaded, and he was left with nothing now.

Nothing but hatred linked to cold despise – a blackness he lay accepting would never break or stop choking him.

"I'm so sorry Shane."
He cried reaching for Shane's forearm when he moved it away as much as he could. He could feel the hate and despise emanating from his dark eyes hitting his skin, it was more painful than the stab to his shoulder.

Mark stepped back nodding, wiping his face as he carefully lowered to the wheelchair again, the nurse quickly aiding him out of the room.
Shane shut his eyes as tears ran down his cheeks, his soul riddled with an anger so vile it bore in it a hate that even he could not comprehend.

****

Using her good arm, Dekka pushed herself up from the armchair carefully as the aching in her back muscles stung.
Hours had gone by, and they were still making very little progress. They'd circled from Carla back to Matt and Maggie, then again sat with Carla – buying time with Eric's request for a lawyer.

"I think we all need some coffee." She looked to her partner, "I'll take mine with milk please."
Malik, knowing the signal managed a smile, "Sure, good idea."
"None for me thanks." Preston said with a wave.
"Oh sir, you're helping me carry." Malik grinned, ushering him by the shoulder towards the door.
Carla's blue eyes scanned Detective Dekka's face as the two men head out shutting the door.

"What is this, girl power talk?" Carla frowned mockingly.

Dekka laughed shaking her head while she carefully moved to the side of the desk, "No definitely no girl power here."

Carla tilted her head with raised eyebrows, "My story won't change Detective."

"I don't expect it to." She carefully sat on the side of the desk holding her casted arm, "Co-incidentally, I believe you."

Carla shook her head, "Look Detective you are wasting your time drilling me and my friends when the killer is still out there."

Dekka nodded, "Maybe, but like my partner explained you are all the only thing linking us to the victims, like I said I do believe that what happened at the hospital really did happen. Whether he attacked your mother and killed the old lady is another thing, I have my doubts. But I'm not like my partners, Miss Wilson."

"Oh yeah? Why's that?"

"Because I faced this son of a bitch one on one. I realized that nothing he does is left to chance, he is prepared."

Carla studied her as she looked at the cast on her arm, recalling the moment the blade tore through and the detective closed her eyes, fluttering them back open while moving to the window behind Carla.

"What I don't believe is that you randomly sought out Eric."

"He was on the news."

"As a suspect. You had no way of knowing if it would be safe going to him or not." She watched the raindrops running down the window, "I think you suspected that you were in danger, all of you. And you began banding together against whoever is doing this."

A smile broke on Carla's face, "So that's why we are here – you think we know who is doing this."

"You know more than you're telling us." Dekka turned from the window, "You all do. What I don't understand is why? Why you won't tell us, so we can help you?"

She rounded the desk back to the armchair where her jacket hung, inside its inner pocket her painkillers.

"I think that, like your friends, you are scared of something, something that ties you all together. I think you are all in over your heads. I think you are trying to protect someone. Colonel Preston thinks its Eric, my partner I don't know what he thinks yet, but my point is Miss Wilson, I think you need more than just your friends to survive this."

She paused tossing the pills to her mouth with a gulp of water from her bottle as Carla sat still now, folding her arms, watching her.

"Let's work together Miss Wilson." She said looking back at her, "Tell me what you all are hiding, let me help you."

"Detective you dont get it do you?" Carla leaned forward, "You can keep at this, but eventually you need to arrest us to keep us here. Nothing is going to change. We don't know who is doing this."

Dekka stepped into the hallway shaking her head at her partner and superior, "Nothing, I can't get anything out of her either. They're all hiding something."

"Or they're apart of this." Malik suggested with a frown, "But we need to make a call for Jansens lawyer, arrest them or we need to let them leave, we can't keep them here any longer."

"It's a miracle they stayed as long as they have." Dekka agreed when she noticed Preston staring off in deep thought, "Sir, what's on your mind? What would you like us to do?"

Everything was on the line for Colonel Preston, if they didn't find the killer, end the speculation and cease the fear spread across the country, the UCU would be closed down and he'd be back in a station like the small cramped, noisy one he had worked so hard to escape in his career. He shook his head, "I have one more thing to say to Mr. Jansen."

He pushed between them, walking briskly as they hurried behind him.

Laying on his arms on the desk, the droning noises from outside as rain hit the building, he was lulled to sleep overtook all the other maddening thoughts plaguing his mind. Heaviness set in over his body just as the door slung open.

"What about Leigh Anne Roos, let's talk about her Mr. Jansen." Preston stormed to the desk, leaning his fists down just as Eric stood up in alarm.

"She's going to wake up any time now, and when she does do you really think she'll protect you like the rest of them?" he snarled, "You and your friends are behind these attacks, what is it? Revenge for a game of spin the bottle gone bad?"

Dekka and Malik paused by the door, equally nervous that they'd be off the case and without jobs soon.

"I already told you..."

"You told us nothing!" he hit the desk hard, "Mr. Jansen I'm placing you under arrest."

"What?" Eric gasped, "Why?"

"You wanted a lawyer; we want the truth." He grinned, "Now sit down and talk or I'll arrest your sorry little ass."

"I think I've seen enough." A voice came from behind him, causing them all to turn to the door where a tall man in a silver suit with accompanying tie stood with short combed back blond hair and a briefcase in his hands.

"Who are you?" asked Malik as he stepped into the middle of the room.

"My name is Simon Alsbury. I'm his lawyer." He grinned, "In fact I'm representing everyone you brought in here with Mr. Jansen at forty minutes past nine this morning. Which is six hours and fifty-five minutes longer than needed considering none of them have justifiable reasons to be detained here, other than Mr. Jansen and Mr. Naicker, am I correct?"

"Simon Alsbury?" Malik gushed almost, "I'm actually a big fan of your' s sir."

Staring at him for a moment blankly, the tall lawyer returned his attention to the confused Eric, nodding at him as he then continued to address the colonel.

"Also, was I correct in hearing you threaten to arrest my client unless he sat down?"

"I wanted…"

"Well, we all want things don't we Colonel." He said with a cold narcissism, "If you have insufficient grounds for an arrest other than my client not wanting to sit down, then we'll be leaving."

A relief washed over Eric as Preston scoffed, "I know who you are Mr. Alsbury, and I'll have you know, all of them came here voluntarily, number one. Number two, we never forced them to stay here. And thirdly, we have ample justification to have detained them."

Simon Alsbury chuckled, "I'm sure you followed all the right protocols Colonel Preston, have any of them been given their rights under constitutional law, criminal law?"

Preston hated the smugness of his face and his teeth clenched staring at him.

"I'll gladly ask you again, are any of them under arrest?"

The colonel's eyes narrowed angrily to the smooth nonchalance Simon Alsbury oozed as he turned to face the two detectives.

"Is there any justification to make any arrests here today?"

"He fled two crime scenes linked to the Province Slayings, that's enough to play this game Simon." Preston stepped forward, "We have sufficient reason to arrest Mr. Jansen and Mr. Naicker on that alone."

Eric's wide eyes watched between the two men anxiously, his gut twisting in fear.

"After five hours, almost six now, you have not been able to make the decision on whether to arrest them. You must be losing your touch Colonel or was that brutish success rate of yours only applicable when you were running a station?"

"I'd pick my words carefully Mr. Alsbury." Preston warned politely.

"Your force had my clients Zain Naicker and Eric Jansen labelled as suspects in the recent killings, one burned up house, and with multiple eyewitnesses placing them nowhere near the scene of last night's attack - I'd say four, excuse me, five hours - should be enough for someone of your grade to make an informed decision, so you tell me Colonel Preston, are you or your detectives making any arrests or not?"

Preston grinned, "Not at this time, no."

"Good, then we're all leaving, we'll find out in court just how well you followed standard legal protocols Colonel Preston."

"Court?" Preston scoffed, "You must be joking, you know what's happening out there."

"I'd be double checking your pension benefits if I were you, Colonel." He mocked, ushering Eric towards him, "It is my advice that my clients sue you and your Unique Crimes Unit for unlawful detention for over 5 hours without any justifiable grounds to make an arrest, particularly Miss Wilson, and Mr. and Miss Jonah – unwed of course, that would be gross, they're brother and sister."

He pushed Eric into the hallway, before turning back, "As for Mr. Jansen and Mr. Naicker, I'd have you know we will be issuing a separate defamation suit against you directly Mr. Preston for allowing confidential case material and information to leave your unit. Such an oversight, imagine there was a special task force around to ensure that unique crimes are handled in a delicate and swiftly manner, wouldn't that be something? I wonder who they'd get to run it. Thoughts?"

Dekka and Malik awkwardly looking between them, the raw hatred seeping from the colonel's face.

Simon Alsbury mockingly shrugged, "Nope? None? Worth a try." And walked off out of sight.

****

"Your buddies are waiting for you outside, oh snap! Except Zain Naicker, I should probably go get him." Simon said stopping at the side entrance door.
"How awkward is that going to be?" he laughed patting Eric's shoulder as he turned back down the passage.
Eric frowned confused and stepped out of the door where in the empty narrow parking stood a gun-metal grey Range Rover with shining silver rims, with Matt, Carla, and Maggie each holding an umbrella as the sun's last visible rays faded to the night.

"Eric, are you ok?" Maggie asked covering him with her umbrella.
"What just happened?"
"That was Simon Alsbury." Carla explained as the rain drummed on the umbrella above her, "The highest paid lawyer in the country, the guy who took down Le Roux and Associates a few years back."
"What's he doing here?"
"I have no idea, but I'm glad to be out of there." Matt huffed from the side.
"Guys we need to know what we're dealing with here, why would he just show up like this?" asked Eric nervously, huddling beside Maggie from the rain.

The door behind them opened Zain stepped out holding a small paper bag, a smile broke across his face as he rushed towards Eric, hugging him.

"Are you ok?"

"I'm exhausted, but I never said anything." Zain said looking to each of them, "I never said anything."

Matt frowned, "Where's the lawyer guy?"

"I don't know." Zain said cramming beside Carla as the cold forced a shiver, "He said to come outside, and that the car would take us anywhere we wanted. Also, he gave me this."

"Our phones." Matt said eagerly re-distributing among them.

"This is too weird." Eric said walking back towards the door when from the side at the entrance to the road, a black Mercedez Maybach honked, and they turned.

At the window in the back seat, Simon Alsbury offered a smile, "You guys best get out of here before you catch a cold. Stay safe alright?"

"Wait…" Maggie rushed forward when he waved as the window rolled up while the Maybach pulled away.

"There's no way I'm getting in that car. Without knowing what the hell this was about." Said Maggie shaking her head, "Where's your car Matty?"

"At the hospital remember. We were escorted here directly from there! God how are you in university when you don't even have logic!" He snarled turning to the Range Rover, "Everyone just get into the damn car. Let's just get out of here! We go back to the hospital so we can talk to Mark and find a way to figure this out."

"I agree." Said Carla moving towards the door.

"Besides, we're four people and this Zain guy, I'm sure we'll be alright." Matt grinned.

CHAPTER SEVEN

By nightfall the hospital lights blared a welcoming contrast against the black stormy sky and dull downpour that continued since the afternoon.

They were all tired, drained, and startled. The short run from the car to the hospital entrance made them all feel as though death itself was chasing behind them.
In their walk towards the elevators, Matt paused.
"Look I need to eat." He said earnestly, "Like I can't anymore. I need to eat."
They all wearily agreed.
As Zain, Eric, and Carla head to Mark's room, Maggie and Matt walked towards the hospital's coffee lounge.

"I'm glad we're talking. Kind of." Maggie started, "I mean, at least we're able to be around one another without trying to kill each other."
"Yeah, we got someone else doing that part." He said abruptly as the smells of coffee, fries and toasted sandwiches filtered the air as they drew closer.
"Dad used to tell me sometimes about how great you're doing at his side and…"
"What do you want Maggie?" he moaned slowing down, "Don't stand here pretending to give a crap, because you don't care about me. If our parents weren't just murdered along with our old friends, you probably wouldn't even have called me back!"
"I just wanted to…"

"What? To be my big sister?" he mocked rudely, "Thanks Mags but I'm good, I'll find a way to keep going without my parents around."
He turned to continue walking.
"You're an asshole!"
"And you're a selfish bitch!"
She gasped, "What if *we* die tomorrow? Then what?" she rushed behind him.
"Could have died a year ago, four years ago. Hell Maggie, this isn't the time for that final bonding moment between estranged brother and sister alright?"
He stopped and turned to face her again defeated - exhausted by the strain it all forced on his mind.

"This all started a long time ago, and you made it clear that you blamed me so…"
"I don't blame you! Where did you even get that?" she asked moving them aside so others could pass them, "I never said that, not once."
"It was in everything you said Maggie and everything you didn't. It was everything and nothing… I get that you had to find a way to deal but making me feel like I was the only one who did anything that day, that wasn't fair."
"But I never blamed you Matt." She urged, "I just…I didn't want to be around anything that reminded me of that day."
He looked down feeling dirtier than ever and she too looked away from him.
"You remember as kids when you started to hang out with us, you were the oldest one of all of us and everyone had you as the big sister? Well Maggie you _are_ my big sister. But you abandoned me to deal alone. I suffered too you know, we all did. Clearly!" he moaned, "But we had each other, or at

least I thought we did. But you didn't want to talk about it or think about it. You didn't want me near you after that, and a part of me understood that. But we had a chance to be different. Look at Mark and Odie, they fell apart."

"They did what we did." She said shaking her head, "Everyone dealt with things the way that worked for them, some worked out and others didn't. But I had my own burdens to carry Matt, I couldn't carry yours too, I just couldn't!"

Tears welled in her eyes, "But after all of this, those images, our old friends…"

She paused as he sighed almost impatiently.

"Matty, I don't want things to be this way. Mom and dad wouldn't have…"

"Maggie just please!" He grabbed her by the shoulders in a loud interruption, "Don't use them, don't you dare use mom and dad."

He stepped back shaking his head, "I'm tired, I'm hungry as hell! I don't want to do this now ok? But you're alive, you're ok and that's enough to just exist knowing nothing bad happened to you. Alright?"

She stared into her brothers' eyes and nod her head, allowing him to continue their expedition for food.

As he walked away, she knew she had no idea who he had become, that she had been selfish all those years never sharing the burdens of what changed their childhood forever.

****

Grateful to have her phone back, Carla called the hospital for an update on her mother as they walked down the long corridor to the ward where Mark had been admitted. Hearing that she had woken up was a delightful relief and she burst into a happy string of tears, quickly giving Eric and Zain the thumbs up to continue ahead without her.

With that, also the realization that her mother now faced charges for the death of the old lady who shared her room, and the relief quickly returned to worry again. The doctor was kind and gentle with all the information regarding her mother's health which on its own was enough, at least for the moment to give her a boost of hope that once they unmasked the killer, the future would be somewhat liveable.

"Thank you so much doctor, thank you. I'll call again tomorrow."
She hung up as she entered the room to find Zain kneeling at Eric's side where he lay scattered on the floor with blood trickling from his lip, Mark standing over him angrily.
"What the hell is going on?" she said stepping to help Zain lift Eric to his feet.
"That was for breaking the pact." Mark scoffed as he limped around to the far side of the room towards the windows where lightning tore the darkness in the distance.

It had been eating at him since their first meeting, but it only sunk in once they'd gone, and everything started to settle in his mind.

"It's fine, I'm ok." Eric stood up holding his cheek, "I suppose I had it coming."

Zain shook his head, moving to the far side of the room to sit quietly on a wooden bench.

"There are already too many people who might be wanting to hunt us down from what happened that day. I just wish we could undo telling anyone." Mark huffed as a weight pressed against his chest. A silence hung as Carla inspected Eric's face, and then Mark turned to face him again.

"It was stupid of me Eric…"

"No Mark it's ok, you have a point." Eric sighed, "Trust me, we've been going over it a hundred times who knew or may have known, but Zain isn't a threat here."

"I know." He huffed looking to Zain, "I'm sorry that wasn't called for actually."

Carla sighed rubbing her temples when Matt and Magaret entered with packets of food, greeting happily before the weight of tension sunk in.

"Wow, who died?" Matt asked stupidly as he began to unpack the food on the tray by the foot of the bed and Carla nudged him.

"Are we good?" Eric asked stepping to Mark as he stared out the window.

Mark paused, frustrated, and exhausted, "You shouldn't have told him, nobody else should be brought into this. Take it from me, telling someone is worse on them than you can ever imagine."

Noticing Maggie bore on her a different sadness, Carla sat beside her on the edge of the bed, "Are you holding up alright?"

She forced a smile and held up her chicken sandwich, "Is anything ever going to be ok again?"

"We need to talk about our next move here." Zain said, "I mean, honestly what's the plan?"

"Look I've been thinking about this…" Eric said, "Anyone who may have a reason to want to do this is either in this room, untraceable or buried."
"Possibly buried…" Matt corrected cocking his head as he handed Eric his food.
"So…this is where we hang out now?"

It was as though a shockwave hit them all seeing Zachary standing at the doorway, managing an awkward smile and for each of them a moment of disbelief shook through them – the boy who once made sure their circle was impenetrable had grown up, and the excitement that fuelled their youth was now dull.

"Oh my god! Zach?" Maggie exclaimed, the first to approach him with a hug.
"Hey Maggie."
"I didn't think I'd ever see you again!"
He smiled as she stepped back, again looking at him top to bottom – rags to riches before her eyes.
"That was you? The lawyer?" Eric asked as he greeted with an awkward hug.
Zach nodded, the sight of his bruised face saddening his smile as he patted his old friend on the shoulder, "I'm glad you are ok man."
Eric's hug was tight, and Zach returned it, his once best friend all grown up.
"Well, it's about time you showed up." Matt teased approaching with food parcels still in his hands, "We've been wondering about you."
Matt greeted him with an elbow-bump, his usual boorish arrogance hadn't changed.
"Good to see you, where the hell have you been bro? If we knew toasted chicken would bring you back, I'd have organized some days ago." Matt

joked, handing Zain his food when Carla stepped forward, her eyes scanning his face in disbelief.

"Hey Carla." A smile broke across his face as she hugged him tightly, embracing that he really was there.
"We've been trying to find you." She said stepping backwards, noticing the glance between him and Mark who offered a shrug behind her, a shrug everyone else noticed.
"Wait you knew where he was this whole time?" Eric turned.
"Talk about a dick move!" grunt Matt biting into his sandwich, mumbling something more which nobody could understand as he plonked onto the armchair.

"When I realized what was going on, what was *really* going on, I got here as quickly as I could." Zach explained looking into Carla's eyes, before moving around her to greet Mark with a handshake hug, "I'm glad you're ok."
"Where the hell have you been? I thought you vanished off the map."
"That was the idea, Eric." Zach offered a smile as he turned to face them all, "I don't really use my phones much…I barely watch the news, so I didn't really know what was going on until Mark let me know about Odie and then…"
He paused, "The killer found me."
"How? What do you mean?" Mark was surprised.
"If you're the only one who had Zach's digits maybe the killer traced your call or something?" suggested Matt, "I've seen that in the movies."
They all listened as the food in their hands grew colder.

Zach shrugged his shoulders shaking his head, "I got a message, from my aunt Chantal. There was a link on it, and I clicked it…it was…"

His voice broke as he explained, "It was just images of Jacques, Odie and other people."

"I got that on email." Eric said softly from the side, "I think we all did."

Zach nodded and Mark put his hand on his shoulder, turning him to face him, "How did he…Is your aunt alive Zach?"

**

Zach dropped the phone to the ground at the foot of the empty bookshelf that stood on the side of his large white bedroom, heart racing as he turned and slunk down on the bed.

The phone rang and he looked up at it laying on the floor.

Why would she even have those pictures? He thought standing up and going towards it, picking it up quickly.

"Why would you send that to me?" The nauseating anger was thick in his voice.

"Finally! I've been waiting for you to click that link. It took you long enough Zachary." The voice came through, a voice he did not know or recognise.

"Who is this?" he felt a coldness now, "Where's Chantal?"

"Oh her, yeah, her body will be discovered soon enough, I'm sure."

Zach froze, gripping the phone tightly in his hand against his ear.

"But now I know exactly where you are!" the voice continued,

"You didn't think you could escape me, did you? You'll never really escape me, Zachary. I am everywhere. You cannot run, you cannot hide, not from me."

"What do you want?"

"I want you to know how it feels to watch everything you've aspired to survive crumbling down while your friends gargle on their blood. Ooohh I'm going to make you pay for what you did to me Zachary. I'm loving every minute of it."

"Who are you?"

"Who are you, Zachary? You're the one who started this all and yet you think you can run forever? It's time for you to pay for what you took from me, again… Or are you willing to keep letting others die?"

"You want me?" he snarled, "Then come and get me! What are you waiting for?"

"No! No Zachary! You don't get to make demands here Zachary!" The voice now roared into the phone angrily, "I'm not one of your slaves! You cannot wave your money here, no one is going to stop me! I'll kill them all…I'm going to savour every second. Nobody is going to end this but you! They'll all die one by one until you come out and face me,

Zachary. The clock is ticking! You know exactly where to find me."

**

"I called the police in Lydenburg almost immediately after the call, and they sent someone to her house." Zach explained morbidly, "She was dead in the bathroom, accidental drowning they said."
"That's awful..." Carla gasped, "I'm so sorry."
Mark squeezed Zach's shoulder, "Yeah, I'm sorry bro."
"So, the link was the tracker, smart." Matt tore into his sandwich.
"That must be why I got my letter the way I did!" Maggie gasped, "Maybe he couldn't tell which campus I was on?"
Matt nodded, "He wanted you to call that number to trace you."
"Maybe he's already tracking all of us." Eric said nervously, "That's how he knows where we are?"
"Look this is about me, something I've done. I'm so sorry you all got caught up in this." Said Zach solemnly, "He made it clear when he called me."
"That doesn't make any sense Zach." Eric shook his head as Zain now too bit into his sandwich beside him, "If this wasn't about what happened that day, then why us? If you've done something, why target a bunch of people from your past."
"I agree." Said Maggie, "This is related to what we did that day."
"More like what we didn't do." Mark huffed, "This cannot be isolated to one individual Zachary. I mean that makes no sense, and I know you..."

Mark stared into his Zach's eyes, "…Don't do this to yourself."

"Unless you're the province slayer just trying to throw us off?" Matt said wiping his mouth, "I mean where were you man? Like nobody could find you and you just show up randomly."

"Don't start that." Mark sighed rolling his eyes when Maggie supported.

"No, he has a point. How do we know you're not the one doing this Zach?"

"Maggie…" Eric huffed when Maggie stood up.

"No! Our friends are dead, our parents are dead!" she snarled, "Eric and Mark have been attacked! But you just show up randomly with some story. How do we know you're telling the truth?"

Everyone's eyes turned to him, each one now letting the logic in her statement linger and battle against their counterintuitive history with him.

"I'm here, aren't I?" Zach said shaking his head, "Look guys I'm not doing this."

"Well until we know for sure, you should keep your distance." Matt warned.

"Guys this isn't answering the question!" Zain huffed, "If we don't do something soon and end this, more people will die, including people in this room."

"Why are you even here?" Matt scoffed shaking his head, "Seriously!"

"Look enough!" Mark raised his voice, "We're all here now, basically where we left off ten years ago. Plus, we have Zach, so that leaves two other people who know."

"Who *maybe* know." Carla corrected, "We've never known if anyone know about that guy."

"We also don't know for sure that Bobby is in fact dead." Matt said again when Eric huffed angrily.

"Stop with the damn Bobby theory already, this isn't some movie."

"You mock me, but I'm not crossing out any names on my list. If they're not dead, they are suspects. Including you Zach Manson, you too Mr. Zain the stranger who is just suddenly a part of the group."

"Will you give it a rest!" Warned Eric when a knock tapped at the door.

"Oh, hello again." Marks doctor smiled entering with a nurse at his side, "I'm sorry but we have to check your wounds again Mark. Would you all mind giving us the room?"

"Visiting hours are actually over." The nurse said, "But we'll give you all another few minutes once we've changed his bandages."

She smiled as they moved towards the door, "I know some of you have travelled far to be here. There's a small lounge down the hall to your left. I'll call you once we're done here."

****

There was a calmness settling in as everyone somehow scattered apart in the waiting lounge, with the uncertainty and distrust in Zach's presence still ringing in the silence as they all dug into their food and soda's.

For a moment it was just the sounds of the hospital as they ate, each allowing the madness to settle, each one's own haunting demons from their shared passed nesting in through their rampant thoughts.

"Would anyone want these? They're untouched but I don't have space to finish it." Zain offered his fries up awkwardly from the side.

Matt got up crossing over, taking it without a thanks before returning to his seat.

Another silence gracelessly settled, reminding them all that they had nothing to talk about other than that which brought them all together again after all these years. He'd forgotten them and as he sat watching them in their own silent spaces, Zach couldn't help but feel a small sense of happiness seeing them all together again, everyone so different to the smaller, younger versions he remembered.

"So…" Zach braved speaking to the untrusting group, "Who are you exactly?"

"Zain. Zain Naicker." He managed a cautious smile, "I'm with Eric."

Eric quickly chewed then stood up defensively, "Zain knows everything. So, if you want to punch or take a swing let's do it and get it over with."

Zach's eyes were dark and shrugged back his shoulders, "Why would you tell?"

All eyes fell on Eric, and he casually shrugged his shoulders, "Because I love him."

Zach nodded while turning to meet Zain's eyes again, "Well, nice meeting you."

"Same." Zain offered a highly awkward wave as Matt also stood up, tossing his trash to the garbage can.

"Yeah, I need some air and a smoke. I'm going to find a balcony or something."

"Same here." Eric said motioning to join him when Matt held his hand outward.

"No offence, but I just need some air. Alone."

"This isn't a good time to be alone anywhere."
Maggie moaned standing up, "Don't be a dick Matt.
Get over it already."
Matt huffed looking down as shame flooded his
face, then still hesitantly forced a smile as he
cocked his head motioning for Zain and Eric to
follow.

"Let's go." Eric said holding his hand out and lifting
Zain from the couch with a proud smile. "I need the
ladies, I'll go with them, you need to come?" Maggie
said heading after them.
"No, I'm good." Carla smiled.
"Are you sure?" Maggie pressed, nervously trying to
signal her to be cautious of Zach. Carla shook her
head laughing, "I'm ok Maggie, thank you I'll be
alright."
Maggie nodded, paused looking at Zach and then
head down the passage after the guys.

"So, this is awkward." Zach managed a laugh, "I'm
not the one doing this, I don't know how to prove it
to anyone but I'm not."
Carla stood up from the seat towards the trash bin,
allowing her thoughts to calm as the quiet lounge
grew still with all the words not said between them
in the two years since they last saw each other.

They had run into each other at a club in Rivonia by
chance, and it was as though nothing had ever
happened - the spark they'd always had for each
other was ignited instantly. They spent the night
talking, again like the same kids they used to be.
Eventually they ended up dancing, but soon their
bodies began to move closer to each other, their
eyes fixed on each other.

Each touch of his hands against her skin lingering as they moved against each other, the noisy club around them fading. They kissed, a long overdue fire. Later making love in unrivalled ecstasy, a burning desire they'd shared since their first meeting but never acted on - falling asleep in each other's arms was the only time they'd both felt safely at peace.

But when she woke up, he was gone and wasn't seen or heard from again.

"So, you stayed in touch with Mark?" she asked carefully, "I almost forgot you mentioned staying in touch with him that night."
He looked down quietly, "I never meant to hurt you."
"You didn't." she braved a smile, "I just spent the last two years wondering why you left without saying a word, and why you chose to disappear. I mean, I know your parents passed away shortly after but, that was a few months after, so it couldn't have been that."
He stood up and cautiously walked to her.
"Carla I wasn't who you thought I was that night." He said staring into her eyes, "I was trying to protect you."
"From what? The truth? Our truth? That wasn't your job Zach, we all carry what we did in our own way, it was never your job to protect me." She said shaking her head, "What we had that one night was more than I had felt… in years, you just left."
She moved around him, "Not a word, nor a number or address. You ran and it reminded me that I'd never wash away what we did as kids. I'd always be stained…stained by what happened."

He took her hand, turning her to face him. His eyes again staring into the dark blue of hers, "I don't see you that way."

He wanted to kiss her lips, every fibre of his body burning for her embrace again.

"But I do Zach, and its worse now than it was before because for the first time I felt alive, like I had a chance at something... but you ran...from me."

"No Carla, I ran from me." he paused, the pain in her eyes ached his heart, "I was scared of what I felt when I was with you."

"So, if we don't deserve happiness at all then...then why are we both living if all we have is numb?"

"I don't know." His eyes welled, his body aching to pull her close and feel her lips.

She stepped away, forcing herself free of the enchanting craving to be with him, tears ran down her face, "I need to live Zach, I can't...I can't stay wallowing in the past anymore, it's suffocating and its controlling. It's killing me."

"I know." Zach said looking up at her again, "It's killing everyone."

****

Magaret exited the bathroom smiling in thanks to Zain who was ready to walk to the exit when she paused.

"Zain I'll head back and stay with Carla. Maybe Mark's ready and we can go see him again, so I'd rather be there."

"Oh, ok." He nodded, "Should I walk you back?"

"No, I'll be fine, it's just down the hall." She smiled as she turned away, "Thank you though.

At the far side of the hospital building, in a narrow street fencing off the darkness of the fields surrounding it, Matt and Eric stood beneath a shade netting that covered a portion of the side structure, over one of the service entrances.

The service door was near the corner, by it stood two large trash containers against the small wall that separated the narrow road from the boundary line near the fence of the hospital.

They stood there sheltering from the drizzle, the big waste containers blocking the frigid air circling in the open, dark fields around the hospital.

They were finishing their cigarettes while Zain was gentlemanly enough to have waited outside the ladies' room for Magaret.

"You really think Zach could do something like this?" asked Eric.

"Who knows, nobody in there is the same person they were ten years ago. What we did, it changed us all."

"Isn't that the truth." Eric sighed, his heart and mind colliding in the turmoil of Zain's participation, "You know I hate myself for saying anything to Zain. If anything were to happen to him that would be on me, another scar to carry for the rest of my life and… I don't know if I can carry anymore."

Matt looked down, pausing as he inhaled.

"Yeah, I understand that. He seems decent, more than decent I guess…I mean he's still here and hasn't said anything to the cops."

Eric nodded proudly, "He is decent, he's a good human being. So just lay off the guy, you're adding to the problem."

"Yeah, I can do that." Matt bellowed his smoke into the air as he spoke, "Guess not everything has changed?"

Eric laughed, "Evidently not. You're still a dickhead." Matt laughed playfully punching him.

The rain drummed against the bins.

The narrow roadway had started to build up large puddles as the water ran down the slope.

"What about you? Do you think Zach's telling the truth?" asked Matt.

"I don't know any more Matty. My brain is fried. I'm so tired." Eric said flicking his cigarette butt into the darkness where the dim lights could not reach.

"Well, he said this was all about him, someone he pissed off."

"Or someone who blames him more than the rest of us for what happened." Said Eric in defeat, the cold wet air now chilling through his clothes.

"You know if it's not him, then there's a big possibility that more people know about this than what we all suspect." Said Matt, his voice shaken, "I'm not starting something here, but you told Zain! Mark told that other guy, his sister's fiancé. I mean... I know I haven't told anyone, but I can't say the same for Maggie and Carla, or even Leigh Anne."

"What are you saying?" Eric stepped to face him, rubbing his aching head.

"I'm saying that someone killed my parents and made it look like suicide, just like Zach's aunt. So, what if everything - from Bobby's accident to God knows what else - is about what we did?"

Tears now broke through his façade, and he huffed to hide his face, "I'm just...I'm scared you know?"

Just then as the door along the side of the building opened, with Zain stepping out into the rain, quickly rushing towards them.

Matt quickly composed himself and Eric nodded, patting his shoulder.
"Like Mark said, we're all together now. We've always been stronger together."
Matt managed a smile, taking the last drag of his cigarette as Zain neared.
"Where's my sister? Matt asked worriedly, also flicking his cigarette into the darkness.
"She went back hoping the doctor was done with Mark."
"Oh, ok look dude." Matt said stepping to face him, "I have no issues with you at all and I think you're a decent guy. Don't read too much into what I say alright? It's just my way. Always has been."
Looking first to Eric who lit up with an impressed smile, Zain nodded, "Thank you, I appreciate that."
"Good." Matt playfully patted his back while he rounded past, "I'll head up to the rest so long. I'll meet you guys up there."
"That was...sweet." Zain smiled while Eric handed him the pack of smokes, watching as Matt hurried towards the door through the puddles.

"He's alright." He laughed, "Are you holding up, ok?"
Zain nodded as the end of his cigarette flared, "I'm the one who should be asking you that, you've taken more hits than me."
"I'm alright." Eric smiled, "Been through worse."
"That's not what I meant." Zain smirked, huddling closer to the trash containers to block the icy air.

"I know how hard it was for me, back at the police station." Zain turned to face him, "I don't know how you lived your life like this."

Eric sighed shaking his head, "I didn't…not really, not until I met you."

Zain leaned forward to kiss him when in the darkness, near the entrance to the narrow roadway the sound of a loud engine tore through the wet air.

It was a familiar sound, a growl almost and they both spun around.

At the entrance to the small street leading to the service entrance, the lights from the black pickup hit them as it sped towards them.

"Run!" Eric said shoving him as they dart towards the door. The old black Ford pickup was a few meters from the shaded cover, the headlights bright in their eyes as the sound of its engine droned down on them.

Eric had just flung open the door when the pickup swerved into the wall, tearing along - ramming both them and the door.

It slammed to a stop against the trash containers that barriered against the low wall - pinning Zain's right leg while flinging Eric and shrapnel from the door off into the wet soaked fire boundary line against the high barrier fence.

The passageway at the end of the hospital was quiet, and it was just as the door to the elevator began to shut that Matt heard a commotion from outside. He flung forward, to try and stop the doors.

"Eric!" Zain cried out, trying to free his leg as he lay sprawled on the bonnet, when the driver's door flung open and the tall, leather clad figure stepped out into the drizzle with the homemade knuckle duster on its black gloved hand.

"No! No!" he yelled trying to force his leg free, calling out for help while the figure stepped to the side of the bonnet.

It stood watching through the black gauze mask before reaching into its coat for the small black handled axe.

"Help!" Zain called out with the axe swinging down just inches from him, contorting his body as far back as he could to escape the blade.

The pinning of his leg ached as he fought in painful cries, pressing his hands against both the bins and bonnet to push himself as far away from the onslaught as possible.

"Time to be quiet now." The figure said swinging it down again, the blade sliding just past his face and into the bonnet again.

"Get away from him!" Eric roared, rounding the containers in a limp.

Leaving the axe embedded in the hood of the pickup, the figure flung towards him, throwing a fast, hard punch. The knuckleduster's sharp ends connected into the side of Eric's face – sending him struggling backwards in a terrible scream as the pain tore through every nerve in his face - from deep in his gums. The blood gushed from his left eye socket as the eye itself fell from the figure's knuckles into a puddle on the road.

"No more of this!" the figure said turning as it removed the large hunting knife from inside its coat.

****

The elevator doors rung open, and Matt stumbled out on the 3rd floor, calling at the top of his lungs for help.

Maggie, Zach, and Carla spun around from the lounge at the sound of his screams. "Stay here!" he ordered as he dashed without thought for the stairs. Still fighting to free his lower leg, Zain cried out for Eric, for help – for anything to end the madness before his eyes.

But shock had already hit, and Eric tumbled in cries as his hand felt for the eye that had been torn out. The figure had sprung forward, stabbing the long thick blade of the hunting knife deep into the centre of his stomach.

Watching as Eric's body got torn apart, the blood spraying everything in the rain, Zain screamed and pushed with all his might to free his leg while the figure continued to stab at Eric's torso - viciously, lunging him backwards with each stab until Eric was up against the fence where the figure kept on stabbing and stabbing.

"Eric!" Matt's voice called from inside, rushing towards the bent door frame.

The figure hurried back towards the opening, dropping Eric's mutilated and blood-soaked body to the ground.

The figure was halfway past the pickup when Matt, two nurses and two security guards stormed out into the rain, stopping dead in their tracks at the site of the black figure standing just feet from them – Eric's blood running down its black forearm, glove, and blade to the puddle on the ground.

Zain leapt down from the bonnet with the axe in his hand, using all he had left to bring the blade down into the figure's back, just off the shoulder. But his leg was not ready and the force with which it hit into the figure was not enough to pierce the thickness of the leather hood. He swung again, but the figure grabbed his arm and delivered a punch into the centre of his chest, crippling him breathlessly down to a puddle.

Screams filled the rain as the nurses rushed back in, the figure slicing at the air in front of Zain who stumbled backwards and down to the ground.
"Stop!" the guard yelled, holding out his taser gun, "Put down the axe!"
"Holy shit!" Matt gasped stepping behind the security guard in disbelief and disappointment as the figure very quickly reached far into the side of the coat - pulling out the detective's 9mm sidearm it had taken in the fire.
Two shots to the upper body had the security guard falling backwards in the rain, the taser going off as his body hit into Matt.
When they hit the hard ground, the live barbs of the taser fell to the water that dammed the roadway - sending the current into them. The figure stood still, its thick rubber boots nulling the current that filled the water.

"Please…" Matt forced the words through the involuntary impulses as the figure stood over him.

Two more guards rushed out of the doorway and the dark figure fired at them, hitting one in the leg as they tried to duck back inside.

"Stay back!" they pushed at Zach who rushed for the door.

"Please…don't…" Matt begged through a clenched jaw, fighting through the spasms cringing his body.

"Sssshhh…" it said aiming the 9mm and firing four shots to Matt's face.

"No!" Zach cried at the doorway, his whole body almost convulsing in pure terror before looking up at the figure who stood in the rain - the dark sky behind its imposing form lighting up as bolts of lightning ripped.

Police sirens rang out through the rain, growing louder the closer they got, and the figure raised its arm and began to fire, forcing Zachary backwards into the building again as the bullets riddled the walls.

The figure hurried back into the matt black pickup, and the vehicle tore backwards, just missing Zain who stood up in a limp as Zach tackled him out of the way. Zach rolled, looking up at the driver – the blackness of its face staring at him, raising its index finger against its mask before spinning its wheels on the wet roadway, turning sharp and crashing through the fence into the darkness as the red and blue lights fluttered with the police cars rounding into the roadway.

It was as though time stopped as Zach moved through the rain, numbed as he watched the red lights disappear into the darkness.

Zain's painful cry tore the drumming in his head, and he turned to see Zain limping - collapsing down beside the body of the bright-eyed boy who once was his best friend – laying in the dirt, the rain drenching his blood-soaked body.

****

'You're the one who started this all and yet you think you can run forever? It's time for you to pay for what you took from me, again… Or are you willing to keep letting others die?'

The words were haunting in the mayhem of his mind as Zach sat motionless on the bench inside the police station, watching as Maggie cried from the pit of her soul into Mark's arms as he and Carla tried to console her. She was now alone in the world, and he was told it was all his fault by the black figure who called him.

Exiting the small office with detectives Dekka and Malik, Eric's sister Celeste and her husband Keith stepped out. He put his hand on her shoulder as she walked trembling and sobbing into a tissue, having to sit she pulled a chair from a desk and just slunk to it, wailing into her hands.
Detective Malik felt her pain radiating from her and he knelt to her side.

"We'll make sure all arrangements to transport your brother back to Pretoria are handled quickly. Again, I'm very sorry for your loss."

The painful tears left Zain who was seated beside his father's sister who had welcomed him when he was chased away from his home by his parents. He watched Eric's sister, looking at them through the eyes of a young man so early battered and torn from happiness, whose future now was shattered. He understood her agony and pain, it was a pain that stole the air from each breath, the warmth from every drop of blood circulating inside a heart that was squeezed so viciously tight by the unbelievable suffering, it barely functioned. The world had never felt so cold.

Detective Malik got up to join Simon Alsbury and his partner at the side and as he stood with his hand on his wife's shoulder, Keith's glare at Zain burnt.
"What are you looking at?" Zain stood up angrily from his aunt's side and walked towards them, "You want to say something to me?"
Celeste turned as Zain approached and Keith shook his head angrily, "Stay away from us."
"Keith…don't." she said taking his hand.
"You don't get to look at me with contempt asshole!" Zain said as tears streamed his face, "You have no right! You made his chance at life harder than it needed to be, you and your judgements! You locked us out when we needed help just like you did all his life, you made everything harder!"
"No, I…" Keith stammered as the words stabbed to his heart, and Zain swung.
The flat handed slap tore across Keith's face, his head spinning to the side as he almost lost balance – a slap so hard that it almost silenced the police station foyer.
"That's enough!" Malik rushed up pulling Zain away.

"Are you holding up, ok?" Simon said sitting beside Zach who sat motionless, just managing a shake to his head.

Simon heaved an awkward sigh, "The detectives want to put everyone under police protection, this thing has blown up really big in the media and…" He paused as Zach still stared at the others, their pain emanating across the room as though pointing to him.

"…look Zach, I'm going to need to know what's going on here. I can't protect you if I don't know everything."

"You need to protect them, not me. That's what I'm paying you for."

Simon Alsbury sighed shaking his head, "Zachary, whatever it is, you can tell me."

Tears filled his eyes as he watched Zain sitting by his aunt again, crying in her arms while Celeste and Keith head out past them.

"That poor guy. He's not even supposed to be here."

"You know who this is don't you?"

Zach leaned forward in his chair, looking down as he shook his head.

"You know why?" asked Simon leaning forward too.

Zach again shook his head.

"You're lying." He said studying his face from the side.

"You make sure they're safe." Zach turned to him, "That's what I'm paying you for." Simon sat back in his seat, shaking his head in frustration.

"Hi, Mr. Alsbury." Carla said walking over to them, "I just wanted to thank you, for everything."

"I'm here to help." Said Simon buttoning the middle of his jacket and looking down at Zach again, "All of you."

Zach slunk back into his chair, looking past them at Dekka and Malik standing in a room talking to Preston and other officers.

Simon turned to him, "I'm staying at a small B&B. I'll see about booking more rooms for the night so everyone can get some rest and sort out any travel tomorrow. Makes things simpler for their protection order too, having everyone in one place."
"Or dangerous."
Simon nodded, "Let me see what I can do."
"That's a good idea."
"Miss Wilson." Simon greeted walking away and allowing room for Carla to sit beside him. "I know you think this is all your fault." She said softly, "It isn't."
"He told me it was." He folded his arms against his chest, "You know when we were kids, all I wanted was for everyone to be together and stay together. Happy."
"You had no idea this would happen. None of us did." Said Carla leaning forward as Mark approached with Maggie under his arm, leaning against his chest sobbing softly.
"Maggie... I'm so sorry." Said Zach standing up. She nodded but barely made eye contact through the water running down her face and the tissue wiping. She just wanted to sleep and wake up from the emptiness of her reality.

"What happens now?" Mark asked Zach behind tormented, lost eyes - as though still young and confused, a look he saw that afternoon when everything changed.
"We have to tell." Said Zach braving back his tears, feeling the emptiness and guilt writhing at his core.

"I know." Said Carla standing up beside him, crossing her arms as a different coldness sunk into her skin, "I'm surprised Zain didn't already say anything."

"I wouldn't do Eric that way." Zain's voice came from behind Mark and Maggie.

"Alright we have something to share with you." Simon said happily rounding the desk as Colonel Preston and detective Dekka stepped towards them.

"We have agreed to the accommodation suggestion, this late in the day it only makes sense." Dekka spoke friendly, "Officers will secure the Scherman House for the next few days while we do our best to wrap things up."

"You mean catch him?" Maggie asked beneath her breath, her disdain thick even through her heartache, "And how will you be doing that since all you did was waste everyone's time yesterday!"

"Maggie." Mark said trying to console her as she began to yell, turning to Preston. "You are to blame! You killed my brother! You did this!" she screamed hitting at his chest when Zach grabbed her and pulled her against him.

He hugged her tight as she broke again, her legs too weak to hold her up as they slunk to the bench.

Preston, riddled with self-loathing stepped back, excusing himself to diffuse the tension as he quietly walked away.

Dekka knelt, taking Maggie's hand in hers and squeezing it tightly.

"We're going to find him Maggie. We've finally got a lead that brings us one step closer to finding him and killing him."

"Don't you mean arresting him?" asked Simon raising his eyebrow.

Dekka looked to him, but shook her head as she stood up again, "We're going to get this bastard, I don't care if death is the easy way Mr. Alsbury."

"What do u mean you have a lead?" Mark urged with anticipation.

"There was a partial capture of the license plate on one of the CCTV camera's when it entered the hospital grounds. My partner detective Malik is following up on it as we speak." She explained, "We also got confirmation of some fibres found…"

Zain's heart sunk as she paused glancing at him, and she quickly finished, "We're going to catch this son of a bitch."

"What about us in the meantime?" Carla asked.

"I confirmed we can book out the Scherman House off the N17." Simon explained, "Detective Dekka and some officers will be providing protection."

"I'm sorry we can't let you leave just yet." Dekka said with true regret, "But until we have a solid grasp on this, it's safer to keep you all together under our watch until we can be sure."

"Be sure? Of what?" asked Zach.

"That he's dead." She said bluntly glancing up at Alsbury, "We'll ready the transport and sweep the building before you arrive."

Simon managed a smile, excusing himself as he pulled Zach to the side away from the others.

"Whatever this is, if you have anything that can help them catch this guy, you need to know that I'll keep you protected, no matter what." He said urging Zach, "Nobody else needs to get hurt anymore. You need to talk to me Zachary, I know it may seem daunting but you're paying me a lot of money and I

need you to understand that I'll do everything I can to keep you out of trouble."
Zach managed a weak smile nodding, "I know Simon, thank you."

"That's ridiculous!" Zain's feisty aunty exclaimed forcing him to sit down beside her again. He managed a smile, "I need to stay aunty."
"I disagree. They've had this case for a week and done nothing but put tags on toes. Your uncle Murray was an officer, I know how they operate they are most likely using taxpayers' money to rent out a place while they continue to do nothing. At home, by me, you will be safe."
"I appreciate that aunty, but they won't let me return to Pretoria just yet." He sighed, too weak to handle her, "Anyway it's not safe to be travelling back to Pretoria this late just to come all the way back if I need to be here."
"I'm not going to some fancy place. I know what places like that charge per night because your uncle Ash was checking for me before I drove out here. It's expensive there, we'll stay on at the B&B I'm at, very nice gentleman running it, and it's self-catering so I will make you a proper warm supper." She said rubbing his hand - the pain in his eyes reminded her of the day he showed up in Pretoria, lost, broken and unwanted.

She sighed shaking her head and put her hand to his face, cupping his cheek,
"You're a good boy Zain, I'm so sorry for this horrible thing that happened to you."
He managed an exhausted smile as tears welled in his eyes as she continued.
"Even your father should be ashamed of himself."

"I love you aunty." He said as her arms hugged him.

****

After being herded to the rear exit, they stood waiting in an awkward silence, each one with a million reasons to talk, scream, shout, and rage anything from the pain to the truth.

"Are you managing?" Zach asked, noticing that Zain was straining with his leg.
He nodded, feeling awkward and out of place among them without Eric - an emptiness he knew he'd never lose.
"I have some news." Said Dekka rounding into the passage with Simon Alsbury at her side, "Your friend Miss Leigh Anne Roos woke up."
"Is she ok?" Carla stepped forward, "What'd she say?"
"We'll have more information a little later, detective Mallik will be flying out to see her. But the good news is she's fine." Dekka smiled, seeing the relief flow across them as Zain stepped up beside the detective.

"Alright look, officers Benjie, Koto and Lucas are escorting you all to the vehicles outside and will stay on site until we have further analysis from the crime scene." Simon explained - seeing the pain engulf Maggie, "They're armed and dangerous, with them by our sides nothing is coming in or out. We'll be safe at the Scherman House until we have further information."

"Us?" Carla frowned, "You're coming with us?"

"Me? No, but detective Dekka is." Simon grinned, "I must get back to the city. Mr. Naicker will also not be joining us, he'll be at another location under guard."

"If the son of a bitch makes a move, there's no place I'd rather be." She said with a certainty stemming from insider her gut.

Zach moved to Zain and pulled him to the side.

"I know you don't know me, and we've met in the worst of situations." Zach spoke softly, "But you don't need to be alone, come with us."

"No thank you, I think it's in my own interests if I stay away from you all." He said shaking his head as he took a step back, "I'm not part of this. Not without Eric."

Zach sighed, "Eric was a good guy."

"He really was." Zain nodded, forcing back the tears which it choked him.

"I'm so sorry Zain." He said pausing, wanting to say so much more, beg forgiveness for causing everything he'd been swept into but not finding the courage or words to explain how responsible he felt in the madness of his thoughts and emotions.

"Zach?" Simon called from the group while three heavily armed uniformed officers rounded the corner towards them.

"Take care of yourself." Zain managed to smile, patting Zach's shoulder.

"You too Zain." He said, stepping back to the group as Dekka continued.

"Now look, it's been raining so it could get a little slippery, but please we need to get you all into the police vehicles quickly, unfortunately the press got wind of this when my guys brought the cars around, so there is going to be press outside. It's going to be loud. It's going to be crude the moment you all step out there, reporters are savages so just keep your heads down and don't make any statements no matter what they throw out alright? Mark, we need you to wear your jacket up, head down and stay beneath the umbrella's, the press still think you're dead."

He sighed rolling his eyes as she continued, "We move quickly, we move together. Heads down, mouths shut."

"Actually, Mark and I will join you all later, we scheduled some time with Mr. Alsbury regarding other matters." Zach issued quickly, but as nonchalant as he could muster. Dekka turned to Simon with surprise, "You didn't mention that?"

"Yes, it was a last-minute request from my client." Simon nodded with an assuring smile, "I'll have them at the location within the hour."

"A few hours." Zach corrected, "Business stuff takes so long, let's be transparent. Besides this makes it easier for Mark to slip out undetected by the media, right?"

As Simon continued to agree, Dekka frowned, "And where will this meeting be taking place?"

Simon turned to Zach who shrugged, "Where are you staying?"

"I was going to head straight back to my offices in Sandton…"

"My advice would be to use an office here at the station. Our primary objective now is to keep them safe Mr. Alsbury." Dekka pushed with a raw irritation.

Zach's eyes pierced Simon and he quickly shook his head, "No that's alright, I must collect my things from the B&B I'm staying at, that would suffice. You can even have officer Koto escort them to and from our meeting place to the secure location, will that work?"

Zach nodded and looked to Mark who stood frowning.
"And this must happen now Mr. Manson?" she frowned in annoyance.
"Well let me remind you detective, there is no warrant for protection order and my clients are all co-operating to follow you to this location, at my client's expense which not only benefits the UCU investigation and spares any humiliation should anyone else be attacked, but also saves in the revenue the UCU so desperately needs to keep its doors open while the media call for action. I'm saying that we will be 2 hours behind you."
She stared at him shaking her head, "Alright but I'm not comfortable with it purely out of a concern for your safety Mr. Manson, Mr. Gallagher. Officer Koto will tail you. Neither of you leave his sight, understood?"
Simon nodded, staring at Zach behind an angry smile as Dekka hesitantly put her hands against the doors again.
"The cruisers are a decoy just in case the slayer is watching. We'll head to the hotel by the casino but change vehicles in the underground basement parking, taking every precaution necessary. You'll switch vehicles at the casino. Ok? Ready?"

The early morning air was cold as the sky remained covered in thick clouds that clung to the sky where the sunrise had yet to peak over the horizon.

As they stepped out of the station the noise and cameras leapt out as they rushed towards the cruisers as officers tried to keep the press at bay.

"What's going on? What's Zach up to?" asked Carla pressing closely to Maggie as the officers hurried them towards the cruisers.
"I don't know."
Everything they anticipated in those short moments before the door flung open happened, but it was more aggressive and louder than they imagined, causing them to almost freeze on the steps wondering if any of the faces were those of the man behind the mask, watching them from the crowd.

****

The roads of Secunda were almost empty, with only some cars moving about as the sun begun its accent behind the string of thick clouds that hung heavily, with summer downpours coming in waves that made the black tar glisten as several under cover vehicles exited Secunda on N17 towards the very small, remote town of Leandra that sat on the boarders between Gauteng and Mpumalanga.

The stretch of emptiness allowed the police ample control over the traffic on either side of the old 'motel stretch' of the otherwise empty and dark N17 highway.
The Scherman House – a 20 room Cape Dutch style hotel was one of three accommodations on the 'motel stretch'.

As the main transport continued, two police vehicles made stops on either side of the stretch about 5 kilometres apart under the guise of being a typical sedan broken down on the side of the road, hiding their checkpoint status for the remainder of the afternoon and night while another standard vehicle cruised on to do the same in the opposite direction until his partner arrived.

"Charlie five confirming we have no tails, and it is safe to proceed." A voice came through on the handset radio from the front seat in Dekka's lap, as the last three vehicles turned off and rolled in at the large white gates of the Scherman House entrance.

"It's so pretty out here where there's nothing." Maggie said lifting her head from Carla's shoulder, looking up to the large main house that stood tall and fashionable as the light from sunrise glimmered against its white façade.
"Your lawyer secured cottages three and four." Dekka explained from the front seat beneath a disguise of a curly perm as the three cars rounded the large water feature before the main house.
In her lap, Carla hurriedly sent a message to the number on Simon Alsbury's business card.

The car drove along the gardens towards two smaller units.

Dekka got out, followed by Maggie, and Carla. Carla scanned the vast emptiness between them, the main house, and the other hotels nearby, "The middle of nowhere seems dangerous to me."

"Please enter the building ma'am." A boorish voice urged, the officer now holding his R5 rifle ushered them towards the stairs that lead up to porch of their cottage.

****

"I don't even have a room!" Simon snarled below his voice to Zach and Mark as the Mercedez Maybach stopped in the parking bays outside the B&B at the heart of Secunda's residential hub.

"Tell me what's going on. What is this about?"

"I need your help to shake the cop." Zach said turning to him with a heavy heart, "Look Simon, I don't want to lie to you so please don't make me."

"Then don't lie, just tell me what's going on?"

"I can't." he sighed, "I just need you to trust me."

Simon shook his head, "You and your father have been very good to me Zach, but this is where I have to draw the line."

"We just need your car, for an hour max."

Mark leaned forward in the back seat, tapping Zach's shoulder as their escorting officer slid into the parking spot beside them on the right.

Simon sighed shaking his head, "You're in over your head here Zachary. This isn't just a misdemeanor that I can sweep away. If you aren't honest with me, I cannot help you and I cannot keep you safe."

"One hour Simon I just need to see something, and I can't have a police officer following us. But I must make sure, we must make sure." Zach said as the officer rounded from his unmarked cruiser.

"Make sure of what?"

"I can't tell you."

"I'm your lawyer, a very expensive lawyer Zach, you can tell me anything."

"Not this." He huffed, "I need one hour, just an hour."

"Is this about who's behind this?" Simon asked as the officer stood by Zachary's door now, "Zachary running around out there makes you an easy target."

He sighed and unclipped his seatbelt, "One hour Simon."

Zach and Mark stepped out to the officer as Simon huffed frustratedly in the car. Mark scanned Zach's face confused still when another car swung into the parking bay behind the officer who stood ushering them to the door of the B&B.

Zain stepped out of the car facing them as his aunty also got out, her face riddled with confusion as they walked behind them into the B&B, where they were greeted by a smiling old man who welcomed them to the small reception desk.

"You go first." Simon said ushering Zain's aunty ahead of him.

"Hi again, my nephew will be staying with me, the ad did say it sleeps two people?" she started to talk while Simon ushered the officer to the side.

"Do me a favor, before we check in – won't you just do a perimeter check for the black pickup or anything out of the ordinary. While we're here we need to know we're safe? I'll keep an eye on them." The officer nodded and headed out the front door, leaving Simon to nod his consent to Zach and Mark as he tossed his keys over.

They quickly exited back outside, rushing to the silver sedan.

"What's going on?" Zain asked stepping out, "Where are you going?"

Zach paused at the driver's door, looking over to Mark who anxiously got into the car, watching for signs of the officer's return.

"We'll be right back." Said Zach getting in and shutting the door.

The car sprung to life when the back door opened to Zain slopping in.

"What the…"

"I'm part of this, for Eric." He said matter-of-factly shutting his door, "So where you go, I go."

"Zain?" his aunty called rushing out, "What's going on?"

"Go! Go! Go!" Zain tapped Zach's shoulder rampantly, as the Maybach swung backwards, veering out just as the officer rushed around the side of the house, watching while the car disappeared down the road.

Standing now beside the fuming aunty, Simon looked to the officer and shrugged, "I don't know …Maybe they needed to buy smokes?"

"In a seven-million-rand car?" the office snarled angrily.

"Zain smokes?" she barked angrily as the officer hurried to his car with Simon rushing behind.

****

In her room inside cottage three, Dekka stood listening into the phone while Colonel Preston gave her the results from the black fibres they'd pulled from Eric's body as he stood in the foyer of the CSI ballistics unit in Pretoria.

She sighed in defeat, "I was almost expecting bad news sir. Every other crime scene was clean so far. What about the license plate, anything come back on that yet?"
"They're busy with it, we do know the car was scrapped about 7 years ago, but that's where it gets murky because the licensing department has eight owners who re-registered in the past three years, all of which have not been digitally captured to the system. But I have a team going through the records as we speak, we'll get something."
"I look forward to hearing from you sir."
"Stay safe Anele. Get some sleep." He said hanging up.

In the open planned entertainment area and kitchen, Maggie sat staring blankly at the early morning infomercials playing on the TV as Carla made her some tea under the watchful eye of the downstairs officer who guarded near the front door. Carla put her cup of tea on the beautiful coffee table as she sat beside her on the couch, "You need to try and get some sleep Maggie, I have something for you to take if you need."
"I don't want to sleep." Maggie stared forward in a daze, "I want to die."
"Don't say that." Tears filled her eyes.
"What have we done Carla?" she looked at her

friend as tears welled, "Look at what one decision has brought on all these people who have died. Why must I live if I have nothing else?"

Carla hugged her against her, and Maggie burst into tears again at the torment of her family home forever being empty. That her brother died without giving her the chance to undo a miserable relationship with him.

"Matt loved you so much." Carla spoke soft, "He had his way, he...was Matty the bull. But he loved you."

"I thought I blamed him." Maggie tried through her snivelling, "I didn't. I never did... now I will never be able to tell him that and make him believe me."

Carla held her tightly as she too felt the tears running down her face - the past ten years flaring through her mind. The pain, the darkness, and the longing to pick up the phone so many times after seeing Zachary to reconnect with everyone, regretting the fear she had that stopped those calls.

****

In Alsbury's sedan Zach clenched the steering wheel nervously.

"So how do you even know any of this?" Mark asked, "I mean you could have said something last night when everyone was accusing you of being the killer."

"I didn't have much opportunity, did I?" Zach huffed, "When you have a lot of money you have a lot of resources."

Mark's eyes narrowed with suspicion, "In this short amount of time? I don't buy that Zach, not for one second."

He shrugged looking away and Mark huffed, tapping him hard on the arm, "You did this before all of this didn't you? You tracked everyone down, didn't you?"

Zach paused with a sigh, "Not everyone, not exactly. I needed to know if everyone's life was ok."

"Bullshit!"

"You're telling me you never wondered?" Zach retaliated, "You never thought about them since you left? Wondered if they were ok, if the trauma they went through matched our guilt? I wanted to know, I had to know."

Mark scoffed in frustration, shaking his head quietly while Zain watched them from the back seat.

"So, if this doesn't pan out, what's next? We're going to dig up Bobby in the middle of the day?" Mark gasped.

"I think the fact that you want to dig up a body takes preference over the time of day it occurs." Zain scoffed sarcastically, looking out the back window to make sure all the detour turns had in fact lost any pursuing officer.

"Eric and Matt said they came back to Secunda to make sure it wasn't Bobby doing this." Zach explained, "But there's others who may have wanted to get some kind of revenge, if it doesn't check out then we finish what Eric and Matty came here to do."

"Who is Bobby anyway?" Zain frowned from the back, "I never understood why Matthew would even think he'd fake his death and do all this. Was he that kind of messed up?"

Mark slumped into his seat as the weight of the past riddled through his mind, replaying the events on the day everything changed.

Exhaustion was setting into detective Malik's posture as he sat slumped on his arm in the chair at the edge of Leigh Anne's hospital bed. Any more coffee would have a negative result to his bowels and the bumpy one-hour flight from Johannesburg to Bloemfontein proved difficult to catch even a moments sleep.

"I want to see them." Leigh Anne said pleadingly behind her tears as she stared at him, "I think we should be together, especially now. God I can't imagine how Maggie feels…or any of them."
Her face ached from the cuts and stitches to her nose and top lip. Her whole body ached from both the bullet wounds and the fall as she lay staring at the ceiling with her tears running down her face.
Malik heaved forward, "Miss Roos, why is someone after you and your friends?"
"I've said everything four times…"
"What are you scared of Miss Roos?" He stood up to the tray at the bottom of her bed, pouring himself water from the jug, "I want to make sure nobody else dies. You've already been attacked, and your friends are thinning out, why won't you just tell me so we can help."
She wiped her face, "I want to see them."
"We can't do that." He said standing with his hands in his pockets.
"Yes, we can." She urged, "Please detective, these are my friends!"

"I mean this with all due respect Miss Roos, but I don't know you, I don't know your work. I don't owe you anything here. I need to do my job."

"I've told you and the first bunch of detectives everything already detective, I don't know what more you want me to say." She burst into tears, covering her face with her hands, "I don't know what you want from me."

He sighed looking down, "I know you've been through a lot, but I want to help you, all of you and I can't do that. I know there is a reason he's after you, but someone needs to be brave enough to tell me so I can help. Let that be you Miss Roos, save your friends because they are refusing to save themselves."

A silence hung and she knew that nothing would ever be the same for her after the attack, the stigma alone in the industry would shatter her dreams of being renowned, not to mention the ghastly scars to her face and body that she wasn't sure would ever heal.

Mark and Zach had protected her all throughout their childhood when her body changed before even Carla's did, and boys would take advantage or throw slanderous comments out about her or Odette.

Maggie was the big sister she never had, and now her world was empty.

She had spent so much of her life trying to run towards something, she had forgotten that she was running away too, and it all flooded back to her, the memories she'd suppressed away behind make-up and hairdo's, designer outfits and shoes – the day she caused their childhood to end.

The memories of that day hurt like a bullet to the heart knowing that she'd never get a chance to apologize for the events that lead to the pain, shame, guilt, and now the deaths of innocent families and people who had nothing to do with what she brought on ten years ago.

"I know you have something to tell me, and I know you're scared. Because I'm scared too Miss Roos." He said softly as she looked to him, "I'm scared because this guy almost killed my partner. He's cutting down people like they mean nothing and so far, nothing can stop him. So, I'm scared Miss Roos that I can't save anyone else, I need to save them. It's my job."

She forced herself into a sitting position, "Detective, take me to my friends and I'll tell you everything. But I don't want to live another day without seeing them, there's too much unsaid for it all to end this way. We were family once. I'll sign whatever you want me to sign, I'll tell you everything. But I need to see them." Malik stared at her, the torment in her eyes was real and he stepped closer.
"Miss Roos, I believe you will. But I want to know this…What you're going to tell me…they already know don't they?"
Her lips quivered and she looked down in shame, nodding slightly.
"Then why would they stay quiet if it could help us catch this guy? What would be so terrible they'd rather watch innocent people die?"

She looked up at him, "I want to see them detective. Then I'll tell you everything."

CHAPTER EIGHT

Sitting in the gardens outside the Scherman House cottages, Carla felt that the sinister events of her reality were relayed to the storm waiting above. A few feet behind her, the two officers stood on watch.

Dekka walked the narrow stone path to Carla's side as the cold air circled.

"Any news?" Carla looked up at her.

"Margaret is still sleeping." She said sitting down beside her, "But there's still no news on Zachary and Marcus."

A smirk broke on her lips, and she looked away hoping Dekka had not caught it.

"Something you want to share with me?"

Carla shook her head, "Just the boys. Nothing changed after all these years."

"You think this is funny? That your friends are out there with a maniac on the loose?" Dekka asked with insult, "Because we cannot protect them if we don't know where they are, so if you know where they went Miss Wilson…"

"I don't know where they are detective." She sighed still smiling, "I'm just smiling because if I don't, I'll break apart and I don't know if I'll ever recover. I think I'm saving that for when this is all over, I can't be useful if I break apart."

Dekka nodded solemnly, "I know the feeling, I've been there."

A silence hung, with Dekka trying to brave the cold that ached at her wounds beneath her clothes.

"Carla, I need to know, do you have any idea where they might have gone?"

"No."

"They're looking for someone aren't they?"

"I don't know detective."

"And if something happens to them, you'll live with not telling me on your shoulders." Dekka said with a shiver, "I know you're tired, and you're scared. Why won't you let me help you?"

Carla brushed her hair aside, "I don't know where they could have gone detective. I'm telling you the truth."

Dekka managed a smile, "I just want to help, I want to end this."

"I know."

Another silence lingered as Dekka watched the dark clouds above slamming into each other, forming the storm that teetered in the cold sky.

"So, have you and Zachary Manson always been a thing?" she finally asked to which Carla frowned turning to her.

"There's an obvious connection between the two of you." She smiled, "I saw how you look at him and how he looked at you. It's clear he's worried about everyone and everything, but there's a little more worry for you."

Carla smiled shrugging, "Yeah its complicated."

"I can imagine." Dekka gave a chuckle.

"What is it that you all are so afraid of?" she asked bluntly, "And I know you won't tell me, but it's bothering me like a splinter that I cannot get out. Why would so many people be afraid of something more than they are about a masked killer."

Carla sighed dropping her head.

"Eventually you will all be arrested, it's a matter of time because my superior knows, like I do, that you are all hiding something. Carla, I need you to understand me when I say this – I really want to help, whatever it is you can let me help you and then maybe nobody else needs to die or get hurt. That poor boy, your friend Odette's fiancé. He'll never walk again, his life is effectively over and he's going to be stuck in this nightmare forever, without escape. I just want to stop it from happening to anyone else."

The wind howled as tears fell down Carla's face, and Dekka put her arm around her, gently hugging her.
"Let me help you, all of you." She said pleadingly, "You need to trust me because its deeper than someone surviving or not, it's about what happens in the years ahead, after all of this. What price is that redemption?"
"I wouldn't…" Carla said choking on her words, "I wouldn't know how to start."
"Anywhere you can." Dekka said turning to her while taking her hands, "Let someone who can help you do that."

****

"How did you find him?" Mark frowned in surprise.
"He never left." Said Zach getting out of the Maybach as the afternoon air howled through the quiet street in front of a brick faced house.

Mark closed his door, "How exactly do you know this?"

Zach sighed and turned to Mark and Zain at the car, "Look when I came into my inheritance, I thought I could do something good you know, and I had a private investigator look into him and this was where he was."

Mark nodded, "That's good of you."

"Hold up, I'm sorry..." Zain huffed, "Since I'm still playing catch up here, just how many people could possibly be doing this?"

Zachary shrugged his shoulders and carefully opened the small gate while heading up to the front door where he knocked.

Inside the bark of a dog sounded as Zain and Mark stepped behind him. The door opened slowly, only halfway. An old woman in a wheelchair blocking the dog between her chair and the door.

"Yes?"

"Mrs. Bekker?" Zach asked cautiously.

"Yes, who are you?" she huffed as the dog continued to bark, "I don't want to buy any bibles."

"We're actually looking for your son, Nathan."

"I have a colourful blanket I would show you." She nodded with a smile, her eyes bright and yet distant at the same time.

"No, I'm sorry I don't think you hear me. we're hoping to see Nathan." Said Zach smiling, "He still lives at home, doesn't he?"

"I don't think..." She sighed looking down, "Are you from Liberty?"

They frowned in confusion.

"Who is it mom?" a deep voice sounded behind her, and the door opened further to a tall, strong 18-year-old teenager.

"Can I help you?" he asked stepping out, "We're not interested in whatever you're selling."
"They came here looking for Nathan." She said struggling to block the old barking dog.
The tall blond with slight freckles frowned looking at the three strangers and then excused himself, quickly helping his mother back inside, closing the door. They listened as he called the dog towards the back and the barking got distant.

The door opened again, and he stepped out, "Sorry, who are you?"
"Old friends of your brother." Said Mark hiding his discomfort.
"I don't recognise you as friends of Nathan, I've met everyone who has ever come here to see him or at least all his friends before the accident."
An awkwardness hung and the boy asked more defensively, "So who are you really? Is this about the money?"
Zachary sighed nervously looking at Mark before digging into his jacket.
"Yeah, in a way it is I suppose…my name is Zachary Manson." He said handing the teenager a certificate – a tax certificate confirming a donation for R2 380 000.00.

The teens eyes lit up and then flew into Zach hugging him very tightly as Mark and Zain gasped in silent surprise.
"I have no way to thank you sir." He stepped back, grabbing Zach's hand and shaking it while he spoke, his eyes filled with tears.
"You don't need to thank me at all."
He smiled, "You have no idea how that money saved us."

Mark and Zain looked at one another confused but the teens face dropped almost immediately as he stepped back.

"I thought you were like the rest of them, showing up out of the woodworks because they heard about money."

"It's alright, I wanted to remain anonymous, I knew it would help your family."

"How did you even know about us?" he stepped back handing the certificate back, "I mean it came through as such a surprise, so randomly and God sent." The teen smiled, "I cannot thank you enough!"

"It's a pleasure." Zach smiled awkwardly trying to avoid the glares from Mark, "I just came by hoping I could have a few words with Nathan."

His face dropped, "I'm sorry to tell you this but Nathan passed away four months ago."

Inside, his mother sat staring at the TV in the lounge, the house smelled almost clinical.

"Mother, this is Zachary Manson." He said smiling. She looked up at him, her eyes distant and she smiled, "Nice to meet you."

Zach smiled and the teen awkwardly ushered them down the passage.

"She's not all where she should be, she's had it pretty rough so she's on a lot of medication too." He explained, "But believe me sir, your donation made the world of difference in our lives, especially Nathan's. If he was alive today it would have made a world of difference meeting you."

****

A coldness filled Zach as he forced a smile before the teen ushered them into the bedroom to the left. "This was Nathan's room." He said heavily while they entered cautiously behind him. The smell profile changed drastically, suddenly the fragrance of antiseptic with undertones of soaps and cleaners filled their noses.

The large rotating bed stood in the centre of the room with the transfer bench beside it and the power assisted quadriplegic wheelchair to the very side sitting empty, cold.

"These were all bought with your money sir." The teen explained, "Thank you."

"What happened?" asked Zach.

"In a nutshell it was the sepsis that got him, it affected his kidneys and liver to an extent that it was beyond any treatment." The teen explained with a strong bravery in his voice, "He couldn't survive it. But he was comfortable in his last days, mainly thanks to you sir."

"I'm sorry to hear that."

"The thing that makes me angry is that it's always been difficult since the accident, it was hard and expensive. Eventually my father just couldn't take the bills anymore, so he left and that's when it got harder and harder to keep my brother healthy and comfortable. It's funny, your donation came at the right time, but I suppose God had other plans for my brother." He paused shaking his head, "It just makes me angry because…never mind it's ugly."

"It's ok, you can tell me." Zach offered a reassuring touch to the teens shoulder. He shrugged, "So much money and effort trying to keep him alive, then my father leaving… It was just…It's been very hard times…then he died anyway. He died when we had the chance to make his life bearable. It just feels so pointless."

A silence hugged the cold room and Zach's guilt ate through him like acid.

"Well, if it's all the same to you sir, I'm trying to get some of this sold so I can take care of my mom." His voice broke the stillness, "Since Nathan she seems to be progressing worse."
"Dementia?" asked Mark, also disgusted with life's unfairness and the guilt he was swimming in. The teen nodded, "It's been a very difficult time having to keep the house going you know, with my mom and everything."
"I can't imagine how difficult this must have been on you, both of you." Zach said solemnly, "I'm so sorry."
He shrugged, "It's not your fault any of this happened, I suppose life had its plan you know?"
"Well, she's lucky to have had you with her through all this." Zain managed a smile.
"I wish she'd see that." He said softly, "Not that I need a thank you, but my whole life has been about my brothers. Nico's death, Nathan's disabilities. Even before the dementia started, I was an afterthought."

The air left the room now, almost suffocating Zach and Mark as Zain could feel their pain radiating loudly behind tears that they both fought to keep at bay.

"But I pray about it, to release myself from feeling resentment. I know it is part of my plan in life, you know? Sorry I shouldn't just be blabbering on and on like this, I don't really get out much having to care for my mother you know?"

"It's alright." Zain offered softly, "Everyone needs to be heard once in a while."

The teen nodded heaving a deep breath, "That is true. Like I said I pray about it a lot, I don't want to be punished some day for all the blame I have against my parents for all of this."

"You blame your parents?" asked Zain.

"All of this is their fault, my mom and dad. It was bound to happen sooner or later that either one or both would end up dead and buried with how reckless they were. So stupid. But Nico and Nathan were the do no wrong twins, got away with everything. They should have been stricter and stopped letting them get away with everything. I mean if you knew them at all, you'd know what I mean."

Mark shook his head confused, "They were reckless?"

The teen gave a soft giggle, "Reckless is an understatement. Look I am 8 years younger than the twins and even I could see that eventually something like this would happen."

Mark looked to Zach and then frowned asking, "I'm sorry to sound blunt but wasn't this as a result of some accident?"

The boy huffed nodding, "It was, but... Nathan would follow Nico anywhere, and it was usually into something crazy. They knew my parents wouldn't touch them, so they abused it, they were the golden boys. Always doing crazy things wherever they went, seeing how far they could push the limits with my parents and anyone else for that matter."

The teens eyes went distant as he recalled their lives before the accident.

"Broken arms, legs, fingers... every month or two new stiches. But still my parents did nothing to stop them, to them it was youthful ignorance or something. I mean sure sometimes my dad would get upset and yell even threaten to whack them with his belt, but then nothing would come of it. No matter what my brothers did, they got off with a warning or some pathetic chore to make up for it. You know they wrote off two motor bikes that they had stolen, on separate occasions. They set our uncles house on fire once during a family visit and they denied it, but I know because I saw them. Once they even put each other in the oven to see how long they'd stay as it heated up!"

Zach turned to Mark in alarm as the teen continued. "You have no idea how many times they'd get home, and I'd be surprised that they were alive. Guess their recklessness finally caught up to them." An uncomfortable silence lingered, and Zach pat him on the shoulder, "I'm so sorry for what your family went through. If there's anything you and your mother need, please call me."

He dug into his jacket and handed him one of Simon Alsbury's cards, "You tell him to put you in touch with me alright?"

"Thank you." He took the card suspiciously frowning, "I appreciate that."

Mark sighed looking to Zach, "We'll get out of your hair then."

They stepped out of the room back into the passage, passing the other room and Mark paused, grabbing Zach's sleeve as he stared into the room.

"Yeah, this was my brother Nico's room. He died in the accident that left Nathan paralyzed from the neck down." Said the teen while Zach and Mark's eyes remained fixed on the picture on the dresser that faced the door – Nathan and his twin with their younger brother all covered in foamy water - washing their dad's pickup – it was the same faces he'd last seen that day when everything spiralled out of control into mayhem that would not leave.

****

Colonel Preston, accompanied by a six-person unit of UCU tactical officers rushed out of the elevators into the basement parking lot of the CSI ballistics unit in Pretoria, and he quickly dialled into his cellular.

Sitting now in the cozy sitting room of the Scherman House cottage, Dekka leaned forward on her knees with her elbows, her chin resting on her hands as she stared at Carla and Maggie. Maggie's face was swollen and puffy from all the crying, her head riddled still in torment and her soul dead to her empty life, cold as she sat with her legs clumped under her and a large mug of coffee in her hands. Between them on the large soft sofa sat a box of tissues.
At the front door, standing outside one of the officers stood smoking.
The silence was deafening as Carla paused to wipe her nose when Dekka's phone rang.
"Colonel." She answered standing up.

"It took 24 hours and a lot of digging but we finally have a break on the black pickup." He smiled as he walked leading them through the parking, "Its last recorded owner was a Corne Brown, who registered ownership of a 2000 Ford Bantam. Brown bought the car from Daan Bekker."

"A Bantam?" she frowned in surprise, "That's not…"

"There's more. Corne Brown and his son Caleb were killed in the same vehicle just over three years ago, in a somewhat mysterious accident."

"Mysterious?"

"Well, his wife tried to claim on his life insurance, assessors determined the brake line had been cut, voiding the claim."

"Alright, I'm following."

"Here's the kicker…" he continued, opening the passenger door to the white van as it filled with his tactical unit, "It's previous owner, Daan Bekker also had a recorded history with the vehicle when it was involved in a MVA 8 years prior, an accident that killed two teenagers."

Dekka frowned nodding, "All in the same car?"

"Exactly, the vehicle was scrapped and basically written off entirely. But it was rebuilt, that's why it's not on the actual registry anymore. Technically the car does not exist."

"Which is why it doesn't look like a Bantam." She nodded as he continued.

"Also, it turns out that Caleb Brown, from the last accident, was also noted as a surviving occupant of the first accident that killed Nico Bekker. And all three of them went to the same school as our victims Jaques Petersen, Odette Gallagher, Eric Jansen and Matthew Jonah."

"Right…" She gasped looking back to the sofa at the two young women.

"We were able to determine after it was scrapped, an individual by the name Robert Minnaar purchased the vehicle shortly after the accident that killed the Brown's, paying by cheque. I've got a tactical team with me and we're heading to the address where the remains of the car were delivered to before it's drastic re-modification. A small body shop in the heart of the central business district. Get this, the body shop hasn't existed or at least has no recorded trading in the past three years but has an active lease with Harmony Rentals. Rent is paid every month, but the business doesn't trade. The last time it traded was three years ago, under then owner Corne Brown."

Her thoughts raced and she stepped to the side entrance door, going out onto the patio, "Have you heard from detective Malik sir?"

"Not since they boarded the flight, they'll be touching down soon at a private air strip just outside Secunda, I've got Clyde waiting for him to debrief and rendezvous with you at the Scherman House. Now listen Anele, I want those three boys found. I want Zachary Manson and Mark Gallagher brought in immediately. All of them have been playing us from the beginning."

"Evidently so." She said clenching the wooden railing angrily.

"Keep a lid on things until we've got the boys, then make an arrest. I'll have the warrant sent through to your cellular."

"Yes sir." She said hanging up, taking a deep breath of the fresh air booming over the vast emptiness.

****

The Secunda cemetery stood in thick gloomy silence on the outskirts of Secunda, the clouds now releasing a faint drizzle as Zach, Mark and Zain stared at the headstones of Nathan Bekker and Nico Bekker, buried side by side.

"This family just suffered one thing after the other." Zach said brushing his long-wet hair aside, "All because of what we did. We did this to them, to everyone."

Zain searched the headstones in the distance, his dark black hair dripping wet while his mind tried to absorb the weight of piecing together details in what Eric had shared with him.

"We didn't do all of this Zachary." Mark said matter-of-factly, a tone and statement he'd never uttered before, surprising even himself.

"I've always carried guilt believing we were the ones responsible for everything that happened, but standing here right now, I don't believe it anymore, not like I used to."

"How can you say that, Mark? Look at what's happening! At all the death and sadness! Look at the lives that have been ripped apart by that day."

"I am looking!" Mark said starting to walk off, "You think I forgot? I haven't forgotten, Odie is dead! My sister is dead, and our friends are dead! I see now how many lives were ruined, shattered because of that day. But I refuse to carry any more guilt. You heard what that kid said, it was a matter of time before Nico or Nathan did something that would kill them! Why should I carry the burden on me if it was bound to happen? I can't do it anymore."

"So, what you just forget about it?"

"No but… Damnit Zach, we were kids. Just dumb kids and some bad stuff happened. But none of us had any control over it how that day went down."

"But we did have control over it, Mark. We left that boy in there to die, we left them to die whether they had a death wish or not." Said Zach sternly staring into his friends' eyes, "We ran when we should have helped. We ran while Nico laying dying… instead of telling those security guys where they were or what happened. I remember reading it took seven minutes for them to even know about Nico and the others. Seven minutes, it could have made a difference."

"So, what is the point then Zach? Why are we fighting to stay alive? Why not just let this killer rip us to shreds and accept our fate? Not me Zach, hearing what that kid just said about his brothers makes me wonder about a lot of things." Mark sighed brushing the water from his face, "It tore us apart and for what? They were daredevils and that other guy was a runaway nobody wanted."

"What are you saying? That he deserved it? That all of them had this coming?"

"I'm not saying that!" he scoffed, "But what else could we have done? Yes, we ran, but there was nothing we could have changed, not really."

"We could have stayed. We *should have* stayed!" A silence hung between them until Zain called out from the side of them.

"I found it! I think this is him." He said looking down at the headstone - the light of day began to lessen, and a heavy downpour released.

"So… what's the plan here Zach? His been in there for three years, how will we know if it's not his body?" asked Mark.

"I don't know."

"Well, you dragged us to that house thinking it was a cripple or whatever, surely now you have some idea what we're doing here?"

"I thought Nathan might be helpful in tracking down Wessel, he's the only other one from that day that my guys couldn't find."

Zain shook his head in frustration, "So why are we here then?"

"I don't know anymore." Zach sighed shaking his head, "I don't know ok, I don't know what we're doing here, or what to do next! I just want this over!"

"Then we need to get back to Carla and Maggie." Mark sighed in defeat, "We're out here wasting time, we're not getting anywhere. We need to look into finding Wess…."

Seeing a folded white paper in the withering flowers by the headstone as the two old friends clashed, Zain carefully knelt to avoid the mud on his knees, resting his hand on the granite block reading 'Robert 'Bobby' Minnaar' as he plucked up the folded paper.

"What is that?" asked Mark as Zain stood up, nervously unfolding a picture.

Zach froze, his eyes not prepared for what they saw in the picture and Mark immediately looked to him, unsure of his reaction to the photograph of a man and woman, bloodied - dead inside a vehicle with the words written below it in black ink:

I KILLED THEM

Zain frowned to the rain beading down his face, "Who are these people?"

****

Dekka went outside following the call from her superior and from the raised porch, instructed the officer to cover the front and side entrances to their small cottage, to get on their radios to inform those in the road to block traffic on either side, check all pickups or suspicious vehicles, individuals and notify her of *any* black pickups.

She called her partner again, watching as the darkness sunk over the vast emptiness around the Scherman House.

"Go for Clayton." He answered stepping out of the small Cessna 182T, carefully aiding Leigh Anne with the umbrella down the few steps as thunder roared above in the dark sky.

"You landed?"

"I just landed yes, we're about forty-five minutes from your location. And I have the model with me." he said as they stepped to the runway. Leigh Anne rolled her eyes and pulled her arm free from him, using her hand to cover the other arm that hung in a sling.

"You haven't received the Colonel's briefing yet?"

"No, I see Clyde Lovington is waiting with a car, why what's going on?"

Dekka sighed shaking her head nervously, "Clayton, I have a bad feeling about these kids. Call me when you've up to speed, but be careful, there's more going on here than meets the eye."

****

Dekka closed the side entrance to the deck that overlooked a large dark pond, and took a deep breath, re-entering the lounge with a bright smile, putting her hands together with a subtle but prominent clap as she walked, "Ladies."
They looked up at her, she asked, "Do the names Nico Bekker and Caleb Brown ring any bells?"
Everything about their posture and facial expressions changed and Dekka sighed shaking her head, "I figured it would ring a bell."
Carla turned to Maggie nervously, then back to her, "What do you mean?"
"Don't play dumb with me Miss Wilson, I saw your reaction. You know them, we know that you all knew each other back in the day, didn't you?"
"They were seniors in our school when we were kids."
"What about Robert Minnaar? Do you know who that is?" Dekka pressed.

****

The UCU's unmarked van was parked outside the dilapidated fencing that aimed to keep trespassers from the small lot in front of the old store that had been boarded up, it's exterior walls covered in graffiti that stood out on its faded, long since painted walls as the city sky saw the last of the sun.

Having already checked the front entrance and discovered that it was completely sealed shut on both the outside and inside, Preston followed three of the tactical officers to the left side of the building while the other four went around the right side.

Both teams circled and met at the back, where a large metal blue door stood with two thick chains intertwined with nine different locks ensuring the chains' place.
"I'll get his open, I need 5 minutes." Said one of the officers quickly holstering his weapon, lowering down his small black bag and digging for tools.
"What about here?" Preston asked, gun in hand, nodding to the small window that had wood strips nailed over it just a few feet from the door.
Quickly placing his weapon away, the other officer pulled a short crowbar out and shoved it in between the wood and walls to pry away the wooden boards.

****

With the black sedan parked a distance from where they disembarked, detective Malik and Leigh Anne huddled beneath the umbrella and carefully wade across the black runway where the rain bounced off the tar at the force in which it fell while the pilot taxied the plane towards the hangars behind them.

Malik opened the backdoor and assisted Leigh Anne in as fast he could, slamming it shut as he round to the other side.

Not realizing that the car's indicator lights flashed as he hopped over the puddles forming, her screams tearing out from inside the car forced him to rush for the door, only to realize it would not open. He dropped the umbrella and lowered to the passenger window where he saw detective Clyde laying head back with his throat slashed.

"Get me out!" Leigh Anne cried, hitting the window when the roar of the black pickup's engine flared, its headlights beaming suddenly out of the darkness from the other side of the tarmac.
He grabbed at the door handle, desperately pulling with no success, rushing to the driver's door, and trying the same as the pickup ripped across the blacktop through the downpour towards them.

"Alright you son of a bitch!" he said turning while unholstering his Glock 19 from under his jacket, firing out at the roaring pickup. With all fifteen rounds spent and the beast still in approach, Leigh Anne screamed and huddled down as the detective flung himself to the side. The front of the black pickup rammed into the side of the sedan – forcing it six feet to the side, its windows shattering, and its airbag detonated into the dead detective's body.

Malik rolled to his knees, quickly digging for his next cartridge as the rain drenched down. The pickup reversed, its thick tyres skidding as it backtracked and spun to a skew stop, facing him.

As desperately as he could between the rain and blood from his cut elbows running down his hand,

Malik got the new cartridge in while stumbling to his feet while the tyres skid forward towards him.
He fired again, five shots but the window would not shatter, and he ran back towards the smashed sedan.
"Hey! Are you ok?" he yelled in, as the pickup roared with its sliding on the runway in it's sharp, skidding turn to chase him.
"Give me your hand!"
The tyres burned as the body of the pickup hopped, slashing through the rain towards him and the car again.

"Shit stay down!" he said running again, firing as best he could at the wheels with no luck as it chased after him across the runway.
Taunting him as he ran, its engine bellowed out, all cylinders fired, and it came just inches from him before it would slow and repeat the same terrifying taunt as he tried to zig zag towards the hangar.

At the crumpled sedan, Leigh Anne used the back seat belt to clear the jagged glass as she began to climb out.
With his legs on fire now, Malik knew he would not make the hangar with the pickup on his heels, playing with him and his agony. He was 9 meters from the hangar when he felt his legs cramping, giving in beneath him.
"Not like this!" he cried pushing himself with the last of his might, "Not like this!"
His body went down, and the wheels of the pickup crunched over him, skidding to a stop just a few meters from the hangar.

The driver's door opened, and the dark figure stepped out, the rain slicking over its hood effortlessly as the big boots walked over to where the detective lay.

The left side of his body was mangled and crushed, with bones jutting out while the rain and blood flooded around him - his hand on his gun, finger twitching as he gargled for life.

"Hush now." It said lowering to take the gun, the detectives final breath drowned by the puddle of red at his face.

It looked back up to the crumpled sedan where Leigh Anne pulled the dead detective free from the deployed airbag.

She tugged at his dead weight, sprawling his body out to the side, quickly reaching for his gun behind his soaked black jacket only to find his holster was empty. She looked up as the door to the pickup closed.

"No!" she cried as she ran towards the small control office on the other side of where their plane had sheltered for the storm - the pickup's tyres tearing into the road in its turn.

"Help me!" she screamed - the cars in the lot came into sight, rushing around the back of the hangar along the fence – the small control tower sitting up two flights of stairs.

She forced open the gate in the fence and entered the parking lot where only three cars stood getting pelted by the downpour, at the very top against the black sky the lights of safety.

She reached the metal stairs, breathlessly trying to find the power to push through the immense pain to keep heading up, when the figure entered the gate. "No!" she cried, scrambling up the stairs.

****

The officers quicky removed the locks, having already picked five by the time the window boards were removed and after instructing them to continue, Preston moved to the small window. "It's concrete sir." Said the officer hitting it with the crowbar, "Someone closed it with concrete." Preston shook his head angrily and head back to the door where three locks remained closed.

The wait felt eternal, and he knew that whoever had gone through the trouble of sealing the windows with concrete certainly wanted whatever was inside to remain private and protected. The team began to undo the thick chains, the scraping of the chains against each other and the metal door was loud, scratching and clanging in the droning of the usual inner-city noise as night set in.

****

Carla sighed looking down and Maggie shifted forward to place her mug down on the table, "Why are you asking us about Bobby?"
"Who is he?" Detective Dekka pushed, "And don't bullshit me, I want the truth."

Carla frowned, "Bobby's dead. He died about three years ago when he was 17."

"Say again?" she cocked her head, "Robert Minnaar, you're sure?"

"Yes, Bobby used to be a good friend to us." Explained Carla anxiously, "Why?"

Dekka's mind began to race, "And he died three years ago you say?"

"Yeah, when he was seventeen." Carla leaned forward worriedly, ""We had all basically lost touch with each other when it happened, but his mother included us all in his funeral notice. He was out driving on his motorbike when he got hit by a car, he didn't make it."

"My parents went to the funeral." Maggie added in a solemn whisper, "My mother and his were still relatively close."

Dekka paused nodding, then looked to them again, "Do either of you know what happened to the driver of the vehicle that hit your friend?"

"No." Carla sighed looking to Maggie.

"It was a hit and run, someone in a pickup who fled the scene. I don't know if they ever found the guy." Dekka raised her phone, walking out of the lounge again.

****

With both thick chains removed, the officer picked the doors lock and then stood up to his Colonel, "That's it, sir we are ready to breach."

"Yes, breach." Preston instructed as he took out his gun again.

They lined the walls on either side of the door as the first officer stepped in front of the door, readying to open it.

He looked back at his Colonel who nodded and with a swift flick at the handle, the large metal door flung inwards, and the six-man tactical unit flurried into the dark building with the torches from their rifles breaching the stale blackness.
Inside the van, on the seat in the back Colonel Preston's cell rang.

He was the last to enter when the blast went off, a pre-rigged trap for any intruders that sent flames sprawling into all directions along with the numerous nails that exploded out of the large blue drums that lined the interior walls – ensuring that the blast would not only be forced inwards and consume every inch of the building in flames and deadly debris, but that the walls too would crack, burst and buckle.

Riddled in nails, with his back and legs alight in the engulfing flames, Preston's screams lowered as he lay dying with his skin sizzling. His head fell with his eyes staring at the wall as the flames shredded through the pictures, drawings and plans the slayer had meticulously plotted out.
The walls groaned loudly then collapsed, the fuel containers in the ceiling bursting on impact with the ground – a final and deleting scorch.

****

"Help me!" Leigh Anne cried breathlessly, reaching the last of the steps towards the tower with the figure making its way up in a slow and teasing pace, only several steps behind her, the scythe grinding along the handrails.

"Help!" she cried pushing through the burning agony up the final steps.
"Yes, call them. Bring them out here." It mocked behind her.
She reached the final three steps, and leapt up to reach the door, barging in before slamming it shut behind her.

"Help me!" she cried to the three men and one woman sitting there in alarm. The pilot of their charter rushed towards her in alarm, "What in the hell is going on?"
"He's out there! He killed the cop!" she cried rushing away from the door, "Please call the police!"
The owner of the airstrip, an 80-year-old man by the name of Earl tapped his wife as he and the control operator hurried towards her, his movements slow and his back hunched, "Tish you better radio this in."
"No!" she warned as the pilot and owner were about to open the door, "Don't let it inside, it'll kill everyone!"
The control operator, a tall 65-year-old with a grey goatee, took her hands, "Ma'am come take a seat while we wait for the police to arrive."
"Do you have a gun?" she asked pushing him away, "We have to protect ourselves, there's no getting out of here."
"Earl, get the gun!" his wife said nodding with the phone in her hand. She was a short, very thin

woman with greying brown hair who knew terror and could see it in how the young girl trembled from her core.

He hurried to the cabinets as the pilot pressed against the glass to see outside.
"There ain 't nobody out here." He said looking through the rain to the darkness, only the runway lit by the lights of the hangar shining out, he then saw the crashed sedan.

"Oh hell! It looks like something went down on the runway! An accident of some kind, that agent's car is all banged up. How far are the police?" He asked turning away from the window to face them when it shattered over his shoulder, the figure reaching in and grabbing him, pulling him outward.
The operator gasped, rushing to pull him back in as he fought to keep his brace against the frame.

"Earl!" his wife cried out, dropping the phone, and rushing to her husband in alarm. Leigh Anne cried into her hands, watching in horror as it pulled and pulled the pilot, knowing nothing would keep it out, keep it at bay or stop it.

The scythe slashed out of his back, slicing the operator's cheek and the pilot fell limp as the scythe retracted, the screams from the owner's wife echoing the small room and Leigh Anne rushed away, immediately seeking another way out.
"Knock, knock!" It mocked leaning in by the window. The operator scrambled backwards on the floor, up against the desk as the figure hoisted itself inside.

The owner slammed the six-shot chamber into place and raised the revolver, his hands and arms shaking while he fired - five shots at the figure hacking down at the operator as the shots hit around it.

"Stay back!" the owner warned aiming the revolver at its dark face, "Get out of here!"

The figure walked towards him, and he fired the final shot, hitting the darkness beneath the face and the figure flung backwards to the floor.

"You got him!" his wife gasped, grasping Leigh Anne as they huddled to the side.

"I think I got him in the neck." Said Earl shaking while he slowly stepped forward.

Leigh Anne stood up shaking her head, "Reload your gun!"

He stared at her, then at the gore within his small control room as tears welled in his old eyes. The figure sprung up, immediately grabbing the old man by the neck, and raising him off his feet.

"No!" his wife screamed as Leigh Anne tried to pull her towards the door.

"Come on! We need to get the hell out of here!"

"Leave him alone!" she cried, pushing herself free from Leigh Anne's grip and rushing to help her husband.

Leigh Anne scrambled to the door, back into the down pour, looking back as the old man's neck jolt to the side before his body dropped down. She screamed and continued her rush down the stairs. Frantically trying not to lose her balance and keep going while straining to see through the rain, Leigh Anne hurried down the slippery stairs.

"Hey!" it called from the top - she turned to look back up. It had Earls wife up in the air over its head in both hands, tossing her body down.

Leigh Anne screamed, trying to cover and block with her arms, but the old lady's body slammed into her - sending her over the handrails - four meters down.

The figure could hear the crack of the two bodies hitting the ground and stepped down the stairs, peering over where she had fallen. Her body was on top of the old lady, and she rolled over gasping to regain the air that was knocked out of her as a pool of blood ran out into the puddles.

****

Dekka's eyes were wide as she leaned against the kitchen counter listening into her phone in disbelief, Maggie and Carla huddled nearby anxiously.
"I understand, please call me the minute you have anything." She turned to face them, allowing the news of the explosion and shock to settle into her mind.
"What's going on?" asked Maggie, "Are we going to be ok here?"
Just then the door slammed open, and they all jumped in fright.

"Zach!" Carla said rushing to him, "Where have you guys been?"
She clung against him as Mark and Zain entered with the officer shutting the door.

"The patrol cars radioed in that they were coming." The short but stocky officer explained, his arms and thighs bulbous beneath the uniform from his time a scrumhalf in minor league rugby.

"Thank you, officer Hyke." Dekka rolled her eyes, turning to face the young adults again.

"Are you ok?" Carla stepped back realizing that her hug and question went nonresponsive, "Mark? Zain? What's going on?"

"Where were you? What happened?" said Dekka rounding to face them as Mark tossed his wet jacket to the rack.

"We found something." Explained Zain realizing then that neither Mark nor Zach had spoken a word since they rushed back to the car from the graveyard, "It's a picture."

Zach looked down shaking his head, "We went to Bobby's grave. It was left there…for us."

"What picture?" Maggie asked worriedly watching them.

"He knew we'd go there." Zach said staring blankly at their faces, "He planned all of this…"

"Bobby's grave?" Dekka pressed, "As in Robert Minnaar's grave?"

"Zachary, please! You need to show them." Mark said putting his hand on his friend's shoulder.

Zachary nodded, forcing himself to withdraw from the spiral in his mind as he dug into his pocket and handed the picture to Carla.

Her blue eyes scanned it, immediately recognising them as she stepped back in alarm as Dekka grabbed it from her.

"Who is this?" she asked looking at the picture and the words below it in black ink.

"That's Zach's parents." Maggie said looking over the detective's shoulder and up at him in confused alarm.

CHAPTER NINE

The rain drizzled down heavily on the grass, rushing beneath the raised cottages and under into its dark shadows like rivers as the sky above groaned to the thunder that followed each vicious lighting strike that tore open the darkness around their cottage.

Inside the air was thick while they all sadly recounted their story about the events ten years ago.

"We swore to never talk about it again." Zach said softly as the lounge rang in silence, "None of us knew how bad it all was until the next morning." Squeezing Maggie's hand, Carla wiped her eyes, "Stefan died before they could get him to the hospital."
"And Nico…he was crushed, he couldn't be saved." Added Mark.
"Nathan was pinned from the chest down…everything was broken." Zach explained solemnly, "Caleb and Wessel made it, but they moved away with their family a month or so after." Silence screamed as Dekka soaked in their story, and she leaned forward, "What about the other boy?"
"We don't know." Said Mark softly, "There was never any talk or reports about him. It's like he wasn't ever there."
"We figured because of the little we knew about him, that his family just took him for a runaway." Said Carla leaning forward.

Dekka heaved a heavy sigh and stood up, "Is that everything?"

"That's everything." Zach wiped the tears away. Zain, now with the full story scouring through him sat forward almost breathlessly, putting his head into his hands.

After a moment of pacing, Dekka turned to face them again.

"Sixteen kids went in that day and only twelve walked out, yet nobody knew you were there? Nobody said anything?" The detective said walking, thinking.

"What about Caleb and his brother Wessel? Why did they never say anything?"

"I don't know." Said Carla wiping her face, "I've wondered that for ten years."

"Me too." Maggie said softly.

Dekka shook her head in confused disbelief, "And did anyone other than you, know about the other boy?"

An ominous uneasiness lingered as they all looked to each other, shaking their heads in silence.

Dekka huffed frowning, "So sixteen kids go in and twelve walk out, then through the years and with the recent killings, eleven who knew but never said anything are dead. Leaving five of the original sixteen." She turned to face them, "Four are in this room, leaving only one nobody can account for."

"Wessel Fouche." Said Maggie clenching her fists when Mark cleared his throat.

"One night after my dad's funeral, Bobby phoned the house, he was really scared." He spoke softly, "He said that Wessel got hold of him and made some threats or something."

"What?" Carla frowned, "You never thought to tell us that?"

"We weren't exactly speaking Carla. By that point we'd all basically gone our own ways." Mark defended, "Besides I left the next day to the Cape with my uncle."

Zach shoved him angrily, "You asshole! You suspected him?"

"No, I didn't." he defended angrily, "I only remembered that right now!"

Maggie sat forward, "Detective, you were asking about Bobby earlier, why?"

Dekka sighed looking down to her phone, the last twenty minutes feeling like an eternity as she waited for dispatch to call her back.

"You said it was a pickup at the hit and run…well it turns out that the pickup at the mall in Midrand is the same pickup that rolled that day out in the fields ten years ago…"

Zach turned to her in confused alarm, "What?"

"We traced its registry, and now with your story I know for sure it ties into what we found. It's been severely modified." She paused, "It's also the same vehicle that Caleb and his father were travelling in when they were pushed off the road and killed three years ago."

Carla's blue eyes glared up in chilling alarm as Zach stood up facing the detective.

"This has been in motion for years. He's been watching, waiting…"

"Why now? Why start with your and Jacques' parents?" Dekka shook her head puzzled, "What makes now the time to come after you all?"

"So, Wessel is the one doing all of this?" Maggie said finally breaking the silence, her voice riddled with anger.

Detective Dekka looked to her phone again, then back up at him, unsure of what to say, trying to find words and thoughts in the chaos of the information within her mind.

The front door opened, the bulky officer stepped in, "We're having issues reaching team two on the radio."

A chill slithered in behind him as the cold wet night air circled into the house.
Dekka sighed nervously and instructed, "Send officer Cambouris out to check. But let's assume the worst so radio team three and let's be alert and ready for anything."
His head nod above his thick neck and he shut the door again while she unholstered her side arm and locked the door.
"We're all going to die." Maggie said staring blankly to the ground. Zain reached over and took her hand.
Dekka's cell phone toned, it was detective Malik.

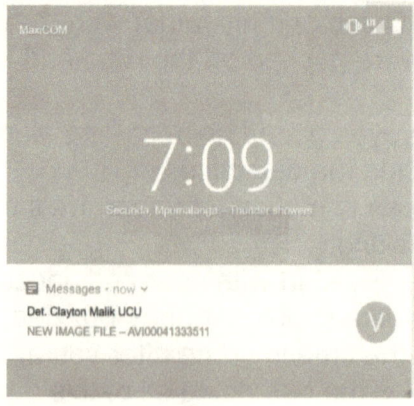

She stepped out of the room clicking to open the message, stopping in her tracks as the chilling image of his body filled her screen and as her hand went up to gasp.

Carla's phone also toned and from inside Maggie's handbag a notification too.
"What is it detective" Asked Mark moving between the two sofas towards her as Maggie dug out her phone and Carla clicked on the image from an unknown sender.
"Oh my god." She gasped looking up in alarm as Maggie too jolted up from the couch holding her phone up.

Zach and Mark both stepped forward staring at the phone, a snapshot of a bloodied Leigh Anne laying in a back seat, hands tied, and her mouth bound, her eyes staring up at the camera operator in silent screams.
"Who is that?" asked Zain as the chill of fear riddled beneath his wet clothes.
Dekka glanced at the phone in her rush towards the front door, hurrying out into the cold.

****

"Wessel's got Leigh Anne!" Maggie cried covering her mouth as she repeated it over and over in disbelief, stumbling onto the couch.
Their phones toned again.
"Open it!" Mark urged as he slunk down beside her, taking her phone to help while Zain, Zach and Carla huddled over the phone in Carla's hands.

"Oh god he's here!" Maggie exclaimed staring at the image on her phone - a snapshot of their cottage taken at a distance.

"We need to be ready." Zach said rushing towards the front door, "Mark, check all the doors and windows, Carla get knives! Get whatever you can for protection."
He rushed outside, the cold air stinging through his wet clothes.
"Detective Dekka?" he called out, not seeing her or officer Hyke as he walked out towards the car.

Mark had just began to double check the latch on the side entrance when the large bulky officer stepped to the door, rapping against it.
"I'm not able to reach anyone on the radio, where's detective Dekka?" he said pushing in as Mark again shut and locked the door.
"Outside with you?"

The night was silent around the two cottages, with only the lights from the Scherman House in the distance. Zach carefully investigated the remaining undercover police car, but it was empty.

The wind howled as it tore through the blackness beneath the cottages from behind the stairs, and he felt eyes peering from all the shadows.
"Zach? What are you doing out here? We need to get back inside!" Dekka urged rushing towards him from the side where the empty cottage stood between them and the main house.
"He's here detective, he knows where we are!"
"I figured! I can't reach anyone either! I've asked officer Hyke to check the..." she started pulling him

with her when she froze as the roar of the black pickup's engine filled the air and they spun around.

Bursting out of the darkness with no lights on, the pickup tore through the flowers and shrubs of the beautiful garden towards them, its engine revving high.
Without hesitation detective Dekka shoved Zachary behind her and immediately started to fire at the pickup.

Officer Hyke rushed out of the front door, his rifle high, firing at the black beast as he walked out to the lawn. The bullet's sprayed the vehicle without success as it tore on, with Dekka and Zach leaping out of its way.

Officer Hyke flung himself out of the way as the front of the pickup crashed through the small stairs, bounced against the wall of the house - over the shrubs in the garden bed and then rolled onwards slowly, coming to a stop a distance away in the field.

"Get inside!" Dekka said shoving Zach towards the house while instructing officer Hyke to follow her to the vehicle.
He rushed to where the steps once were as the front door flung open with Mark and Maggie coming outside.

"Zach, are you alright?" asked Maggie watching while the two officers head towards the darkness where the pickup hummed.

Inside, Zain tapped a rolling pin to his hand and Carla took out three of the largest knives she could find from the kitchen drawer.

"Yeah, I'm fine." Said Zach carefully moving through the shards of wood and reaching up, "Give me a hand, will you?"

Mark knelt and reached out for his hand as Carla and Zain rushed around the counter towards the door.

Officer Hyke flung open the driver's door to find a rock laying by the pedals and Leigh Anne stuffed in the gap behind the seats begging behind the tape over her mouth.

With Zain and Carla just inches from the door, the banging of the figure's heavy boots on the floor behind them shook the wooden flooring, they flung around just as the blackness slammed between them - sending them both to the ground with their weapon utensils.

Mark pulled Zach upwards when Maggie screamed. Mark turned the figure milled into him, sending him and Zach down into the broken wooden debris below.

Maggie screamed again rushing for the door when the scythe slashed in front of her, the figure kicking it shut just as Zain tried to rush out – the blow forcing him inside again and Carla tore open the curtains.

"Maggie! Run!" she screamed banging against the window when the scythe swung and tore into her stomach.

Using its hook like blade, the figure plucked her closer as blood spooled from her open mouth.

"No!" Carla cried while Zain tried desperately to pull open the door – it's interior handle now useless. Maggie's body swung, slumping up against the window when the figure ripped the blade out of her stomach – her blood spraying to the window where Carla's hands hit the glass.

As her friends' dying eyes stared at her, Carla screamed through her tears "No!"
The figure gutted the blade through Maggie's back twice more, and with a final cough of dark blood, Maggie dropped to the ground.
Carla looked up into the black gauze, her face riddled with complete rage when bullets tore out - Zain diving her down r to the ground.

Firing rapidly from his rifle, officer Hyke sprayed the front of the cottage as the dark hooded figure scrambled along the porch - three shots finally spraying blood from the figures arm - flinging it to the wall and tumbled over the side railing to the darkness below.

"Are you alright?" Dekka said moving carefully through the shattered beams and poles towards them with her sidearm up beside her as officer Hyke hurried on to where the body had fallen over, carefully checking beneath the cottage as he moved along the side.
"We're ok." Zach confirmed pulling Mark up to his feet.
Zain hauled Carla up - together they rushed to the door, pulling, and banging at it while frantically calling for Dekka, Mark and Zach.

Pulling himself up to the porch with ease, Mark rolled onto the porch moving towards the door before he even stood up - stopping in nauseated horror at the sight of Maggie's dead body in a pool of blood.

"Hello?" officer Hyke's knock rapped at the side entrance, to which Zain quickly rushed as Mark tried to open the door by Carla.

"He's wounded! The trail leads to this door." Hyke said looking at the trail of blood with Zain pulling the door open for him.

Officer Hyke lowered his rifle as he stepped inside when from behind, the figure opened fire from detective Malik's gun while it climbed the steps. The shots tore into the officer's thick tactical vest, with one shot hitting his shoulder as he turned, sending the rifle to the ground – the officer's big body jolting backward with each shot until the figure stopped, raised its arm, aiming directly at the officer's face and fired three bullets to it.

"Shit I can't get up! I can't grip it!" Zach moaned desperately trying to grip the wet patio as he dropped and turned to the detective, "Get up into my hand!"

She quickly put her foot in his clenched hands. Zain scurried around the wall towards the front just as Mark kicked the door inwards, "We need to get out of here!"

"Get down!" Mark said, flinging himself back outside with the figure rounding into the living room, firing the last two shots of the clip. Still in Zachs hands, Dekka forced through the pain of her wounds to get on to the patio when a bolt of lightning tore through the sky with a loud crack causing her to flinch and almost slip.

Mark rushed for the door and the figure slipped the new cartridge into the gun, firing three shots again, forcing Mark back outside to the deck.

From the floor, Mark looked up just as the figure ran, kicking hard into his side and sending him flying into the detective sending them both down the side.

"Run!" screamed Carla, darting up the stairs with Zain as the figure chased behind them, slipping the gun back inside the thick coat.

They slammed the door to the bedroom shut, but with one hard slam of its shoulder the figure burst through, and Carla screamed - the scythe slicing the air just inches from her as she scrambled over the bed.

"Get away from her!" Zain grabbed it by arm and punching as hard as he could.

"No!" it snarled, grabbing him by the neck and began ramming his head into the wall, again and again.

Carla scrambled to the dresser, grabbing the provided hairdryer, quickly scrambling over the bed and wrapping its chord around the figure's neck, pulling him backwards away from Zain who propped down to the ground gasping, holding his head to stop the disorientation.

The figure reached over, grabbing a handful of Carla's hair over its shoulder, and chucking her into the dresser.

She screamed when her body slammed into the mirror – shattering it as the figure chopped down at her with the scythe - just missing.

Mark cried out into the pouring rain, his hands over a shard of wood jutting into his thigh and Zach rolled to his feet, quickly huddling by the detective who lay in pain from her wounds.

Carla grabbed the potpourri vase from the bedside table, smashing it into the figure's face and flinging a kick into its side. With all her might she screamed as she threw a strong right punch that landed hard to the mask and she tackled into it up against the dresser, her hands fighting to rip off the mask when a punch from its shredding knuckleduster forced her to whelp and grab at her side as she stepped back, and it raised the scythe above her.

"Hey! Dickhead!" Zach snarled from the doorway, running in with a thick piece of the stairs in his hands, slamming it hard into its head with every ounce he had, swinging again and again anywhere he could land a blow as the figure stumbled backwards into the dresser – the scythe falling to the ground.

Mark cringed and his body bent as he yanked the wood from his leg, gripping at the wound in agony while detective Dekka carefully pulled herself to her feet - the rain pouring over them.
"They're inside!" Mark groaned as she stumbled over the debris past him to the side of the house, trying not to slip.

Zach flung backwards into the wall with a bang as the figure reached into its long black leather coat, pulling out the large hunting blade.
Carla tried to run for the door, but it slashed at her with an effortless swing, and she stepped

backwards, ducking down - the blade tearing through the air just inches from her scalp. Again, she tried scrambling for the door, screaming for help but the figure grabbed her by the hair again, and flung her.

She slammed into the window hard, her body forcing the blinds to crash down -her weight cracking the glass and buckling the wooden criss-cross frame.
Still hazy, Zain stumbled over Zach pulling him to his feet as the figures boot slammed into Carla's chest sending her through the window, slamming down to the mud below.

"Carla!" Zach yelled as Zain pulled him out of the room with the figure angrily giving chase. Rushing over to Carla who lay limp in the mud, detective Dekka quickly felt at her neck for a pulse.
They scurried down the stairs, grabbing at the front door that would not budge as the figure prowled down the stairs.

"Mark!" Zach called banging on the window while Mark rolled up onto the porch on his side near Maggie's body.
The figure swung the blade and Zach flung himself aside sending the figure's blade smashing outward as Mark slammed against the door, trying desperately to open it.

"Run!" yelled Zach grabbing Zain – with both stalling in alarm as they spun towards detective Dekka who stood aiming, drenched in water that ran down even the barrel of her gun.

"Now you freeze you son of a bitch!" she snarled through her teeth, firing six shots one after the other, with four hitting into the dark figure, slinging its body backwards.

Outside, one of the bullets shattered through the door, hitting Mark's left shoulder and he cried out as he fell to the ground.
The figure dropped to the stairs.

****

Silence filtered through the cottage, the ringing in their ears subdued to the sound of their own gasping breathlessness and the drumming of the downpour.
They stood up again, Zain's eyes fixed on the motionless dark mass and Zach turned to the detective.
"Thanks."
"Just doing my job." She said holstering her weapon and stepping forward when the front door smashed open with a flash of lighting, and they all jolted in fright.
Mark heaved breathlessly, holding his shoulder as he looked to the figure on the stairs then back to them in alarmed confusion.

"Don't worry we got the son of a bitch this time." Dekka said almost grinning as she limped towards the figure.
"Are you sure?" Mark said leaning against the wall.
"Son of a bitch killed my partner." Dekka said kicking at the dark mass's leg - hard.

"Is he dead?" asked Zain anxiously, "Like properly dead?"

Zach stumbled to help Mark who collapsed against the wall, "Are you ok?"

Mark moaned, "Where's Carla?"

"She's alright." Dekka said wincing as she lowered to kneel beside the body, "Will probably have a killer headache but she's ok, found her out in the mud. Your friend Leigh Anne is safe too, she's in the pickup tied up."

A rush of relief filled them as they lowered Mark to the chair as he clutched his leg in agony. Zach turned towards the side entrance, "I need to help Carla!"

"Let's see who's under this mask." She said tossing the hunting knife aside as Zach rushed outside. Zain lowered to help Dekka who tugged the long black coat to turn the heavy body facing up.

She pulled at the coat, prying it open to reveal a set of two bullet proof vests and another thick padding beneath it, inside the coat holsters for all its weapons.

"It's just a man." She said almost in disbelief, seeing the neck of the unstoppable slayer was that of a white man. Mark scowled in disgust, "Just a man." She felt her fingers trembling as she placed them under the rim of the thick gauze mask, its metal cold.

Outside the engine from the black pickup roared and its headlights flared on against the house, lighting up their faces as it revved loudly.

"What the hell?" Said Mark rushing to the window.

"Who the hell is that?" Zain exclaimed, "Is that Zach?"

The engine lowered to an idle, humming when an agonizing scream filtered through the rain.
"Carla!" Mark said rushing to the door again, frivolously trying to open it.
"Screw this!" said Dekka, readying to fire out of the shattered window when the attacker lunged up from the stairs, its jagged knuckleduster deep against her side as her gun fell to the ground.

The attacker twisted his fist - grinding the nails and screws against her ribs and she screamed out. Mark and Zain barely had time to react when he attacked, swiftly slamming his foot up into Zain sending him backwards into the kitchen counter. He then punched Mark who blocked, the knuckleduster tearing open his forearm.

The attacker then kick-stomped at Mark's wounded leg before grabbing him while shoving him backwards into the front door with a bang as he slammed his elbow to Marks face in two rapid blows before standing back - ramming him into the door again, and again. By the fourth time, the wooden door cracked, and Mark flopped to the ground on his knees gasping.
"Hush now." sneered the attacker, launching a kick to his ribs, sending him down without air.

The masked attacker flung his opened coat away and he turned to detective Dekka who reached for her gun with her trembling, bloody hand.
"I don't think so." He said swooping down and grabbing the gun.

He turned his attention to the window where the black pickup stood rumbling, its headlights bright against the gauze mask.

Then looked back down to Mark who lay almost balled up against the wall, and back to the detective as she gasped holding her side, her body shivering to the cold of death that began to crawl over her body. He cocked his head to a tilt watching her through the mask, aiming the gun first at her face, then at her chest -toying with her.

"Goodbye detective." he said aiming for her head. With a yell, he lunged forward but Zain already had the hunting blade gripped in both hands, driving it deep into the attacker's side.
The attacker screamed and slammed the handle of the gun in his fist into the side of Zain's face, sending him down to the floor as he carefully pulled the blade out of his side.
Zain fumbled himself up, disorientated with his fists in front of him, "Let's go asshole."
The attacker raised the gun, shooting twice - slinging Zain backwards before he fell to the ground.

The attacker stumbled, holding its side as blood oozed over the black gloves, leaning by the window in pain to stare out to the pickup.
Mark fought to push himself up and the attacker turned to him, slashing at his strong bicep and forcing him down in a cry.

"What do you want?" Mark cried out, his defeat burning, "Why are you doing this!"

The attacker reached into his open coat and dropped a note to the floor before kicking down at his face knocking him out.

The attacker turned, still clutching the wound at his side as he smashed the hunting blade against the remaining glass at the window, clearing it before launching himself out.

The cottage was silent, with just the rain droning against the roof as the lights from the pickup dimmed while it pulled away into the blackness of the night - sirens sounding distance.

"Mark!" Zain called as the pain to his shoulder ripped through his body, the smell of hot flesh lingering from the oozing wound.

"Mark! Get up! Please!" he said trying to roll himself to his knees as the agony of the bullet hole demanded every fibre of his being to push through the pain.

"Son of a bitch!" he yelled through the hurt as he finally propped onto his knees, holding his shoulder, "Mark! Get up!"

Mark moved his head, everything hurting from his face to his leg.

"Get up Mark!" Zain urged, "Please!"

"Mark!" detective Dekka said softly, forcing words through her dry voice. Zain leapt forward in alarm, scrambling to her side.

"I thought you were dead!" he cried, pressing his other hand over her side, "Stay still ok, I hear the sirens coming for us."

She nodded, fighting to keep her eyes open and Zain turned to Mark again, yelling his name loudly.

"Zain..." Mark said pushing himself up - blood seeping through the gash on his upper arm.

"Mark! Get up! They took Carla!" he urged, "Please get up!"

"Leigh Anne…" Dekka said trying to fight the cold sleep that lingered beneath her skin, "In the car…"

Mark slumped up and reached for the note the attacker had dropped.

YOU KNOW WHERE TO END THIS!

Zain shook his head and tears fell down his face, "No, don't do this Mark."

Mark forced himself up, "I'm not leaving Carla or Leigh Anne."

Zain stared at him as he stumbled out towards the side entrance where he looked around the outside of the cottage as the rain cooled the burning from his pain.

"There's no sign of Zach, I think they have him too." He said finally coming back inside, limping in his walk.

"Or Zach's part of this!" Zain urged.

"I need a car and a gun." Mark said looking down at the detective.

"No! Don't do this Mark! Wait for the police!"

"I'm not leaving my friends!" He said standing over the detective, "Do you have a secondary weapon?"

"This is crazy, if you know where they are, take the police with you!" Zain said pushing down on the detectives wound, "Stop trying to end this yourselves! Look where it got you all! All your friends are dead!"

"No Zain! Not all of them. This ends now! Tonight!" Mark snarled, "No one else dies, no one else!"

The heater inside the car was barely doing much to dry Mark's heavily soaked clothes as he turned onto the long dark 15km stretch of road linking Secunda with its neighbouring town Evander.
The rain danced against the car while lightning flared, briefly opening the darkness that clung to the dense fields.

It had been ten years, but he could still hear the echoes of their victorious giggles as they peddled up this road.

The fields were dark and the grass now even higher than he remembered, struggling with remembering where to turn, the downpour making everything harder to see as his mind was racing in both fear and pain, his heart resounding loud like the racing wipers.

CHAPTER TEN

With the beautiful blue sky above and scorching summer sun beckoning, 17-year-old Nico Bekker couldn't pass up the opportunity to take his father's keys from his pocket as he lay sprawled out on the sofa snoring loudly.

"This is a bad idea." Nathan whispered, "Maybe we shouldn't, its dad's favourite thing Nico!"
Nico held his hand up over his lips, "Sssshhh, you'll wake him!"
Nathan shook his head grinning as Nico carefully went for the keys.

As they rushed out the back door, Nathan grabbed his brother's arm, "To be sure, we're doing this because *we* want to right? And not to impress Wessel?"
"Are you jealous of Wessel?"
"We just don't get to do fun and exciting stuff anymore since he's around. All you do now is get drunk."
"So, maybe I'm growing up." He grinned moving to the door when Nathan tugged him back. He sighed to calm his building frustration, trying to remind himself that in their 17 years, twin brotherhood was important, and he had to give Nathan reason to relax, or the afternoon would be spoiled.

"We're brothers, twins!" he laughed grabbing the back of his brother's neck and tugging him playfully, "If you want to do some crazy stuff, let's do it you

know I'm game. But today let's have a few drinks and chat with a couple of girls, alright?"
Nathan smiled nodding, "Ok good because I have tons of fireworks, I want us to experiment with."
"So? Why not bring them today? We can light a few in the girls change rooms and watch them scatter!" laughed Nico as they walked out into the hot sun where their younger brother sat cooling off in the small splash pool, their mother on the grass beneath the shade, reading.

"We're going to the pool with Stefan and Caleb." Nico explained flicking his blonde hair, "What time is dad due back at work?"
"Seven as always." His mother smiled, "You don't want to take Norman with you?"
"And baby sit? No thank you." Nathan shook his head with a laugh, "That's your job, you're the mother, right?"
"I suppose, I was just asking." She rolled her eyes.
"What time are you waking him up for supper?" Nico pressed again.
"What are you boys up to this time? No trouble again please."
"No trouble mom!" he rolled his eyes, "I told you! We don't know what happened to Mrs. Thorpes cat. You must learn to trust us!" Nico knelt to kiss her on the cheek, "So what time will you be waking dad up? We want to know so we are home in time."

From the side, their little brother Norman watched them with scornful eyes.
She turned to her other son who also walked down to the wash line and took a towel for himself, "At six, and Nico you better not be hanging out with Wessel,

you know what we said about you two mixing with that rubbish."

"We won't mom." Nico smiled with expert nonchalant while taking his bicycle from the side of the house, waving as he and his twin head around the side of the house.

In the driveway, they quickly propped their bikes up on the back of the stained yellow Bantam.

"Ok let's roll it out and start down the street like we did last time."

"Why do you insist we hang out with Wessel after what he did to Karen?"

Nico shrugged, "Why not? Caleb and Stefan like him, so do I. He's cool."

"Mom's right, he's a troublemaker." Nathan said opening the passenger door as his brother dropped the handbrake.

"Wow, since when do you side with mom on anything? Where's your sense of adventure?" Nico scoffed while they pushed the pickup along the driveway, "We're supposed to be twins, you like what I like isn't it?"

"I don't like how we don't do cool stuff anymore. I mean stealing dad's car is done and its old. We had so many plans for the holiday and now all you want to do is get drunk."

Nico steered the car into a turn as it rolled into the street and he pressed for it to stop, "He's made us popular! Everyone knows us now. We're the guys to watch out for, the guys to make way for in the passages at school. It beats being the wankers we were a few months ago. I mean yes…"

He paused while Nathan quickly rounded to the back to push.

"...The Yolanda thing was not cool, but he admitted it was a mistake and that he went too far."

"More like rape."

"You better watch your mouth Nathan, if he hears you say that you'd be dead meat, and I won't stop him." Nico huffed as the Bantam rolled forward past their neighbours' house, "There comes a point in life where you have to grow up and start thinking about girls."

Nathan shook his head rolling his eyes as he pushed the heavy two-seater along.

"And yes sure, we read dad's old magazines all the time and we have our little fantasies about girls, but Wessel is our ticket to actually having a girl!"

"Rape isn't a fantasy of mine, that's jail time." Nathan pant as the sun forced sweat to run down his face.

"At least we got to see real life tits!" Nico laughed, quickly hopping into the driver's seat.

Nathan rushed to the side, opened the door, and gave one more hard push as the car reached the slope in their road, rolling faster now.

The engine sprung to life and Nathan leapt up into the passenger seat.

****

11-year-old Carla Wilson watched as her friend Maggie carefully lay her towel to the grass beneath a thatched shade umbrella just a few feet from the large public swimming pool. The heat had most youngsters and teens poolside while some families occupied the benches.

Since Maggie's breasts developed, she had noticed how the boys were always peaking over, especially at the pool.

"You're so lucky, yours are all out and stuff." She sighed sitting cross legged on her towel.

"You're three years younger than me Carla." Maggie laughed playfully, "You're getting there just be patient."

Leigh Anne, a distance from them in the sun, sat up to turn around for the sun to warm her back that was still cold from the water.

"Are you guys talking about boobs?"

"Yes Leigh Anne, but you and Odette are only nine, somethings we need to be mindful of around you, we can't have another incident with your mom, or she won't let you hang out with us anymore."

Leigh Anne rolled her eyes in a giggle.

"So, are you guys really going to move to Joburg?" Carla asked laying back on her elbows with her legs out in the sun, "Because that would really be sad."

Maggie sighed, "I don't know, not for certain anyway but my dad is talking about starting his own company. He says he's done making money for other people and wants to start a construction company of his own. We'll see."

"I hope you don't." Leigh Anne said with a sadness, "It won't be the same without you and Matt."

Maggie sat up - it was the opportunity she'd been waiting for.

"There's something I actually wanted to also point out, on that note." she said cautiously, "So, even if we don't move, you do know I can't always stay friends with you guys, right?"

"What do you mean?"

"Well, I'll be sixteen in a few weeks and my parents think it would be good if I started hanging around girls my own age." She said cautiously, "I mean we'll always be friends but…"

"You can't be hanging around kids anymore, got it." Carla rolled her eyes.

"Don't say it like that, I just mean that I'm older and I need to be doing different things, hanging out with people my age."

Leigh Anne shook her head, "With Belinda and Tammy?"

"They're actually nice." Maggie defended, "I'm just saying that I won't always be heading off into some adventure with you guys because I'm growing up. But I will always be your friend, always."

"Change sucks!" Carla huffed, "Why can't they just hang out with us? What's so wrong with us?"

Maggie sighed dropping her head.

"I know what you mean." Leigh Anne said looking at her, "When I'm a famous actress I probably will also want to hang out with other celebrities."

Carla laughed shaking her head, "Totally different thing Leigh Anne."

"But we'll still be friends." She smiled, flipping her long blonde hair over her shoulder as Odette and her brother Mark walked towards them greeting with bright, eager smiles.

They were both thin, and being three years younger than her brother, Odette's little 9-year-old body seemed even more frail against his scrawniness.

"They guys went to buy sodas." Carla said looking up Marks skinny body while he pulled his shirt over his head, immediately seeing a bruising beneath his arm against his chest, "Your dad again?"
He sighed and pulled his shirt back on, "It's nothing."
Leigh Anne sat up looking to Odette, "And you?"
"It's nothing." Odette managed a smile as she flayed her faded green and yellow dress out before sitting down beside her.

A heaviness hung over them as Mark and Odette awkwardly tried to avoid talking about their sordid life at home.

"I have some sandwiches for you if you want them?" Carla offered, opening a plastic packet she'd brought with, "It's nothing special, just some left over chicken."
Their eyes widened and Mark took the four saran-wrapped sandwiches, "Thank you so much! Chicken is great, thanks!"
Odette smiled and gave her thanks to Carla as her brother handed her a sandwich, and he sat down beside his sister biting into the bread eagerly.
"We only had coffee for dinner so we're pretty hungry." Odette said behind her chewing, "Marcus forgot to sweep the garage, so daddy wasn't very happy last night."
"You guys don't deserve this." Maggie scoffed angrily.
"Is that why you won't take off your dress?" Leigh Anne said looking to Odette, "Did he hurt you too?"

She shook her head as she chewed and swallowed, "He works hard, he just needs help around the house. You guys know how it goes."
"We don't need to talk about it." Mark said swallowing the last of his sandwich, his voice harsh and impatient. Maggie reached out and squeezed his arm with a reassuring smile.

Each with their hands full of soda cans, and with the two youngest in front of them, Matt, Zach and Eric head out of the store scheming the days adventure while Jacques and Bobby spoke about games they'd want to play in the pool.
The paving at their feet began to burn, and the boys hurriedly hopped over the road and onto the grass, laughing at one another as Matt casually continued to walk to them frowning with a mocking grin.

"That was hot!" Bobby exclaimed shoving his feet to the grass beside Jacques.
Matt laughed, "Such babies, it wasn't that hot."
"Not all of us live our lives barefoot like you." Eric laughed, "Some of us care about our feet, right boys?"
Jacques nodded up at him with wide eyes as Bobby shrugged, "Someday I'll be big like you and it won't hurt me then either right?"
Matt smiled nodding, "You bet kid."

Seeing his best friends nearing, Mark got up and rushed to them, greeting happily as he took the sodas from little Jacques and Bobby.
"We can see you drooling…" Maggie giggled, nudging Carla who stared at them.
She turned to her laughing, "Please, it's not like that."

"Yes, it is." Leigh Anne giggled, "We all know it."

"It's not like that! I'm just thankful that he stood up for me with Caleb the other day." she insisted as the boys approached.

Leigh Anne shook her head, "I cannot believe Caleb turned out to be such a jerk."

"I almost got marked for detention because of him. Luckily Zach took the blame, can you imagine what my mom would do to me if I got detention?" Carla huffed.

Maggie laughed shaking her head, "I'm sure there's more to this."

"We got colas for everyone, the cheap stuff obviously." Zach said smiling down at the girls and handing Carla hers - a smile that brightened even the hottest of days in the Secunda summer.

"We have some money left so we were thinking maybe later we'll get some ice pops and split them." Added Matt as he handed the drinks to the girls, "My idea."

"Thanks." Leigh Anne taking her soda from Eric and looking at the scrapes on his arms, "How's your arm feeling?"

He slumped to the grass with a sigh, "It hurts when I use it."

"What did you tell your parents?" asked Mark taking a sip from his can.

Eric shook his head with a shrug, "That I fell off my bike."

"You're such a baby." Matt remarked rolling his eyes as he tipped back his head to gulp from his can.

"Well, it's the same thing I told my parents." Zach agreed, "The day will come when enough will be enough!"

"I seriously hate them, all of them." Odette huffed, "People like them should just go straight to the army and learn some manners."

"I hate them too!" Jacques added with an angry grimace over his face.

"What I don't understand and never will…" Matt said slumping to the grass in the shade, "Why does Caleb even like hanging out with those guys? They're nothing like us!"

"Neither is Caleb." Snarled Mark, "That's why he didn't fit in with us."

"Yes, he just wants to do adult things." Bobby huffed shaking his head, "Smoking and drinking beer, he's not even cool!"

"And the twins are?" Matt laughed mockingly, "Look whatever, they just need to leave us alone and its better we don't split up."

"Agreed, like we said yesterday…" Zach said sternly, "We always stay in groups."

For a moment they all went silent and the sounds of joy around the pool beamed. "Ok let's all swim!" exclaimed Jacques' 9-year-old voice, shrieking as he leapt up from the grass, taking off his shirt and tossed it aside mid-run.

"Hey! Are you guys going to swim with us or what?"

"Yes! Let's have some fun!" Matt laughed running towards the end of the pool and diving in while the rest also happily rushed into the water behind him.

****

With Stefan and Caleb in the back with his brother, the Bantam rolled along the street towards the public pool with music blaring poorly from the speakers inside. 17-year-old Wessel Fouche sat with his feet up out the window smoking - his long dark hair hanging across his face as he blew kisses to any girl walking near the car while Nico drove, holding a beer low by his seat.

In the back, Nathan sat comfortably in the corner with his legs out to the middle soaking the sun that beat down while 16-year-old Stefan Campbell stood up holding the roof. With them was Caleb, Wessels younger brother who quickly caught on to his influencer's lifestyle. His slender 15-year-old body huddled down sipping from the beer the three of them shared, and smoking low in the back where nobody would see.

The pickup rolled into a parking bay, the music disrupting the sounds of happiness around the pool and garnering attention.

Maggie rolled her eyes to Bobby and Eric, "The pee-stain is here."
From the water with 9-year-old Odette on his shoulders, Mark paused their water fight as an uneasiness fell over the crowded lawn surrounding the pool as the music roared from the parking.

"We should just leave." Sighed Odette as she saw Caleb hopping off the back of the pickup, her heart sinking and her stomach almost immediately trembling. "They always ruin everything!" huffed Jacques from up top of Matt's shoulders looking down at Zach their game's referee, "Do we have to go?"

Zach looked to Mark and then back to Odette, his stomach nauseated, "I think we should head out of here, find some adventure."

"But we were here first!" moaned Jacques, "I'm sick of them hurting us all the time! We can never do anything without being scared of them."

Zach sighed shaking his head, "We're done here ok, let's get out now!"

Mark stared at Caleb angrily, his blood boiling and he turned to his sister in disgust, and she looked away in shame.

Stefan hurriedly took off his shirt to cover the six pack of beers, prompting Caleb to do the same, glancing over his shoulder and seeing Mark and Zach from the pool glaring at him in pure hatred and he sighed shaking his head.

"Relax, if they were going to say anything, they would have." Stefan smirked patting Caleb on the back, "You're good, you're with us now."

"Agreed." Nathan grinned hopping down too, "Let's have some fun!"

Caleb nodded, his heart racing in fear that it would come out from his previous group of friends that he had forced his fingers into Odette's panties while playing, the day he no longer was tolerated in their company.

"There's Donna and her pal Letticia." Wessel pointed as Nico quickly finished his beer and shoved it under the seat.

"Ooohhh, I want that on me like white on rice. Let's go take what's ours" He grinned, his dark slick blond hair almost glistening with the sweat.

Nathan nudged Caleb from the side, "Better just make sure we have permission next time huh?"

Caleb looked past his friend and backed away as Nathan turned into Wessels hand gripping his neck, pushing him backwards as his fingers pressed into his throat.

"What did you say?"

"Hey man, leave my brother." Nico sighed as he shut the door.

"You trying to say something to me?" he asked again, squeezing harder. Seeing his twin start to choke and redden, Nico hurried around the car and pushed between them.

"This is not going to get us anywhere." He said shoving his coughing brother in the chest, "Show some respect, some things are not worth joking about!"

Wessel nodded, staring at Nathan's shocked face, and he laughed, "I was only playing around like brothers do."

Nico laughed and wrapped his arm around Wessel as they head off towards the lawn around the large bustling swimming pool.

"I need the bathroom. Anyone want to come with me?" Leigh Anne asked as she pushed herself up from her towel beside the pool.

"Not me." Maggie smiled as Leigh Anne flung up - unknowingly knocking the shirt from Caleb's hands, sending it down to the cement around the pool.

"What is that?" she frowned at the golden liquid running to the concrete.

"You idiot!" Wessel said shoving her, "Look what you did!"

"Hey!" a chorus erupted from Eric, Maggie, and Carla as they sprung up.

Nico and Stefan stood forward to provide cover.

"Cool it, take it easy. We've got eyes on us."
"You owe me a six-pack blondie." Wessel said reaching to touch her face when she pulled away.

"Get away from her creep!" Eric said as Nico grabbed him by his shirt.
"What did you say? You have a mouth on you don't you Jansen?"
"Get off me!"
"Can't you guys get another hobby?" Maggie scoffed to Nathan, who she secretly had a crush on, "Just leave us alone."
"Yeah, let's move on guys, we have another six." He said turning to his boys, "Nico, leave him. It's not worth our time and we got a lot of people curious here."
"I disagree Nathan because you didn't pay for it. I did." Wessel said glaring at him.
"Really?" Mark said picking up the shirt as the glass inside clangored out, "They're so cool, remind me to get brain damage to be like them when I'm seventeen."
"Are you calling us stupid?" Caleb snarled shoving him.
Zach stepped over the glass, "This isn't allowed here so why don't you move along, and we'll pretend we don't know what you guys smuggled in here."
"Yes, just go and leave us alone." Added Jacques bravely.

Nico looked to the side, confirming that the lifeguard had not yet seen anything.

"Why don't you put a shirt on porky, nobody wants to see that here!" scoffed Caleb pointing at Jacques, "You're so fat it makes me dizzy!"

"You want to start this?" Zach snarled stepping forward.

"Yes! Maybe I do!" Caleb shoved him with a cocky grin.

"Oh, big words with a lifeguard behind you." Stefan laughed stepping to Zach, "Big mouth when you know we won't do anything to you here."

"No see I know how you guys operate - everyone knows. You only bully people smaller than you, in places where nobody can see. Because you are cowards." Quipped Zach with a brave grin hoping his legs were not trembling as much as his stomach.

"Watch your mouth if you know what's good for you." Warned Nico.

Eric pipped up behind them, "Big scary cowards the lot of you, just go away and we'll pretend we didn't see anything."

"We don't need your favours piss ant!" Said Nathan shoving him backwards as more attention drew to their huddle.

"Cool it, the lifeguard is looking." Said Caleb grabbing Odette's towel and quickly laying it back down over the broken glass.

"You still owe me a six-pack blondie." Wessel said staring at Leigh Anne.

"Just back off already." Maggie huffed rolling her eyes, "This is boring."

"But we have nothing to drink now." Wessel taunt, "And we want our beer back."

"I have some money for sodas, that's all we have." Zach explained.

"We don't want sodas." Caleb huffed mockingly, "Sodas are for kids, like you."

"Mr. Big shot!" Maggie laughed sarcastically when Caleb shoved her shoulder.

"How about you stop playing with dolls and start hanging out with us?" Nico grinned to Maggie, licking his bottom lip, "We can help you outgrow these losers."

"Get away from my sister!" Said Matt rushing to stand between his sister and Nico, "If you want to get away with sneaking booze in here, you better keep stepping."

The older boys laughed to the stares from the other kids who were all to relieved that they were not in their firing line, and like a viper strike – Nico slapped Matt in the face.

"Don't think so tough guy."

"I'll get my money back from you." Wessel continued, still staring into Leigh Anne's eyes, "I can even think of a few ways you can sort that out."

"Pig!" Carla just swung with the words leaving her lips, a left hook that flew high in the air with her body as she stepped forward, punching him dead in the centre of his mouth.

Instinct kicked in and without thinking, Zach swung too, hitting him in the eye as his head turned from her blow - then tackled into him. Within seconds, everyone was in some form of tussle to both grab at each other and block the commotion from the onlookers. Jacques and Odette grabbed at Stefan, shoving him towards the pool – the shirt in his hands slipping and crashing the second six pack of beers to the ground as the three of them toppled into the water.

Everyone paused at the sound of the shattering glass.

The 17-year old's blow to his 12-year-old face felt like a horse kick and as Mark slung down to the ground, with Wessel reaching over with his fists in the air and pounding his fist into his stomach.
"Stop!" Leigh Anne yelled as she and Bobby leapt up onto Wessel's back, pulling him down to the side off Zach.
Nico hit the ground with Eric on top of him, while Maggie swung her bag at Caleb, connecting a few blows to his head as he tried desperately to cover with his arm.
Zach and Matt tried pinning Nathan, with Jacques kicking at his legs and inner thighs as he scuffed Eric from him.

The lifeguard's whistle blew as he hurried down his ladder from the far side of the pool, a cluster of kids hurried to see the scuffle.

"Get off of me!" Wessel said shoving Bobby to the ground as he stood up, leaving Zach breathless on the ground beside Mark.
"I'll beat you like daddy." He snarled, punching down hard, and knocking Bobby to the floor.
"Hey!" Carla called stammering out of the pool, grabbing an unbroken bottle from the mash of glass and throwing it into his crotch and sending him down to his knees in a yelp.

The whistle sounded again, with the lifeguard rushing angrily around the shallow end towards them. Zach lunged, grabbed a fist full of fabric and pulled down – dragging Nico's shorts to his ankles.

"Come on!" Said Zach breathlessly laughing, pulling Bobby to his feet as Nico flopped about trying to re-dress while the onlookers erupted in giggles.
"Run! Run!" urged Leigh Anne as they all scurried away, quickly grabbing their stuff as they ran towards the bicycle post in the parking.

"Get up!" Nico panted breathlessly, pulling Wessel up while he and his crew also began to rush towards the parking lot just as the younger group fled on their bicycles.

****

The Bantam swung out of the parking, Nico trying to drive with his legs trembling from humiliation and anger.
"You better get them for that!" Wessel sat uncomfortably holding his beer wet crotch, "You cannot let them get away with it!"
"There goes us ever going back to the pool again!" Stefan huffed through the small window facing the back.
"Shut up Stefan!" Nathan growled angrily, leaning in by the glass, "We need to do to them what we did to that cat!"
"Damn straight!" Nico snarled, clenching the steering wheel as he watched their bicycles round through the park.
"You're going to chase them, right?" Wessel scoffed, "You aren't going to let a bunch of kids embarrass us like that are you?"
Nico swung the wheel, and the Bantams tyres screeched as it flung the corner – sending Stephan

and Caleb banging into each other against the side of the bin.

"There!" Nathan pointed across the park.

The Bantam swung a turn sharply across the road, almost hitting the oncoming sedan who braked and honked.

"You don't have to prove anything." Stefan yelled at the window, "It's over we lost this one, but we'll get them back."

"Shut up!" Nico and Nathan yelled as the Bantam circled the park, rounding just as their fleet of bicycles left the park – their eyes shooting wide in alarm when they saw the stained yellow Bantam heading towards them.

"This way!" Zach said leading them towards Barnes Avenue South, a long one-way road, all downhill that head past the town centre and towards the town exit. Heading this way would mean gaining enough time ahead of them, as the Bantam would need to circle and get onto Madison North to catch up with them from their current path on Main Road.

"You got a small chance to get them, push it!" Wessel barked as Nico pressed the pedal to the floor. Nathan huffed angrily, shaking his head to the cars honking at their erratic driving and sped to catch them before their bikes hit Madison Road.

"Damn it!" Nico hit the steering wheel as the fleet of bikes flung off the pavement, veered between cars at the stop light, and swung down the long one way.

"Go to St. Andrews, that's their only way back in!" Nathan yelled from the back.

"They must take St. Andrews back into Secunda, they won't dare ride towards Evander. They're too lame for that!" Caleb said yelling through the window.

"Caleb is right." Nico said as the car rolled to a slow.

"That's my guy!" Wessel laughed, howling out the window as the Bantam swung a U-turn.

****

"Can you believe we did that?" exclaimed Jacques.

"I'm so sorry guys, if I was just looking, I never would have bumped them." Leigh Anne said.

"You have nothing to apologize for Leigh Anne!" Zach smiled, "This was our time!"

"That was incredible!" exclaimed Carla from the side as her black and purple mountain bike chased alongside her friends – their laughter and cheers echoed to the nothingness that spanned around the empty fields outside of the small town.

The heat from the tar slung up against their legs as their bikes sped around the bend that linked Secunda to its neighbouring town Evander – a 15km stretch. Panting, breathless and with muscles aching, the ten of them were still revelling in their triumph, hair, and shorts still wet as they peddled.

"Oh no! They're coming! Zach! They're right behind us!" yelled Jacques looking back in alarm as the stained yellow Ford Bantam rounded the turn and began to barrel down after them on the long empty stretch of road.

Laughing, Zach flung around and raised himself on his pedals, his legs already exhausted but the adrenaline still fuelling.

"Keep going! We've got this!"

He darted his bike to the left, raising his front wheels as he flung off the tar and onto the gravel fire boundary – his friends all following the same manoeuvre as he led them towards the gate to a farm that covered a large stretch of the fields before the mine ahead.

Mark peddled his red and white 6 gear mountain bike as fast as his 12-year-old legs could, burning from heel to thigh already with him forcing himself to push on and maintain speed with the rest of the group, his little sister Odette clutched her arms around his waist, too afraid to look back as the sound of the car's engine sounded over the stillness that surrounded them.

Their wheels skid on the dirt, with Matt and Eric pouncing off their bikes that fell to the dirt, and they scrambled to open the old, rusted gate.

"They're going to kill me!" Bobby said turning to Zach with wide eyes, his face still bloodied from the punch to his nose. Of the whole group, Bobby was the youngest at 7 years old, dark hair and dark eyes complimenting his tanned skin.
"It'll be ok." Said Maggie, brushing the side of his face with her hand, "We'll be ok Bobby."
"Let's go, let's go!" urged Leigh Anne with a bright grin over her face as she cycled through the gate while everyone else rushed to follow. Even as a 10-year-old, her dust covered, symmetrical face was designed for future covers.

Zach shut the gate, dropping its heavy rusted slot down, laughing through the dread as he quickly scurried back onto his bicycle that Jacques held up for him, pedalling as hard and as fast as they could to catch up with the others on the old farm road before the older boys caught up with them.

****

The yellow Bantam rolled off the blacktop and onto the dirt road, skidding in the dirt at the closed gate as the dust from their bicycles settled.

"Get the damn gate open!" scoffed Nico Bekker who sat wet in the driver's seat, fuming.

Caleb and Stefan, still both shirtless, leapt from the back, quickly ripping open the gate and slinging it open while the Bantam sped in almost clipping the frame.

Nathan slammed his hand on the roof as the car slowed for the two boys to jump in again, "Let's go kill those bitches!"

"Let's kick their asses!" his brother yelled, flooring the pedal down and kicking up sand and stones as the Bantam tore after them.

From deep into the field, the ten friends laid low with their bikes as the Bantam seared through the dirt past them.

"They think we went to old man Piet's house."

Giggled Odette as high-fives burst in the air among them with soft, victorious giggles.

Carefully, Zach stood up and peered out the grass watching as dust flung up in the distance towards the old farmhouse deep in the field.

"Alright see Bobby." Zach smiled and lowered, "We're ok little brother, you have nothing to be afraid of."

Bobby's eyes lit up at him and he nodded with the rest of the group all forming a large hug over his scrawny body.

Like Mark and Odette who lived under dread of their drunk father, Bobby's parents were both zero tolerant, very strict members of the church and believed very firmly in physical punishment for any wrongdoing, and they all knew that any sign of blood on his face or shirt would result in a few days of difficult sitting.

"We can get you cleaned up." Said Maggie spitting on the very tip of her skirt to wipe his face. Zach, Eric, and Mark huddled up, carefully ensuring their surroundings were clear.

"That was awesome what you did." Zach said pulling Carla up to him, smiling with bright eyes, "That was legendary!"

She smirked bravely.

Leigh Anne giggled, "Agreed that was epic! I don't think anyone expected that! Wham!"

They all laughed, grinning proudly from their spots in the tall grass.

"We're all sick of them bullying us," Carla smiled proudly, "They had it coming."

"Yeah, nobody picks on us, any of us! Not again!" Zach said playfully scrounging through Jacques and Bobby's hair, "Especially our little brothers over here."

"I can't get this out." Maggie sighed, "Quite the blow you took Bobby. I'm surprised your nose isn't broken."

"We should go now." Said Eric hopping down, "They're by the house."

"Will only be a few minutes before they realize we're hiding." Mark added.

"They'll see us if we take the road." Jacques sighed in defeat as tears welled in his eyes, "What are we going to do? How do we get out of this?"

Leigh Anne smiled and took his hand, "It's ok, it's going to be ok."

Mark and Eric propped back up, peering through the grass. In the distance a shimmer caught Eric's eye, and a while behind it the blackness of a road that rounded the fields opposite from the large white tailing dams that ran towards the gold mines further away.

"There!" said Eric pulling Mark with excitement.

****

Frustrated and suspicious that the old fat farmer was hiding the kids from them, Nico asked again, "So you haven't seen them."

"Listen boy, I know who you are, and I know what troublemakers you and your friends are, next time you or anyone passes my gate I'll shoot you. Now piss of my property before I get my gun." The sweaty, dirty farmer snarled impatiently, waving them away as he turned back to his workers by the tractors.

Nico and Nathan turned back to the Bantam where the other three teens waited.

"This is bullshit." Nico plucked at the door angrily whipping it open, "I want to make them pay!"

Nico slunk into the car and the boys leapt in the back again, the farmer again waving at them to leave.

"They humiliated us. We're going to find them and we're going to make them very sorry for it." He snarled, shifting into gear, and turning the pickup around.

"This was a shit day." Caleb huffed in the back.

"We'll get them boys, don't worry." Wessel called out the small window, "They're out here somewhere. Keep your eyes peeled. They're out here…"

****

Hunched down, pushing their bikes carefully through the long grass, they giggled in whispers about their victory.

The air around the open field was quiet, with the sun beating down on them as they steadily crept to a slower pace to keep their wheels from crunching the grass.

A droning sounded in the distance, humming and moaning through the silence.

"What is that?" Whispered Maggie.

"Could be a mine pump?" Matt answered softly, "I have no idea. Maybe something from the farm?"

"Where are we?" said Jacques standing up.

The small pickups tyres slid on the dusty road and Caleb raised his hand over his eyes, scanning the heat that bounced off the field, "I think I saw something."

****

A drumming, slushing sound filled the air as they stepped out of the high grass to a more comfortable, knee high veldt a few feet from a large shed that stood near dilapidation.

"Looks like a hangar." Said Mark looking up at it, everyone's eyes lighting up with excitement and adventure.
"Let's go check it out!" urged Zach with a smile, as they lowered their bikes to the ground, rushing through the grass towards the building.
They lived on adventure and would often spend full days out in the fields between Secunda and its little neighbour Trichardt, but these fields were uncharted territory and adrenaline was high with excitement.

The grass around the old building was relatively flatter the closer they got, the field becoming more of an uneven ground that once was a dirt road now being slowly overtaken by weeds and grass patches. The droning sound was louder, coming from inside the building, the large glimmering white slime dams from the gold mine standing out prominently in the distance behind it.

The doors were large, but were sealed closed with a thick, rusty metal chain and locks, the windows covered in dirt making it near impossible to see into its dark bowls. The droning, slushing was louder now, clearly from inside.
A large, faded sign hung on the door.

"We can climb up to the roof and see if we can't get in there?" Leigh Anne said as Mark and Zach tried pulling at the large, rusted locks.

"Maybe this isn't a good idea." Said Matt staring at the sign.

"Oh, live a little." Zach laughed shrugging him off, "We won't break anything."

"Hey! Look here, someone broke this out." Said Carla rushing to a window.

"Looks like a pumping station." Maggie said peering inside as the echo of the pumping hummed inside the vast building.

"What's a pumping station?" asked Bobby tugging on Zach's arm.

"I have no idea, what is Maggie?"

She smiled, "They pump water to the mines."

"Looks haunted to me!" Eric frowned as a nervousness set in.

Jacques and Leigh Anne giggled, "Let's go check it out!"

Eric turned to Carla, "You're the flame that leads the way, after you."

****

One by one they carefully helped each other into the small window, careful to not cut or scratch themselves on the glass remnants jutting out, with Zach and Mark being the last to manoeuvre inside.

It was colder inside, and very dimly lit only by rays of light that broke through its tattered corrugated iron roofing sheets, some sheets dangerously hanging down, creaking as the air passed through.

The flooring was predominantly concrete on the main layer, with stairs heading lower to a very thick grid plated flooring in the centre and huge metal pipes and tubes lining the sides all from one central point in the middle of the building.

It was clear that the droning emanated from the massive pumps inside the building, pumping water from the centre of the building to the huge pipes that led to the slime dams in the distance.

They carefully head down the long grid metal stairs to the grid flooring below, the droning hum louder and louder the closer they got. To the right against the side was a long ladder going up to the ceiling, and beside it two large, orange control hubs with switches and panels behind glass. They could smell the water, and the sound was deafening as the force of the pumps vibrated up into their feet while they all stepped onto the grid that covered a concrete floor a few inches beneath it.
"This is crazy!" laughed Mark. "It's awesome!" added Carla as they all stood with the vibration tremoring through them, the loudness almost deafening.

"I wonder what's down there?" Zach pointed to the centre of the room where the concrete beneath the grid sloped down to a dark blackness with only a massive steal pipe coming out and splitting to the pipes on the sides.

With enough sense of adventure thriving within the excitement, they all very carefully walked across the grid towards the darkness, covering their ears now with the loud drumming of water inside the pipes boomed.

A few feet from the main pipe, they stopped, just where the concrete sloped into the dark hole where glistening water could be seen almost ten feet down, splashing against the thick silver pipe that vacuumed it up.

The vibrating hum was so powerful that they stood dead still, scared that the thick grid would cave in, and they'd be lost to the pit forever.
It pulsated and droned, the water being pumped from somewhere deep below into the pipes, vibrating and shivering through their small bodies and then – silence.

They lowered their hands from their ears in alarmed confusion as silence screamed out across the building, just the remaining water in the pipes gulping.

They stared at one another, and then around the building.

"Boo!" a loud voice echoed, startling them all into jumps, Leigh Anne and Bobby connecting and toppling to the hard grid.

Coming out of the darkness behind one of the massive pipes was another boy, dressed in shorts and a T-shirt with very short brown military style hair.

He was older than them, grinning from ear to ear as he stepped towards them with his hands in his pockets.

"You guys shouldn't be down here." He said looking Maggie up and down as he walked, "It's dangerous here...for kids."

"Who are you?" Matt asked bravely stepping in front of his sister.

Maggie rolled her eyes and pushed him aside.

The stranger smiled and scanned them all closer than he could from the shadows watching as they tiptoed to the middle of the room.

"If we're not allowed here, why are you here?" Zach stepped up to him readying defending his friends behind him.

"I'm Dillon." He said reaching out his hand, "I found this place a few days ago, I come here to get away from my uncle and the work on the farm."

"Farmer Piet?" asked Eric shaking his hand too.

"Yes. I'm supposed to live by them until I learn manners. It's been two days, and I can barely take it." He grinned arrogantly, "So what brings you guys out here?"

"We were running from..." Jacques started when Carla nudged him.

"We heard the sound, so we came to take look that's all." She shrugged, "But we're leaving so…"
"This runs for about thirty minutes every twenty minutes or so." Dillon said, "It's pretty awesome how powerful it is."
"So, you come here to hide from your uncle?" Bobby asked intrigued.

The boy looked at him, the bruises on his wrists clearly older than the blood on his face.

"In the day yes. At night it stops running at around seven, so I stay here for some peace and quiet." He lowered, "What happened to your face?"
"We had a run in with some idiots." Maggie said brushing her hair back behind her ear, "We didn't mean to interrupt you, Dillon."
"No problem, I don't mind the company." He smiled.
"We didn't think anyone would be here." Matt said rolling his eyes at his sisters flirting, the fear of the outside signage still rattling him.
"Well beats pretending to be a farmer and ducking my uncles' belt." He laughed walking casually towards the centre and spitting down, "Besides they don't care where I am, so why should I be where they expect me to be, you know what I mean?"
Bobby smiled, he knew exactly what he meant and admired that he could be so defiant and brave to stay here, alone at night.
"You're spitting into drinking water, that's messed up." Matt huffed.
"That's sick, oh god I'm going to be sick." Said Carla shaking her head when he laughed, a chuckle that echoed in the silence of the walls.
"It's not drinking water! It gets flushed into the mine's slime dams."

Carla sighed in relief as he knelt to the grid, putting his fingers through, and pulling with all his might while the heavy grid slowly lifted.

"What are you doing?" asked Jacques stepping back in alarm.
"Sssshhh..." he gestured as the flap slammed down in a booming echo.

****

Out in the field, carefully making their way through the bumpy old road, the Bantam carefully rolled on into the nothingness that surrounded the wide long building.
"We probably need to get home before dad wakes up." Nathan urged tapping on the roof, "We don't have time for this Nico!"
"We're not leaving here without getting payback." Wessel snarled, "Quit moaning like a school bitch!"
Stefan sighed anxiously, "I kind of agree, we should not be out here."
"Then go back!"
Nico looked up at the sky, knowing his brother was right, but continued to carefully steer the vehicle along the old forgotten path.

****

"The other day I made a bunch of these little paper jets." Dillion said walking to the side where a pile of old newspapers stood stacked near an old, faded pillow and some cans of food.

"And I toss them in there, so a part of my experience here will always be out there in the mine." He explained with a bright smile, "See this huge pipe here pumps all the water down there up into the slime dams by the mine, so whatever I throw in will always be there buried."

"That's cool. Can I try?" asked Bobby eagerly.

"Sure."

"No, I think we should get going." Carla smiled, "We have a long way back."

"Ah just one?" Jacques also asked.

"Yeah man, just one and we can go." Matt grinned taking a paper.

"Be careful, if you go down there, we'll never see you again." Dillon warned as Mark carefully hunched towards the opening with his paper jet in his hand.

He nodded and tossed it down into the depth of the hole, where it landed on the water.

"How do we know it will get taken up anyway?" he said carefully moving away.

Dillon shrugged his shoulders back, "That's a lot of force pumping, it's definitely going to go don't you worry."

Matt, Maggie, Leigh Anne, and Bobby all carefully moved to the opening in the grid and tossed their planes down.

"This is so cool!" Bobby laughed, "I wonder what else we can throw down there?"

"I've tossed a few things down, there's bins of old bolts and nuts, huge things that I've chucked in, but they go straight down it's hard to know if they actually get pumped in or not."

To the side of where he had made a cozy spot for himself was a few old containers and bins full of old nails, screws and bolts – all large industrial types. "Here, do another one! This time write your name on it." Dillon grinned handing him a pencil as Zach, Eric and Mark took to the opening with their jets. "So doesn't your uncle come looking for you out here?" asked Maggie with a shy smile. Dillon shrugged, "No, half the time they don't even know I'm alive unless they need to take their frustrations out on me."

"So, you're a runaway?" asked Matt frowning, Bobby's attention glaring up at him.

Dillon shrugged, "I was, kind of. But my mother forced me to come stay with my uncle so technically I have a home I just don't want to be there."

"I know how you feel." Bobby said softly when Zach hugged him tightly.

Just then the sound of an engine outside drifted like an ominous hum through the walls and they all turned.

"Oh no." sighed Carla carefully stepping to the doors. "It can't be, could it?" Zach frowned as he strained his ears and Bobby grabbed onto his arm. Dillon stood still, his ears pricked in expectation of hearing his uncle's bellowing voice and losing his freedom.

A car door slammed, and the echo caused Bobby to jump, dropping the paper and his pencil – the pencil falling through the grid onto the slanting concrete that slowly rolled to a stop just inches from the drop.

"Come out, come out wherever you are." Wessel voice teased from outside where he kicked the wheel of Zach's bicycle, "We know you're here."

"Look I don't want to get involved and lose my sanctuary." Dillon huffed angrily, "You better get out of here and take them with you."

Outside by the door, Wessel shook at the chain angrily while Nathan and Stefan waited by the car. "Are we really taking their bikes?" Caleb asked with an evil laugh, pushing Carla's bike to the back of the pickup, "If we do, they're going to be out here in the dark with no way home."
"I can smell them in there." Wessel grinned, "We have a chance now, out here we can really give it to them good. Even take the girls if we wanted to."

A nervous silence paused across the boys and Caleb dropped the bike to the ground, "I say we go in there and we kick their teeth in!"
"Yeah!" roared Stefan when a loud 'clunk' sounded, something hit into the passenger door.

"What the hell was that?" Nico gasped rushing to the door when another 'clunk' hit, and a large bolt rock bounced off the front of the Bantam.
"Hey losers." Zach called from the roof, his hands full of large bolts and nuts, "Are you sure you want to do this?"
"Get your ass down here!" Nico yelled angrily.
"You little shit! Look what you did to my dads' car!" roared Nathan, "You're going to pay for this!"

"You should leave, now!" Warned Carla joining him as Mark and Matt helped Eric and Leigh Anne out through the roof beside a large sheet that dangled. "You want your bikes? Come get them or we're taking them!" Wessel laughed.
"Screw this!" Zach scoffed, tossing a handful of the bolts and screws at them.

They stung hard, tearing skin and bashing bones as the shrapnel hit down on the boys and the car.
"Stop! Please!"
Carla began throwing too, a rain of pain began slamming on them as they all tried blocking and ducking down in cover as the hard metal objects hailed down - clanging down onto the car's bonnet and roof and hitting down on them like painful rain.

Wessel hurriedly grabbed at the rocks and stones on the ground, throwing them up at them – with Caleb, Nathan and Stefan following suit.

"Be careful!" Maggie warned, holding Bobby and Jacques by her as Dillon dropped on the grating, trying to reach at the opening for his pencil.
Mark pulled Leigh Anne up and Eric rushed to the edge, digging into his pockets to join the attack, but a rock hit into his face just as he flung a fist full of bolts to the air. He stumbled, tripping and hitting the roof in a roll, slamming into Mark who just hoisted Matt up.

Matt grabbed the metal frame as Mark and Eric toppled back inwards, hitting the dangling chunk of roofing before slamming down on top of one of the large orange control hubs.

Jacques looked up in alarm while Matt plucked himself safely onto the roof with the help of Leigh Anne.

"Look out!" Bobby screamed pointing up at the sheet of roofing that came tearing down, bringing two other pieces with it.

Mark and Eric rolled off the hub just as the sheet ploughed into it, causing the glass by its panels to burst outwards and its relays to trip – sending out a faint beep with a small light flashing.

Two other large sheets of corrugated iron crashed inward, sliding and grating down on the ladder and the large water pipes, hitting the floor with a loud bang as they hit the grid flooring – spinning and then sliding – forcing Maggie, Bobby and Jacques to leap aside.

"Get in the car! Get in the car!" Nico said as the bolts tore down again, denting and scuffing their bodies and the Bantam's paint.

He scrambled around the car as Zach, Carla and Eric launched fistful after fistful of bolts into the air at them. Wessel leapt into the car and shut the door when bolts hit the window, smashing the glass onto him.

"Get in!" Nico said starting the engine, "Nathan!" Stefan and Caleb scrambled from their cover against the building towards the car as Eric pelted at them.

The tyres spun in the gravel, veering forward in a turn as they quickly dug the last of the bolts from their pockets, and Nico finally saw his brother beside the building near the shattered window, his face bleeding.

"Nathan! Get in!" he yelled as Zach's fist let go of its arsenal.

Nathan stood up, eyes frightened in alarm before running to the car while the screws and bolts beat down on him from above, quickly leaping into the back of the pickup.

Eric and Carla continued to release their last bombardment at the car as it sped away wounded, dented, and scuffed like its occupants.

"We did it!" Eric exclaimed with raw excitement watching while the yellow Bantam sped off in a trail of dust.

"That'll teach them to…" Carla's words barely left her mouth when the Bantam turned, slipped, and started to roll – flinging the three boys off the back as it tumbled into the field.

"Oh shit!" Gasped Zach as a coldness fell over him, "We need to go help them!"

"Is that police?" Eric said grabbing his arm in alarm pointing towards the distance where a group of orange lights moved with three white vehicles in a row.

"Mine security." Carla said worriedly.

"Guys!" Matt called in alarm from the opening in the roof, "We have a problem!"

****

Carefully clambering back down, Zach, Eric and Carla leapt down against the grid floor, rushing over to Bobby and Matt who were desperately trying to lift the large grid door from the opening. The corrugated roofing had slid and hit Dillon into the water below, slamming the grid door shut.

"Help me!" Dillon screamed wading the water, trying to reach for a part of the pipe that held a small set of steps.

"Matt! Help us!" called Mark, as everyone rushed to help tug at the grid.

With all their might, they all pulled at the grid, but it was too much for them. The slam caused rust and dirt to wedge it against the side slots making it even heavier to get open.

"Help me out of here you, guys!" Dillon urged with wide, terrified eyes.

"We can't lift it!" Zach pant breathlessly, as they all continued to pull the heavy grid with their weak arms. "It's stuck!" Carla yelled to him, "We cannot open it."

"My dad is going to murder me." Bobby burst out crying.

"We cannot be here! That sign out there…if our dad, or Bobby's… we have to go!"

Urged Odette behind her tears.

Leigh Anne pulled at Zach's arm, "Please, we have to get out of here!"

"Hey guys, what's happening? I need you to get me out of here please!"

Maggie sighed, "Look he said it comes on every twenty minutes, right? It's been longer and it's not coming on."

"I think that thing is broken." Jacques pointed at the old beeping hub as tears ran down his frightened face.

"We can't leave him." Mark said sternly, "We cannot do that!"

"What about Nico and them? For all we know they're dead out there!" Carla urged as tears filled her eyes, "Zach, we need to go!"

"Then you guys go, I'll catch up later." Said Zach looking at them while Dillon continued to call out from the water below, "I cannot leave him down there."

"I'll stay." Eric agreed.

"No, we either all stay, or we all go." Said Mark sternly, "No other way."

"Hello?" Dillon called up, "Hey! Please open the gate!"

"Security is on the way! We must get out of here!" said Odette pulling at her brother, "Dad's going to kill us if we get arrested!"

Bobby's sobbing forced Eric to stand up and turn to Mark and Zach, "We need to get out of here."

Zach looked down at Dillon again, the strangers' eyes glaring up in desperation. "Don't leave me here!"

"Security is on the way, hang tight, ok?"

"No! No! No! You cannot leave me here! Hey! Please help me!" Dillon cried.

"I'm sorry we cannot lift it! The mine's security is on the way, ok? Hang tight! I'm sorry!" Zach said hurriedly getting up as Eric pulled him and rushing after the others towards the small window.

"Don't leave me! Don't leave me!"

Outside, they grabbed their bicycles as fast as their trembling arms and legs would allow, darting towards the long grass, pushing in just as the three mine security vehicles grind onto the old road.

"I hear yelling!" Leigh Anne said breathlessly, "That means they're ok right?"
The security van sped across the bumpy, uneven ground and skidded to a stop outside the water house.

They kept running, pushing their bikes as fast as their trembling legs could carry them through the shaking dread, while in the distance they could hear calls and screams from the rolled Bantam.

And through the roaring of their terrified heartbeats within their chests, the droning sounded behind them as the pumps started up.

CHAPTER ELEVEN

Zach fell to the floor, the force stealing his air and forcing him to open his eyes.

His head ached like something he'd never felt before, his ears ringing from the throbbing pain and a soft murmur somewhere in the pulsing headache.

He could taste the rust with each breath, forcing himself out of the daze after remembering rushing past the large officer who lay dead near the side entrance before everything went black.

The murmuring began to elevate as the ringing subdued, a more pronounced and muffled mixture of silent screams. He forced himself to his knees, looking through a haze from the blow to his head and the blood that had run down above his eye. The room was cold but familiar and he stood up, wobbling as he realized where he was, and the muffled screams and moans became clear – his body riddled with instant terror.

****

Shivering from both pain and the dampness to his clothes, Mark slowed the car to a roll along the wet tar as the desolate darkness swallowed everything beyond the car's lights.

He clenched the steering wheel, trying to force his legs to stop shaking while the car eased forward - scanning the left side of the road through the downpour.

Finally, he saw the remnants of the old gravel path and he turned in, expecting to see the old, rusted gate but only its posts still stood buckled over into the long grass.
He carefully let the car roll forward into the darkness, seeing only the vague muddy path of the road that was now almost walled in by the grass as his eyes strained to see more.

****

Older, taller and stronger now than he was standing there as a 12-year-old, the longstanding, dilapidated water house seemed larger, lit only by a few bulbs that still hung from the remains of its ceiling.

The grid over the concrete by his feet even more ominous and scathing to his mind – the open grate and black pit almost screaming as the wind that tore through the derelict building howled through like screams from history.

He turned to find Carla gagged and tied against one of the large steel pipes, her arms stretched around either side and bound with a black rope and in fright he ran to her.
"Carla are you ok?" he said ripping the tape from her mouth and brushing her long red hair from her dirty face.

****

The car stopped and he sighed, laying his head down for a moment as he fought to catch his breath and regroup his screaming thoughts.

Mark stepped out into the rain again, the night beyond the car lights a blackness that hissed as the water beat down to the grass. He carefully got up onto the hood of the car, wincing through the pain in his leg while he carefully hauled over the windshield onto the roof.
With his hands covering his eyes, he stared out to the blackness searching – when he finally saw a faint light.

He lowered his hands, his heart now slamming so hard against his chest he felt almost breathless, remembering how Eric had seen the old water house ten years ago. He carefully slid down the windshield onto the bonnet, and down the side, parting the grass to step into the field.

****

"You need to get out of here, run!" Carla warned as he spun around looking for anything sharp enough to cut through the rope.
"Oh god is that…" he said seeing the battered blonde tied up against the old orange hub, the ceiling sheets to the side of it still laying there since the last time he stood inside those walls, the roof above it still missing with rain falling in.
"Yes, but Zach you need to go, get out now!" she urged.
"I'd listen to her if I were you, Zachary." A voice came from out of the shadows to the right of him.

He stepped towards the centre of the grid flooring, his eyes scanning the darkness.

"Where are you?" he growled, "Come out and show your face, let's finish this!"
"Don't leave me!" the voice now yelled from the other side, and he spun.
"Stop! Please!" it came from the opposite corner now and he scanned the darkness.
"Don't leave me! Please!" the voice now near the shadows by Carla, and he stepped towards her, desperately searching the thick shadows.
"Please stop!" this time from behind him and he spun around again as the voice whimpered, "Please! Please! Please!"
His heart raced and his eyes wide staring into the dark, "Who the hell are you huh? Come out and show your face asshole!"
The lights went out, and in the seconds, it took for his pupils to adjust to the night, the figure tore out at him, like a dark blur – slashing into his back through his jacket. He had barely cried out when again, the figure tore past and slashed at his arm. He cried out, and Carla screamed.

Another blur in the darkness as the figure whipped past, punching hard into his back with its shrapnel fist, then another from the side into his lower abdomen.
Reaching out in front and around him with one hand, he tried to grab onto the dark assailant, but the punches continued – his shoulder, his upper thigh and forearm and he fell to his knees crying out with a scream, a scream from the depths of his frustration and exhaustion, guilt and remorse to end all the chaos inside.

The building fell to silence as his echoing scream softened, and Leigh Anne opened her eyes with the flickering of the lights coming back on.

The dark figure stepped out of the darkness towards him.

"Stop please!" Carla begged behind her tears, "Who the hell are you?"

"Sssshhh." It said putting its finger over the mask before removing the knuckle duster and tossing it to the ground, its fall resounding in faint echo to the large dark pit beneath.

"You! You! You! All this because of you! An immoral human being who just refuses to suffer like everyone else!" it said as Zach stumbled to his feet. "Zach Manson, a spineless fucking coward! A worthless nobody hiding behind daddy's money! You don't deserve any of it!" it said clipping its mask off.

A horrific shock and realization clobbered Zach as he stared into his eyes, the face he knew and had trusted.

He tossed the mask to the floor and turned to face each of the girls before looking back at Zach, cocking his head with a grin.

"Hi, remember me?" He smiled removing the black gloves.

Zach shook his head, trying to retain his balance as his wounds leached his strength. His mind raced, unable to fathom the horrifying truth.

"Caleb..."

He smiled, "Alive and in the flesh."

"But...they said you were..." Carla stammered in awe.

"Dead? Died with daddy in a crash? Yes, yes - I know. Or at least, so the story goes." Caleb smirked, his eyes dark and filled with hatred, "You should know… I mean, stories can be told, manipulated and hell, even sealed behind a pact for decades."

Zach stumbled breathlessly.

"You'll be surprised what you can do when you have the right motivation." Caleb grinned as he turned towards the shadows where another tall dark figure emerged.

"And the right partner." It said stepping towards the middle of the floor as Caleb removed the hood from his thick leather coat revealing the sparing helmet.

The figure stayed still, staring from behind the black gauze mask.

"I really hate you Zach, more than anyone else, I hate you." He said adamantly, his eyes ablaze with pure evil despise.

"Why? Why are you doing this?" Zach said staring at him still in disbelief.

Caleb grabbed him and started hitting him, again and again – face, head, chest, stomach as hard as he could, even screaming as the rage within him unleashed.

Tortured and bleeding, Zach fell to the grid on his hands and knees as blood dripped from his mouth.

"Caleb please! Stop!" Cried Carla pulling at the ropes that bound her wrists.

"Shut up bitch!" the masked figure warned pointing the scythe at her.

"As you can see Zachary, not everything is as it seems, is it?" Caleb continued to remove his long coat, exposing the dual layered bullet proof vests that was riddled with holes and arm protector pads. "Oh yeah, at lot of thought has gone into this." Caleb smiled taking the hunting knife from inside the coat, turning to Carla as he unclipped the vests and pulled off the arm guards, "To make this decade anniversary special and memorable just for all of you...My dear old friends."

"Why are you doing this?" cried Carla as he neared her, his eyes staring deeply into hers.

The other figure stood still watching as their faces winced in disbelief and horror.

"The flaming fire that is our leader...what was it again?" Caleb grinned touching her face while he stared into her eyes.

Then his face softened, "God I had the biggest crush on you...I can't do this."

The figure stood watching as Caleb looked up at it.

"Sorry we cannot kill Carla, I'm serious. I mean...it's Carla Wilson! Look at her, she's gorgeous!"

A silence lingered as the masked figure stared at Caleb, and then finally it stepped forward giving a nod.

"Then let her go."

Caleb smiled and turned to Leigh Anne, "No offence, I mean you look great...or at least you used to have something going for you. But Carla..."

He put the knife to the rope and looked at her grinning, "You're my wet dream."

Caleb sliced the rope and Carla flopped down as the blood rushed to her arms and shoulders again, stinging.

"Have you been paying attention Carla?" Caleb asked touching her face with his bloodied hand and asking again, "Have you been paying attention?"
"What do you want?" she cried looking up at him. He smiled and cocked his head to the side, "Like I said, nothing… is as it seems!"
She frowned and he grabbed the rope dangling from her left hand and wrapped it around her neck, putting his foot up against her chest as he pulled her face towards him.
"Sorry about your mom." He snarled with a cold grin.
"Please! Don't do this!" cried Zach as tears ran down his bloodied face.
"Sssshhh!" Caleb put his finger to his grinning lips and Zach screamed.

****

Rushing through the darkness towards the scream, Mark stumbled to the mud, clambering to his feet through the pain in his leg and kept running until he burst out the long grass and toppled down into the mud, looking up to a haunting history that loomed above him in erosion -

NO TRESPASSING

No unauthorized access whatsoever.
VIOLATIONS WILL BE CHARGED IN
ACCORDANCE WITH CRIMINAL CODE
AND WILL BE PROSECUTED TO THE FULLEST EXTENT OF THE LAW.

-ZERO TOLERANCE-

As he reached the rusted decrepit doors, he paused almost to his memories flashing through his mind of how carefree they all were, filled with wonder to open and enter the unknown. He shook his head and pulled the doors open.

Carefully he moved down the creaking stairs, scanning the dimly lit place that forever changed their lives until he saw Zach laying in the centre of the grid flooring, and he rushed down.
"Zach!" he said kneeling over him, "Zach! Zach wake up!"
He slapped at his face as Zach's eyes opened when suddenly a foot slammed into his face, and he flung backwards.

"Welcome to the reunion Marcus." Caleb mocked while Mark quickly stumbled to his feet, reaching down to his pants for the detective's secondary weapon - a small six shot Colt Revolver which she had around her ankle.
"Caleb? he exclaimed when from behind the masked figure rounded and grabbed his arm, stabbing into his shoulder.
Mark screamed as the gun hit the grid and flopped to the ground as the two maniacs stepped over him and started kicking and stomping down at him until he lay foetal.

"Thanks for this Marcus, we'll keep it safe for you." The masked figure said opening its coat to put the gun away, pausing first and then firing a shot into his leg.
Mark squealed as the blast echoed into the rain, and he clasped at his leg, crying in screams as he rolled on the rusted grid.

"No!" said the masked figure, stepping down on his neck and raising his finger over the mask, "Sssshhh…"
Caleb laughed up into the air, "Wow!"
Staring up at them, the disbelief and shock of an old friend's evil smile - he knew his time had come, then he saw Leigh Anne tied to the old hub.
"Carla's here too." Smirked Caleb raising his eyebrows to the side, slowly lifting his boot off from Mark's neck.

He rolled to the side coughing, grabbing his leg again while he looked up as Carla lay on her side against the massive pipe - the ropes loose at her wrists and her eyes pleading with him as she lay defeated, breathing heavily.

"My God! You people all look so damn shocked!" Caleb laughed again while moving to Zach who managed to get to his knees, "I mean come on! You are all the kings of deception! Why is it so hard to believe that I'm alive?"
He reached down and grabbed Zach by the hair, plucking him upwards, holding tightly as Zach dropped to his knees in front of him.
"You want to know who that is?" he mocked looking to his masked partner as it unclipped its cloak and tossed it aside.

"Do you want to know who killed your sister Mark?" Caleb laughed.
Mark rolled and grabbed at the figures legs angrily yelling as the figure kicked him in the stomach. The wound at its side from Zain's stab seeped blood through its vests.

"What about you Zach?" asked Caleb pulling him by his hair to his feet, "Little rich boy, do you want to know who forced your parents off the road and then made sure they were dead?"
Zach stared up as the figure dropped the mask and headgear to the ground by Mark.

"Hey buddy."
Zach gasped and Caleb grabbed his hair tighter.
"You know, we were angry at all of you for a very long time." He explained stepping forward with a smile and toying with the scythe, "And sure, we wanted revenge, we were angry, we had our moments. But we had no idea how much we'd enjoy any of this."
"And boy! Did we enjoy it!" Caleb laughed winking over at Leigh Anne.
"Why?" Zach asked staring at his friend's face, "Why are you doing this?"
"Because you deserve it!" he snarled slamming a punch into Zach's stomach, with Caleb letting him drop to floor again.

"You all deserved this." A friendly face looked down at Mark as the scythe hung over his face, "Some more than others, in my opinion at least."
Caleb smirked as his partner walked over to Leigh Anne, grabbing her face in his hands, "You're such a fighter Leigh Anne, who would have thought under all that make up was such a spirited survivor!"
She screamed behind the tape, and he ripped it off.
"Fuck you!" she snarled when he stabbed into her stomach, putting his hand to her lips, "Sssshhh."
"I like your will to survive Leigh Anne." He turned looking at Caleb.

"She's a tough one!" grinned Caleb, "Not like Odette, she was pathetic."

"Go to hell!" Mark snarled from the floor.

"Oh, I've been in hell for ten years Mark. This is our cleansing if you will." Caleb said kicking down at his leg.

"Why?" Zach said looking up at them, "Why would you do this to us?"

"Why?" the other snarled, stomping over and grabbing Zachary upwards and wrapping his hands around his throat, "You dare ask us why?"

Zach clawed at his friend's hands choking at his neck with a vile rage staring into his eyes as he screamed, pushing him back up against the central pipe.

"Where were you when families broke apart and people died? Where were you when I needed you? Where were you?"

"Please…" Zach choked, his arms dropping. His friend released and dropped him to the ground against the pipe where he gasped breathlessly, slumping over as he choked for air.

"I thought you were my friends!" he screamed, "Brothers and sisters! But you deserted me, left me alone with the guilt of a boy drowning in the pipes! Afraid everyday that Caleb or Wessel would come after me!"

Bobby Minnaar stepped back grinning.

"I was nine! And you all decided we had to leave Dillon to die. Nine!" he screamed angrily, his face wicked and tormented while he began to pace and catch his breath again.

"My life spiralled faster than I could accept what we did that day. And I had nobody, you all shut each other down, split and went your own ways while I was fucking drowning in guilt and confusion! Seven years! Seven years with this eating at me!"

His voice echoed as Caleb stood beside him and put his hand on his shoulder.
He heaved a deep breath, smiling with an adorning nod, "But Caleb and I, see we found a way to get retribution and redemption. We share a lot of the same interests."
"Yes, we do. I probably would have been good friends with Bobby if you all didn't have sticks up your asses about me!" Caleb agreed as he walked over to Mark, "That's the thing, isn't it? You thought I wasn't worthy to be part of your little group. See Mark, Nathan saw that boy going into the hole over there. But he was basically screwed, wasn't he? A miner's son what chance did he have after the accident? But he held on, and unlike you bunch of assholes…"
Caleb screamed kneeling down by Mark, "Wessel and I stayed in touch with our friends. Yeah, see we cared about Nathan because I mean, everyone else died that day, didn't they? You killed every single friend we made, didn't you?"
"It was an accident." Mark stammered.
"We defended ourselves." Zach added breathlessly, trying to keep his blood from leaving his body.
Bobby laughed out loudly and turned to Caleb, shaking his head to instruct him to refrain from snapping.
"So, we checked in on Nathan." Caleb said looking back down to Mark, "And then one day, he finally manages to tell my brother what he saw. A boy nobody had ever heard of or even spoken of. And of course, Wessel tells me and then it clicks!"

Bobby looked at Carla angrily, "And I get a visit, I get my ass kicked! I was beaten so badly. My ass was handed to me six ways from Sunday by Wessel and Caleb, demanding I tell them what happened to the boy we abandoned in this very hole!" he said pointing down at the darkness.

"That's when it started." Caleb's eyes lit up, "The plan to make sure that your silence would be eternal."
"So that's what you want?" Mark asked, "For us to tell the truth?"
Bobby laughed, "That's irrelevant now, whether Jacques or Odie – hell even if you had a press conference, we'd have found a way to finish what we've put together."
Caleb stood up again, his face beaming with crazed excitement as Bobby continued.
"But eventually it became clear that Wessel didn't share Caleb's passion for vengeance and mayhem."
"But I did." Bobby smirked looking down at Zach, "I got my wounds healed up and I went looking for them, and at first Caleb wasn't convinced, but I proved it by running your parents off the road."
Zach bit down, glaring up at him in vile hatred.
"That's when brother dearest got cold feet. Surprising for a drug addict, isn't it? He was so far gone I grew tired of waiting for him to want to do this with me." Caleb smirked, "So Bobby and I put him in the car with my dad and made it look like it was me who died, I mean why would mother think anything else? And then Wessel just disappears to the streets with his drugs, and nobody is any wiser. Nobody cared!"

"And of course to make sure we had enough practise we scored a body from the morgue and made it look like I had an awful motorbike accident." Bobby smirked, "The dead cannot be suspects, can they?"

Caleb laughed, "And all this with the same car that ended my friend's lives!"

"And mine." Bobby stared at Leigh Anne who fought to stay focused, "And just like that we had the freedom to carry out our plan, our retribution against the gang that turned their backs on everything and carried on with their lives."

"You think it was easy on us?" Zach gasped slumping against the pipe breathlessly.

"Oh, we watched you all Zach." Said Caleb walking to him with the hunting knife out towards Zach's face, "Leigh Anne was making money, travelling. Matt and Maggie, my god they had a decent go at it didn't they?"

"And you Carla…" Said Bobby turning to her where she lay, "You had it going with your little well-paying job didn't you? Oh, Odie was in love."

"So romantic!" Caleb laughed.

"And Jacques, ok that was tough, but it needed to happen." Bobby said turning back to Mark and kneeling, "And we cannot forget about you can we Mark? Mr. Vid-Tube star with your followers and your cutesy little videos! Every time I saw your face I wanted to scream because you, you forgot about everything, and your smile showed it."

Bobby's eyes were dark as he put the tip of the scythe down on Mark's stomach, his knees on either side of him clamping his arms down.

"Every one of you had moved on with your lives, like it didn't matter that Dillon had been sucked into the pump and washed out into the slime dams, buried and forgotten. Or that three people died in that crash!"

"A crash you caused!" Caleb said stabbing into Zach's shoulder and sending him down to his knees again crying out in pain beside the opening in the ground.

"And poor Nathan, you caused that poor guy ten years of suffering and still you said nothing to the police, that you were there, hurling bolts and screws, chasing them into that accident!" Bobby snarled as he screamed, "And you left a nine-year-old to deal with it on his own, what kind of monsters are you?"

"I hate you Zach." Caleb said kneeling over him, "Because unlike the rest of them, your parent's death just opened a world of cash to you and that isn't fair, no Zachary Manson that isn't fair! It isn't fair that you forgot about the boy you left! It's not fair that you forgot about Nico or Nathan or Stefan! I'm going to make you suffer!"

"And now we're at the end, and we need to end this now." Bobby said pushing the tip of the scythe down into Marks stomach just below his ribs.

He screamed as blood pooled around the curving blade and Bobby put his finger over his lips, "Sssshhh."

****

"We..." Zach said breathlessly over Marks screams, "We all make mistakes..."

"Mistakes?" Bobby's head turned as he stopped sliding the blade into Mark.

"What you all did was a mistake?" he scoffed, "A mistake!"

Again, his roaring voice echoed.

Zach gasped, "You…I was talking…about you!"

Zach said forcing the words out, "Your mistakes!"

"What mistakes Zach?" Frowned Bobby.

"You…" Zach said finding the will to stay alive weakening at the exhaustion of his battered body, "You…"

"What's he saying?" Scoffed Bobby angrily as Caleb lowered closer to Zach's face.

"We don't make mistakes!"

"You forgot…" Zach said softly, "You dropped this!"

Taking everything, he had left, Zach flung upwards, the treacherous knuckleduster gripped on his fist – flying right up under Calebs jaw and piercing into his gums and tongue. Zach ripped his fist away and blood spewed out of Calebs chin as he fell to his knees grabbing his throat and face, when Zach kicked him down and got on top of him, hitting and hitting with all his might.

Bobby leapt up from Mark, who pushed the last of his endurance to a kick, tripping Bobby down to the grid – the scythe sliding across the floor as Zach screamed, slamming down his fist repeatedly at Calebs face, neck, throat and chest.

"No!" Bobby said grabbing the hunting knife and lunging at Zach, who grabbed at his hands, fighting to keep the blade away as Bobby rammed him backwards into the pipe just inches from the opening to the darkness below.

Zach's eyes flared as he stared into Bobby's crazed eyes, but he was depleted now, and his hand's grip began to loosen, and the blade tore down into his chest.

Bobby put his finger to his lips as Zach screamed out in pain.

"Hush now Zach." He grinned, before tossing Zach to the ground where he slammed into the grid before Bobby kicked him down into the dark water below.

Carla wrapped the ropes at her wrist around his neck, pulling with all her might as he tried slashing at her. She clenched and pulled as he rammed her against the pipe, again and again until she finally subdued and slunk down beside him to the ground, her legs sliding through the open grid and pulling him down.

He grabbed frantically at the rope still around his neck, fighting to keep himself from falling in as she dangled down.

"Let me go bitch!" he gargled as he dropped to his knees, bracing himself as she looked up at him from inside the darkness above the water where Zach floated.

He desperately reached for the scythe, but Leigh Anne stumbled and grabbed it.

"Don't…you dare…bitch!"

"Oh, shush you mother fucker!" she swung it down at his neck, chopping its blade deep into his tissue.

The blood splashed down to Carla, and she screamed, when her weight tore his head off and sent her and his head down into the water.

Leigh Anne stumbled to the ground on her knees, holding her stomach as the cold of death crawled over her skin.

****

The darkness of the night remained into the early morning hours, as the rain continued to drone down, watering the vast span of fields and the strong winds howled along the tall grass.

Lightning lit the dark clouds above as the cold wind slithered over the puddles of mud, up along the old pillars holding the ominous warning sign that creaked to its power and continued along the water house's decrepit walls and hissing through the gaps as it funnelled inside and sloped down the stairs and along the rusty grid.

The cold airstream moaned in chilling whispers as it meandered along the grid floor and down into the opening, circling the vast surface of dark water in chilling silent screams.

HUSH
THE SILENT SCREAM

Lynel Coetzer is a South African author and small business owner.

His first publication of the suspense / adventure series 'Soul Break' was released in 2016. In addition to writing mystery / suspense novels, he has also released the online chronical series, 'Apparition', a dystopian story centring on characters seemingly trapped within a world inside their minds.

With the first part in the 'Soul Break' series being called *"A romantic, charming and dramatic suspense thriller that keeps you hooked until the end"* - further parts of the series are set to be released.
Other works to look out for include the crime thriller 'The Fields of Obsession' and romantic comedy "Jack & Julie".

Lynel lives in Southbroom, South Africa with his wife and their two children, and four border collies.

www.lynelcoetzer.co.za
info.lynelcoetzer@gmail.com
https://web.facebook.com/lynelc.coetzer
https: //www.facebook.com/AuthorLynelCoetzer
https://www.wattpad.com/myworks/69066566-apparition-the-chronicles-of-darkness

I cannot thank my faithful, loving 'co-writer' and trusted partner Sidney enough. My now 6-month-old Collie who continuously sat on my lap and watched me type, often typing and spacing with curious and wonderful eyes. My hug-loving, brown 4-legged boy.

While I write for everyone to have a glimpse into the worlds of my imagination, I always write to make one person proud enough to still be with me...
My best friend and wife Soreen. Without your constant support, I would have all these stories bubbling inside of me without anyone ever knowing.

And of course, to my daughter Hailey, who nagged me night after night for updates on how far I was with this story after reading chapter 1. I'm so happy you liked it and enjoyed the ride.

And Dylan, my son - I hope I have impressed you, because your sense of adventure is so inspiring to me and like your mom, pushes me to jot down these things even when I'm doubtful.

Even if nobody were to ever read this, except these 3 human beings who my world revolves around, at least I know that they did - and that is enough.

To anyone reading this, there's an alternate ending. Perhaps the silence will scream again?

Contact me if you'd like to check it out.

On the afternoon of his 8th birthday, he went upstairs and was not seen again for 9 years. Treated and rehabilitated, Kyle Evans is now a young man ready to begin his journey out of the darkness and explore the possibility of living a normal life after his return, labelled as 'Boy X' by the media. With the silent hope that no one would realize who he is, he gradually begins to break free of the past, surrounded by other's who have ghosts of their own haunting them from the shadows.

Heir to the family millions, Joel McDonald's darkness exists in the fact that his place in the world has been predefined. But there is a new face in town, someone whose darkness brings him out of his own. Unaware that their paths have crossed before, Joel realizes that he is only reaching the crux of his journey to break free of the chains that have so long caged him to the family fortune.

Life has never been the same for Michael Harper, not since the murder. Everything is spiralling out of control for him and long-time friend Jessie as they continue to do the bidding of two dirty cops to stay out of prison. Their lives were ruined by a chain of events they are yet to uncover, when the reopening of an old mine shaft brings to surface a shocking revelation and prompts Michael to look deeper into the past.

As the chaos surrounding the old E Shaft draws further attention across the nation, detectives Jordan and Underwood find themselves desperate for clues to unravel the enigma within the shaft as the body count begins to rise.

While the dangerous secrets of the past surface, everyone quickly finds themselves in the middle of a conspiracy designed by the mysterious 'Corporation' and carried out by its agents in black who strive to silence anyone in their way of them reaching the Corporation's ultimate goal.

In Part One, the turbulent past begins to collide with the present in a race to free themselves of their inner darkness as they begin to scratch the surface of the dangerous truth buried within the old mine…